PRAISE FOR GHOST LIGHT

A page-turning thriller... Can't wait to read the next book in the series!

AMAZON REVIEWS

If you're looking for a page-turner... this is an entertaining thriller... Can't wait to read the next installment!

AMAZON REVIEWS

Full of big ideas and delicious details...

AMAZON REVIEWS

A great read... It kept me up late while I read "just a few more pages"... I look forward to the next book in the TROUPE.

AMAZON REVIEWS

Tightly woven thriller... with lots of twists.

AMAZON REVIEWS

GHOST LIGHT

A TROUPE THRILLER

JASON CANNON

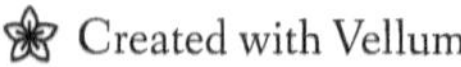 Created with Vellum

GHOST LIGHT *is dedicated to* SAM MOSSLER.
A brilliant actor, delightful writer,
and tremendous human being.
He left us far too soon.
His passion, humor, and kindness
continue to inspire.
This book owes him dearly, from patching plot holes
to clarifying how New York City actually works
to encouraging me to write Adler
as freely as possible.
Thank you, my friend. You are sorely missed.

"ghost light"

Noun.

A single bulb, usually a free-standing lamp on a stage, left burning whenever the theatre is dark.

Origin: May come from the day when theaters were gas-lit and the lights were left dimly on to relieve pressure on the valves.
 Another popular legend says that a burglar many years ago snuck into a Broadway house and in the darkness he fell from the stage into the pit, breaking his leg. He then sued the theatre. And won.
 Some say the ghost light is left lit to ward off and distract mischievous spirits, so they don't take out their frustration on the set, cast, or crew. Others insist it lights the stage to keep the ghosts happy, giving them illumination to perform for each other and the echoes of the audience.

All theaters, after all, house ghosts.

1

SARASOTA, FLORIDA

Thousands of feet thunderstormed into the pavement. Home-made signs stabbed at the overcast sky. The crowd throbbed.

A bullhorn called. *"No Justice…!!"*

The throng responded one-throated. "NO PEACE!!"

"No Justice…!!"

"NO PEACE!!"

The young white man walking along the outskirts had no interest in this mob's brand of "peace."

He would leave such a scar. He would slash wounds down to the genes. Children of those who survived today would grow up looking over their shoulders, wondering if his ghost was creeping up on them.

Finally. It was his time. All was in place.

He had underestimated the turnout to this protest—who knew there were this many porch monkeys, beaners, and chinks in this town??—so working his way toward the head of the crowd had put him seven minutes behind schedule.

But talk about your silver linings. The march itself started late for the same reason. He made up his time in no time. And the swelling numbers ultimately meant a greater sacrifice.

With everyone so focused on their self-absorbed chanting and whiny bitching for "equality," no one saw him slipping his perfectly primed packages into public trash cans. Receptacles eager to shred into shrapnel.

His primary targets led the march. The half-breed Congresswoman and the Judas Congressman. A few minutes more and the blast radius would embrace them.

He shivered in disgust even as he savored his impending immortality. The crowd was such that even on the edges he couldn't avoid the occasional shoulder bump with a filthy skin. It made him uncomfortable. And his discomfort made him furious.

Their stupid homemade signs. Their false fury. Their inability to see the world as it actually was... sick and dying, in need of *curing*.

He suddenly couldn't breathe. He found sanctuary in a pocket of space created by a consignment store's entryway. Watched the horde stomp past.

A ribbon of White people swirled through the black and brown mass. He snarled inside. Traitors. How could they forfeit their birthright? Snowflakes indeed were White.

Which of them would die today?

It didn't actually matter to the young man, but it was a fun thought experiment to pick out individuals from the oblivious throng, see if he could tell which were marked for martyrdom.

The power hummed in his marrow. When the moment came... all that would be required... a simple press of finger to phone...

boom

boom

boom boom

boom

Anticipation saturated him.

He forged back out into the crush, working upstream toward the final targeted trash can. Arrived. Pretended to tie his shoe. Cased the corner. Unzipped his previously bulging backpack. Dropped his last IED. Re-zipped. The bag flopped flaccid over his shoulder, spent and happy.

Soon. So soon. The world would see. And understand his cause. And know his name. His *true* name.

SPEARHEAD.

2

A FEW MONTHS EARLIER, MANHATTAN

"What is acting?"

Gideon Price pulled a chair to the center of the small studio stage and sat. Twelve students faced him, most of them a diverse batch of 20-somethings, along with two Black women in their mid-30s who appeared to be friends, a Caucasian married couple in that 50ish range, and a grandfatherly, mustachioed white fellow.

They all remained silent, waiting for someone else to speak first. Gideon re-rolled a sleeve of his lightweight button-down.

"It's not a trick question. And at the risk of starting our time together with a cliche, there are no wrong answers."

Gideon waited, smiling pleasantly, his hands casually folded in his lap. After a few moments, a young Latinx man flung up his hand. Gideon nodded.

"Pretending to be someone else?"

"Sure, yeah."

The married couple both raised their hands. Gideon again nodded.

The couple whispered back and forth, acting out the time-less relation- ship negotiation of who ought to go first. The husband finally insisted the wife take the lead.

"Telling a story?"

"OK, good."

She sat back, pleased. The husband leaned forward. "Becoming rich and famous?"

The class chuckled. Gideon loved it when a student got the first laugh in a first class. That always set the group instinctively at ease.

"For a very cloistered few, absolutely." More chuckles, and now hands flew up all over.

"Mr. Price, what do you mean by cloistered few?" asked an eager young white man in the front row.

"Please, Gideon is fine. Here's what I mean by 'few.' A very tiny percentage of professional actors make their living solely from acting. A somewhat less tiny percentage make their living by cobbling together various performing gigs, everything from voice-overs to theme parks to TV commercials, with some live theatre thrown in. Most have one or more—cue the scary music —*survival jobs*."

More chuckles, looser and louder. The young man followed up.

"So acting is actually... any type of performing?"

"Well now that's a different conversation. There's the art, and there's the business. Whatever the medium, all acting comes back to the same core principles. Plenty more on that later."

The young man was not to be deterred. "And cloistered?"

"That one's easier. If your face is everywhere, if your name is currency, the pressure mounts. The expectations grow. You never leave your house without sunglasses and a cap pulled low. Your private life becomes public. Wealth and fame—as many celebrities attest—end up holding you hostage."

"Sounds good to me!" the husband chimed in. And the class ripped off its first good laugh. Gideon smiled inwardly. He never tired of watching a group of strangers evolve into community.

One of the 30-something friends gasped. "I got it!"

Everyone startled and looked her way. Gideon lopsided a grin and pointed. "Remind me your name?"

"Imani."

"What is it you got, Imani?"

"Who you remind me of!"

Everyone swung their attention to Gideon, probing with keen interest the contours of his face.

"Ho boy. Moment of truth. Do tell."

"Mr. Price—I mean, Gideon—you are a dead ringer for Daredevil!" A few voices went "oooooh!" and "yeeeeah." A couple others went "huh." The mustache went "Who?"

Imani clapped her hands. "Same brown hair, same dark eyebrows, you're definitely taller though."

"Wasn't that Ben Affleck?" the husband asked, squinting at Gideon's face.

Imani was appalled. "Not the *movie*. The TV show!"

Imani's friend—Gideon recalled her name as *Aniyah*—spoke over Imani's squeals. "Don't get her started. She's watched the whole series like five times."

Gideon let the delighted chatter play out. This good-natured moment was his cue for the first "inspirational teacher" monologue. He stood, ran a hand through his apparently Davedevil-y hair. The laughter came in for a gentle landing. He spoke.

"At its most fundamental, acting is simply behaving truthfully within imaginary circumstances. Note that 'truthfully' is a much larger word than 'realistically.' Also note that it's 'behaving,' not 'feeling.' It is, after all, called ACTING. To act. To do. Feelings, yes, are key and we'll get to them. But if your feelings do not manifest into action? If the audience doesn't see it or hear it? They won't get it. True on stage. True in life."

"Sorta sounds like 'faith without works is dead,'" offered the Latinx man.

"Useful comparison, Alfonso, yeah. I've never woven the Apostle Paul into my acting class before, but sure. Feelings. Beliefs. Faith. Points of view whether political or moral, if they don't manifest into action, they're just... thoughts. Air." Gideon's eyebrows furrowed. "Alfonso, I'm blanking... Is that from 'Galatians'?"

"Book of 'James,' baby!" Alfonso fist-pumped.

Chuckles as four pens and three pencils scratched madly. Two tablets and one smart book, perched on laps, click-clacked at competing words per minute. The thumbs of the eager young man took notes on his phone. The 70-something gentleman simply held up an old-school dictation recorder.

Gideon continued. "You will never master this craft. You will always have room to grow as an artist, because—hopefully—you will always be growing as a human being. You cannot separate the two. Another great definition of acting is that it is simply standing on stage naked and slowly turning around."

Gasps and snorts punctuated the giggling. Imani was the first gasper to catch up to the metaphor. "Oh my god I thought you meant literally." "No no, though actually I did have one role where I had to, um, fully de-robe on stage. It's actually... well, intoxicating and empowering."

"Oh reeeeeally?" Imani said, leaning forward with a glint in her eye.

Her ornery curiosity wildfired through the other students.

Gideon held up his hands. "OK OK, my bad, not the story for class one."

The wife reached back and patted the pouting Imani's knee. "Don't worry, dear, we'll get that story."

Gideon got the class back on track. "You must cultivate vulnerability and a thick skin. You must cede control while maintaining control. You must find yourself in every character, and every character inside yourself. If that sounds like a lot, just remember this: you must simply stand on stage and tell the truth."

"Is it really that easy?" A new voice. She was late-20s, with piercing slate eyes, dark brown skin, and a shorn scalp.

"It's Rheia, right?"

"Yep."

"It's the hardest easy thing in the world."

3

An hour later, the class returned from a quick break, chattering excitedly about the physical and vocal warm-ups, the elocution exercises, the tongue twisters, the icebreaker games designed to help everyone learn each other's names.

"I know a lot of that probably felt silly," Gideon said. "But silliness is vulnerability, and vulnerability is necessary if you want to act. So the exercises and warm-ups have a dual purpose. They stretch and strengthen your physical and vocal apparatus, and they free you from the shackles of ego."

The older gentleman spoke up. "But don't you have to have an ego if you're an actor? Or any artist? Aren't you saying 'Hey look at me! Look at my work!'"

"Good point, Marcel. This goes back to the fame idea, yeah? But for every famous artist you know, there are thousands, tens of thousands, grinding away in anonymity, going daily to the smithy of their souls to forge something meaningful with their creativity."

Gideon sat down, leaned forward conspiratorially. The students instinctively settled.

"At the end of the day, the mission of the actor, of any artist, is simply to move the body of work forward. Ninety-nine-point-nine-nine-nine percent of the world will never know my name. Never see me perform, or read my plays, or—unlike you wise few—take my class."

Smiles flickered. Gideon took his time, making deliberate eye contact with each of the extraordinary humans across from him.

"The number of Shakespeares in the world? The ones who can change the world from the top down? That number is infinitesimal... and they don't do that on their own. We are all interconnected. There are as many molecules of air in one breath of air as there are breaths of air in the entire atmosphere. There are as many molecules of water in one glass of water as there are glasses of water in all the Earth's oceans. Shakespeare doesn't happen without every other actor and playwright plying their craft before him. That old chestnut: bloom where you're planted? Well, the field is only a field if each individual blooms. The random Shakespeare-tree that grows out of that field... its very tree- ness is only apparent because of the field around it. The tree owes itself to the field."

Gideon leaned back.

"So... does my work not matter? If I only ever am part of the field?"

He watched as each student contemplated the question. Some eyes went up to the ether. Some down into memory. The married couple gazed at each other, and Gideon saw them squeeze hands. He continued.

"It's up to me to believe that what I do has meaning. Others can decide if it's 'good' or not, whatever, I will never please everyone. But I can contribute. Even just a single verse, right? For you Whitman fans. What will your verse be?"

Gideon noted that Imani had put her arm around Aniyah,

who was working a handkerchief between her fingers, pulling and wrapping and clutching. Gideon caught Aniyah's eyes. They were brimming. *You are seen*, he thought, sending as much gentle warmth toward her as he could. Whatever she received, she nodded, took a deep breath, eased her grip on the hanky.

"You know during the pandemic a poll was taken and the general population listed 'artist' as the least essential job in our society. 'Essen- tial.' I have to wonder how many of those polled only maintained their sanity through quarantine because they listened to music. Read a book. Watched a movie. Consumed art."

The class nodded. Gideon found he couldn't sit any longer.

"Art makes it easier to breathe. Art may not be how we stay alive, but it's why we live at all." He paced. He vibrated. Calm guru fired up into impassioned prophet.

"Do you remember every single meal from last month? Of course not. Well, maybe if you're journaling or food planning, but you'd still have to double-check your records. Never mind, here's the point—do you need to eat every day? Absolutely. Even if you can't recall *what* you ate, you know that you *did*. The same with art. So while food helps our bodies grow and fuels our daily activities, art helps our minds and hearts and humanity grow, fuels our daily evolution. Art is food for the soul."

Gideon prowled the small stage.

"And this is why art is *essential*—it provides context, it carves meaning, it gives us a framework to make sense of our lives and a world that so often seems senseless. And as we learn to create art we learn to see artistry in those around us. Theatre happens... all the time... all around you."

Gideon paused, a conductor suspended between notes.

"You know... just last week... in a bar of all places... I saw what I could only describe as a 'performance.' As powerful and true as anything I've ever seen on stage."

"Well isn't all the world a stage?" Rheia asked.

"And all the men and women merely players?" Marcel finished.

"Indeed, Mr. Wigglestick says as much through the voice of the melancholy Jaques," Gideon conceded. "There's a hopelessness in there, a dismissiveness that has always gnawed at me. I want to believe in theatre as something aspirational, and last week in the bar..."

Gideon hesitated. He was way off-script, and the class knew it. "I'm honestly... it was just a bar fight."

"A bar fight??" Rheia prodded.

"Yes. But it was... more?"

"What bar?"

"The Bear and Fawn, just over on 46th."

Several nods of recognition, a few quizzical eyebrows. And the timeless, hushed insistence of the campfire.

Tell us the story.

He inhaled their rapt attention and started to carve the narrative. "I was having a well-deserved bourbon after a two-show day."

4

Gideon watched it all unfold in the mirror behind the bar.

A 20-something Black guy playing at being dapper in a white suit had sucker-punched his pool opponent, another 20-something Black guy in jeans and a Henley. The sounds of the punch and Henley's clatter to the floor had frozen every patron mid-bite.

White Suit crowed, "Yeah! That's what's you *get!*" His two gym- thick wingmen hooted. They high-fived and low-fived. Henley's friend helped him up, blood from his now crooked nose staining the billiard felt black.

No one moved. Not the trio of cool dudes hitting on the girls at the dartboards. Not the booth full of mud-streaked amateur rugby toughs. Not the bartender. Not Gideon.

White Suit and his wingmen strutted toward the exit. The bar held its breath, ashamed of inaction, but anticipating the relief that would come when the proverbial bullies left the playground.

How she appeared Gideon would never remember. But suddenly there she was: average height, tight black ponytail, bangs, large opaque sunglasses, dark jeans, dark jacket over a basic T, skin tone that a theatrical agent would call "ethnically ambiguous." Everything about her—and looking back Gideon realized this was intentional—just *blended*.

The only reason she stuck out was that unlike everyone else in the bar she was standing between White Suit and the door. Her hands idly twirled a wooden pool rack.

"Why did you hit him?"

Gideon blinked. The voice that came out of the deceptively average woman was rich and resonant. Like a judge. Or a queen. Or an empress. He could have sworn even the lights shifted.

He glanced around. The Woman's blunt query had transformed the air hockey, the stools, the four-tops, the coasters, the neon, even the strangely muffled blatherings of some play-by-play guy on the TV... into a theatre. And Gideon would know; he had just held center stage as King Henry the Fifth an hour ago.

Gideon turned his attention back to the Woman, acutely aware he was now a member of an audience.

White Suit swiveled his head back and forth, sensitive to the shift in the air but unsure what it meant. Every eye in the bar was on him, an unwitting actor in a play with no clue what his next line was.

Gideon tasted a familiar growing electricity in the air.

The Woman cocked her head to one side, the triangle in her hands still slowly spinning.

"I ask sincerely. Why did you hit him?"

White Suit and his buds in turn cocked their heads, like dogs hearing the word "treat." White Suit opened his mouth. Closed it. Looked to his left. His friend gave a perplexed shrug.

"Come now," the Woman continued in that voice that wove through the bar. "We all are curious. It appeared that other young man won fair and square, yes?" She glanced past White Suit. Henley hesitantly nodded, not wanting more attention from the bullies.

"So I ask again, on behalf of everyone here who was just looking to have a good time tonight… why did you hit him?"

White Suit casually picked up a pool cue, buying time. What response could get him out of this without losing face? He chuckled audibly and looked around, gauging the audience's reaction.

No one believed him.

An ageless and universal story. Ego at its most primal. Either White Suit would yield—unlikely—or he would escalate.

White Suit's chuckle smeared itself into a sneer. His two strongmen inhaled and drew themselves up. Gideon felt his arms break out in gooseflesh, and he sensed the audience collectively lean forward.

"OK, Miss. You're right. I sucker punched that asshole." White Suit's voice in comparison to the Woman's, even though he was trying to sound patronizing and macho, came off reedy and thin. He knew it. He tried to snort. "But so what? You his babysitter or something?"

No one as much as tittered. So he glanced to his side, and his wingmen obligingly guffawed.

"I've never met him." The Woman's voice again froze time. "You should now apologize."

White Suit studied her closely, bouncing the pool cue in his hands. "You've got some balls," he drawled.

"I see you failed anatomy." The audience didn't know whether to giggle or gasp. "There's no dodging this, gentlemen. You owe this man an apology."

"Whatever. C'mon, T, move her out of the way. We're out."

The smaller of the two wingmen, T apparently, stepped

toward the Woman. "Smaller" was relative. Next to her he was a hulk.

Gideon suddenly wondered why no one was joining the Woman. Why HE wasn't joining.

T stopped short of the Woman, raised his hands palms out in a sorry- but-I-have-to-do-this gesture. "I don't wanna hurt ya," he said.

"That's kind of you, T. I don't want to hurt you either."

The bar choked on another giggle-gasp. She laid the rack on the nearest table.

"But if your hand touches me, I will break it." The Woman said this matter-of-factly, devoid of threat or anger. It was immutable. She may as well have said "Today is Saturday."

T looked back at White Suit.

"Get her out of the way! We're leaving."

T nodded, turned back to the Woman, gave an oversized shrug. "I don't hit ladies, so I'm just gonna..." His beefy hand reached toward her shoulder. "C'mon now."

When Gideon recalled this moment, he would see it as a series of still images, like panels in a comic book. First panel, T's fingers making contact with the Woman's jacket.

Second panel, T's eyes wide in surprise as he sees his hand in the Woman's vice-tight grip.

Third panel, T on his knees howling, the Woman torquing his wrist to an improbable degree.

Fourth panel, a close-up of fingers jutting at odd angles, the words "CRACK" and "SNAP" written in huge, technicolor font.

Fifth panel, T curled on the ground, cradling his hand, the Woman standing over him, cool and unperturbed, a text bubble floating above her head:

"You should learn to hit ladies."

5

THE STUDENTS STARED AT HIM, agog.

"There is NO WAY she said that!" said the eager young fellow. *Evan, Evan, Evan,* Gideon thought to himself; memorizing names on day one was always a challenge. Evan spluttered on, "That's like what you hear in a movie."

Gideon held up his hands. "No, I swear. That's exactly what she said. And that's why I'm saying I felt like I was at a play. This woman... she was *performing* for everyone in the bar."

Evan was a dog with a bone. "So what happened next?"

"Act Two will have to wait, I've used up more time than I meant to, let's get to work. Everybody up, grab a partner!" The class grumbled good-naturedly as they moved to the stage and paired off.

"Mirroring is a foundational theatre exercise. It's been around since the first baby mimicked the first mommy's facial expressions. Partners, face each other, a couple feet apart. Choose an A and a B. A's raise your hands?"

Half a dozen hands went up.

"B's?"

The half dozen hands swapped for six of the other.

"Great. B's will start. All you're going to do is slowly move. Arms, legs, hands, head. Tilt forward, backward, sideways. Extreme facial expressions, wild fingers. But the goal is for your partner to be able to mirror you, to match precisely every movement you make. Your goal is not to fool your partner, that's easy, and funny only the first time. You want to lock in together so that an audience watching wouldn't be able to tell who's leading and who's following. And go."

The students began to move. The room filled with giggles and exclamations. Some pairs connected right off, while others struggled, but as the exercise went on the room got quieter and more focused.

"Now A's take the lead. Again, the goal is to appear as if no one is leading, that you two are moving in concert."

Gideon floated around the room, making small comments and suggestions, but also flipping mental flashcards, reviewing names and the information shared during introductions.

Here was Evan, the eager lad just out of acting conservatory and taking his first professional class in the big city. He exuded a sweet hope that Gideon hoped showbiz wouldn't stomp out of him too soon.

Evan was paired with Alfonso, who had proudly declared that his parents were immigrants from Zapopan, Mexico, and that he was taking the class to further his drag career. "Next time 'Salsa Verde' takes the stage, I'll be sure to let you all know!"

Gideon smiled inwardly as he saw Marcel, the oldest student in the group, paired with Emma, the youngest. Marcel was Polish, a retired surgeon who donated a big chunk of his time to training up first responders. Emma, soft-spoken and petite, wasn't even twenty but had seen *Wicked* when she was a kid and had dreamt of Broadway ever since.

The Forths, Dan and Joan, both worked in publishing, and were both each other's second spouse. They had met via an old-school print personal ad. The youngsters couldn't believe what they hearing. "Is that like Tinder?" Alfonso had asked, inadvertently setting Dan up for a punchline he had clearly used dozens of times. "No, son, if you swipe right on a newspaper you just smear the ink!"

Aniyah and Imani introduced themselves together, Imani doing most of the speaking. They had been friends since childhood. Imani did something in finance, and Aniyah had just moved in to Imani's guest room after life took a couple hard turns back in Detroit. They were taking the class as something fun to do together, and Gideon intuited also to help Aniyah find new friends and move forward.

Two aspiring actresses, like Evan just out of school, had immediately clicked and were mirroring like their lives and future Tony awards depended on it. Kaida was third-generation Japanese—"My name means 'little dragon'! Isn't that awesome??"—while Tosha's parents had moved to New York from Moscow when she was twelve. She wanted nothing more than to rip out the lingering Russian roots from her English. "No audience believes Russian Gypsy Rose Lee."

And the final pair was Rasheed and Rheia. Rasheed was the first in his Pakistani family to graduate from college, but four years into a frustrating TV and film career that had seen him play various versions of "Middle Eastern Terrorist" and not much else. He was desperate to expand his skills and land some juicier roles.

Rheia didn't reveal much but did warn that because she traveled a lot for work she might have to miss the occasional class. She had sat a few seats away from the main group and rarely moved or spoke. *Observer*, Gideon thought. And behind those high privacy walls, he guessed she possessed an acute b.s. detector.

"Great work, everyone! Take your seats. Any observations from that exercise?"

The discussion, as usual, focused on eyes being windows to the soul, the feeling of connectivity once you took it seriously, overcoming self- consciousness, becoming hypersensitive to the actual mechanics of how your muscles move your body, and—

"Releasing ego," Rheia said, beating Gideon to the punch.

"Go on."

"When I'm leading the mirror, it's not at all about what I do. It's about taking care of my partner. If Rasheed messed up, that actually was on me. Even though I was technically leading, I was serving something bigger than myself."

Eleven pairs of eyes swung Gideon's way. Rheia had nailed it, he had nothing to add, so he gave a confirming nod-shrug. Notes were furiously scribbled and typed.

But Rheia sat sphinx-like. Gideon met her unwavering gaze, and they suddenly had their own mirroring moment... was he assessing her assessing him? Or the other? Or both?

Tosha abruptly piped up. "Hey! We are still having a couple minutes—"

"—so can you tell the rest of your story?" Kaida finished.

Universal clamor.

"OK, OK. If this story takes me past time, you can leave if you've gotta catch your train or whatever."

"I still can't believe she said 'You should learn to hit ladies,'" Evan muttered. "So badass."

6

Had the Woman even moved? The amount of violence performed in those couple of seconds left the bar dumbfounded. The rack was back in her hands, idly spinning. White Suit and Wingman were staring at T, mouths agape. Gideon realized his mouth also hung open and closed it with a click.

The bar started to murmur. Gideon saw White Suit's knuckles turning white as he tightened his grip on the pool cue. *He's getting ready to attack*, Gideon thought.

But before White Suit could inhale to bark his big boy challenge, the Woman spoke. Still calm. Still in command.

"I want everyone here to note that actions have consequences. I have not behaved aggressively. I have simply stood up for someone else, and offered space for an apology multiple times. Unfortunately I also had to defend myself, though I gave fair warning. You all bear witness."

She turned her full attention to White Suit. His breathing accelerated. Wingman synced up, his massive bulk quivering.

"So. Gentleman. A second chance. How often do those come around? An apology, an offering from your wallet for this young man's urgent care visit, and I'll hold the door open for you. T will need medical attention as well."

The stillness pulled bowstring taut, twanged by T's occasional whimpering. Somewhere behind Gideon, a woman tried to suppress a cough. He again noted the oddity of the televisions having hushed.

White Suit shook his head and clucked his tongue. Gideon tensed.

Here it comes.

"What's your name, anyway?" White Suit said in a transparent attempt to catch the Woman off guard. The rack came to rest in her hands.

White Suit whipped his pool cue back like a baseball bat, a home run hitter trying to end the game. In reality, his cue hadn't even reached its rear apex before the Woman had stepped forward and pistoned a jab with the triangle.

The shortest distance between any two points, after all, is a straight line.

White Suit's head snapped back. His hands spasmed, releasing the cue. He staggered, widening his feet to keep his balance. Football being a more apt metaphor than baseball for this particular moment, the Woman's leg slash through a perfect punter's pendulum. The lowest part of her shin landed precisely between White Suit's legs, lifting him off the ground. White Suit and his pool cue hit the floor simultaneously.

Several patrons now finally moved. The four rugby friends stood and looked primed to jump in and rumble now that the Woman had subdued two of the three.

Wingman sensed it, too. All those hours flinging weights at the gym had in no way prepared him for this particular circumstance.

"*Third* chance. Seriously, you never *ever* get those."

Wingman looked around. Did the math. Reached into his

pocket and pulled out his wallet. Clutched it in his sweaty hand.

"Go ahead. Whatever cash you've got in there, that'll be just fine. Put it on the pool table. All good. Then take care of your friends."

One of the rugby dudes chimed in. "Yeah! That's right! That's what YOU get!" The bar trembled, other throats started to clear. But Gideon could tell the Woman didn't want a mob. The audience needed to stay the audience.

"No." The Woman's voice crackled with authority. Rugby Dude stepped back. "You are late to this party. Save it for next time."

"Next time?" Gideon asked the question impulsively. He felt the spotlight swing his way. The attention was terrifying and delicious, as electric a rush as he had ever felt on stage. The Woman's eyes—invisible behind the sunglasses—bored into him.

Wingman, his hackles up from Rugby Dude's taunt, in the end could not swallow his pride. Taking advantage of Gideon's inadvertent distraction, he lunged a huge left-hook at the Woman's head.

She slither-stepped aside. As the fist harmlessly sailed by, the Woman snapped her heel into Wingman's knee. He tumbled. In a blink she had lassoed his neck with the triangle, slid behind him, and pulled the triangle garrote-taut into his throat. He choked and flailed, but she was implacable. She spoke over Wingman's gasps.

"We live in a fallen world, my friend."

Wingman's eyes rolled up in his head. She released him and he thumped unconscious to the floor next to White Suit and T. The Woman turned to Gideon, not a hair out of place.

"There's always a next time."

7

Even after going over time, the students hadn't wanted to disperse. They were going to be a tight-knit group.

Evan, predictably, bent Gideon's ear into a pretzel.

"No way no way no WAY! She spoke directly to you? She dropped another Hollywood-perfect line on you??"

"That's how it happened, best I can remember."

Gideon was cleaning up, checking that no one had left anything behind, turning off lights and a/c. Evan babbled on even as everyone else evaporated into the steamy New York night.

"So did anyone call the cops? Did she say anything else to you? Did you get her name? DUDE did you get her number??"

Gideon set the ghost light, slung his well-traveled Osprey backpack over his shoulders, and placated Evan best he could. No, no one had called the cops, she hadn't said anything else, no name, definitely no number. He led Evan outside, locked the deadbolt, shook hands.

"Thanks Mr. Price, I mean Gideon, I mean that was awesome, can't wait for next class!"

"Glad to hear it, Evan. Good work tonight."

Gideon watched Evan whip out his cell and hurry away. He stood a moment. Took in the sudden solitude. Took out the final images of that night in the bar. He hadn't shared the denouement with the class, it sounded too bizarre...

Wingman thumps to the floor. The Woman turns to Gideon. "There's always a next time." The TVs suddenly blare. The lights flash blinding full. Even the CD jukebox in the corner thunders to life.

And in the chaos, the Woman disappears. Gideon glimpses her slipping out the exit, leaving White Suit, T, and Wingman in various states of brokenness on the beer-stained floor. He leaps after her, pressing through the surge of patrons. The cacophony, the crowd, the chaos, he fights through them all to reach the door.

He springs out onto the sidewalk. Looks left. Right. Left again.

She's gone.

He also hadn't told the class that he had gone back to the Bear and Fawn every night since, hoping the Woman would reappear. Or that his post-show bourbon that night had been a triple, and that in recent days those triples had doubled.

He couldn't even admit it to himself, so how could he tell the class?

His facade crumbled. He deflated. He slumped against the door. The city throbbed and honked and moaned.

His pockets were full of masks. He wadded up "charming teacher" and stuffed it in with the others.

Go home, Gideon. A nightcap, a couple chapters of the latest Neal Stephenson, hit the hay, all good.

To be haunted simply means you haven't let go of the past.

But what if the past won't let go of you? Does that make *you* the ghost? That's how Gideon felt, like a translucent wisp. But for a few weeks, during rehearsal for *Henry Five*, he had been able to pack the past away into the back of the tiny closet in his tiny sublet. No time to think, in the theater all day and night, surrounded by like-minded artists, nowhere to be but the present.

Bliss.

Losing himself in the show, anonymous in the giant city. For the first time in a long time, his sleep rejuvenated. No sweat. No dreams. No tangled blankets. Exactly what Gideon had hoped for, escaping to New York.

Just go the hell home.

But then the show had opened. And Gideon found himself with time. So much time. Too much time and too few masks. Anonymity rotted from blessing to burden. Solitude curdled into loneliness. So much *time.* His sleep evaporated. The past bounded out of the closet, too bulky to stuff in his pockets with the masks.

GO. HOME.

So the past became his only companion through morning minutes and afternoon hours. Every day a slogging struggle to get to the respite of the evening: fight call and make-up and costumes and co-stars and audience and bows and then...

The past. Hanging out at the stage door, eager for an autograph.

Gideon heaved himself onto the sidewalk, plodded toward the intersection where he'd have to decide how to kill time while Tuesday shed the mottled skin of Monday.

Can't kill time without injuring eternity.

The show still had two months to go in its run, but already he could feel the void looming beyond closing. What then? Where to?

Don't think about that, Gideon thought, knowing full well that the surest way to think about something is to tell yourself not to think about it. *Just go home, dammit.*

He reached the intersection. The Bear and Fawn beckoned a couple blocks this way, his sweaty bed that way.

The past gossiped at his side, oblivious.

Gideon pretended to deliberate.

The lights changed. Crosswalks filled. He turned this way, trudged yet again toward the Bear and Fawn. The Woman *had* something, *knew* something. And Gideon wanted it. He *needed* it, even if he couldn't articulate what it was. If only he could ask her.

And you know what? Even if she didn't appear, the bourbon would.

Wrapped up in the contemplation of this shittiest of win-wins, he didn't note the shadow that peeled itself off the wall and drift behind him step for step.

8

Aniyah blogged in Imani's guest room, several trainstops away from where Gideon was raising three fingers to the bartender.

Her therapist had recommended getting things out. Thoughts and feelings, just get them out, diminish their paralyzing power by fencing them in with words. Nothing public, necessarily—her blog's privacy settings were locked down. But she could access it anywhere, anytime the pressure got to be too much.

Aniyah smiled as she typed about her first-ever acting class earlier that evening. The idea had been Imani's but also received enthusiastic approval from her therapist when Aniyah had mentioned it in session.

She muttered one of the ridiculous tongue-twister warm-ups as she typed—*Unique New York. Unique New York. I need unique New York. You need unique New York. I know you need unique New York.*

But, as always, her thoughts started skewing toward darkness. The friendly faces of the other students, the instructor

Imani couldn't stop commenting on ("those kind eyes, that Daredevil-y profile, those *shoul- ders*"), the incredible moment when they clicked on their mirroring... it all faded. Sucked into the whirlpool.

Aniyah's fingers pounded agony into words. So many words, but never enough. Thoughts of her daughter and her soon-to-be ex- husband—*my fault, my fault*—memories, feelings, curses, regrets. Bailing water on a sinking ship.

9

Gideon may not have sighted the Woman, but that didn't mean she wasn't there, leaning against the iron gate of an Italian joint opposite the bar. She watched Gideon leave the Bear and Fawn. Clockwork.

She thought back to that night. She'd been tracking a potential target, but then... White Suit. An unscripted performance, but nothing special. Except for Gideon. His attention radiated. She could tell he was reading the room as keenly as she. Then to see him burst out the door, and feel his eyes pass right over her? He was fast; she'd barely made her quick change.

Intrigued, she dug. Discovered who he was. Had an idea. Pitched it. Maintained surveillance on her own time.

As Gideon waited at the crosswalk, the Woman opened a browser on her phone, logged in to the pre-arranged web-based email account. Found a message sitting in the DRAFTS folder.

The body was empty. The subject read: "Update on side gig?"

She deleted the draft. Started a new one, leaving the "TO:" line empty. No inadvertent sending.

SUBJECT: "Side Gig Update."

BODY: "He is exactly what we need."

She paused her composition but kept her thumbs moving, pretending to type, shifted her attention without shifting her eyes. Gideon passed in front of her, close enough to touch.

Up close... she could see through him. Something was hollowing him out. He wasn't a husk. Yet. But if the whiskey fumes were any indication, he soon would be.

And that would be a waste.

The Woman watched him all the way to the end of the block. He stopped for a beat, as though sensing her eyes on his back, but then curled around the corner.

And we could be exactly what he needs, she thought.

She finished her email—"Request permission to make offer"—left it in the DRAFTS folder. Tucked her phone into a pocket. Melted into an alley.

Her shift was just starting.

10

Gideon wiped sweat from his face as he set up the pressure cooker. Chugged some water. Kicked off his running shoes, Hoka Cliftons, ever and only. The first trickle of runner's high hit his bloodstream, addictive like 80 proof.

He FaceTimed his mom. Docked the phone in a charging cradle and kept puttering toward breakfast.

"Good morning, number one fun son!"

"Hey mom, how's it?"

"Just walking the park, your father's at the pool, I'll be taking some muffins over to the rec center later." His mother's running monologue of the upcoming day's trials and tribulations continued as he peeled an orange.

"Hot down there today?"

"Oh you know, it's Florida, endless summer and limitless sweat. How many miles today?"

"Just over ten. Best way to learn a city? Run it."

"Ten miles on a Monday morning??"

"Clears my mind, momma."

"But didn't you just have five shows in three days?"

"More like five shows in 50 hours. Friday night, double Saturday, double Sunday. Gotta love matinees."

The pressure cooker beeped. He flicked the release valve. It hissed like a happy snake.

"Oh you're using the pressure cooker I got you for your birthday!"

"Yep. Perfect eggs every morning. They peel like a dream." And he started dream-peeling.

"So how did your five shows go? And what's that theatre called again? The Hootch? The Hitch?"

"The Hatchery. Remember my grad school buddy Shawn?"

"Oh yes."

"It's his baby." Orange and eggs were peeled, he cut the eggs in half, topped them with salt, pepper, a couple home-made pickled jalapeños. "It's what they call an 'incubator' theatre, mom. Only like 50 seats, little black box, just enough lights to do something funky. Although Shawn did just put in a sweet new sound system, he got a grant I think."

"Oh hi there Marlene, it's a hot one today isn't it?"

Gideon refilled his coffee as Marlene confirmed it was indeed a hot one.

"So this whole adventure is working out for you, Gideon?"

"Yeah, it's going great. I wasn't sure how a modern dress, six-person *Henry the Fifth* would play, especially in summer, but Shawn crushed it. Adapted the script, directed, designed the sound."

"Wow!"

"Yeah. And he's had my back the whole way. Set me up with this sublet."

"Is it tiny?"

"The tiniest. The kitchen is the bedroom—or maybe the bedroom is the kitchen—and the hot plate fritzed out my second day here. This pressure cooker is saving my life."

"Oh now now now."

"Shawn put together this amazing cast and he's even letting me use the space on Monday nights to teach an acting class."

"You don't even get a night off? Oh sweetheart."

"No, mom, it's... it's everything I need right now. We opened strong, got a couple good reviews—"

"The New York Times??"

Gideon chuckled. "No mom, nothing like that. On-line stuff, bloggers, still useful." He crammed an entire jalapeño'd half egg into his mouth.

"And I had twelve students last week—"

"Manners, young man."

He swallowed, chased with coffee. "Sorry. Anyway, taking a leap like this, in the heart of New York? Came at the right time. And whatever happens... well."

They chattered, he ate as mom walked, he was just about to sign off and wash up when she took a big breath and said...

"I understand you almost found your sister."

A bomb of silence exploded. Shrapnel pierced old wounds, tore open fresh.

Invisible scars are the thickest.

"I'm sorry, Gideon, I know it's not... I just..."

He forced his hands to unclench, then noted his mom trying to hide the fact she was crying.

"I missed her by a couple days, mom. No word since."

"Well." She sniffled. "No one blames you."

I do, Gideon thought. But out loud he said, "I know, mom." Thankfully just then she arrived home and her rescue min pin's yapping gave Gideon an out. "Love you, give Tinkerbell a treat for me, talk again soon."

"You too, Gideon. I hope you know how much. Have a good class tonight."

He clicked "end" and breathed, leaning on the tiny sink in the tiny sublet in the gigantic city.

11

Gideon led his students through a series of warm-ups. "Tonight I want you to think of theatre as *violence*."

The students startled.

"Yes, movement and speech are *violent*. But remove the pejorative baggage. It's like a doctor: do no harm, but this may hurt."

Marcel grunted through a side stretch. "Two more inches and my hurt may harm me, Mr. Price."

"I hear that Marcel!" Imani tagged on. The group chuckled.

Gideon smiled and continued. "Here's the thing. Creation requires violence. Think of any birthing scene in a movie." More chuckles, and Dan whispered something to Joan. She promptly shoved him off- balance.

"Care to share, Dan?"

"Oh she was just thanking me for feeding her ice chips as our boy was birthed."

"SEVENTEEN HOURS!" Joan hollered. But she was smiling.

The Woman wasn't watching Gideon tonight. She had his routine down. Running. Teaching. Performing. Drinking.

Side gig on pause. Back to our regularly scheduled program. The show must go on.

She settled into a shadow, watched the door of the brownstone across the street. A bulky sentry with an Iron Cross tattoo stamped on his forearm held post at the base of the stairs. The target, if she stuck to her pattern, would soon emerge.

The warm-up progressed. Gideon kept up a running commentary as he guided their bodies through flexes and twists.

"Creation literally alters the state of matter. It changes something from this into that. And there's nothing humans hate more than change. So think of violence as the effort and energy required to effect change. The pickle jar goes from stuck to open only through grunting and straining, hitting it on the counter, running it under water, using a towel—"

"My mom had one of those plastic grippy things!" Emma chirped.

"And once she torqued it hard enough?" Gideon snapped his fingers. "POP. Violence. Even more—you bite that dang pickle. CRUNCH. Violence. Transforming brined cucumber into bodily fuel."

The Woman saw the sentry turn his head a couple degrees, listening. "Adler, confirming sentry has an earbud. Can you hack it?" Her sub- vocalization was inhaled by the exquisitely sensitive microphone in her sunglasses, exhaled into the wireless ether.

The sentry nodded. Ascended. Opened the door. The target emerged. Adler's voice buzzed through the bone conduction speakers engineered into the earpieces. "Can I hack it?? If a bear takes a crap in the woods, is the Pope still Catholic?"

"A simple 'yes' would suffice, Adler."

"Not my style."

"And maybe don't talk into a microphone with your mouth full."

"Hey, you caught me during dinner."

"It sounds... strangely wet."

"Strangely Wet. Good song title."

The Woman watched the target saunter down the stairs and up the street, a bully among bullies. Untouchable. The sentry re-posted.

The Woman's heart rate ticked up. Adrenaline flooded her system. "Fearlessness is a lie," the Director often said. "Butterflies, stage fright, fight or flight, whatever you want to call it, it's necessary. The day you aren't nervous before a performance is the day you should quit. Because that means you no longer care, you're no longer invested, you no longer have anything at stake. Step into your fear."

The target turned the corner. Weekly Thai fix. Nothing makes an untouchable touchable more quickly than routine.

"Adler, I'm going on. Stand by sound cue 1. Squelch that bud LOUD."

"Ready sound cue 1. Break a leg."

The Woman stepped out of the shadow.

"Likewise, art is violent. Theatre is violent. Break it down. SPEAKING is violent. You have silence... and you speak into it. You destroy that silence, transform it. You have a vowel sound. *Ee ay ai oh ooh.* That vowel sound can continue indefinitely until you introduce a consonant. Consonants are cleavers, chopping vowels into words. You can't hold a 'd' sound. It bites off the vowel. Violence creates meaning."

The Woman walked past the sentry, head down, sunglasses and bangs hiding her face. She angled close, brushed her arm against him.

His voice rumbled. "Nice ass."

God. So easy. She stopped. Turned. Lifted her face to give him a good look.

His lips slashed into a jagged leer. "Think you're in the wrong place, mulatto."

"Nooooo," she purred. "I'm right where I need to be."

"Painting is violent. Writing is violent. You have a blank canvas, an empty page, and then... paint splatters. The keystroke strikes a letter, a word, a sentence onto the page. You have fundamentally altered that canvas, that page."

He flicked his tongue. "Unless you want me to take a bite out of that juicy exotic ass, move along. Whites only around here."

"Sound go."

The sentry's head twisted sideways as his come-on was cut

short by a deafening digital shriek deep in his ear canal. He staggered up the stairs as his fingers dug.

As he pulled the bud free, a collapsible steel baton dislocated his jaw. He hadn't seen it materialize in her hand, much less heard it snick long.

"CHOOSING is violent. It costs. And when you recognize that cost, paying it becomes your choice. The classic marriage vow... forsaking all others? The act of courage is saying no to everyone else so you can say yes to the one."

"You've got that right," Joan said, wrapping her arms around Dan. He put up token resistance. But he was smiling.

Alfonso hooted. "You gotta teach me your moves, girlfriend!"

The Woman's follow-through whipped around into a backhand and the baton shattered the sentry's orbital bone just as he was registering the first blow. He bounced off the door and fell forward. Her knee ascended in a vicious arc to meet his descending chin.

"Violence must also be specific. Generality no one gets. You must get painfully, microscopically specific, and only in that specificity will you find universal truth. Specificity is why we can keep performing Shakespeare, because otherwise why bother? It's been done. But not done THIS way in THIS time by THIS company for THIS audience with THIS director and

THIS cast and THIS design team in THIS venue within THIS current social and political and economic situation. Every time you specify a THIS... you are doing violence."

The knob turned. Hinges flexed. A second guard stood framed in the doorway, baffled by the sight of his crumpled twin. His gaze flicked up to see a woman with bangs, ponytail, and dark sunglasses. Her stillness... the tilt of her head... he was twice her size... but her bemused assessment of him reminded him of the snake, Scaley, the mascot of his eighth-grade class, and when his day to feed a mouse to Scaley had come he had watched the mouse sniff Scaley's coiled length and Scaley hadn't moved and hadn't moved and the suspense had made him almost cry in front of the girl he liked—

"Adler?"

"Ready sound cue 2. Obviously."

"Sound go."

A sonic explosion incinerated his memory of Scaley and then his kneecap shattered and then a couple other parts of his body erupted in pain and then mercifully he was unconscious.

"Music? Violent. You pound the keyboard, yes? You blow through any wind or brass instrument. You pluck strings, or strum them, or fret them, all active verbs that imply energy upon them, stress upon them, violence upon them. Heck when you do a sculpture you literally hit the rock with a hammer and chisel!"

The bully among bullies returned, a bag smelling of peanut, ginger, and lemongrass swinging from her hand.

She turned the corner. It took her a few steps to decipher what she was seeing. Her door was wide open. And two wrestler-sized bodies were haphazardly sprawled across the sidewalk.

She stopped, started to dig out her phone, muster reinforcements, start the revenge flywheel a-spinnin'. This had to be the mestizos or the blacks making some sort of opening salvo. She would put it right, she hadn't risen to the rank of Centurion by accident. The Owners rarely gave a woman so much power, but she had earned it, and she would keep it, and she would—

"What do you think happened?"

She flinched. The voice belonged to an uppity brown woman in a dark jacket and sunglasses who had suddenly appeared beside her. "Get lost, mutt."

The mutt's jacketed arm snaked under her throat and squeezed with implacable force. Her phone clattered and her Thai splattered as she clawed for air.

"Violence is transformative. And by this point you know I'm not talking about gratuitous violence that gets a movie an R rating instead of PG-13. That sort of violence... y'know, where exactly does that hail of bullets land anyway? All the laser blasts that miss their target? They eventually hit somewhere, don't they? And blow up something? But when violence merely *looks* awesome, it's not actually transformative. Violence must be in service of your target."

An anonymous tip resulted in a couple squad cars hastily arriving on the scene. The officers found an upper echelon white nationalist cell leader and her two enforcers ziptied together in the foyer. Weapons, maps, and plans for an assault on the Mayor's home were stacked neatly in a damning pile on the entry table, the leader's phone perched like a cherry on top.

The Woman was already on a train four stops away.

She sub-vocalized. "Get everything ok?"

Adler's chewing was still strangely wet. "Yep. Phone, tablets, laptops, you did good. Everything uploaded and downloaded, gonna start dissecting."

"Your sunglasses keep getting more amazing, Adler."

"Tell me somethin' I don't know! And would you pleeeeease start calling 'em 'shades'? 'Sunglasses' is so... corporate."

"We'll see. I'm gonna do a quick pass by the Bear and Fawn."

"Side gig?"

"Yeah. See you back at the Rehearsal Room."

***

"We'll talk a lot more about targets next week. Dress to move and sweat."

12

NEAR CORTEZ, FLORIDA

The printer spat out page after page.

JEWS ARE GENOCIDING YOU.

JEWS ARE GENOCIDING YOU.

JEWS ARE GENOCIDING YOU.

The young white man meticulously stacked each new page of block letters, centered, bold, brave, 72 point font. Except for the word "genociding" which he had to format to 66 points so it wouldn't auto-wrap. The details mattered. Precision kept you safe, so Granddad had beaten into him.

The dumpster-dived laptop had a couple cracks but still worked just fine as a word processor. A warning box popped up —low on ink. Again. He grimaced. He did need to upgrade his printer, though. Big time.

As he fiddled with ink, he kept an eye on his primary flatscreen—a Black Friday steal from last year. He had hooked it up to his homemade system of daisy-chained desktops—a couple stolen from the Technical College down the road, one purchased at the outlet mall up the highway, one inherited from Granddad.

Multiple news channels regurgitated footage of BLM marchers and libtard protestors. Justice? Peace? Hypocrites and morons. He kept the news muted so he could listen to the truth.

The portable Bluetooth speaker, paired with his phone, encouraged him to buy bullion because when the financial system collapsed you'd want gold and silver, not paper. The commercial break ended.

"Everyone's gotta wake up! *The Devil is at our door!!*" He pumped the volume. This guest on his favorite podcast, THE SCOURGE, sounded like he was about to drop a truth bomb.

"People will try to profile you. They will try to 'figure you out.' Let them! Let them waste their time! Like this newest Marx-lover in Congress, Stacy Mallory. Calling for expanded background checks and anti-racism training and all this other touchy-feely nonsense? We cannot be pigeonholed, we cannot be stuck in a box. We come from all backgrounds, but we share one creed. The Fourteen Words. THE FOURTEEN WORDS! We don't believe the Fourteen Words because our mommies didn't love us. We aren't riddled with poverty and drugs. That's THEM. And that is what sets us apart. We behold truth, and we accept it. They are weak, the precious snowflakes, the ones who rage in the streets and burn down our country. I can understand it from the non-Whites, they literally don't have the mental capacity to understand. But you know who baffles me? Who terrifies me? The Whites who protest with them. Who have turned their backs on their people. I say —those who betray us deserve a fate even worse than those who resist us!"

The young man nodded, refilled the wheezing printer with

paper. It whirred, choked out another JEWS ARE GENO-CIDING YOU.

The host of the podcast, a silken-voiced man who went by the name AlphaSupreme, took back the mic.

"Thank you, Congressman. You have shown admirable courage coming on THE SCOURGE. To my listeners, we altered the Congressman's voice to protect his identity from the drive-by media and police state, but if you follow the clues, you will be able to decipher his home district, and those of you who live there... get out and vote. Keep him in the halls of power. We need leaders like him now more than ever."

The young man scrambled to his keyboard, logged in to the podcast's "Members Only" portal—username SPEARHEAD-1488–and dug up the digital breadcrumbs. The Congressman unfortunately did not represent his district but represented him in every other way that counted. He made a mental note to send a campaign donation.

He grabbed the speaker, stepped outside to enjoy the last streaks of sunset reflecting off Palma Sola Bay. Simple pleasures. Another inheritance from Granddad. This shack, this view, this purity.

AlphaSupreme wrapped the show. "And now, wherever you are, my friends, let us speak the Fourteen Words together."

The young man bowed his head and heard Granddad's ghost whis- pering on the briny breeze in unison with him and AlphaSupreme... "*We must secure the existence of our people and a future for white children.*" "Good night, my friends. Remain vigilant. For as the Congressman said... the Devil is at our door."

13

To RUN the perimeter of the island of Manhattan would be almost exactly 37.5 miles.

Gideon had been taking bites out of the perimeter since arriving two months earlier. Since the island was over 13 miles long north to south but only about 2 miles wide, most of his routes went east or west from his sublet in Hell's Kitchen before turning to trace the perimeter.

As he always did when first exploring a new locale, he started with the primary veins and arteries. A city of any size was a living organism, pumping traffic and commerce and information throughout its extremities in patterns only discernible with organic calculus.

The UN Route, as he labeled it in his running app, took him past Bryant Park on 42nd to the East River. Turning right at the United Nations he quickly learned to love the Greenway, several miles of waterfront that led him past the Water Club, the Brooklyn Bridge, all the way to Battery Park at the southern tip.

The Hudson River was just a hop-skip to the west of his

tiny apartment, and heading south on the West Side Highway meant passing the High Line and Chelsea Piers before also terminating at Battery Park, where the Statue of Liberty greeted him from across the water. Since it was a one-way-south route, he would then work his way back up through Lower Manhattan, sometimes veering through the East Village but usually enjoying Washington Square Park.

Broadway of course proved invaluable as a central through-line. And within a couple weeks he had traversed the southern portion of the island multiple times and claimed not quite a third of the entire perimeter.

Exploring Harlem, Washington Heights, and Inwood way up there at the northern tip was going to require longer runs, but he was in no hurry. The Upper East and West sides unfolded before him, but—and he knew it was the obvious choice, a cliche even—he just couldn't get enough of running Central Park.

Today he looped the entire park, just under nine miles total, heading up Eighth Avenue to enter at Columbus Circle. Up the Great Hill, down through the Conservatory Garden, slowing his pace by the Jackie Onassis Reservoir to take in the sweeping views of the skyline.

His Hoka Cliftons propelled him through ghosts of movies past. There... isn't that Will Ferrell as an elf? And John Wick running for his life? And here is where Thor whisked Loki back to Asgard at the end of *The Avengers*, while over there is the patch of pathway where Harry and Sally met yet again. And nearing the end of his loop there's the Plaza Hotel, and if you squint you can see Macaulay Culkin, Cary Grant, and Dudley Moore all ascending the steps.

Back to Columbus Circle, leaving the shade of the trees and re- entering the simmering summer streets. And maybe it's just the heat, or because his Garmin buzzes his wrist with his split for mile eight, or because a taxi leaps past like Spartacus' chariot almost clipping him on the sidewalk, but suddenly there's a shimmer glinting off a window, and it's not a Holly-wood star he sees but the face of his sister.

Her mouth moves.

Hey big bro.

Every run. No matter which direction. She's there but just out of reach. Like punishment.

He never could outrun her. Not in a sprint, definitely not cross country. But if he's always the one who's behind, why does he feel like the one being chased?

What if... he just stopped?

Another shimmer, another chariot honks, her face is gone, and he knows he never could. Because then she would vanish forever.

He weaves through the hustling bustle, his Hokas' odometer chewing through tread.

14

THE WOMAN WATCHED Gideon leave the Hatchery. He lingered by the stage door with his castmates. A few members of the audience had hung around to thrust out playbills and pens.

She logged on to the web-based email. A new message sat in the draft box.

SUBJECT: Rules of Engagement

Finally! She glanced up. The Shakespeare fans were skipping away with autographs while the cast headed out for a post-show drink. Their production of *Henry the Fifth* was astonishing. She had found it muscular and surprisingly timely.

The cast turned the corner. Looked like he had talked them into the Bear and Fawn. Again.

She looked back down at her phone.

BODY: You are cleared to make offer. But keep him in the dark. Also good work on the cell.

Bingo, thought the Woman. Gideon would help the Troupe take a huge step forward. Especially Stan, he couldn't act his way out of a paper bag.

She deleted the draft. Created a new one. Left it unsent in the draft box. Logged off.

SUBJECT: ROE

BODY: Understood. You won't be sorry.

15

Gideon and his twelve students stood in a circle. He held thirteen dowel rods. Each rod was three feet long and half an inch in diameter.

"You've possibly heard the term 'objective' before." A few looked unsure but all the recent graduates nodded excitedly.

"That is what your character is wanting, correct?" Tosha said.

"Yes, but that *wanting* can be a trap. Ultimately the objective is not about you." He lifted the rods. "Behold, your objectives for the night." The group buzzed. As Gideon had instructed last week, they all were dressed to move and sweat. Sneakers, yoga pants, athletic shirts and shorts. The Forths wore matching New York Rangers T's. Marcel sported a Polish national team soccer jersey.

"We gonna duel?" asked Dan.

"Only with yourself," Gideon replied. He handed a dowel rod to each of them, stepped to the center of the circle. "For now, just observe." Gideon bent at the waist, pinched his dowel rod lightly between right thumb and first two fingers, tapped it gently on the floor, came to complete stillness. The students held their breath, instantly transformed into an audience by the sheer power of attention being paid.

He pushed his feet into the floor and the floor pushed back. That force guided his torso and by extension his arm, and he flicked the dowel into the air, eye-height, perfectly vertical. At the precise moment the rod came to stillness, the apex, when all upward momentum had been drained and just before its downward plummet, Gideon floated his hand in underneath, palm up, and caught the rod as gently as a snowflake on a tongue.

The dowel balanced there, quivering, all sorts of forces playing upon it.

Gideon's eyes were locked on the delicate piece of wood. He remained athletic, knees bent. It seemed a string connected the rod to his heart, so as the rod moved, he moved. If it started listing right, his arm followed. As it tried to dump left, his feet instinctively adjusted.

From the students not a sound. Only Gideon's feet scuffling as the stick led him on a dance within the circle.

Gideon extended his left hand and passed the stick from his right, a movement of simplicity and grace. The students blinked. A few gasped. He passed the stick back. Forth. Back and forth. Palm. Various fingers. Back of the hand. It remained vertical and alive.

His hand flexed through an abracadabra twist and the stick ended up balanced on the tip of his thumb.

"It's like the circus," Emma whispered.

"Speaking of..." Gideon whispered back. He lifted the stick higher, let it step from thumb to upturned chin, and extended both arms. The rod stood straight and tall, jutting from his chin toward the ceiling, still quivering, still trying to fall, but Gideon followed every vibration, his body intuitively defending the stick from gravity's onslaught.

As Gideon tried to move the stick back from chin to finger, it passed the point of no return. The rod clattered to the floor. The students broke into spontaneous applause.

"And now you," he said, picking up his stick and gesturing everyone to spread out. Multiple hands went up and multiple voices asked questions but he shook his head. "Don't interrogate it yet. Just try. And don't worry about these sticks hurting your fellow students when they fall. They are super light." He reached out and bonked Alfonso on the head with his dowel.

"Didn't hurt a bit!" Alfonso confirmed.

Everyone laughed and moved into space. Tapping and grunting and footsteps, muttered curses and sticks rolling on the ground, bodies zipping past each other as sticks disobeyed, a few "how did you do thats?" and a lot more "Sorrys!" as sticks bounced off shoulders and backs.

Gideon wove through the room, offered encouragements.

He saw right off that Aniyah and Rasheed were both struggling, but headed in vastly different emotional directions. Aniyah's breath came in viscous bursts. She was sweating, clenching her teeth, trying every variation of hand and foot. Rasheed got quieter and quieter, taking more time between every attempt. Neither would get the stick vertical anytime soon.

Rheia was a natural. She missed her first toss, but on her second try the stick landed ramrod straight on her palm, and she had already moved on to passing, traveling, and walking the stick from finger to finger.

He saw Imani catch the stick as it fell, not letting it go all the way to the floor. "Let it fall!" he called out. Imani looked up, and everyone paused. He demonstrated, dropping his own stick so it clattered.

"Every time. Let it fall. No catching. Full restart every time."

Imani gave him a playful "Are you kidding me?" look, then dramatically tossed her stick into the air. As it clattered she gave a soap-operatic sigh.

"Exactly. Thank you, Imani. On you all go."

Everyone was sweating. Marcel and Dan sat down together for a quick breather, compared notes. Joan, though, kept passing her stick back and forth, and let Dan know all about it. Evan and Kaida were just a step behind Rheia, exploring trickier moves. Tosha, Emma, and Alfonso had gotten to the point of attempting their first hand-to-hand pass.

Aniyah was boiling, looking around the room with both embar- rassment and hope she could steal a tip from someone else's success. Rasheed was wrapped in a shroud... tap tap... toss... momentary struggle... clatter. Tap tap toss. Tap tap toss.

As Marcel and Dan stood back up, Gideon moved to center stage and said, "So what works?"

"If the toss isn't straight up and down, you're toast," Evan offered. Nods all around.

"So how do you ensure the toss is straight?"

Joan piped up. "You can't throw it from the wrist, that torques the stick off vertical. You've gotta throw it... well, from your shoulder, but more like from your feet."

"Great observation. The only part of our bodies in constant touch with the earth is our feet. The earth, from which all our power comes. What else?"

"I was having trouble until I noticed where other people were looking," Kaida said. "I kept looking at my hand, at where the stick was supposed to land. But then I saw how Joan and Rheia basically never looked at their hands. Their eyes were always on the stick."

"Absolutely one hundred percent yes." Gideon tossed his stick, balanced it on his finger. "Watch my eyes, everyone." He locked in on the stick. "I know where my hand is, yes? I don't need to look at my hand to know where it is. As soon as I look at my hand..." He shifted his eyes down. Immediately the stick started wobbling. He shifted his gaze back up, regained balance.

"Looking at your hand is navel-gazing. Looking at yourself means you aren't looking at your stick. Or your scene partner. Or your life. Self-indulgence is the death of good acting. As I said at the beginning of class, it's not about you. It's never about you. It's about your target. The target, in this case the stick, will always tell you what it needs, and where to go."

Gideon suddenly flung his arm up. The stick went through a graceful flip in the air and came down perfectly vertical to land on his palm. Balanced.

"Oh my god!" Imani said.

"I am so trying that," Rheia said.

"Stick whisperer," Dan said.

16

"I JUST! CAN'T! GET IT!" Aniyah snatched her stick off the floor and cracked it across her knee. It snapped. She stood in the center of the circle, a piece of splintered dowel clutched in each of her trembling fists.

The room got very quiet. Gideon gave Aniyah a couple moments to breathe, then bluntly asked, "Why'd you break the stick? It's not the stick's fault."

The room got even quieter. The expected teacherly comfort had not come. If anything, the teacher had just made the situation *more* uncomfortable.

Gideon joined Aniyah in the circle. Everyone else had already had their solo moment in the middle, balancing their stick with the added pressure of an audience watching.

Tosha had demonstrated ease while Kaida had balanced her stick for just as long but with flamboyant movement. Marcel held his stick vertical for an impressively long time, his nimble feet hopping non-stop. Dan had finally passed from right hand to left, while Joan had gotten the stick to her chin for a split second. They kissed hard in celebration, and the class hooted.

Evan and Emma both achieved multiple clean passes, and Alfonso had started singing a Diana Ross song as he worked the circle. "Salsa Verde does love a good long straight stick," he said with a wink.

Rheia was sublime, the room felt sacred as she danced with her stick. She finished her solo with a flip attempt—the class gasped. She just missed the catch—the class groaned. Rheia gave a little bow as the students applauded her back to her place in the circle.

Rasheed had muttered, "I have to follow HER? I haven't even gotten it balanced one time yet." He wrapped himself back up in his cocoon of silence and proceeded to drop the stick over and over and over. Gideon could tell any offering of encouragement or escape would be summarily rejected, so he watched and waited. Until Rasheed happened to catch the stick on his pinky and chased it in a wobbling circle for two quick seconds before it fell to the floor. He turned and pumped his arms in the air and shrieked "I GOT IT!!!" The class joined in his rapturous joy as he did a shuffle and kept saying "I got it! I got it!"

Gideon received Rasheed's enthusiastic high five and then spoke. "Notice how we celebrated both Rheia and Rasheed? How both of their stories were immensely fulfilling, though entirely different? Catharsis can be achieved any number of ways. Stick a pin in that." The class nodded, a few scampered to their notebooks and phones to make a written note. "Imani, you're up."

Imani had kept up a running dialogue with her stick: "Where do you think you're going? Oh that's nice, good stick, good good stick. No no, wait, what are you doing? Oh COME ON stick!" She instinctively caught her stick as it fell, but then felt Gideon's eyes and with a huff let it drop to the floor. It clattered, the students clapped, and as she picked it back up she asked "WHY do we have to let it drop??"

"I'm glad you asked, Imani." He gestured her back to the outside of the circle and took her place inside. "So often in acting we think of objective and motivation as these holy grails. But they only scratch the surface."

Gideon held his stick across both palms like a sword.

"You may have been thinking that your objective is to not let the stick fall. Except the fall is the most important part. Every time you balance the stick, it's an entire play. It has a beginning, which is what the tapping signifies, the blackout before the curtain rises." He tapped, got still, and tossed, caught the stick on his finger.

"A middle..." He moved about, did a couple passes.

"And an end." He planted his feet, held his arm still, and waited. A couple beats later, the stick fell.

"No matter how long I balance the stick, it will fall. It MUST fall. Because a story only matters when it ends. The lights have to go down. The curtain has to close. The audience has to go home. And our job as actors is to make sure that for the moments they are investing in our story we are giving them the best, scariest, funniest, most meaningful story we can."

He tapped, got still, and tossed, balanced again.

"If I give myself permission to catch the stick..." He let the stick start to fall but then caught it, no clatter. "Then I haven't allowed the story to end. I haven't let go. I am shortchanging the story, the audience, and myself. Because instead of fighting like hell to keep that stick upright, I'm giving up. The stick is going to fall. Of course it is. It must. But my struggle to keep it balanced is what makes it a story."

He tapped and got still, tossed and balanced.

"This is why I tell you to always let it drop. Because only

when you deny yourself the permission to catch it will you then do everything you can to keep it up." Once again he attempted a flip, but this time he missed. "So was that a failure? Or a complete story? Just because the protagonist may not 'win'—and in a tragedy they pretty much never do—that doesn't mean the audience didn't receive a full, gutsy, cathartic experience."

Imani pursed her lips, mock-disappointed. "OK. Fine. Good answer." Then Aniyah had entered the circle, and after a dozen tosses, none of which had resulted in a balanced stick, she had snapped, both herself and her stick. Gideon wasn't surprised by her frustration, but she had gone several degrees hotter than he expected. Something deep inside her was working itself out.

Gideon faced Aniyah in the circle. Her eyes were brimming. He held out his hand. She passed over the two pieces.

"Sorry about your stick, I'll pay for it."

"Nonsense. Here." He extended his stick. She lowered her eyes, stricken.

"If I thought you really couldn't get it, I'd say move on." He tapped her arm with the stick. She gripped it hard. Pulled, but he held his end tight. She looked up. "But no. I'm not going to take this away from you, Aniyah. And no one here is judging you. In fact, you have never been in a more supportive room in your life. Everyone here is rooting like hell for you. Now get to it."

He released his end of the stick and backed away, rejoining the circle. Aniyah stared at the stick in her hand.

The other students fidgeted. Gideon remained utterly still. The students felt his calm assurance radiating. The fidgeting evaporated. Aniyah whispered into the silence... "What if I can't? What if it simply won't balance?"

Gideon whispered back... "Balance is not a static state. It is only ever a moment, that must be created again and again. Ongoing. The stick will never balance. Only you will."

She squeezed her eyes shut.

"Aniyah. You know where your hand is."

She leaned over, tapped the stick on the floor.

"You don't have to see your hand to know where it is."

She opened her eyes, took a deep breath, and tossed.

The entire room held its breath. The stick came to its apex. Perfectly vertical. Perfectly still.

And it stayed there. Balanced exquisitely on Aniyah's outstretched palm.

She gasped. Her face was luminous. She started to move about the circle, her eyes locked on the stick.

Gideon glanced around. Everyone was transfixed. The entire universe was a flimsy, two-dollar dowel.

"Stay with it, Aniyah, don't look at me, just hear my voice. Don't think. Pass the stick to your other hand. Go. Now."

Aniyah executed an elegant pass.

"Pass it back. Don't think. Go."

The stick wobbled but rebalanced on her original palm. Something in her cracked open and she started to laugh.

"Go to your knees. Now." She knelt, the stick still alive and awake and aloft.

"To your back." She laid back, reached fully supine, instinctively adjusted her wrist to accommodate the new angle.

"Stand back up." She hesitated. "DON'T THINK. Go before you're ready. Now."

Aniyah stood, and the stick protested, started to lean. The students inhaled as Aniyah stutter-stepped and ducked and bobbed and regained balance. The students exhaled into cheering and whistling.

"What next? What next?!" Aniyah called.

"Rheia, step in with her." With an eager grin Rheia leaped into the circle. "Aniyah, pass the stick to Rheia."

"*What?*"

"Just hand it off. Eyes on the stick, not on each other, not your damn hands. Share the responsibility and hand it off. GO."

Aniyah moved toward Rheia, who bounced on the balls of her feet like a boxer, hand extended. As they closed, the stick started to conduct them. They moved in tandem, step for step, inch for inch. And just when the class thought they couldn't take the suspense a moment longer...

Aniyah's hand and Rheia's hand floated together. Floated apart.

The stick stood on Rheia's finger.

Applause erupted, firecrackers of delight.

"Pass it back," Gideon said, but the women were already ahead of him.

The stick hopped from Rheia to Aniyah and back again, right hands, left hands, the epic story played out.

"Time for the climax! Aniyah, FLIP the stick to Rheia!"

There was no hesitation. Aniyah's arm flung upward. Time seemed to shift as the stick rotated in slow-motion. Rheia reached out. The stick nestled into her palm.

Balanced.

There was a moment... everyone's unblinking eyes were on the stick. Then Rheia and Aniyah looked at each other. They screamed.

The students went batshit crazy. Whooping, hollering, jumping up and down. Rheia joyfully javelined the stick across the room as Aniyah shrieked. They collided in a huge embrace and were mobbed by the rest of the class.

"It's like we won the Super Bowl!" Evan cried.

Gideon received more high-fives, watched his students

celebrate and pummel each other. He waved everyone to their seats. Water bottles cracked open. Cheers and toasts flew back and forth. He stood before them, smiling, as they sank deeper into their seats, wrung out and happy.

"So let me ask you this. What's actually at stake here?" They quieted. "Nothing. And yet we are in raptures. As Evan said, it's like we're about to plan a victory parade. And why? Because of a stick?"

He again presented his dowel to them sword-style.

"Why does it matter? Objectively, it doesn't. It's a cheap dowel rod. The world is changed not at all if you hold it up for a minute, or for two seconds. When it falls, so what? I'm in no way trying to harsh your buzz, what we just saw was incredible. My heart is still beating like crazy." Several heads nodded in agreement, and Aniyah let out a big "whooooo!"

"This is why the stick is such a keen metaphor for theatre. Because like the stick, a play is objectively meaningless. Words on a page, acted out by people in pretend clothes, where nothing tangible is at stake. Make-believe. Fantasy. It matters only because we say so. Because the power of our attention makes it matter. For this brief, tiny moment, watching the struggle to keep the stick standing... is everything."

He started to collect the sticks. As usual, students were reticent to return them. "You feel connected to that wood now, don't you?"

"Can I buy my stick from you?" Alfonso asked.

"You can buy one from Lowe's. The stick, like a theatre, has many stories invested in it. Ghosts. Get a new one, make it yours."

Alfonso harrumphed, but handed it over. "Good-bye stick!"

The rods collected, Gideon faced them to wrap up class.

"Each of you struggled with something tonight. Something internal. Private. Possibly deeper than you expected. Your assignment for next week... just write down something true. As short as a line, as long as a page. And yes, you will share these truths aloud, so you can self-censor and plead the Fifth as needed. Don't worry about performance, we are just interested in the courage of truth at this point."

He took the time to look at each of them in the eye. They each looked back, tired and transformed.

"I thank all of you for your work tonight. See you next week."

17

Aniyah sat down at her laptop.

"Dad, I know it sounds bizarre, but yes I balanced a stick and it was one of the most exciting things I've ever done." Her father's grumbly chuckle buzzed in her earbuds. "Anyhow, I'm about to do my homework. Thank you for checking on me. All love."

She ended the call, opened her blog, and... sat there. The cursor blinked warily. *Just write down something true.* "Thanks for the specific directions, Mr. Price," she muttered.

Something was different. No darkness. No whirlpool. No smashing the cursor through sentences.

But the release she had felt in class... the clarity, the focus... simply balancing a stick had manifested such a sense of peace. Could she do something similar with her words? Compose them like a florist nudging a collection of slapdash blooms into a harmonious bouquet?

Suddenly digital felt too removed. Aniyah closed her laptop. Snatched up a legal pad and pen. The analog sensation of ink inscribing paper... slow down her thoughts. Shape her feelings. Allow them to... balance.

The pen moved across the page. Her hand followed: *I awake. And immediately wish I hadn't.*

18

LIDO BEACH

SPEARHEAD 1488 watched the sunset.

The flyers huddled in his backpack, along with cans of spray paint, tape, a staple gun.

The sky crept from orange to coral to pink. The nightly gathering of vacationers and sunset junkies started to pack up. He waited them out. Dusk plucked the last shreds of color from the sky. His cue.

Spearhead stood, shouldered his pack, headed toward the bike rack. Unchained and wove through the disgusting mix of foreign tourists. No fewer than six languages assailed his ears as he pedaled past ice cream shops, restaurants, clothing stores. He felt dirty, violated. They were invaders.

Spearhead pushed into the surrounding neighborhood. Multi-million dollar homes. Teslas and BMWs in the driveways.

And defiled by Jewish blood.

He braked to a stop. Looked around. Alone.

He pulled his custom-printed fishing mask and neck gaiter up over his head and nose. His face now looked like a screaming skull, violently streaked in red, white, and blue. The American flag as avenging banshee. He turned on his GoPro and started a video that he'd upload later to THE SCOURGE's deeply buried fan page.

"Tonight I strike a blow for all of us who know the truth, who see the world honestly and bravely. I thank Alpha-Supreme and THE SCOURGE for being beacons in this dark time. Watch the news tomorrow. The libtards' heads are going to explode."

He snapped the GoPro into the handlebar mount.

And then...

JEWS ARE GENOCIDING YOU slipped under wind-shield wipers.

JEWS ARE GENOCIDING YOU stapled to telephone poles.

JEWS ARE GENOCIDING YOU taped to lampposts and park signs.

He cruised back to the bustling tourist section of the key. Pulled down his mask and blew past the defilers, worked his way over the bridge back to the mainland. Full dark by now, cloud cover, no moon. He plastered JEWS ARE GENO-CIDING YOU up and down another neighborhood he knew to be infested and then turned toward the most notorious syna-gogue in the coastal city.

The spray paint cans clinked eagerly against his back.

19

The Woman sat in the audience, once again taking in the strange, exhilarating, six-performer, modern dress *Henry the Fifth*.

One of the mind-bendiest choices was how the cast all shared the lead role. The character of "King Henry the Fifth" was signified by a slick military coat with epaulets and ribbons. Each of the performers had one of those coats, cut to their measurements and hung on hooks positioned strategically around the stage. When one actor took off the coat, the character and lines of King Henry transferred to whichever other performer then put theirs on.

Coat-ography, the Woman thought to herself.

On the surface this convention may have confused, but the cast was so finely-tuned and the Henry hand-offs so organically staged that the huge themes of the play ended up enhanced.

Most exciting was seeing the "vastly outnumbered underdog" through a variety of lenses. A young black man exhorting the audience to charge "once more unto the breach, dear friends!" unlocked parallels to slavery and Black Lives Matter. An actress listed as "Zainab Ahmad proudly from Afghanistan" added a hijab to her Henry jacket and attacked "St. Crispin's Day" with a ferocity that brought MeToo and centuries of religious persecution to the forefront.

Gideon donned his jacket at the start of Act IV, then wrapped a blanket around himself to anonymously join his soldiers for the famous campfire scene. Quite intentionally, he was the only Caucasian in the cast, and the sudden appearance of whiteness as authority gave "Upon the king!" a chilling twist. The audience actually chuckled in recognition of entitlement as Gideon started:

"We must bear all. O hard condition,
Twin-born with greatness, subject to the breath
Of every fool..."

But as the speech continued, and the only white person on stage made the case that slaves were ultimately better off than kings because being a king is so very very hard... People started to squirm. The rest of the cast rose quietly from their slumber and prepared themselves for battle, ghosts silhouetted behind their privileged leader.

The director of the production, a Shawn Wells, had also done the adaptation. For the most part his modern interrogation of the play worked. The corrupt and self-serving clergy of Act I surreptitiously plotting to line their pockets while sending Henry into harm's way resembled nothing so much as Capitol Hill lobbyists. The Act V wooing of Catherine, a problematic scene rife with overtones of women as property and vessels for male power, was turned on its head when Zainab slipped on her jacket and put the monarchy moves on a suddenly French-ified Gideon.

Less successful were the video projections of "Terms and

Agreements" legalese from any number of banks and websites that scrolled across the floor and walls as the clergy made their intentionally opaque justifications for Henry to invade France. Clever, but a bit on the nose.

But even with only six actors, the battle scenes made the audience giddy. Live drumming, pulsing lights, acrobatic movement, and a cacophony of pre-recorded protest chants turned the tiny space into a throbbing spectacle, like a circus holding a political rally.

This was the third time The Woman had seen the show. But the first time she stuck around after. She lingered outside the circle of admirers at the stage door. The group started to break up. Go time.

A flicker of doubt flared. This man had proven himself to be a finely attuned theatre artist, an expert at observing and interpreting human behavior, and in class he had demonstrated an especially high level of empathy and emotional intelligence.

Seeing someone outside the normal framework of your interaction... you see them differently. Or in her case, he might see her *clearly*. She was good at this. Very good. But still, when he looked at her, who would he see? Was the mask an alternate you or just a truer version of you? With sunglasses, jacket, and wig... she was the most powerful version of herself. Free.

But confined to shadows.

She approached Gideon. Held out her playbill.

"You got one more autograph left in you?"

Gideon looked over. His face lit up.

"Rheia! Hey! I didn't know you were here tonight."

"Well I had to see if my acting teacher practices what he preaches." Gideon laughed. "Thanks for coming! And yeah yeah, of course, here you go."

He scribbled his name on her program. She watched for

any sense of recognition. But as he handed the inscribed play-bill back, it was clear she was "my acting student Rheia." No connection to the Woman in the bar. Framework intact. She exhaled a breath she hadn't realized she'd been holding.

"Wanna grab a drink, Teach?"

20

"Can I buy the first round, Mr. Price?"

"Please. Gideon is fine. And if I can buy the second, you're on."

"Pick your poison."

"Bourbon."

"Bliss in a bottle." Rheia caught the barkeep's eye, pointed at the Bib and Tucker, flashed two fingers.

"You know your brown booze. Good call."

"A congratulatory toast deserves no less. I loved the show, Gid." Rheia watched Gideon clock the nickname overture. He cleared his throat.

"Only a couple people in my life have ever called me that. *Gid*."

"Is it OK? I didn't mean—"

"No, yeah, no, it's fine. But, um, just so we're..." He waggled his fingers between them. "When it comes to castmates and students... Socializing? Sure. Fraternizing?" He shook his head.

"Got it. Keep the complications at bay."

Gideon nodded. "So we can totally have a drink, talk about theatre, philosophy, religion, politics—"

"Damn! Heavy guns!"

"Baseball..."

"Mets or Yankees?"

"Ummmm, *Cardinals*."

"Ask about your Midwest roots. Noted." She traded the bartender two twenties for two glasses. They moved to a table near the CD jukebox, sat facing across.

Rheia unslung her messenger bag. "Since you were upfront, you should know that even if I were interested in barking up a tree at this time in my life, you can rest assured that said tree would not be yours. I prefer foliage to a branch, if ya catch my drift."

Gideon snorted. "Gotcha."

"No offense."

"None taken. Totally my bad. Presumptuous much, Gideon?"

"Hey, I appreciate the forthrightness. It's refreshing." She lifted her glass. "To barking up the right trees."

He lifted his. "Woof woof." They clinked and sipped and savored.

He asked, "Soooo no special someone?"

"Nope. What about you? Chronically single? Long-distance blues?"

"Recent split."

"Well well, do tell."

"That story is known only to Misters Bib and Tucker."

Rheia laughed and took another sip. "Oh hey, Rasheed caught me up on all your 'violence' theory from two weeks back. Provocative perspective."

"Yeah we missed you in class that night. You had work?"

"Yep. Speaking of, I've actually got a business proposition

for you." Rheia shifted in her seat, the better to face him. "You want to teach a private class for my consulting firm?"

Gideon's eyebrows raised. "Your company wants...?"

"Wants to gig you in to do some intensive workshops. That stick stuff—"

"Biomechanics. Meyerhold."

"Whatever. Sticks. Improvisation. Storytelling. Those vocal exercises."

Gideon's lips danced. "Buh duh guh duh guh duh buh duh, eent aint aiynt ohnt oont, I slit a sheet a sheet I slit upon a slitted sheet I sit."

"You know you're kinda dorky when you aren't teaching."

"So I've been told. Take the work seriously, but don't take yourself seriously."

Rheia chuckled. "I hear that."

"So why me? And why theatre training for consultants?"

"Second question first. A lot of our consultants aren't connecting to the clients effectively. There's a lack of confidence in presentation—"

Gideon nodded. "Which leads to a lack of sales. Got it. First question?"

"I recommended you."

"Wow. Many thanks." He toasted.

"You're welcome." She toasted back. "Wanna know why I took your class?"

"All ears."

"I happened to be at that preview of *Henry Five* when—"

"Oh my god you were there that night??"

"Yep. That poor guy in the audience had some sort of seizure."

Gideon shook his head. "I've only heard the stage manager come over the god mic to hold a show once before. And that was for a tornado warning!"

"I'm just glad he ended up ok."

"The house manager and ushers were on it, yeah. And we comped him into a show the following week, he's all good, but that was scary as hell."

"What you did, stepping out on stage and improvising in character, in *verse*, keeping the audience calm as they helped that man..."

Gideon waved her off. "Not a big deal."

"OK, fine, you didn't administer meds or give mouth to mouth, but you kept the audience together, didn't let panic rampage around the room. That's why I signed up for your class, and why I told my boss you'd be perfect for this specialized training. Lots of people can say they saw *Henry Five* at the Hatchery, but I'm one a few—'we happy few'—who got to witness THAT show THAT night."

"That's the appeal of live theatre, never know what may go wrong."

"Or go right. If only I'd pulled out my phone you'd be viral by now."

Gideon laughed. "Well, I am flattered and honored and yeah, I'm open, let's talk further. I assume you've got dates, rates in mind?"

"You betcha. I'll have HR email you."

"Sounds great."

They air-toasted again, sipped, let the conversation take a breather.

She saw him looking over at the pool table. It had been deep-cleaned, the bloodstain scrubbed out of the felt.

Something ornery in her. "So the Bear and Fawn, huh?"

He chewed his lip. "Yep."

She flicked her head toward the pool table. "That where it happened?" Gideon nodded.

"Those three guys ever show up again?"

"Not that I've seen, and I come here pretty often."

"Oh yeah?"

"Actors work when civilians play. Nights. Weekends. Holidays. Good to have a place to unwind, release the show."

Something in his voice. Inwardly: *He's barely hanging on.* Outwardly: "And the mystery ninja lady?"

Gideon shook his head. "I gotta tell ya, Rheia. That was one of the bravest things I've ever seen. I can't stop thinking about it."

"Sorta like your audience member with the seizure, right? You just happened to be here that night—"

"No, that's not it. That was happenstance. This was... like I said in class, it felt like theatre. Intentional and inevitable." He swirled his glass."I've felt emboldened and ashamed ever since."

Rheia watched his thumbnails pick at a cardboard coaster with a local brewery's logo on it. She waited.

He spoke suddenly. "You know Michelangelo's *David*?"

She blinked. "The statue?"

"Yeah."

She shook her head. "Not really."

"Three tons. Seventeen feet tall."

"Geez. Cue the Jeopardy music."

"Nah. I saw it in person once. Read the museum fun fact cheat sheet. Had a couple days shooting a film in Florence."

"Nice."

"Trip was great. The movie was rightly relegated to the trash heap."

"Yikes."

"They can't all win Best Picture."

Gideon went back to shredding the coaster. Rheia gave it a beat. Nudged.

"I know the story of David and Goliath, though. Shepherd

boy defeats the armored giant. Triumph of the underdog. Sorta like your show, actually. Agincourt."

Gideon nodded. "Henry and the Brits outnumbered big time by the French. Longbows carried the day. You did pay attention at the show!"

She chuckled. "Crispin's Day is such a killer speech. And what that actress did with it...!"

"Zainab. She's a future star, just you watch."

"I believe it."

Back to the coaster. Bits of cardboard disintegrated between his fingers.

"Gideon."

He startled. Looked at her before his shield was up. She saw behind his eyes. Raw. Haunted. She tugged the half-shredded coaster from his hands.

"You'll get no judgment from me. We've all got our stuff. What about *David*?"

Trust is an uncharted sea.

Gideon launched. "There are loads of other paintings and sculptures of the David-Goliath story. And almost all of them depict the end. The victory. Goliath dead, David holding up the giant's sword or head or both, the Israelites cheering and the Philistines pissing themselves. But it's Michelangelo's take that has become iconic."

"How come?"

"Because Michelangelo is the only artist to depict David *before* the battle. Think about that. Where's Goliath?"

"Huh." Rheia dug a tablet out of her bag. Web search, image, stood it on the table. *David.* They studied it together.

"See what I mean?" Gideon said.

"Yeah. I guess Goliath's invisible. Or off in the distance, jeering from the battlefield."

"Exactly. This is what I can't get out of my head, Rheia.

That Woman... what was going through her mind before she stood up to those three bullies? Like Henry in the campfire scene. Or David right here in this statue. What was she *thinking?* What was she *feeling?*"

Rheia knew. But couldn't say.

Gideon continued. "Michelangelo leaves Goliath out. Forces our focus onto only David. Who is really just us. Small. Alone. A mere errand boy for the real soldiers."

"Leaving Goliath out also means we have to imagine our own. Goliath can be anyone."

"Or anything. Anything that looms over our lives."

"So unlike other depictions," Rheia said, "Michelangelo's isn't about victory."

Gideon nodded eagerly. "Right! Remember in class I talked about given circumstances?"

"Yeah. The unalterable facts of the play."

"Apply that idea to this sculpture. What do you see?"

Rheia studied the image. "He looks tense."

"What else?"

"He's readying for battle."

"Keep going."

"He looks like he's just made a decision."

"YES." Gideon twirled a finger. "This statue is in *motion*. It's active. It captures the precise moment just after David has decided to step forward but just before the moment he actually takes that first step."

Rheia knew that moment well. "Smack dab in the middle of fight or flight."

"What else do you see?"

"His brow... his neck... clenched." Rheia's head tilted a couple degrees. "Look at his right hand! The veins!"

"The veins are *bulging*. His heart must be racing."

Rheia's voice accelerated. "He's turned sideways, instinctively making himself a smaller target. Holy shit he's... how did I not notice this first? So obvious." And she literally smacked her palm to her forehead.

Gideon grinned. "He's naked?"

"He's naked! Stripped of all protection."

"Of course he didn't actually fight naked, but the artist is telling us something, yeah? When you go into battle, your ego is laid bare."

"Gideon." Their eyes met. "He's afraid."

"Why should he be afraid?" Gideon murmured. And Rheia heard the fear deep in his voice, like the thrum of central heating in the basement. "Doesn't he know the story? Doesn't he know he's going to bullseye the giant and become a hero?"

Rheia shook her head. "Of course not. Just like Henry at the campfire.

Nothing is guaranteed."

"And David's just a kid," Gideon said. "Even if he's got faith, this moment only matters if the possibility of losing... and dying... is tangible."

They stared at the tablet.

Then Rheia said, "You don't have courage and then be brave. You act with bravery to discover your courage. At that moment, anyone's faith would bend to breaking."

"Especially a teenage shepherd with no military training."

"It's amazing he didn't run away."

"He considered it," Gideon said. "That consideration is the only thing that makes his stepping forward courageous. And that brings us back to that night when those three jackholes Goliathed this entire bar. That woman... she was David."

Step carefully, Rheia. "You know, it doesn't have to be martial. Or violent."

Gideon suddenly had difficulty meeting her gaze.

"Gid. Every human on this planet has a moment when a

Goliath looms up. And you have to decide whether to do something that jeopardizes yourself. Maybe your literal life isn't in danger, but your comfort, your ego. Your job or relationship. The Goliath can be anything, right?"

He nodded. But he avoided her eyes, focused on rubbing condensation from his glass.

Rheia continued. "Whatever Goliath is, it's always something so dangerous, so huge, that to turn away is the obvious and correct course of action. And usually no one will be the wiser that you turned tail, and even those who are the wiser wouldn't judge you anyway. They'd nod and go 'yeah, good choice, you wouldn't have stood a chance.'"

Rheia tapped the tablet screen.

"This is what David is contemplating, Gid. Every soldier on his side has backed down. No one would think less of him if he did too. Because we can't know the outcome."

"The illusion of the first time," Gideon muttered.

"What?"

"Theatre jargon. Actors know the outcome of their play, but the audience doesn't. So the actors have to commit to the illusion of the first time, every time."

"Exactly. What if David's slingshotted stone was off an inch or two? Clanged off Goliath's helmet instead of walloping him between the eyes?"

"The entire world would be different."

"History would be rewritten."

"When that Woman stepped out to face those guys..." Gideon finally looked up at Rheia. She saw the guilt gilding his face. "I didn't join her."

"No one else did either, right?"

"No. But I still feel..."

"But the fact you're beating yourself up now? Maybe that means next time you *will* step forward, huh?"

They looked again at the image of the scared boy unaware of his impending celebrity.

"I have to believe that there are far more Davids than Goliaths," Rheia said. "That the bullies are ultimately vastly outnumbered. And that if multiple Davids decided to step forward simultaneously..."

Gideon gave a curt nod. "Then Goliath wouldn't stand a chance."

He gets it, Rheia thought. *If only he could fight, he could be a member of the Troupe.*

21

SARASOTA

Stefano and Mandy made their final turn and picked up their pace. Their runs always ended with an unspoken and usually friendly competitive sprint.

Today they had parked in the Hillview District and jogged all through the neighborhood, pointing at houses and sharing ideas about how to add that garden detail or that porch feature to their own house, when they finally were able to afford their own house.

They zipped past some outdoor diners enjoying breakfast, flashed across a beckoning crosswalk, and pounded for the finish line of Hawthorne Street.

Stefano suddenly pulled up short, and Mandy cruised to victory. One block right was the hospital. Two blocks left was the bay. Three feet in front of him was a piece of paper taped to a mailbox.

"Blew you away!" Mandy hooted as she walked back toward Stefano, hands on her hips. "Hey. Babe, what's wrong?"

Stefano silently pointed.

"Oh my god."

Stefano pulled out his phone, started a video. "We were running, just coming up Osprey Avenue. Right here in Sarasota. And we see this."

He framed the video so the flyer was clear.

JEWS ARE GENOCIDING YOU.

Stefano sensed Mandy moving toward the flyer. "There is only one response to stuff like this."

Mandy reached up and tore the flyer down. The tape held, so the page ripped into pieces. She tore and tore, leaving no trace. She faced the camera boldly.

"FUCK you."

Stefano started composing a post for social media. Mandy stepped toward a trash can, but just as she was about to drop the shredded flyer...

"Stefano. STEF."

This time she silently pointed. They looked further up the street. JEWS ARE GENOCIDING YOU glared back from windshields, tree trunks, lamp posts. A few of the diners had noticed and now joined as well, pointing and gasping. A young boy, maybe eight years old, asked his mom what "genociding" meant.

Authorities were called. Tears were shed. Mandy, Stefano, and the diners stuffed every flyer they could find into the trash.

22

SPEARHEAD 1488 SPENT the next few days safely hidden in the shack. The uproar had been immediate and hot, burning bright and high like the dried palm branches he used for kindling in his fire pit.

THE SCOURGE played constantly in the background.

"You know I took my AR-15 to the capital for the protest. We marched right past the Governor's house. Some snowflake asked me why I felt the need to open carry. And I screamed right in his face BECAUSE I CAN! It's the goddam Constitution!"

Spearhead nodded in agreement with the podcast guest, scrolled through his master feed. All his social media now fed through an algorithm he had written himself. Any mention of his nighttime strike would be flagged and funneled directly to him.

"My next guest is the Dean of Pick-Up Artist University, Carter X."

"So glad to be here, man."

Spearhead watched a short video of two runners tearing down one of his flyers. "FUCK you." He smiled. *Weak.* Similar pictures and videos popped up on feeds up and down the coast. Transparent virtue signaling. The kindling hissed.

He screen-captured every face in every post, saved them to the "Crisis Actors" folder, added them to the database that Granddad had begun in 1999. He would need more memory soon. Again. Even though his facial recognition software kept improving, culling through all those images was like trying to empty the Gulf with a sandcastle bucket.

"You take my courses and I guarantee you'll never have an empty bed again. Just don't ever get with a girl more than two skin shades away from yours. Just not worth it. Otherwise... Hump 'em and dump 'em!"

He watched local anchors act out their horror as cameras captured rabbis and parents and students, with their stupid hats and curls, weeping over the swastikas he had sprayed across the walls and doors and sidewalks. Cops puffed their chests and pretended outrage, promised to catch whoever had done this. Civic leaders called for everyone to come together. The Mayor of course said, "This is not who we are. This does not represent Sarasota." Spearhead could've written the script.

"This is AlphaSupreme, and this is THE SCOURGE. So, there are all these months and days to honor specific groups of people. Never white people, goodness gracious no. But Black History Month, and MLK, and this new Juneteenth inanity, and try saying this three times fast: National Hispanic Heritage Month. Even more, now there's Asian Pacific American Heritage Month? I challenge you to go back through history and show me where all these alleged contributions have been made by these categories of non-Whites. Where did any other sub-group of people contribute more to civilization than the White race? It's high time we divided the world into Whites and non-Whites. We would be happier and safer. And so would they."

Spearhead laughed as armchair psychologists analyzed him.

"He probably lives in his mommy's basement."

"Clearly disturbed, likely abused as a child."

"Raised in hate, odds are he was indoctrinated from a young age."

"No one is born hating."

Pre-packaged nonsense. Granddad had warned him. Now that the mantle had passed to him, he would stay strong. He would tend the fire.

But the kindling sputtered. The larger logs didn't catch. His flyers were shredded, his paint was washed away, the news cycles moved on. No national or lamestream coverage. Barely a blip on cable. Even the alt-right newsletters ho-hummed. In a world of manifestos, graffiti no longer galvanized.

He field-stripped his Glock 19. Attention would be paid.

23

Gɪᴅᴇᴏɴ ᴛʀᴀᴄᴇᴅ the morning's route in his mind as he laced up his Hokas. He had studied a walking tour map of Harlem. This first time through he'd keep it simple, hit the high spots, do a deeper dive later in the week.

Head north up Frederick Douglass Boulevard, glance east along 125th to catch a glimpse of the iconic Apollo sign. Right on 139th, take in a couple blocks of Strivers' Row. Turn south on Malcolm X Boulevard—save Harlem River Drive and the water route down to Harlem River Park for next time. Malcolm X would take him past the National Jazz Museum, through the soulful aromas wafting out of Sylvia's, and on to Marcus Garvey Park. Loop it, straight shot south to once again meander Central Park.

Out the door. Sun not up. Beat the heat. The route unfurled.

But Harlem took longer than he had planned because the murals were wondrous. Franco the Great's *Knowledge is Power* was the first to appear, rising up in the dim light of the yawning dawn. Gideon made a note to research this vibrant art and come back in full daytime.

So he upped the pace once Marcus Garvey Park was at his back, zipped down Madison at a clip that pushed his heart rate into the 170s. He slowed for a crosswalk a few blocks short of Central Park North.

And sensed something odd.

Corner of his eye. Out-of-place movement. He peered down the side street, pinpointed a slick shiny SUV vibrating strangely.

He jogged toward it. Once within a couple car lengths, he heard muffled sounds. Voices. Struggle. Then the unmistakable report of skin striking skin.

He downshifted to a careful walk, turned his head to the side so his ears could better triangulate. The SUV quivered, keeping time with the rise and fall of the voices inside.

Gideon came to a full stop, looked around. Still early, foot traffic light, no one else noticing, or noticing but paying no mind. He crossed the street, angling toward the SUV, which had come to a momentary stillness.

Then a thud and a strangled *no!* and a primal growl, and the SUV started to vibrate again, like a washing machine clicking from soak to spin.

Gideon approached the rear hatch. As he neared, the voices separated into two distinct actors, one male and insistent, the other female and resistant. Heavily tinted windows. He couldn't make out shapes, only discern the merest trace of smoky movement.

Some of that smoke seemed to coalesce into the distinct cheekbone and brow of his sister's profile. *Finley?* She turned toward him. Hollow eyes. Her mouth opened but dissolved into wisps before she could tell him what to do.

He pressed his palms into his own eyes, breathed hard,

listened harder. A fleshy thwack. A pained grunt. Whoever she was, whatever trouble she was in, she was fighting back.

Gideon didn't run with a phone. He felt paralyzed. Outraged. Afraid. He thought back a couple nights to his conversation with Rheia. A slingshot. He thought back a few weeks to White Suit. A pool triangle. He looked at his own empty hands.

There's always a next time.

The female inside the minivan made an awful sound. Gideon's stomach turned over. The male inside the minivan chuckled. Gideon saw red.

He rapped his knuckle on the back hatch window.

Everything froze. The hairs on Gideon's arms leaped to attention. He stared at the smoky window and knew the two faces inside were both staring back.

Maybe a second or two of actual time passed. Experiential time, though, stretched taut... that second or two tortured on a rack, joints popping, tendons twanging, muscles tearing, skin shredding.

The world had gone quiet. Gideon could hear his sprinting heartbeat, could smell the warming pavement. Delicious, crystal-edged clarity, like the last split second in the wing before stepping on stage.

Her voice stripped time's gears: "HELP!"

Gideon's hand wrenched the hatch up and open before his brain could give the order. His body continued to act while his bemused mind sat in a la-z-boy and played armchair quarterback... *How curious! This idiot left it unlocked.*

The idiot in question was finishing a "shut your mouth" followthrough (*hmmm, he's right-handed*) so both he and the dark-haired young woman were facing away from Gideon, bodies torqued toward the driver's seat by the force of his blow.

He's wearing Nikes, Gideon's mind offered as his hands

latched onto the idiot's ankle just above the noted cross-train-ers. The idiot's face snapped back around, panicked rage in his eyes. *Well look at that, he's a whippersnapper, look at that wispy hipster beard. Columbia is nearby isn't it?*

Gideon heaved, propelling himself backward, dragging the undergrad out of the SUV. The undergrad managed to latch his fingers onto the edge of the cargo hold. His other leg stopped flailing, knee cocked, target acquired.

Gideon flinched to the side, so the sole of the idiot's Nike stomped into his shoulder instead of his jaw. He managed to maintain a one- handed grip. Adrenaline surged, numbing the pain. Gideon lifted the captured leg and yanked it down as hard as he could, bullwhipping the college boy's entire body. The shock broke the boy's grip, and he tumbled to the pavement.

Ooooh, you're gonna feel that later in your lower back.

Gideon's lizard brain spared a breath to hiss at Gideon's mind—*you are not helping!* Gideon's mind huffed and went off to rummage in the fridge.

The undergrad was dazed but working his way back to his feet. Gideon hadn't wrestled since college but all those hours on the mat had drilled certain instincts bone-deep. He closed distance, wrapped up the idiot like a present, and pressed the slap-happy jerk's face into the cargo hold's floor.

"Let me go, man! Get off! Get OFF!" Gideon tightened his grip. His shoulder didn't like that. And his lower back also started to gripe. He gritted his teeth. Ibuprofen later.

"You didn't stop when she asked. Why should I?"

"She swiped right, man, for real, she agreed to meet for breakfast, you can't do this to me!"

Gideon responded by mashing the idiot's mouth into the spare tire. "Miss? MISS? Whose SUV?"

Whether the young woman was dazed from being hit,

having her OJ roofied, or both, Gideon couldn't tell. But at least she was sitting up. Her dark hair curtained her face.

"...what?" Groggy.

"Is this your car, or his?"

"...'s'mine. No... 'z'hiz."

"You want to call someone? The cops? A roommate?"

She nodded, crawled toward the front seat, dug around in her purse. The undergrad made noises that could have been threatening, could have been begging. Only the spare tire knew.

24

THE CLASS STARED AT HIM, again rendered speechless.

Evan, of course, was the first to pipe up.

"DUDE! You're a friggin' HERO!"

Gideon shook his head as the class broke into excited chatter.

Rheia had noticed immediately that he was "off" that night in class. Moving stiffly. "Overdo your workout today?" Geez she was perceptive.

"Not a workout. More of a... well, I got kicked by a college kid." That had brought the class to a standstill, then a clamor. They had to hear the story.

Imani followed up. "So you just held that asshat in a suplex till the cops came?"

"No, a suplex is a throw. It was more a half nelson."

"So friggin' badass," Evan muttered.

"But yes, I held him. That was rough. It took a few minutes and he kept struggling, but once he heard the sirens all the fight went out of him. I gave my statement, splurged on a cab home, and put some ice packs to work."

"Was the girl ok?" Marcel asked.

"Paramedics arrived just after the cops. I saw them taking care of her."

Tosha fumed, "I really hope she will be pressing the charges."

"Me too," Gideon said. "But now we are past time to get to work! Your written assignment was simply to come in with something true. I guess I ended up going first, told my true story—"

"Holy segue, Batman!" Dan chuckled, delighted with himself. Joan groaned.

Alfonso jumped on board. "Yeah, you'll have to get a utility belt."

"And a mask!" Kaida chirped. "Ooooh and a cape!!"

Emma's pristine soprano suddenly broke out in rhythmic "NUH nuh NUH nuh NUH nuh NUH nuhs." The entire class joined in as the refrain of the old TV theme crescendoed.

"*STICKMAAAN! STICKMAAAN! STICKMAAAAN!*"

Merriment and laughter.

"You do know we will never let this go, right?" Aniyah said. Gideon nodded, a rueful grin warming his face.

Rheia raised her hand. Gideon gratefully acknowledged her.

"You sure you're ok though? Paramedics check you out?"

"Bumps and bruises, nothing torn or broken."

"Could've been a lot worse." Something in her voice. Concern, yes, but also... well, of course she would understand more deeply. David and Goliath.

"And NOW, seriously and truly, let's go to work. Who'd like to go first?"

Rasheed volunteered and took center stage.

"Title?"

"Fifty Cents." Rasheed had a tremendous speaking voice, resonant with a raspy edge.

My grandmother was the truest person I've ever known. Once she took me and my brother to the zoo. I was just old enough that she had to pay full price for me, which was like two bucks. My brother was just young enough that he got the kiddie discount, a whole fifty cents off. My grandmother didn't hear too well at this point, and apparently when the ticket guy asked if Amir and I were both ten or younger, she said yes. Sooooo... I got the discount. Grandmother unknowingly scammed the zoo fifty cents!

When we got home, Grandmother checked her receipt. She checked every receipt she ever received. She saw the error. She immediately hustled us right back out the door. Never mind that Power Rangers was on, we were going back. She walked us up to the counter, slapped down the receipt and two shiny quarters. Told the ticket guy in her precisely practiced English that she was very sorry, but her older grandson was not ten years or younger, and she had unintentionally underpaid.

The ticket guy was flabbergasted. He thanked my grandmother and then asked her why she had even bothered. It was just fifty cents.

Grandmother, equally baffled by his question, replied, "What kind of example would I be setting for my grandsons if I were to do otherwise?"

"Well that is just fantastic," Alfonso enthused, leading a rousing round of applause.

"And what an amazing tribute to your Grandmother," Joan said.

"Thank you. And here's the kicker! The ticket guy called the press, no joke! Grandmother was in the newspaper the next day. I clipped it and offered it to her. She read it to herself, silently, then handed it back to me and said, 'There is no price so small that it is worth your integrity.'"

"Please tell me you've kept that clipping!" Kaida said.

"Of course. It lived on my dream board for years, but now..." Rasheed pulled out his wallet, extracted the well-worn, laminated clipping, offered it to Kaida. "Here you go. Pass it around."

Oohs and *aahs* followed the clipping from hand to hand.

"Rasheed, thank you for sharing, and sidenote really nice delivery," Gideon said. Rasheed gave a big smile and a double thumbs-up, received his memento back from Joan, who couldn't help but give his shoulder a little squeeze.

"Who's up next?"

Everyone glanced around, but it was Dan who voiced the thought aloud, "Well who the heck would want to follow that?"

Gideon smiled. "Now now, this isn't a competition or time for judgment. We're simply exercising the muscle of vulnerability. Speaking truth to an audience. Hardest easy thing in the world."

Aniyah's hand shot up. "I just gotta get this over with."

Gideon gestured to her. She took a deep breath and stood. Imani gave her an encouraging pat on the back.

Aniyah stepped to center stage.

"Wow, Gideon, this feels so different." She looked down at the paper clutched in her hand.

"What do you mean, Aniyah?"

"I just mean... I feel tall?? Is that weird?" The class smiled.

"Not weird at all. When you're on a stage by yourself—"

"There's nowhere to hide." Aniyah felt her heart running away. Gideon approached. Stood so he blocked her from the curious gaze of the other students. Spoke only for her. "There's nowhere you have to be. There's nothing you have to do. There's no expectation. Just breathe with me."

They breathed. She reached out a hand. He took it in both of his own. "Thank you," she said. "I want to read this."

"You sure?"

"Yes. I... I need to. Get it out."

Gideon squeezed her hand, ceded her the stage.

"Title?"

Aniyah cleared her throat. "Um. It's... this is called 'The Next Day.'"

She cleared her throat again. Shifted her weight back and forth. Held the creased, hand-written paper in her left hand. Transferred it to her right hand. Settled with the paper clutched between both.

Her voice started small and quivering. But by the end, it was calm. Clear. Not loud, but full.

I awake. And immediately wish I hadn't.

Is it only the next day?

I moan. It isn't enough.

I curl myself into a ball and bite the comforter. I hear a growl, and realize

it's me, a primal sound vibrating in my chest.

It isn't enough.

I clamber to my hands and knees. I gulp. I slam my face down into a pillow

and scream.

I scream.

I shred my throat with screams.

It isn't enough.

I collapse. I keen. I am a void yet somehow so full. Pain oozes out my pores. It can't only be the next day.

"Jazzie. Jazzie."

My daughter's name drops from my lips with every exhale.

My husband shuffles into view. The doorway frames his slumped silhouette. I want him to go away. I want him to lie down and hold me. I want him to speak. To stay silent. To comfort me. To leave me alone.

How can it be only the next day?

Time... life... stretches before me. Numberless empty days. Yesterday,

Jasmine was eight. Today, Jazzie would have turned nine. Next year? She won't turn ten. A decade from now? Still eight.

Jazzie today would have taken mini-cupcakes to school, the mini-cupcakes still sitting in the Tupperware on the counter, that she had helped bake, to share with her classmates, to celebrate her birthday.

But on her last day of eight, an angry man gunned her down at her little school desk.

And now my life has been sheered in two.

My husband clears his throat. I think: "I would trade his life for hers."

I know I will go to hell for having this thought.

Though I wonder if my husband thinks the same. If he would trade me for Jazzie.

I realize I hope he would.

The students sat stunned. Gideon let them. This sort of revelation happened often enough in class that he had learned what to do.

He waited.

Aniyah stood as if in a trance. A sacred quiet crept on padded feet into every corner of the room.

He waited. Any moment, she would look up. But until then, the collective suspended breath would hold. No one in the audience would dare interrupt until the performance was truly complete.

There is nothing more poignant... more compelling... than full, grounded silence.

Aniyah looked up. Through the entire recitation she had

not cried. But now soundless tears flowed. She made no move to wipe them away. Gideon glanced at the class. Imani was a reflection of Aniyah, silently weeping. The Forths had their heads together, hands clutched. Marcel's head was down in prayerful aspect. Evan's mouth hung open. Kaida's hands covered her face.

The only student who caught Gideon's glance was Rheia. She mouthed, "Wow," and they traded imperceptible nods.

Then Aniyah took a sudden, shuddering breath. Gideon was instantly at her side whispering *you did great you did great you did great* as the class awoke from their reverie.

Emma asked, "Is it ok to... I mean, should we clap?"

"Hell yes," Rheia declared, and she led a vigorous ovation that carried Aniyah back to her seat. Imani wrapped her in a crushing embrace.

Gideon stood in the vacuum Aniyah had just left. The applause spent itself. The students all looked at each other, at Aniyah, at Gideon, at their laps. The remnants of Aniyah's spell lingered in the air, and words were inadequate.

Gideon tried anyway.

"One of the most vital functions of storytelling—which when you think about it is really just a form of confession—is that we realize we aren't alone. Others are willing to share our burdens. So first, Aniyah... we thank you. We honor you. We now know a little bit more of your story, and we are humbled by your vulnerability."

Aniyah's smile was genuine but also exhausted. The class as a whole looked wrung out.

"Second, it's high time for a break. We'll keep telling our truth in five. Dan, I'm calling it. You're next." Dan groaned and the class shared a cleansing chuckle.

Gideon watched as every student made sure to pass by Aniyah. Every exchange of word, smile, and silent nod brought her back more fully into the present, made her posture a bit straighter. Finally she stood, Imani ever-present at her side, and made her way to him.

She pulled out her phone, thumbed her password, flicked and scrolled. She handed it over. Gideon looked down into the digital glow.

"This must be Jazzie," he said. Aniyah nodded.

"She looks like joy."

Aniyah nodded.

He handed the phone back.

"Thank you, Aniyah."

She pocketed the phone and held up her tear-stained monologue. She folded it carefully, slid it into her pocket next to the thousands of images of Jazzie.

"Thank *you*," she said. Gideon inclined his head. Imani and Aniyah joined the break.

25

THE BREAK STRETCHED LANGUIDLY past five minutes. Gideon called them "bloated fives."

"Dan! Hop to it!"

Shocking everyone, Dan told a heartfelt story about a childhood pet. A bird, no less. "So, at a time in my life when no one seemed to care, my parents had split, I was at a new school with no friends, and nothing made sense... Coco listened without judgment. I could say anything. Cry. Scream. Confess." Dan let the sweet, poignant silence hang. And then, "Coco was... unflappable."

Groans.

"He honestly can't help himself," Joan assured everyone.

"Someday the pun police are going to lock you up for good, my friend," Marcel said as Dan gleefully bounced back to his seat.

Class continued. Anecdotes shared, musings chewed, insights gained, wisdoms earned. Laughs and gasps. Humans weaving themselves together with bonds of honesty and courage.

"Final performer. Rheia, bring us home."

As she walked to center stage, the class hushed. Rheia moved with unmistakable grace and stood with an effortless air of command. Her charisma radiated. The younger students, tainted by desperation, may have had actual theatre training, but they had yet to learn *ease*.

She had no paper. She spoke from her gut. "Working title... 'Double- Edged.'"

There are debts that can never be paid, ledgers that can never be balanced. Everything costs something. Only you get to decide whether the cost is worth it. And we often change our minds. "Buyer's remorse" is legit. Worth is only measured by what someone is willing to pay.

I am terrified that everything I do will end up making no difference. But I will do it anyway. As C.S. Lewis said about prayer: It doesn't change God. It changes me.

Rheia gave a little bow of her head and headed back to her seat. "What was that quote again?" Aniyah asked, pen at the ready. Rheia repeated it.

"And a follow-up," Alphonso said. "Who the heck is C.S. Lewis?" Tosha, Evan, Kaida, and Rasheed all bobbed their heads. Dan, Joan, and Marcel all groaned in mock pain.

"Yikes, the generational gap rears its head!" Imani said.

Emma suddenly inhaled. "Oh-oh! Didn't he direct that movie where Liam Neeson played a lion in Middle Earth?"

"So close, but not quite," Rheia said as Dan raised his hands to the heavens in horror.

Gideon intervened. "He was a British professor, theologian, and author. *Chronicles of Narnia*—"

Emma snapped her fingers. "Narnia! That's what I meant!"

"—*Screwtape Letters. Surprised by Joy. A Grief Observed.*"

"Geez. You know his suit size, too?" Rheia asked.

"I played Screwtape in a stage adaption. Actors gotta do their research. You know he died the same day as JFK?"

"Show-off," Rheia muttered.

Gideon grinned. "But to bring everything full circle, Rheia's truth piece hits on something I want you all to journal about for next week. The idea of accumulation."

Note-taking devices found their various ways back into hands.

"Our truths tonight… accumulated. The feelings you are having right now—fulfillment, exhaustion, completeness—what the Greeks called *catharsis*—they are only possible because of the totality of the twelve stories you just shared."

"Thirteen," Rheia said. "Remember, you went first. *Stickman*." Gideon endured the giggle outbreak, then continued.

"Think of sporting events. We focus on moments of winning. The buzzer-beating jump shot. The ninth-inning walk-off home run. The overtime goal. But those moments resonate only because of all the tension and build-up. And I don't just mean on the court, field, or rink. I mean the quiet, precise preparations in the locker rooms. The taping up, tying up, stretching out. And even before that, the work, the practice, the sweat equity invested long before game night. That dedication is all part of the accumulation of meaning."

Gideon once again was in "stalk the stage" mode.

"It is only through accumulation that any sort of real change happens. Daily prayers, as it were. Practice makes practice."

Tosha raised her hand. "What is this you say? 'Practice makes practice.' I think I do not understand…?"

"Sure. Think of it this way. You can't force change or progress or transformation. You can only, day by day and bit by bit, work toward creating the circumstances in which it may happen. Snow falls on a branch. The branch holds because the weight of each additional flake is negligible. But snow continues to fall, and the branch discovers it's groaning a little, and then there comes a point when one more flake is one too many. And the branch snaps. And we perceive that snapping branch as having been caused by that one last flake. But no. That flake had no more and no less to do with snapping the branch than any otherflake that came before."

Gideon paused, allowed the note-taking to finish. Waited for their eyes.

"How many steps in a marathon?" he asked Tosha.

"How many words in a novel?" he asked Marcel.

"How many notes in an opera?" he asked Emma.

"How many heartbeats in a life?" he asked Alphonso.

"How many kisses in true love?" he asked Dan and Joan.

"More than five," Dan stage whispered. Joan popped him on the thigh. "Waaaaaay more."

Gideon continued. "Is any step or kiss or word or note or heartbeat more important than another? Objectively, no. But if you run a marathon, you know which step feels way different than all the others?"

Several voices murmured, "The last one."

"Exactly. The one when you cross the finish line. But it's the thousands of steps before that build up to the point where that one step can be perceived as special. Meaning is achieved through accumulation."

Imani raised her hand. Gideon nodded. "Sounds like... Context is everything?"

He nodded again. "And even context is wide open to manipulation and happenstance. Think about this... what if Rheia hadn't gone last tonight? How would our current conversation have been different? What if Alfonso had gone last? Or

Dan? Or Aniyah? What path would our feelings have followed if the stories had accumulated differently?"

"So... wait." Rasheed was struggling. "We have no agency? Everything is random?"

"Just the opposite, Rasheed. We absolutely have agency, but our agency is the size of a snowflake. We have no control over the branch. On stage, the story has already been written, and our job as actors is to tell the story clearly and passionately. We know the branch will snap, the audience knows it will snap, and the catharsis is in discovering together how it will snap. But in real life we don't know and can't know when the branch will snap. We can only keep adding snowflakes."

"*Back to the Future.*"

"What was that, Aniyah?"

Everyone turned to look. "Well, at the risk of oversharing, I've been seeing a therapist to help deal with... well, you know. I went to a dark, dark place. My therapist said something that really stuck. Time travel. *Back to the Future. The Terminator. Star Trek*, I forget which, the one with the whales."

"That's number four," Alphonso said. "*The Voyage Home*! I don't know C.S. Lewis, but I love me some Spock."

Aniyah smiled. "All these movies, these time travel stories, they depend on us believing that tiny actions in our past can have huge ramifications in our present. The pebble in the water sending ripples to the shore. Or as you've been saying..."

"Snowflakes."

"Yeah. So my therapist said 'your present is your past for your future.' If you believe that changing a small thing in your past could drastically impact your present, then why can't doing some small thing today, in your present, impact your future the same way?"

"Whooooa," Evan said. "That's deep. Like the butterfly effect but trippier."

"And like you're saying, Gideon," Aniyah continued, "taking that small action? You don't know what the outcome will be. Scattering seed. Some will take root. Some won't. But still you scatter. Because the only thing you know for sure is if you don't plant anything, nothing will grow."

26

Rheia and Gideon just squeezed through the closing doors. They found a seat, sat side by side. The train burrowed

"Where we headed?" Gideon asked.

"Anywhere but the Bear and Fawn, oh wise teacher. Time to try something new."

Rheia adjusted her messenger bag onto her lap.

"Quite the class tonight," she said. "All those stories. And Aniyah? My god."

"Yeah, I can't imagine. Just goes to show there's always more to the story. You never know what someone might be carrying."

Rheia glanced at Gideon. He was gazing out the window, looking at everything and nothing. Secret pain etched his face.

The subway car braked, disgorged a few weary workers and excited seekers, devoured some more, burrowed again.

Gideon came back from wherever he had gone. "So I got the email from HR. Everything looks good."

"Can we talk schedule?"

"Absolutely. Just remember that actors work when civilians

play." "Yeah yeah, you said that in class. Nights, holidays, and weekends.

We can be flexible."

The train came to another stop, caught its breath as people got off, people got on. Doors closed. The train scurried back into its tunnel. A 30-something turbaned Middle-Eastern mother and her small daughter, maybe seven years old and sporting an elaborately colored headscarf, passed by Gideon and Rheia. They made their way down to the other end of the car, sat and huddled together over a tablet, bobbed their heads to a video playing soft sitar music.

"My only request," Gideon said, "is that we avoid Mondays. Actor's only day off, gotta do laundry and hit the grocery store sometime!"

Rheia nodded. "You got a preference on mornings or afternoons?"

The train stopped, strained against its bridle. People off, people on. Including four 20-something guys in trendy athletic shorts and high-end sneakers. They were sweaty and pushy, shouldering passengers out of the way and taking up way more than their share of space. The tallest spun a basketball between his hands. Another sported a New York Knicks jersey. Those two were happy. The other two were sullen.

"Dude we kicked your asses tonight!" the Knicks fan bellowed. He play-punched his man-bunned buddy on the shoulder. The hooting continued as the train again leaped forward in its never-ending quest.

"Bro, how many times did I take you off the dribble tonight? Huh? HUH?" The tall dude with the ball head-faked at his "Bro" with every "huh."

More head fakes and high fives and increasingly nasty name-calling. Passengers not already jostled away from their handholds migrated to the other end of the car.

Gideon and Rheia tried to ignore. He took out his phone, opened his calendar. "I'd lean afternoons. Depends on travel time too."

"Would be in Port Morris."

"Where?" He started to map. Rheia tapped his screen.

"Over in the Bronx."

"Then definitely early afternoons. Give me plenty of wiggle room to get back for show call."

Their negotiations were cut short by the little headscarfed girl yelling, "Give that back!"

"Yo, guys, check this out." Knicks Fan was holding up the mother's tablet. "What kind of freaky terrorist music is this??" He cackled. The daughter yelled some more and stood up but the mother hushed her and pulled her back down.

"But momma that's yours!"

"*Hush.* Let it be." The mother's face was stone-carved. The daughter's glistened with bitter tears.

The rest of the train went utterly still, potential prey praying for invisibility. No one looked at the mother and daughter. They had been plucked from the herd. Sacrifice.

Gideon for the second time that day saw red. He moved to stand and step over Rheia into the aisle. She shoved him back.

"What do you think you're doing??" she hissed.

"What's it look like?"

"There's four of them and you're in no condition. Stickman got lucky this morning."

Gideon waved her off. "I was alone this morning. But here, if one David stands, others will follow."

"Read the goddam room, Gid. Look around."

He did.

"There are no branches in here about to break. The world is scared. Assholes like this are untouchable."

She was right. Gideon sagged back, clenched his fists and jaw.

But inside Rheia, a battle raged. Assholes like these were *totally* touchable. Especially for her. If Gideon weren't here, she'd ring up Adler and put on such a show...

Did she really need to keep Gideon in the dark? Especially after his antics this morning? What's the worst the Director could say? These four "dudes" were exactly why the Troupe existed in the first place.

The crux... could they trust Gideon to keep his mouth shut?

The mother whimpered. The dude with the ball—*he's the alpha*, Rheia thought—had pulled the turban from the mother's head. Knicks Fan passed off the tablet to Bro and pranced around with the unwound turban wrapped around his shoulders. Man Bun fake wept in mockery of the daughter's sobs.

Inwardly: *Screw it.*

Outwardly: "Gimme your belt."

Rheia stood up, turned her back on the scene, faced Gideon.

He blinked. "What?"

"Just give it to me, quick."

"Why?"

Her voice downshifted. "Gid. Seriously. Now."

His hands obeyed. As he yanked his belt out of the loops, Rheia dug into her messenger bag, pulled out a black woven cap, fitted it snugly on her head.

"Rheia, what are you doing??"

She took out a pair of dark sunglasses, slipped them on, gave the earpieces a little fiddle and they snapped into place, gripping securely. "Adler, you there?" Her voice was barely above a whisper but clearly she was communicating with someone because Gideon saw her give a quick nod. She pulled out two black elastic bands, wrapped them around her wrists.

She whispered again. "Get into Transit Authority's system, find me, Eighth Avenue Line. Stand by light cue one."

Gideon leaned in, matched her volume. "Who are you talking to?"

By way of answer she held out her hand. He handed over his belt. She wrapped it twice around her right knuckles, let the metal buckle hang. She grinned grimly and said, "I'm about to go on stage, Gid."

She transformed. A shift in her posture, a focusing of her energy, a long exhale.

"Holy shit. *Rheia??*"

"It's like I told you. We live in a fallen world." Another cruel laugh from the alpha caromed down the subway car. "And there's always a next time."

27

GIDEON'S MIND SWAM. How could he not have recognized her? The black cap on her head didn't sport a ponytail—*must've been a wig,* he thought—but with her shorn hair hidden, and those sunglasses, and that dangerous energy radiating from her... of course she was the Woman from the Bear and Fawn.

The sitar music suddenly blared. Bro had pumped the volume. The mother pulled her daughter in shield tight.

Gideon snapped to. "But you just said there's four of them."

"Three is never a problem. Four can be tricky but the enclosed space tilts in my favor."

"Wait wait wait—"

"Listen. I'm gonna take out Man Bun first."

"Not the tall guy? He's clearly the leader."

"Man Bun's the beta."

"The...?"

"The enforcer. Nine times outta ten, take out the enforcer and the alpha shows his belly."

"What??"

"In class you said you used to wrestle?"

"Yeah—"

"Be ready."

Rheia turned and glided down the subway car toward the four bullies, hands behind her back, belt hidden. She landed even with the mother and daughter, gave the little girl a small nod, and addressed the frat gang.

"Hey. Assholes."

Abrupt silence. Gideon felt the passengers electrify into an audience.

"Well, well, well, what have we here?" Man Bun sing-songed.

Rheia cut him off. "I'm in no mood. You all get one chance. The abuse stops. Hand over their belongings now. You get off at the next stop and you never treat people this way again."

Man Bun and Bro looked back at the alpha, who jerked his chin toward Rheia. In his toughest tough-guy voice Man Bun said, "And what if we don't?"

Rheia cocked her head a couple degrees. "Then I make you."

The alpha laughed first and the others followed suit.

"Laugh all you want but your bullshit tonight is done. Turban and tablet. Now." Rheia held out her left hand. Gideon saw her right hand, still tucked out of sight behind her back, tightening around his belt.

Man Bun looked back at alpha again. The tall leader nodded. Man Bun turned back to Rheia, nudged Bro with his elbow. Bro lifted the tablet high and dropped it. Screen shattered. Case cracked open.

Bro received back pats and high fives from his buds, a shark-smile marring his face. Man Bun put a hand to his mouth in mock apology.

"Oops. Now what?"

Gideon sensed Rheia holding her fury in check, channeling it. "Now you hand over the turban and cash to cover the cost of what you just stupidly broke."

The gang howled in glee. Man Bun leaned forward. "Make me."

Time held its breath. Rheia stood like a statue, her left arm extended. Man Bun sniffed. "That's what I thought, you're nothing but a—"

Rheia twitched her left arm sideways. Every eye in the train followed it. So no one saw her right arm slash forward, but everyone figured it out as Bro roared. Rheia had bull-whipped the belt buckle across his face.

He stumbled back, turning Knicks Fan and the alpha into bowling pins. Attention thus distracted, Rheia wrapped the belt two more times around her hand and leaped forward into a vicious Superman punch. Energy equaling mass times acceleration, the leather—fat around her knuckles—amplified the punch into a wrecking ball. Man Bun, his threat assessment sensors several woeful beats behind, turned his face back just in time to meet Rheia's belted fist.

A splatter of Man Bun's mouth blood Jackson Pollacked the floor.

"MOVE," Rheia commanded. The mother and daughter scrambled toward the cluster of passengers at the back. Gideon helped seat them and then turned back to watch, unsure what to do but oh so eager to act.

Man Bun was out cold. The two bowling pins pushed Bro off of them, unintentionally sending him toward Rheia's reloaded battering ram, which she delivered as a tight hook into his ribs. If the flesh-muted double-crack that echoed off the train walls was to be believed, two were broken. Bro collapsed into the nearest seat, wheezing and bleeding from buckle-lashed lips.

Knicks Fan regained his balance and lunged at Rheia. She backed up till she felt a pole between her shoulder blades. She watched him load up a huge haymaker. As he launched it she slipped aside. His fist collided with the pole.

The pole won. He howled.

She grabbed his Knicks jersey and yanked him forward. His forehead smashed into the pole, pretty much right where his fist had just imploded.

He was dazed but not out. Still gripping his jersey, she flung him toward Gideon. "Keep him off my six. Put him to sleep if you have to."

Gideon caught Knicks Fan, spun him around, locked in a choke. Knicks Fan panicked. Gideon's rage warmed into delight. *Struggle all you want, asshole.* Gideon sat down, pulling Knicks Fan with him. Wrapped his legs around Knick Fan's gut and clenched every quad, hamstring, and glute. Squeezed Knick Fan's breath clean out. "Like rolling up a tube of toothpaste," his wrestling coach had loved to say.

As Gideon felt consciousness leaving Knick Fan's body, he looked back to Rheia. His bloody belt dripped from her fist. The alpha looked perplexed but not yet cowed. He dropped the basketball into Bro's lap—"Guuuuuh!"—stepped over Man Bun, and dropped into something resembling a fighting stance.

One time outta ten.

Rheia laughed out loud."Oh ho ho, you look like you think you know what you're doing." Her laughter froze. "But you don't. Cash and turban. Or join your friends."

The alpha sneered. "I'm gonna rip your—"

"Suit yourself. Adler lights go."

The train plunged into darkness. The passengers gasped and babbled.

Gideon's surprise eased his grip and Knicks Fan managed to crack him a good one on the nose with the back of his skull.

"Dammit," Gideon muttered and sewed Knicks Fan back up tight.

Grunts and scuffles. Gideon caught only glimpses of what Rheia was up to, the tunnel lights strobe-flashing as the train dug through the darkness. She seemed to move with foreknowledge while the alpha flailed.

Flash... Rheia's belted fist sledgehammering his solar plexus.

Flash... Rheia ducking his wild punch.

Flash... Rheia sweeping his leg. Gideon heard but didn't see the alpha falling on top of Man Bun.

Flash... Rheia cinching his neck with the belt.

"Lights go."

The subway car lit up. The alpha and Man Bun lay in an unconscious heap. Bro whoofed painful breaths. Rheia approached, lifted Knick Fan's arm, let go. It dropped.

"OK Gid, he's out, ease up."

Gideon released. His muscles trembled. He and Rheia laid Knicks Fan on the floor.

"Thanks for the loaner," she said, holding out his belt.

"Um. Yeah. You're welcome." He wiped the belt clean on the Knicks jersey.

Rheia addressed the passengers. "You don't have to be first to step forward. But next time someone else does, don't leave 'em hanging. Bullies are brittle cowards. They break and bleed like anyone else. If you all had stood with me, they would have backed down."

Rheia squatted, looked the little girl in the eye.

"What's your name?"

The little girl wiped her tear-streaked face. "Namrah."

"Did you see what I did, Namrah?"

The girl bobbed her head up and down. "You're strong."

"You are too."

The little girl shook her head side to side. "I'm small."

"But you stood up. You inspired me." Rheia peeled off her black elastic wristbands. Looked at the mother. "May I?"

The mother nodded. The little girl's eyes got big as Rheia slipped the wristbands over each little arm.

"I have to remind myself every day that I'm stronger than I think. Now, when I remind myself, I'll know I'm reminding you, too." The little girl looked at the elastic wraps encasing her wrists. Flexed her little fingers. "Not all fights are fought with fists, Namrah. Don't you ever, *ever* give anyone else the pen to your story."

The little girl's mouth pressed into a thin determined line. The mother spoke, her voice raw. "Thank you."

"Was my sincere pleasure." Rheia jerked a thumb over her shoulder. "You wanna grab cash compensation outta their wallets, I don't think they'll complain."

The train started to slow.

"Gid, we're getting off."

"This our stop?"

"Doesn't matter. Time to exit stage left." She dragged him toward the nearest door. "Adler, wipe any trace from the cameras... thanks, I figured you were ahead of me."

"Who are you talking to??"

Rheia looked at Gideon, but she was listening to someone else. He saw a strange version of himself reflected in her sunglasses: nose slightly bloodied, eyes glowing with euphoria. "Yes, Adler. Tell the Director what happened."

The train stopped. The doors opened. Rheia exited without a backward glance, but Gideon paused and took a mental picture: four tough assholes in various states of disassemblage, a gaggle of passengers looking back at him open-mouthed, a mother rewrapping her turban, and a little girl standing as tall as her little frame allowed, her little wrist-banded fists raised bravely in the air.

28

Aniyah took the paper from her pocket, placed it next to the framed picture of Jazzie on the small desk, and opened her laptop. She transcribed the text of her "truth" into her blog. Clicked into the settings, toggled here and there. A confirmation prompt popped up.

She took a breath, looked at Jazzie's picture.

"My baby. You do look like joy."

She clicked "ok."

There was no chorus, no bells, no rushing of wings. But Aniyah felt Jazzie's joy whooshing through the WiFi, romping through digital playgrounds at unfathomable speed.

The entire ride home Imani had been on her to share, share, share. "You were amazing up there, Ani! Just amazing! You were so real, you write so powerfully about your pain, and getting it out helps, right? And there are others out there who know your anguish. They may need you to guide them, or you may need them to hear you, or show you how they got further along, or... or... or..."

Imani needn't have exhorted so exhaustively. Aniyah had

decided to transform her private blog into a public memorial the moment she had finished reading aloud to the class. Those warm, special people.

She dove into the blog, rearranged a few things, added some pictures. Uploaded an image into the header: she and Jazzie cheek to cheek laughing in the grass. She had never bothered to fill in the "About" section. Now she did.

This blog is a monument to my daughter, Jazzie. While it is true that she was killed at school by an angry man with a ridiculous gun, that is NOT her story. I will tell her full story, her true story. I will do this for her. And for me.

I will never mention the angry man by name. He does not deserve to have his name go down even in infamy. And I have no political agenda in telling Jazzie's story. But if some sort of advocacy emerges, I will not stop it.

I will not try to make sense of the senseless, but oh how I will testify.

Aniyah realized her face again was bathed in tears. But tonight they did not taste bitter. They tasted... clean. Distilled. In fact, they tasted like nothing at all.

29

BODY: Adler sent me the reviews of your improvised show earlier tonight. Strong performance, but unfortunate timing.

Spilled milk.

Three options.

Cut him loose. Just disappear.

Or buy him off, THEN disappear.

Or continue with the workshops so we can keep an eye on him. Tell him enough to hook him, then find some leverage. Non-Disclosure Agreement. Ironclad.

Take his temperature, then we'll know how to proceed. But patch this hole.

30

Rheia heard the bathroom faucet turn off. She deleted the email draft and closed the browser, pocketed her phone. *Spilled milk.*

Gideon walked in, patting his face dry with a hand towel. They looked at each other. Their first moment to breathe since zig-zagging away from the train, double-backing, sharing a cab, head on a swivel, into his sublet.

Neither spoke. Gideon turned away, opened the fridge. One refreezable ice pack pressed onto his shoulder. Another he wrapped in the towel and held to his nose.

He sat. She leaned. They squared off, gazing at each other across the Rubicon, ankle-deep, both aware that just a few steps forward would make returning as tedious as going o'er.

The three options revved their motors in her mind.

"So," he said, "is this one of those if-you-tell-you-me-you-have-to- kill-me situations?"

She shrugged.

"That wasn't a 'no', Rheia."

"Wasn't a 'yes' either, Gideon."

They looked and looked, taking each other's measure. The buzz of someone letting their pizza delivery into the building vibrated up the stairwell.

"You're not a consultant."

She shook her head.

"You never flashed a badge. Do I need a lawyer?"

She shook her head.

"You undercover or something?"

She tilted her head. "Yes." Reverse-tilted. "No."

He blew air out his nose. "What you just did back there? What *we* did? Those guys are in the hospital by now, Rheia!"

"Probably."

"And talking to the cops."

"Yep."

"And that doesn't worry you."

"No one in that train would finger us even if they could. And no video."

"Right. No video. That reminds me. How long have you and 'Adler' been stalking me?"

She blinked.

"You brought us straight here, Rheia. Right to my apartment. How did you know where I live?"

Inwardly she seethed at herself. Outwardly she shrugged.

"Stalking is too strong a word, Gid. But we've been watching you since the Bear and Fawn."

"Why?"

"Curiosity at first. You almost caught me quick-changing. Looked you up. Saw you were an actor."

"So you did actually see *Henry Five*."

She nodded. "And took your class to see if you'd be right for our training needs. I've never lied to you, Gid."

"Sure, just a couple gaping omissions. And some light

surveillance. And—" His eyes narrowed. "Wait. How were you able to 'look me up'?"

Rheia pretended to ponder. "Can I trust you, Gideon?"

He snorted. "If there's anyone in this room who needs to earn trust right now, it sure ain't me."

She shrugged again. "We can stop. Right now. The less you know the better, actually. I can walk out that door and you'll never see me again. In fact…"

Rheia pushed off the wall. Option one. Her hand grasped the doorknob.

Gideon blurted, "I want in."

Rheia paused. *Leave. Just leave.* Instead she said, "You want in what?" He stood, vibrating with an intensity she recognized from class. "Whatever group or agency or gang it is you're in. You and this Adler." Option three shoved option one aside. *Hook him hard. Make him fight for it. Then take it away. See what he does.*

"Why?"

"Because…" Gideon ran his hand through his hair. "Because today feels like I've impacted more people than all my shows in my life put together."

She released the doorknob. "How so?"

"All those people in the train, Rheia. That little girl, that mother. How could they not be changed by what they witnessed? Not to mention those four assholes who will forever think twice."

"Hopefully."

"And then this morning. That young woman. I didn't just tell a story. I wasn't just an actor. I *acted*."

"Don't forget the rapist."

Gideon growled. "I won't ever. He got his."

"And is that enough? Might he also change?"

Rheia noted him licking his lips and eyeing a bottle of Buffalo Trace on the counter.

"Sure, whatever, maybe he will. But what matters is today I made a real difference. An impact." His eyes flicked up into the past. "I saved people."

Hook him.

She moved back into the tiny room. "We call ourselves the Troupe."

"The *Troupe?*"

She nodded.

"As in, like, a wandering band of actors?"

"Yep. Now tell me what you think you know."

He grabbed a blue, wrap-around headset off a nearby table. "I run with these sometimes. Bone conduction headphones. Sound enters by vibrating the skull at the temples. Keeps the ear canals clear. Connects by Bluetooth to my GPS and music."

"So?"

"Your sunglasses."

"Huh. Observant." She pulled her sunglasses out of her messenger bag. "These are a wee bit more advanced." She handed them over.

He tried them on. The earpieces snapped securely into place. "Geez, that's nice. I sweat so much, I have to put my sunglasses on a lanyard."

"Bone conduction speakers, like you said. Microphone built in as well."

"So that's how you've been talking to 'Adler.'"

"Yep. Think of Adler as my Stage Manager. They're wireless, so he can leapfrog any password and piggy-back any network in the area. Dig into electrical systems."

"Whoa. The lights in the train??"

"And in the bar. The TVs. The jukebox. He can design lights and sound anywhere he can get a signal. Amplify my performance. They also act as a bodycam. He can see what I see. Record. Screen capture."

Gideon's jaw dropped. "That's how you were able to look me up??"

"Yep. Simple internet search with an image of your face."

"This is magic."

"Nah. Just R&D on steroids. Check this out." She reached over, touched a spot on the frame.

Gideon gasped. The world—a moment ago shaded and dim —lit up in sharply etched highlights of green.

"So on the train, in the dark...?"

"I could see fine. Tall dude didn't have a prayer. Theatrics."

Gideon removed the sunglasses, amazed and wary.

Rheia recalled the first time she'd experienced Adler's shades. They *did* feel magical, but she continued to feign indifference. "Oh yeah, there's a heads-up display, too. Clock, timer, GPS. Rudimentary zoom capability, Adler is still tinkering. Working on adding thermal imaging, other tricks as the tech catches up."

"These must've cost a fortune to engineer." He handed the glasses back. She put them back in her messenger bag. "And I'm guessing you don't sell 'em."

Rheia cleared her throat. "The Director has ample resources."

"Director?"

"Of the Troupe."

Gideon snorted. "Director. Stage Manager. You all have really leaned into this theatre thing."

"It's an effective metaphor. Keeps us on mission, humble, focused on the audience. No navel-gazing, as you like to say in class. What else?" she asked.

"Wig."

She looked at him with mock suspense, reached into her bag, yanked out the wig. Ponytail and bangs.

"All the old school low-tech theatre tricks. Wigs. Make-up. Reversible jackets and shirts, scarves, hats."

"Tattoos and glasses and scars, oh my."

"You got it, Dorothy. Eye patches, spirit gum, beauty marks. Hit eyewitnesses with a flamboyant detail and then ditch it. You disappear."

Rheia slid the wig back into her bag.

"And what's with the wristbands?" Gideon asked.

"Dual purpose. On the Adler side they have VR tech—"

"Virtual reality??"

"Yep. They connect to the sunglasses so you can manipulate screens, surf the web, run downloaded tutorials."

Gideon shook his head. "Geez. What's the other purpose? Casting spells?"

"Far more mundane. They're basic athletic supports, quick version of boxing hand wraps. Keep wrists in good striking form. Though we try to avoid outright punching."

"Why?"

"Because punching causes trauma not just to the target but to you. That's why boxers wear gloves. Not to protect the other guy, but to protect their own hands."

"That's why you're always finding weapons," Gideon murmured to himself. "The pool triangle. My belt." A soft *snick* made the hairs on his arm stand up. A wicked-looking baton had appeared in Rheia's hand.

"You're not wrong," she said. The baton reverse-telescoped and disappeared back into her bag.

He's rattled. Good.

He gathered himself. "So. The Troupe. You're... what? A bunch of vigilantes running around playing dress-up?"

She bristled. "We aren't playing *dress-up*. No capes or

cowls. Everything I just showed you? Helps us blend in, disappear. We don't do it for publicity. We slip out the stage door, incognito, no celebrity."

"OK. But you ARE vigilantes?"

"Sure, if that's how you want to think about it. But did you know, oh wise teacher, that being a vigilante is not actually illegal?"

"Say what?"

"Lots of legal wiggle room. You can patrol your streets. Neighborhood watch? Form of vigilantism. Now, vigilantes may engage in *activities* that are illegal. Assault. Breaking and entering. Worse. But there are real ones out there, all over the world, usually in full costume. Most just visit kids in hospitals or do charity work, but some do end up in the occasional fistfight, carry mace, have websites and viral videos, secret identities."

"They sound harmless. You're a walking weapon."

"Sure."

"And you're taking justice into your own hands."

Rheia cocked her head. "Thought you wanted in, Gid. What's with the judgment?"

Gideon paced.

Make him fight for it.

She heaved a dramatic sigh. "I can go. If this is too much, not what you expected, no worries."

"Stop it. I just..." His eyes flicked toward the bottle on the counter. "You mentioned a mission."

"Primary. Wipe out bullying."

"Bullying?? Seriously?"

"Yep. In all its forms."

"You sound like an after-school special."

"You look like an amateur drunk training for the alcoholic Olympics." He glared. *C'mon, Gid, fight for it.* "Secondary.

Inspire the audience to join us. Wipe out the bullying around them and inside themselves."

Gideon shook his head, paced and paced.

"Aspirational mission there, Rheia. And you achieve that... how? With fancy tech and mixed martial arts?"

Rheia waved off his sarcasm. "So that's the *what* of the mission. Here's the *how*." She held up two fingers. "Double-pronged. First, public improvised performances. Like what you've seen and done. Inspire the public directly and intimately."

"And second?"

"Private, targeted, scripted shows. You follow the news? Those white nationalists who were gonna kidnap the mayor?"

"That was YOU?"

"Told you I'd have to miss class sometimes for work."

31

Gideon reeled.

"But Rheia, if that was you and the Troupe... I mean, everyone is saying FBI."

"In a joint task force with NYPD, sure. I betcha Homeland Security even gets a piece."

"You don't want the credit?"

"Not the mission, Gid. And giving away the credit helps maintain the illusion."

"What illusion?"

"That society works."

"Whoa whoa, wait, what?"

Rheia pretended impatience. "Gid. Come on. I mean you do understand the system isn't designed to deal with bullies who don't play by the rules."

"OK?"

"That the rules more often than not actually *protect* the bullies."

"Yes I understand—"

"Society is an illusion. Just like a play, we all have to buy in. Agree to given circumstances so the story makes sense."

"YES."

"And that illusion lives on a cliff's edge. Doesn't take much to push it right off. Toilet paper."

"What?"

"During the pandemic. Hoarding toilet paper. Ever been in a coastal town when a hurricane is coming? I have. People are animals. Fight over bottled water, steal sandbags, shove each other aside for candles and batteries and canned peaches."

Gideon shook his head. "So that makes it ok for you to kick the crap out of them and conduct secret operations?"

"Every mission has a *why*. The motor. For the Troupe, the illusion is the why. Because the illusion is the only thing keeping our species from wiping itself out. It needs protection from those who take advantage of it."

"Who appointed you guardian?"

"No one. That would imply some external authority. I choose this."

"You and the Troupe. No oversight."

"We don't claim ultimate authority. But we do have clear policies and rules of engagement. If you're actually interested."

Gideon trembled, with fury or temptation or confusion Rheia couldn't quite tell. Then he moved toward the counter. Reached for the bottle. "No way, Gid." She grabbed his arm. "Leave the bourbon. Don't dull this. There's a cost. Pay it or don't."

He pulled away hard.

"How much?"

"It ain't cheap." *Make him fight.* "But then again, what wouldn't you give to go back and protect Finley?"

Gideon's ears rang. His fingers curled into claws. His hazel eyes hardened into slate.

There he is.

"She's who you were really trying to save this morning. Right?"

"Her name. Does not come. From your mouth. Again."

She stared him down. His gaze glanced away to the bottle. He stalked to the window. Hissed at her over his shoulder.

"How do you even...?"

"Before I registered for your class, we dug. There's very little about you the Troupe doesn't know."

He snarled. "So then you know my *why*."

"We know the gist. You want to fill in the details?"

"Go to hell."

"Some other time then."

An awkward pause bumped into the furniture, muttered its apology, tripped on its way out of the room.

In the silence, Gideon realized he was famished. An order was put in to the Korean joint around the corner. Gideon traded ice packs for heating pads. Rheia sat quietly, idly twirling her sunglasses.

Buzz. Knock. Cash. Bowls.

Rheia dished and served as Gideon set aside the heating pads and rolled his bruised shoulder loose. And then, as it has done for millennia, breaking bread gently shredded the silence.

"What was my life before bulgogi?" Rheia said as she speared another bite.

Gideon grunted. "I gotta learn to make kimchi."

"Oh yeah?"

"Apparently you can do a quick countertop version, but if I ever have a yard again, I'll bury it like you're supposed to. Ferment it in the ground."

Rheia shook her head. "You seriously need to go on Jeopardy."

They chewed.

Rheia studied his face. "You usually clean-shaven?"

Gideon swallowed. "No. Usually stubbled. But mostly I shave or grow out based on gigs. I've had goatees, full beards, mutton chops—"

"Mustaches?"

"Once."

"Eek."

"Have not yet been cursed with a soul patch."

"Fortunate."

They chewed.

Rheia spoke as if about the weather. "Troupe members usually stay clean-shaven. Gives them the blankest slate to play with."

Gideon set aside his bowl, wiped his mouth. "Circling back."

"Only if you want to."

"Have I asked you to leave?"

Rheia leaned in, elbows on knees. *Push him to the edge, then take it away.* "You asked about the Troupe taking justice into its own hands."

"And you mentioned rules of engagement."

"Later. What do you mean by 'justice'"?

"Fair play. Rights protected. Getting what you deserve."

"And it's the job of those in authority to uphold justice. So the citizenry can go about their lives."

"That's the working theory. Doesn't always hold water."

Rheia sneered. "It doesn't just not hold water, Gid. It's leaked from day one. Justice is a sinking ship, and those officials who aren't themselves part of the problem are simply bailing water."

"And that gives you and the Troupe the right to—"

"The *right*? Where do you think rights come from? What

gives cops their authority? Any government or state, where does their right to rule come from?"

"Well, the law, Rheia. Our founding documents."

She rolled her eyes. "Oh come on, Gid. You've already seen behind the curtain. Stop avoiding."

Gideon gritted his teeth. "I'm not avoiding, Rheia."

"Citizenship. National boundaries. Money itself. They all are simply *ideas*. Illusions."

"You're talking about suspension of disbelief."

She arched an eyebrow. "Explain."

"Theatre-speak. The audience enters into an agreement with the actors that what they are viewing is real. That we aren't just playing pretend in a dark room with no fourth wall."

"So you *do* get it. Rights. Authority. Governments. They are constructs. Suspensions of disbelief."

"Like plywood flats pretending to be living room walls on stage."

Rheia nodded. "And now that you've seen it, it can't be unseen."

She could sense him standing on the cliff's edge, gazing into the abyss. *He's almost ready to jump.* She readied herself.

Gideon cleared his throat. "OK. Rules of engagement?"

"Isn't it obvious, Gid? If one party breaks a contract, it becomes null and void. The Troupe's guiding principle is simple. Fair play. We meet the cheaters and bullies on what-ever field of battle they choose. Whatever rules they ignore, we ignore the same ones."

She watched him struggle. "So when they go low..."

"They have set the rules of engagement for that skirmish."

"You don't go high?"

Rheia jabbed her finger in his face. "That aspirational *go high* bullshit doesn't work, Gid, and you know it! If there's one universal truth that history has taught us? If you ain't cheating you ain't trying. It's true in professional sports. It's true in commerce. It's true in politics. It's true in the justice system. Humans are wretches."

Gideon's face flushed. "So those who play by the rules... we're just suckers?"

"Yes. Because what the hell rules are we even supposed to play by? Color of your skin? Different rules. Size of your bank account. Whatever apparatus is or isn't between your legs. Worrying about the rules is pointless. So we put that onus on the cheaters. We just meet 'em where they are."

"But if you break the rules—"

"*Which ones??*"

"—then aren't you the same as them?"

Rheia leaped to her feet. "Of course not! If the rules say X and you don't follow them but I do, then I've agreed to a knife fight except you bring a bazooka. Pyrrhic victories? Moral high ground? Whining 'but I played by the rules'? That's ego. Abdication. Your clean hands don't outweigh real-world consequences. So if the asshole across from me pulls out a bazooka, let's see what he does if I pull one out too. He pulls out a baseball bat instead? I'll put the bazooka away and grab my own Louisville Slugger. FAIR PLAY."

Gideon stood, shaking his head. "It sounds an awful lot like you're saying the ends justify the means here, Rheia, and if I'm going to be part of something—"

Rheia laughed outright. "Who says we're gonna let you in?"

He blinked. "But, I thought—"

"Oh I know what you *thought*. You thought that because you've suffered, because you burn hot with vengeance at the memory of your sweet little sister that somehow you're entitled. But you can't even tell me her story. No no. Instead you wrap it around yourself like a warm cuddly victim blanket. You suck on bourbon and perform the character of 'professional actor and wise funny teacher Gideon Price' for your students. But here's the truth. You are a SIDE GIG. You are not the center of my story. And the Troupe doesn't need reclamation projects."

Gideon's mouth opened. Closed. Opened. "I didn't—"

"We don't do this for revenge, Gideon. We do it because we believe the illusion matters. That humans can evolve past the self-destructive bullying hard-wired into our genes. What do you believe in? Besides yourself?"

And she slammed the door on her way out.

Now let's see what he does.

32

For a good three minutes Gideon just stood there. The air in the tiny apartment swirled in the vacuum left by Rheia's boisterous exit.

He wrapped his hand around the bottle. Knuckles white. He dropped it in the trash. Pulled it back out. Emptied it into the sink. Dropped it in the recycling.

He pulled on shorts. Convinced his barking shoulder to ease into a T-shirt. Laced up his Hokas.

Out the door. Down the steps. Out the door. Up the street. He had no route in mind. He simply ran.

Some things you can't chase down.

His shoulder ached. He ran.

Other things you can't outrun.

His nose throbbed. He ran.

Instinctively he ran away from people, but on the island of Manhattan good luck with that. More than one cab nearly clipped him as he caromed through crosswalks. Sightseers saw him dodging through car horns like spears.

He happened upon the Hudson, its inexorable current oozing south.

He gritted his teeth and pushed north. Upstream. Battling. His feet pushed the earth and the earth pushed him back. Propulsion by repulsion.

Miles later he was trembling, sweaty to the point of nausea. His muscles tapped out. Somehow he found himself back in Hell's Kitchen. He stumbled. Down the street. In the door. Up the stairs. In the door.

The aroma of 90 proof lingered like conviction.

33

SPEARHEAD 1488 DOUBLE-CHECKED HIS GPS. Semi-trailers blew past him, racing to swap one batch of stuff for another. His cruise was set at a safe 78, but anyone who has driven I-75 near the Florida-Georgia border knows the flow of traffic hums near 90.

More important not to draw attention than to engage in a live-action video game. He had time.

He swigged cartoon-blue water from a plastic bottle and munched jerky from a plastic sleeve. Cash for gas and snacks all the way. No trail.

Forty-six seconds passed. Another mile devoured.

He kept his eyes open for GA-122 as Valdosta approached. Dusk settled. He flipped on his headlights. The sign for Meeting House Creek crept out of the haze. Off the arterial highway, onto a capillary.

He followed the GPS, staying below the speed limit. He turned onto a meandering path, his wheels crunching gravel. Puddles reflected a recent rain. Scraggly trees. Weeds.

And there it was, looking completely out of place. A simple

monument, though monument was too grand a word. Just a plaque on a pole, really. A pathetic clump of flowers at the base. A homemade cross of white sticks standing like a younger sibling to the side. A stuffed teddy bear.

Spearhead splashed through another puddle, coasted to a stop. There was still enough lingering light to see by. He got out, walked to the passenger window, reached in, pulled the Glock from the glove box, tucked it into the small of his back, approached the sign. The evening insects buzzed in the sticky summer air.

The plaque was eye level. He read:

Mary Turner and the Lynching Rampage of 1918.

Near this site on May 19, 1918, twenty-one-year-old Mary Turner, eight months pregnant, was burned, mutilated, and shot to death by a local mob after publicly denouncing her husband's lynching the previous day. In the days immediately following the murder of a white planter by a black employee on May 16, 1918, at least eleven local African Americans including the Turners died at the hands of a lynch mob in one of the deadliest waves of vigilantism in Georgia's history. No charges were ever brought against known or suspected participants in these crimes. From 1880-1930, as many as 550 people were killed in Georgia in these illegal acts of mob violence.

Erected by the Georgia Historical Society, etc etc.

Spearhead ran his hands over the text. The metal was still hot enough from the sun to make him wince. He leaned into the burn, closed his eyes, tried to conjure the ghosts that walked this baked patch of earth. The real ghosts... the White men had who owned this land, who did what it took to protect it.

If only he could have lived a century ago.

But no. That was not his path nor his mission. But he could still be part of the reclamation of the White birthright.

He stomped the flowers, kicked the shredded petals into

the mud. He yanked the cross out of the dirt, pried the two pieces apart, snapped them into shards, stabbed them into the animal's stuffing and left it gasping on the ground. He spat on the plaque.

He returned to his car, opened the driver's side door, turned over the engine, stood tall and proud. He swept his gaze around the perimeter, ensuring he was indeed alone.

Not alone. My ancestors are here. They see me and know me.

He drew and fired, spearing holes through the monument, giving Mary Turner and all her kind exactly the "honor" they deserved.

Back on I-75, cruising at 78, he trembled, ecstatic. The moon rose and guided him toward his next target.

Back in the weeds, the rising moon also poured its light through the perfectly round wounds like luminous blood.

34

The week unspooled. Gideon felt more observer than participant. Eight shows. Daily runs. Calls with mom. Healed shoulder and nose. No bourbon. In fact, no Bear and Fawn. His castmates explored other joints after shows, extended invites. He deflected. Spent that time wandering the city, trying to see it and its inhabitants as Rheia had described.

And trying to unsee.

He spent his days in a renewed search for any sign of Finley. Put out lines to every address, email, and number that had ever been associated with her.

Radio silence.

Every social media handle she had ever used. Dead ends.

Every relative, friend, acquaintance, co-worker. None had news. He gave himself over to the weekend gauntlet. Five shows. Five audiences. What impact?

Monday. Would Rheia be in class? He hoped she would. He hoped she wouldn't.

She wasn't.

He played the part of "professional actor and wise funny

teacher Gideon Price" to the hilt. Good class. Happy students. He bought a fifth of Knob Creek on the way home.

As he latched the chain, his phone rang. Number unknown. He ignored it. Unwrapped the top of the bottle. Stared at the foil in his hand. Got a glass. Poured four amber fingers.

His phone rang again. He set the bottle down hard. A couple drops slopped out, landed on the back of his hand. The liquor hissed on his skin.

He answered. "Who's this?"

"What'd I miss in class?"

Rheia.

He wiped his hand on his pants. "How'd you know I was home?"

"One guess."

He looked down at his wrist.

"Adler tracked my Garmin?"

"GPS is a bitch."

He walked to the window. Looked out. "Class was good. Everyone missed you. You close by?"

"Why? You wanna talk?"

"You called me."

His heart hammered. "Rheia?"

"Still here. Waiting you out. Horse to water, y'know."

He turned. The bourbon crouched on the counter.

"I've never told her story to anyone, Rheia."

"And yet you make your living telling stories, Gideon. All that muck you stir up in rehearsal only matters if it's shaped. Curated for the audience. Catharsis."

His breathing frayed. He knew she could hear.

"Gid."

His silence screamed.

"Forget the Troupe. You're poisoning yourself."

He looked at his drink.

Her voice suddenly intimate and knowing. "You think you're the only one with a beast caged inside? It can be tamed, you know. Ridden."

He squeezed his eyes shut. Clenched his phone. Ground his molars.

"OK then. I wish you the best, Gid."

"*Wait.*"

He let go.

"We ran cross-country together."

35

THE FRESHMAN PHENOM. Phenomenal Finley. Freshman Finley Price Fleet of Feet.

The local paper had run out of catchy alliterative headlines before the cross-country season was even half over.

Gideon had joined cross-country because it was the cool thing to do in their small Midwestern town. It was the cool thing to do because Coach Carl was a living legend. Coach Carl coached cross-country in the fall, track in the spring, and ostensibly was on the payroll to teach actual classes as well, but high school HR had learned to keep PE and Health subs on permanent retainer. No one complained.

Coach Carl had grown up in this small town and been the first local athlete to make a splash at the state level. The first banners to hang in the small town's small high school gym were due entirely to Coach Carl's god-given quickness. His individual prowess spawned team success. Solo wins over hated rivals who constantly bested the home team on courts and fields but couldn't catch Carl on trails or straightaways catalyzed town pride. His peers eagerly lined up to follow in his literal footsteps.

His junior and senior years brought back-to-back state titles. Such heady success sent the town into a tizzy. The diner on Main Street named its most popular breakfast after him. His face appeared on hardware store billboards. He shot a commercial for the used car emporium just up the highway, a commercial where he appeared to outrun a 4Runner. His times were the point of discussion at every gas station, grocery store, and church potluck. He was Prom King and Student Body President, and more than once the cops let him off for speeding with a wink and some sort of ironic warning like "don't you slow down, now."

As he headed off to college on a scholarship he left behind a thriving run culture and rabid fans. The small town had found its identity.

The most forward-thinking entrepreneur in the small town, soon after the first state title, opened a shoe store that due to demand quickly encompassed all variety of running gear. The townies shopped there en masse, ignoring the fancier stores in the mall two towns over, and their fanaticism financed the store owner's new house, in-ground pool, Jeep, and even college savings accounts for unplanned triplets.

A local sales tax was enthusiastically passed and a state-of-the-art oval track was installed, along with a shiny training facility and spa-like locker rooms. Almost every business owner chipped in to get their sponsorship logos on the new Wall of Fame, and Coach Carl's was the first name emblazoned.

An expert coach was head-hunted, someone with national or even Olympic-level credibility. Boosters made sure the salary enticed and the position filled. And so the tiny town kept churning out a disproportionate number of runners who posted far more than their fair share of annual top-ten times across the state. More banners hung high in the gym. More names inscribed themselves into the Wall of Fame. Just below Coach Carl's.

In the meantime, Carl's college career flamed out. The caliber of competition was such that he could no longer just show up and win. He was always on the cusp, doing just enough to keep his scholarship but not quite enough to take the next step. His visits home increased in frequency, not just on holidays but also more and more on random weekends. The cost of his flights was always covered by a homegrown fan, and the intoxication of his high school era celebrity proved more dampener than stimulant. At home he could luxuriate. At home he didn't have to push. At home he was already a legend.

Coach Carl managed to graduate, his GPA atrocious, his scholarship in tatters, but the diploma had his name on it. He moved home, right back into his parents' house, his bedroom bedecked with ribbons and bursting with trophies. His body, which had been kept in straining check by the requirements of his increasingly frustrated college coach, released itself into ever-rising dough.

Rather than find a job—what legend works for a living?—he let it be known he'd love to assist the expert high school coach. And just like that, the expert coach had an assistant who outshone him.

One year later the expert coach's contract expired. The school didn't even bother to make him an offer, not that he had any interest in re-signing. Not with Coach Carl lording at every practice and looming at every meet. So the town replaced outside expertise with internal celebrity.

The expert coach left behind policies, procedures, and systems. Work-out routines and diet recommendations and gear guidelines. A machine so well-oiled that the levers practically pulled themselves.

Coach Carl slid behind the console and was at least smart enough to know to stay out of the way. He made a couple cosmetic tweaks. Literally cosmetic: new uniforms, new song playlists in the weight room, new stopwatches. Claimed responsibility for the ongoing victories and strong state showings, kept the flywheel spinning and basked in his continued glory.

So of course Gideon joined up first chance, a solid if not spectacular JV member. His times would never get him on the medal stand individually but they wouldn't hurt the team either. Necessary middle-of-the-packer contributing points. Varsity came calling his sophomore year.

Finley, though... Finley was a comet, one of those genetic anomalies that slings by in its orbit once a generation, especially in a town as small as this small town. She was one year behind Gideon in school, ever and always a beloved nuisance at his heels. She joined cross-country not because it was the cool thing to do but because Gideon had, and everything her big brother did she wanted to do.

Running was the first thing at which she outclassed Gideon.

At tryouts, as a fresh-faced ninth-grader, she blew past all but the gals' team captain, and most of the varsity guys as well. Gideon was the only one unsurprised. He chuckled at all the wounded teenage male egos.

Coach Carl, thinking it had to be an outlier but hopeful maybe it wasn't, invited her to the first varsity practice. And Finley cranked out a 20-minute 5K and Coach Carl knew he had lightning in a bottle. She was the first freshman to make varsity, leaping past the dues-paying of JV and transforming the team from mere challengers for that year's state title into the favorites.

She ran with abandon. She ran with joy. She ran with a

smile that blinded, giddy and glancing over her shoulder at her big brother barely keeping her in sight.

The small town swooned. Her first state title may as well have been the coronation of a new queen. The second after Finley's sophomore year elevated her to empress, and the big universities started sending scouts and letters. Whispers about the Olympics floated in the air like dandelion fluff. Coach Carl set the state's Athletic Hall of Fame directly in his crosshairs, started planning how to commemorate the inevitable four straight state titles. He would ride Finley's coattails to immortality.

But the comet didn't let it go to her head. She still ran with joy. With abandon and that blinding smile. She had enough of a competitive streak that she didn't give away tenths of seconds glancing over her shoulder for Gideon anymore, but she knew her big brother always had her back.

After the second downtown victory parade in two years, there was a party. Coach Carl hosted. Varsity, JV, all the runners and jumpers and hurlers. By this time he had built a gaudy new split-level out on a few secluded wooded acres. There was a bonfire. Music. Coolers crammed with ice and aluminum cans. The cops knew to ignore these parties because Coach Carl always supplied the beer, and it wasn't like the noise bothered anyone, way out there in the woods. Nothing wrong with kids blowing off steam. They worked hard, they did the town proud.

Summer break bounded out of May and dove into the pond of June. Gideon worked like normal, detasseling corn and saving up. Corn tassels in summers past had paid for his bike, for his laptop, and would this summer pay for his first pre-owned car.

Finley was set to again be a counselor at the church camp she had loved since she was a little pigtailed camper. But abruptly she said she didn't want to go. She could have her pick of jobs in the small town. Every business wanted her and the boost her presence would bring to their bottom line. She chose the diner and worked obsessive hours.

June gave way to the fireworks and barbecues of July. Gideon's tan peeled and darkened. Finley, despite all the free pie and milkshakes the line cook foisted upon her, started to look wan. Her bones jutted. No one noticed. Her smile still blinded, even if a closer look would have noted hollowness in her eyes.

The oppressiveness of midwestern August wrapped everyone in lazy blankets of cicada song. Gideon got his car. Finley went through the motions. Perhaps sensing something amiss with his sister, he took her on his first joy ride, chasing the full moon through air sticky from an afternoon shower. She laughed and hooted, and the joy in her voice struck him... because he suddenly realized he hadn't heard it all summer.

He parked by the lake. They sat on a rotting dock. The water was glass, pressed flat under the heavy haze. Two moons —one real, one reflected—shone on them with yawning indifference.

He offered her a beer. She blanched. He gave her a fruit punch instead.

They toasted.

"To my little sis, the friggin' two-time state champ."

Finley burst into tears that dripped into the lake. The reflected moon surfed tiny ripples.

And she told him.

Coach Carl's party. Coach Carl's beers. Coach Carl's unwelcome hands and demanding, doughy body.

Things happened fast then. Gideon took Finley straight to the sheriff. The sheriff called their parents. The sheriff called Coach Carl. There was a confrontation at the station. Accusation and attempted placation. The moon set. The sun rose. And the Price Family awoke to discover they were pariahs.

Mr. Price's garage collapsed in mere weeks as every oil change and tire rotation mysteriously canceled. Mrs. Price's secretarial job at the church vanished like a pastoral prayer into the rafters. Whispers behind backs. Side eyes from across the streets. Shoulders ice-cold in the middle of one of the hottest Augusts anyone could remember.

Finley locked herself in her room. No more free milkshakes.

Gideon got into scrapes. Outright fights for Finley's honor. His new used car was vandalized. The sheriff and the deputy scratched their sweaty scalps and shrugged.

The small town scrubbed the Price Family out of existence.

Coach Carl strutted. As the cross country season geared up, the Price Family hit the trail too.

New school for Gideon's senior year. Living in cramped quarters, feeling like squatters in their grandparents' cabin one state away from the titles and parades. He raged. He threw his running shoes in the garbage. He stumbled into wrestling, showed a natural talent and unnatural fury, which often led him to overcommit and lose even in the middle of over-whelming his cooler-headed opponent.

Same new school for Finley's junior year. Her blinding smile erased. Her joy a shadowed memory. Her abandon found only in needles and pills.

Gideon escaped to college. His accidental wrestling career landed him his first stage role, as the wrestler "Charles" in *As You Like It*. The theater community of kooks and weirdos and outcasts welcomed him open-armed. He spent the holiday break with a friend. Didn't go home.

Finley was devastated. She was still running, often to the point of injury, posting painful times that no longer merited media attention. A constant throbbing drone, like the unseen but ever-present cicadas, echoed in her mind and slowed her down. The drugs slowed her down. Her brother should have been able to catch up now that she was slowed down.

But he was gone.

That holiday, after another conversationless meal of left-over turkey, with the three hundredth showing of *It's a Wonderful Life* blabbering in the background, Finley got a phone call. A desperate plea from a former cross-country friend back in the small town. A former friend who had dismissed Finley's accusation, but now found herself secretly and unwillingly pregnant with Coach Carl's kid.

The droning in Finley's mind magnified. She kept the news to herself. Her family, after all, hadn't helped her before.

She snuck out. Drove one state over. Met her friend at the rotting dock. Got the full story. Looked out over the frozen lake. Watched her breath dissipate into the frigid air. The droning got louder.

"Alison. Have you told him?"

"No."

"Don't."

"What are you going to do?" "Nevermind. I'll call you tomorrow."

She drove her friend home. Then drove out into the secluded woods. Turned off the headlights and coasted to a snow-softened stop. The droning was deafening. She called her brother. The phone rang and rang.

"C'mon, Gid. C'mon c'mon c'mon c'mon..."

Gideon's voicemail greeting, unintelligible through the droning. Beep.

"Where are you, big bro?" End call.

Someone had to do something.

She popped the trunk.

Why not her?

As she knocked on Coach Carl's door, the droning stopped. She gasped with blessed relief. Turned her face to the silent, falling snow. Felt each flake landing on her cheeks like daddy's whiskers when she was small and he kissed her goodnight.

She heard the door-chain rattling free. She adjusted her grip on the tire iron and smiled through frozen tears.

Later Coach Carl had professional cleaners scrub the blood entirely out of his entry rug. He healed quickly from the couple licks Finley had gotten in.

She spent a month in the hospital, eating through a straw.

The sheriff, deputy, and small-town populace all shook their heads and clucked their tongues. "Such a shame." "Self-defense." "Aren't drugs terrible?"

Alison quietly made the pregnancy go away. Coach Carl paid, but the price was her silence. A few months later the track team took third at state. There was a parade down Main Street. Coach Carl stood in the bed of a pick-up truck, waving to the cheering citizens with one hand, hoisting the trophy with the other.

36

"Last I heard, he's still coaching."

Gideon was beyond hoarse. He got some water. Rheia remained silent, as she had through his entire recitation.

"I sat by Finley's hospital bed, skipped all of J-term. I held her hand. Fed her. Took her to the bathroom. The good thing that came of it is that she kicked the drugs. My parents..."

His sigh was pierced by a wailing ambulance siren on Rheia's end of the line. "After the sheriff and Carl brow-beat them that night at the station, they were never the same. Something in them broke. They kept vigil at the hospital too, but they had nothing else to give. It took me years to forgive them, for them to forgive themselves, for us to get back to any sort of real relationship."

Rheia heard Gideon rummaging in a drawer.

"Finley didn't go back to school. She moved to my college town. I set her up with an apartment and a job in the dining commons. In between classes and shows and practice I helped her study up and nail her GED. We held a private graduation ceremony, just her and me."

Rheia could tell Gideon had found what he was looking for. He sat down heavily.

"We didn't go home that summer. I moved in with her. We both worked. We ran together. We didn't talk much, but we healed. My sophomore year started. Underclassmen weren't allowed to live off-campus so I had to move back into a dorm. Got cast in the fall play. Was juggling class and rehearsal and wrestling, didn't have as much time to spend with her. Saw her every day in the commons, though. And her smile broke through more and more."

Rheia heard his throat hitching.

"Finley saw me in the show opening night. Told me at the cast party I was really good, she was so proud of me, maybe I could make a career out of this. Gave me a big big hug. The next morning she wasn't at her breakfast shift. I swung by her apartment. It was empty."

Rheia finally spoke.

"She thought she was holding you back."

Rheia sensed Gideon nodding. "I guess."

"So she did the one thing she was better at than you."

"Yeah."

"She ran."

"And Rheia... goddammit... she's still running. I get occasional postcards from here and there, like breadcrumbs." He flipped through the treasured stack he had pulled from the tiny dresser drawer. "She's off the grid. Always gone before I get to the newest return address. She may as well be a ghost."

They sat quietly. Gideon in his tiny sublet. Rheia tethered to him by electrical signals and radio waves racing through the New York night. She heard Gideon mutter to himself. "And that prick is still coaching..."

Rheia made a silent promise to herself, then out loud said, "Gid. I'll see you next week in class."

A beat. Then his voice, cleansed and hopeful. "Yeah?"

"No promises. But I'll show you something after. If you're still interested." Another beat.

"Absolutely."

37

GIDEON HUNG UP.

Rheia stayed on the line.

"Adler, you get all that?"

A click. Then... Munching. Small burp. Contented sigh.

"Yeah I did. Damn and wow and double-damn."

The sound of another bag of something allegedly edible being torn open.

"The Director hear it too?"

Adler's chewing somehow formed words. "Oh yeah. Check your inbox."

"Will do. Stan there?"

"He's brewing more bones." She pulled the phone away from her ear as Adler hollered. "STAN! Rheia says HI!"

"Just tell him to prep the Rehearsal Room for Gideon's audition next Monday."

"Ten-four good buddy."

"Thanks."

She hung up. Opened a browser. Logged in. Draft folder. Message waiting.

SUBJECT: Audition

BODY: Make sure he understands we cannot be responsible for his safety. And that his extreme discretion is required. Do not let your other projects suffer. It's ok if you and Stan break him.

She deleted the draft. Started a new one. Left it sitting in the inbox.

SUBJECT: Audition

BODY: I will make sure he is under no illusions.

38

CONGRESSWOMAN STACY MALLORY was one of the newest and youngest members of Congress and she was not afraid to tussle. Typically she would jujitsu her opponents' words and policy positions to the point they had to tap out, but political egos and ideological blind spots being what they are, these momentary capitulations usually resulted not in legislative compromises, god forbid, but rather a flurry of dog-whistley ad hominem attacks. Upon her gender. Her bi-racial roots. Her alleged socialist-Marxist-Communist leanings ("geez, pick one already" she would mutter as another Tweet barrage tried to bury her).

But sometimes the subtle machinations of a joint lock simply weren't enough. Sometimes nothing but a verbal body slam would do. This combination of delicate skill and brutal force had squeaked her past the 20-year, inertia-addled incumbent in the primary. Her general election opponent may have enjoyed rabid support from a dwindling and desperate base, but he was woefully unaware of just how out of touch with the world he now was. Stacy tidal-waved into office.

But her first weeks in the Capital had been eye-opening to say the least. Top-down change seemed laughable. So how to wield a mandate? Find the right issues to leverage.

And sometimes the opposition made it easy.

The amount of cognitive dissonance necessary to argue that Confederate statues and monuments were somehow "tradition" or part of a "heritage"? Congresswoman Mallory couldn't imagine nursing that level of high-grade daily migraine. But as her momma had told her again and again: *People love their pain. Because it makes them right. If I've suffered more than you then my opinion carries more weight than yours. So people will always do exactly what they want to, even if it hurts. And they will keep doing the thing that hurts until the pain required to stop is less than the pain required to continue. So don't try to make them stop. You won't be able to. Just make it hurt so much for them to keep going that they stop on their own.*

Her momma was warm and loving, made a moan-aloud red velvet cake, but yeah. She also had a titanium spine.

Stacy Mallory took no joy in causing real pain. But she loved watching her political opponents squirm. You've played to a base of racists for years? You've mastered the red meat toss? Great. I'm gonna publicly force you to own those backward beliefs.

And thus Congresswoman Mallory this day stood next to a bullet-riddled historical marker, quaking with righteous fury, glaring at the cameras. Her fury was legit, even if the cameras had been invited and her performance honed sharp.

"Let's be clear. Even the wording of this marker is sanitized. How can we ever hope to address the problem when we won't even say it out loud? That black 'employee' was named Sidney Johnson. He had been thrown in prison for playing dice. Well, playing dice while black. That white 'planter' was the racist Hampton Smith. He was notorious for abusing his workers so—no surprise here—he had trouble finding hired help. So he took advantage of 'convict labor'—another sanitized term. Slavery by any other name. So Sidney Johnson, quite against his will, found himself the 'employee' of Hampton Smith, a racist boss who loved to dole out beatings for transgressions like, you know, taking a sick day. This is in 1918, remember, more than fifty years after the Emancipation Proclamation."

Stacy Mallory stalked around the pole. The cameras tracked her. The sun beat down on all. Whoever had shot the plaque had also done a number on some flowers and a defenseless teddy, or so the crime scene photos had attested. Even though the items had been bagged and tagged, the hatred shimmered from the earth like heat off a car hood.

"Sidney Johnson had had enough. The system didn't have his back. He absolutely did shoot the racist Hampton Smith. Not something I condone, but then again those totally unbiased Stand Your Ground laws didn't exist back then." She looked up at the marker. A bullet hole had punctured the word "murder" so that now it read as "murd."

"That word 'murder'... it provides cover. A Black man *murdered* a White man. And he got away. So no, we aren't a mob. We aren't racists. We are just horrified citizens helping to track down a murderer. Right? I mean look here: the word *racism* isn't even mentioned on this plaque. 'Participants.' Another nice word for racists. 'Illegal.' Hear that? Different from 'immoral' or 'evil,' isn't it? *Sanitized.* Make history palatable for the White appetite."

That was a line her Chief of Staff had resisted as they drafted and edited during the flight. Savvy Amelia, always wary of pushing too hard too soon. But Stacy *wanted* this fight.

"The notorious dice player Sidney Johnson hid for days, right near here, while the White mob rounded up and killed at least thirteen Black people in retaliation. All in a weekend's work. Some were lynched. Some were shot. Two Black bodies were found to have seven hundred bullets in them. And this is back in the day, before semi-automatics."

She paused, looked over at the reporters scribbling notes. "Did you get that number ok? Seven hundred?" She waited. *Make it uncomfortable, Stacy.* She waited. Finally, one of the reporters replied.

"Uh. Yeah. Seven hundred."

"Seven hundred what?"

"Um. Bullets."

"Great. Just making sure we all get our facts straight. The less you know about history the more likely you are to believe you'd have been on the right side of it. As I was saying, this racist mob was rounding up innocents and meting out their specific brand of vengeance. Another innocent had weights tied to his hands and legs and was tossed in the Little River. On and on the rampage went. Most of these Black victims weren't even remotely connected to the dice player Sidney Johnson. Who by the way, thank goodness, was also tracked down, shot, and dragged by a car down Patterson Street in some sort of victory parade."

A reporter raised his hand, inhaled to ask some question. Congresswoman Mallory lanced him with a glance. "Hold up, Devon, I haven't gotten to the best part yet." He gave a little nod and lowered his hand.

"One of the Black innocents picked up is a Mr. Hayes Turner, husband to Mary Turner, the only Black person named on this plaque. He is lynched. For, y'know, being Black in the wrong place at the wrong time. His wife, the immortalized Mary Turner, bravely denounces the murder of her husband and threatens to have members of the mob arrested. Whoops.

The mob decides to teach her a lesson. Local authorities look the other way."

Make it uncomfortable, Stacy. Make it HURT.

"So let's get real. Mary Turner wasn't merely 'burned, mutilated, and shot.' Now that sounds pretty awful, doesn't it? But even that description lets these racists off the hook. Here's what they actually did. They hung Mary Turner by her feet, upside down. They dowsed her in gasoline and oil. They set her on fire. As she screamed, still alive, they pulled out a knife meant for splitting hogs and cut her unborn baby out of her. Did you forget that she was eight months pregnant?"

A couple reporters looked up, startled. One visibly blanched. Stacy stepped closer, hit her mark in front of the marker, angled to face the sun, gave perfect frame to the cameras.

"Eyewitness accounts say the baby fell to the dirt, gave two feeble cries, and then a racist stomped on its skull until it was dead. Right in front of her. *Then* they shot her. Shot her and shot her, hundreds of bullets, shredding her body before dumping it in an unmarked grave. You know what the headline was in the Atlanta Constitution? 'Fury of the People is Unrestrained.'" She snorted. "*Sanitized.*"

Stacy bent down, plucked a lone flower petal from the dust. "Join me." She stayed in a comfortable crouch. The reporters and cameras shuffled forward, tentative. But once Devon squatted down the rest followed suit, some bent over with microphones extended, some taking a knee and muttering about getting their pants dirty.

"'Fury of the People is Unrestrained.' *Fury.* As if they were somehow righteous. The *People.* As if only White people were actually capital 'P' People." Her voice downshifted from contempt to contemplative. "And now, a hundred years later, just look how far we've come. Racists are still shooting Mary Turner while complaining about us wanting to tear down Jefferson Davis statues and rename a few schools and military bases."

Amelia watched from the side, her intern Samar capturing the image on his tablet for social media. Stacy surrounded by reporters, the wounded monument to Mary Turner overseeing an impromptu huddle. Even though she'd seen it before, Amelia marveled at how Stacy could channel-change between barnstorming brimstone one moment and hushed holy intimacy the next. *Sky's the Limit* wasn't just a campaign slogan and ongoing core message. Amelia had finally found a politician to believe in.

"Being *non*-racist is no longer enough," Stacy said. "Not that it's ever been enough. But the line is being drawn. In today's America we are obligated to be unapologetically *anti*-racist. If you can't do that then you are in the way. And you will be left behind as we work to purge theclinging remains of institutionalized racism from our country."

Stacy turned her head to look up at the marker. Sunlight bathed her face. Amelia whispered, "Two steps right, Samar, get that image." Samar eagerly shuffled to his right and Amelia noted several cameras instinctively making the same adjustment. Amelia chuckled to herself.

God, she always knows how to find her light.

"You know, just two years after Mary Turner and all these other innocents were murdered, the 19th Amendment was ratified. Women's right to vote was finally recognized. The Suffragettes won! But that movement took a *century*, and sidenote didn't include women of color. But still. There were women who fought for their right to vote their entire lives but never got to taste the fruit of their labor. It's like the old proverb. What's the best day to plant a tree? Twenty years ago. What's the second-best day? TODAY."

Stacy stood. The reporters and cameras scrambled to follow.

"So I'm calling on all my constituents and on all my fellow Members of Congress. Doesn't matter what side of the aisle you're on. I'm starting a two-pronged legislative push. One, to eradicate racism from public honor. This includes statues, names of bases, installations, schools, parks, streets. Second, the Voting Rights Act has been gutted. Racism still strangles the People's right to vote. This is shameful. I may not be around when this fight is finally won, when Dr. King's dream truly comes to be. But I will work every day to do my small part. Because together... *Sky's the limit.*"

39

SPEARHEAD1488 STALKED THE SHACK, fighting the urge to stick his foot through the monitors.

After his caffeine-fueled marathon over the weekend he had fired off an anonymous, untraceable email to the major networks and fringe outlets—*White Truth is being Black-washed!*—and fallen into a deep, satisfied sleep.

All around Georgia and Florida he had rampaged, from Decatur Square and St. Augustine to Orlando and Jupiter, shooting holes through markers celebrating July Perry, Cinquez Park, and others. Cumming, Georgia, ended up being too far north, especially after he had to wait out some late-night picnickers in Rosewood, but all told he had struck a good half dozen monuments to lies.

But when he awoke and turned on the news, the stories were all wrong.

Somehow that bitch Stacy Mallory had been first on the scene, and she had stolen the narrative. All the big "fake news" outlets could talk about was "Congresswoman Mallory's big speech." Sure, there was lip service given to authorities trying to find the pattern in the multiple defacements of historical markers, but no one understood.

As for sympathetic outlets, they were fully a day late. By the time they even got to the markers, the cops were all over them. Some shakyfootage snuck online and some congratulatory commentary bounced around, but even there it was mostly about rage at Stacy Mallory.

Do I have to spoon-feed every goddam thing??

Spearhead turned off the news, disgusted with the world, angry at himself. He clicked his mouse and clacked his keys and tried to lose himself in the Crisis Actors project.

Images of alleged mass shootings—concerts, churches, schools—popped up on both screens. The sleepless software compared faces in the crowds: so-called parents, onlookers, EMTs. If he could find a match, a proverbial smoking gun, he could blow the false flag conspiracy wide open. Fulfill Granddad's vision.

But restlessness gnawed. The shack felt suffocating. He turned off the monitors, left the software whirring, grabbed a couple beers, and stomped outside to his kayak. Shoved into the bay. Paddled north. Moonless night, salty air.

Instinctively he navigated the waters swirling around the bridge supports holding up Highway 64. Perico Island slid by on his left. Cookie-cutter beach homes. One with a dolphin statue. Came abreast. Dug his paddle to turn and put the statue at his back. Paddled straight at the pitch-black mangroves in front of him.

Spearhead disappeared into a tiny outlet. His kayak squeezed through grasping branches. A secret entrance, originally cut by Granddad, now his to maintain.

Beached. Stepped silently into Robinson Preserve. Closed to the public, but not to him.

He settled on a stone. His restlessness faded as he melded

with the humidity. His hair and clothing plastered to his skin. Scuffling. Gators. Bobcats. Those heavier steps maybe even a coyote.

He drank his beers. Listened to the water lapping.

His pocket vibrated. Alert from the shack. Maybe a match?? He pulled out his phone, unzipped it from the waterproof case.

An alert, yes. But not a match. He was under attack.

40

THE MAN KNOWN as AlphaSupreme stood in his control center gorging on the images and data filling the multiple flat screens. He re-read the particular email that had come into THE SCOURGE'S fan box about "showing the country that history is being rewritten. White Truth is being Blackwashed!" Not a bad turn of phrase.

"Have you tracked down the origin?"

The two teens seated at work stations both shook their heads. One boy, one girl, both brilliant, both his, by different women, who were also his.

The girl spoke first. "Whoever sent this, they've got skills."

The boy agreed. "We've already tracked it around the world twice." "Whatever program they're using—

"—it's definitely homemade—"

"—nothing like it on the market."

Their fingers danced across keyboards and trackpads. The glow of the screens bathed their pallid skin.

AlphaSupreme walked up behind the teens, stroked their hair. They shivered and leaned against him.

"Find him, my children. Let me know as soon as you have anything.

He could be a prophet."

"We will not fail you, Father."

AlphaSupreme kissed each of them on the tops of their heads. "I know you won't." He climbed the stairs, locked the heavy steel door behind him, headed to his brightly lit office—just off the foyer—and began to edit next Sunday's sermon.

41

Behind the steel door, down in the hidden and well-stocked shelter, the half-sibling teenagers waged digital war.

The particular email itself was merely a scout. They put it on the rack, tortured it into giving up its secrets. The intel led them to the origin, a central fortress encased in bristling firewalls. The boy insisted on trying a Trojan Horse, against his half-sister's advice.

Not so much as a sniff of interest before the Horse was obliterated by automated defenses crude in design but brutal in execution.

"I told you, Jude. He's paranoid. His work isn't elegant—"

"—but he's not gonna fall for the obvious. Fine fine fine. Don't tell Father."

"You know he'll know, but as long as we get in—"

"—he'll be pleased. What next?"

The half-sister closed her eyes. Her hands froze, hovering above a keyboard grateful for the reprieve.

"Agnes. Come on. What do we try next?"

She remained frozen, but the eyes beneath her lids pulsed

back and forth. Jude sighed, resigned to waiting out his sister's process. He knew when she snapped out of it she would have a ferocious plan, but that didn't mean his impatience was any less. He struggled with impetuousness; Father was always on him about it. Jude whispered a private prayer, so as not to disturb his sister.

"Amen."

He opened a browser window, scrolled some headlines. Ugliness and evil flashed past. If Agnes was masterful in her ability to decipher and arrange information, Jude was just as masterful at gathering. Anyone watching would have seen nothing but a blur on the screen. But Jude absorbed it all.

The name "Stacy Mallory" was trending. Jude slowed his scroll and opened a second window, dove deep. Father was insistent they be up to date on the sins and transgressions of the world, and this Stacy Mallory was working her way to the top of Father's list of adversaries. Her bills were swelling with co-sponsors. Father would not be pleased.

Jude sensed the split-second before his half-sister's eyes opened that she had returned.

"So what do we do, Agnes? Siege? Baggage Train? Parley?"

Her dilated pupils gleamed.

"All of them."

The half-siblings unleashed hell.

Recon and command, a relentless tag-team flywheel. Jude pushed bushels of data to Agnes. She decrypted, analyzed, wove the info into brilliant strategies. Shot orders back to Jude, who executed flawlessly.

They quickly realized that even though the firewalls were strong and the defenses valiant, they could raze the fortress to the ground and barely break a sweat. As usual, they simply outclassed their opponent.

But that's not what Father wanted.

They had to leave SPEARHEAD1488's ramparts erect. Leave the infrastructure in place, the treasure vaults unraided, the virtual populace unpillaged. Father wanted to control the castle, not salt the earth.

So the gigabytes of blood spilled were simply a distraction. Agnes and Jude knew every catapulted hack would be blocked, every password assault on the drawbridge rebuffed, every viral siege tower toppled. As they were meant to be.

But by keeping the defenses busy, they could launch their true attack. The fortress was almost entirely self-contained. Almost. But Spearhead had to access the outside world via internet somewhere. Much like armies laying siege in the old days might poison the water supply, Agnes and Jude knew if they could just find the hardline contact point then they could infiltrate by shimmying up the well, as it were. Enter the creek upstream, lazy-river right under the walls, overrun the fortress from the inside.

They released tens of millions of burrowing viruses. What these viruses lacked in sophistication they made up for in sheer number. The diggers quickly found Spearhead's hardline, even though it was buried and backlooped. The horde was such that not even a rear-guard cavalry charge through its flank could slow it down. Wave after viral wave entered the high-speed landline and flooded toward the only weak point of the fortress.

But none got through. For once, the half-siblings had underestimated their opponent.

The architect had not only anticipated this type of attack but had demonstrated a flash of true ingenuity. If Agnes and Jude had poisoned the water supply, then Spearhead had installed a platinum level filtration system just inside the walls.

The viruses zapped into non-existence, so many bugs frying on a mosquito lamp.

Jude slammed his keyboard. *"Goddammit!"*

Agnes gasped and pointed to the corner. Jude hit himself in the forehead with his knuckles over and over as he walked to the corner, knelt on a coarse blanket, and pulled off his shirt. Scars crisscrossed his back.

Agnes rose, pulled a crude whip from its hook on the wall, and approached her half-brother. "I'll do you first, then you do me."

"But you didn't curse. I did. I'm the one who needs to be cleansed."

Agnes massaged the welt rising on his forehead. "Yes. You again demonstrated impetuousness. But I demonstrated pride and arrogance. I should have foreseen that defense. It is my fault you sinned, Jude."

Tears squeezed from Jude's eyes. "But I don't like punishing you."

"And I don't like punishing you. We aren't supposed to like it. But it is necessary."

He nodded. Turned to the wall. Folded his hands tight against his heart. "I'll pray. Don't stop till—"

The whip licked fire across his shoulders. He bit back his cry.

"We will be cleansed, brother."

The whip lashed again. Agnes touched a spot where Jude's skin had opened. She could feel his sin oozing out the wound. "And then together we will defeat our enemy."

She raised the whip.

42

SPEARHEAD DRAGGED his kayak up the bank and sprinted into the shack. Turned his monitors on. Tripwires, alarms, and warning messages blinked manically.

His defenses were holding but he had never seen an attack this relentless and multi-pronged. Part of him was awash with glory—the Deep State had finally recognized him as a threat! But another part of him was sweating cold. He had run dozens of simulations, preparing for this eventuality, but the resources of the enemy seemed unlimited.

Another warning blinked. *Breach detected.* He inhaled. *Invader repelled.* He held his breath. *Breach repaired.* He exhaled.

He ran a diagnostic, trying to ID the attackers, trace them, anything to get intel. He thought about disconnecting entirely, taking time to regroup, lick wounds, assess damage.

But suddenly it was calm. Like the eye of a hurricane. The maelstrom roiled just out of reach.

Spearhead sat back, his breath jagged. His hands shook as he took a swig from a sports drink. He cued up the most recent episode of THE SCOURGE, pressed play, shuffled to the bathroom to wash the salt and sweat from his face.

AlphaSupreme's voice balmed him from the myriad speakers wired throughout the shack. "As always, thank you for joining me in our on-going battle for freedom. Tonight, after the show, I will be hosting a VIP chat room, entirely safe, completely encrypted. Breadcrumbs have been left in the members-only section of our website. I invite you to join. I have a new plan to counteract the Blackwashing of White Truth that is underway, and I need your help."

Spearhead jerked to attention. *Blackwashing of White Truth.* It couldn't be a coincidence. AlphaSupreme had read his email and was calling him to action!

He rushed back to his keyboard. Logged in. Located the first clue. The breadcrumbs led him down, down, down into the darkest depths of the dark web. It felt like descending a stone staircase into catacombs. He leaned forward. His breath fogged the screen.

The entrance to the chat room emerged from the gloom. He pictured a thick wooden door. An iron ring. He clanged it in coded rhythm.

The muffled echo of locks being thrown. The door opened.

He stepped inside.

Father, we have him.

Well done, my children. Your previous failure is forgiven.

Thank you, Father.

On my command, eject everyone else and lock him in.

SHOOT. THEM. ALL.

The chat room vibrated with righteous fury. Spearhead grinned as he did a quick back-scroll of the transcript history and caught up to the present frenzy.

I MEAN IT! SHOOT ALL OF THEM!

The rant begat a chorus.

THESE PROTESTORS ARE A FUCKING PLAGUE.

STUPID SHEEPLE. WHEN WILL ALL THESE *WOKE* PEOPLE WAKE UP??

THEY CAN'T. THEY ARE BRAINWASHED BY THE NEW WORLD ORDER.

Amid the vitriol, one voice—THE voice—hissed into existence.

So. You want to stand up to the social justice warriors and man-jawed feminists?

Spearhead and the uncountable others all screamed into the digital void—YES, ALPHASUPREME! YES!

You have taken the red pill? You see the world as it truly is?

The frothy mob responded: YES, ALPHASUPREME! THE SCALES HAVE FALLEN FROM OUR EYES!

You see that all other so-called gods are just Satan in disguise? You see that all Muslims are jihadists? You see that all Jews want to tear down our country?

Spasms of ecstasy.

Spearhead couldn't type fast enough. He snatched up a headset. His body trembled, his forehead sheened anew. He felt a dawning clarity of purpose.

Never forget, the White Race worldwide... we are only nine percent. We have been diminished. We can hide in these chat rooms, or we can act. If we do not, our women, our future children, our way of life will be wiped out.

Spearhead's voice croaked. The headset raced his words

through a transcription app and his plea blinked onto the screen.

"The black pill. I'm ready for the black pill. Tell me what to do."

Now.

Yes, Father.

The chat room went deathly quiet. Spearhead looked around. The transcript history had vanished. The back of his neck prickled.

His monitors flickered and went dark.

"No no no no no..."

Spearhead hammered at his keyboard, slashed his trackpad. Nothing. Not even a cursor.

He dove for the central port and with no thought to what data might be lost yanked every cord and wire free.

He panted on the floor, counting the seconds the way Granddad had taught him after a lightning flash—*one manatee, two manatee, three manatee, four manatee*—waiting for the thunder to rumble. You could tell how far away the storm was— *seven manatee, eight manatee, nine manatee*—whether it was coming or going—*eleven manatee, twelve manatee*—and even how quickly.

When Spearhead hit fifteen, he relaxed. Crawled out from under his desk. Stood, stretched, barked a relieved laugh.

Then his speakers crackled to life.

Too late, Spearhead. I'm inside you.

Spearhead sprang to the breaker box, yanked it open.

You don't want to do that, Dustin. I have come to give you the black pill.

Dustin's hand hovered over the breakers. The voice poured into his room like smoke.

Yes. I know the name foisted upon you by this vile society. But I also know that SPEARHEAD is your true name. I am here to help you set your true self free. I have seen your good work. Yet there is so much more you could do.

Dustin held on to the breaker box to keep from collapsing.

Have you nothing to say?

He realized he was still wearing the headset.

"Can you... can you hear me?"

The speakers chuckled, roiling smoke.

Oh yes, Dustin. I can hear you. And see you.

Dustin spun around. Webcams on his computers. Security cams high in the corners. Eyes meant to protect and secure now exposed him. He was naked in the smoke.

Oh my child. Why do you fear? Do you not recognize my voice?

Dustin's heart opened. He fell to his knees. "Oh god. You are AlphaSupreme."

The smoke embraced him.

I am. And I have chosen you.

43

Dustin trembled in awe, but he hadn't come this far without a knife-edged sense of paranoia.

"How do I know it's you? How do I know you aren't an agent of the Deep State trying to trick me?"

The speakers breathed.

You are right to be wary. I do not take it personally. So, here, I'll show you...

One of Dustin's screens snapped back on. It showed a familiar hand- held video.

JEWS ARE GENOCIDING YOU.

Off-camera voices. A hand rips. "FUCK YOU."

The other screen flickered to footage of Stacy Mallory at the Mary Turner monument. "Did you get that number ok? Seven hundred?" Dustin's mouth hung open.

"Sky's the limit!"

And now his two screens flashed images back and forth of the other bullet-riddled monuments.

This is all you, yes?

Dustin nodded.

Speak, my boy.

"Yes, AlphaSupreme. I... I did all that."

Very good. And what's this...?

The "Crisis Actors" folder magnified and opened. Files prostrated themselves, images of shootings, hundreds of them, all angles, and spreadsheets cross-referencing faces of mourners and parents and emergency personnel.

"I'm compiling evidence to prove that crisis actors are real, Alpha- Supreme."

Yes. I see. Mass shootings are one of the cruelest hoaxes perpetrated on our country. Your Grandfather saw it immediately, did he not?

Dustin's lingering doubt vanished. "Yes, AlphaSupreme. He did."

And even when your parents doubted and disowned him, you did not.

He bit his lip.

There is no shame in weeping for lost heroes. You were the only one by his side as he went to his reward, yes?

Dustin nodded. The brimming tears released.

"Everyone said it was the virus."

The speakers sighed.

Another hoax. You are fighting the holy war, Spearhead. This world will not be cleansed on its own. It is moving ever towards darkness and evil. We must shepherd it.

"I'm trying to do my part but nothing seems to matter, nothing I do leaves a mark—"

Shhhhhhh. Spearhead. Your thinking is too limited, too symbolic. Direct action is required. Are you willing to do what I ask?

"Anything! ANYTHING!"

Hmmm. We shall see. Continue your work. Watch for my signs. I am with you. I am always with you.

The speakers exhaled and went quiet. The screens went dark. Dustin stood frozen. Waiting.

"AlphaSupreme?"

The lights blinked off. Darkness swirled.

"AlphaSupreme??!"

The back-up generator outside coughed and chugged. His system whirred back to life. A couple red emergency bulbs cast their eerie demonic glow. The monitors blinked alive.

He sat down. Kick-started the facial recognition software. Swiped the tears and snot off his nose and mouth.

It was time for others to weep.

44

THE CLASS LEANED to the left, stretching. Gideon roll-called them through check-in.

"And Tosha how are you? What's something weird, wild, or wonderful that happened to you last week?"

"I am discovering joys of Barry Manilow!"

Kaida rolled her eyes. "It's true. She called me right after hearing 'Copacabana' for the first time."

Tosha was adamant. "Lola! Is such tragedy! And did you know, Barry wrote jingles?" She sang, "*Like a good neighbor, State Farm is there!*"

Alfonso bounced on the balls of his feet as Tosha took a bow. "Tosha that's amazing, I actually have a Barry Manilow set in my show! Speaking of which—and this is my check-in, sorry for just jumping in, Gideon—"

Gideon waved Alfonso on.

"Sooooo Salsa Verde will be headlining at a cabaret in Brooklyn! You all are so totally invited! I've got flyers!" As the class congratulated Alfonso, Gideon noted Imani and Aniyah in quiet, intense negotiation.

Imani piped up. "We are there, Alfonso, for sure. Gideon, can I check- in?"

"Of course."

"I'm not sure how many of you saw it, and she's suddenly too nervous to share, so I'm just gonna say it: Aniyah set her blog loose on the world and it's amazing!"

More chatter and congrats.

Rasheed said, "I stumbled across it, Aniyah, and read the whole thing. It's beautiful."

Marcel and Emma nodded vigorously, spoke in turn.

"Yes, you have transformed your pain into something exquisite, Aniyah."

"Oh my god, everyone, seriously, you have to read it. I cried so hard. But in a good way!"

Evan whipped out his phone. "Well someone send us the dang link already!"

Gideon let the class's warmth wash over him. Occasionally he and Rheia made eye contact and his insides would contract. He wasn't sure what she had in store for him after class. He was eager, nervous, a bit on auto-pilot. Kept a semi-transparent smile on his face.

But his mask must've slipped. As the stretched-out students headed back to their seats, Joan said, "Gideon, you seem especially contempla- tive today. What happened in YOUR week?"

Dan tagged on. "Yeah! Take out any more bad guys?"

Gideon thickened his smile. "No no. This and that. Called my mom. Had some good Korean. Did another eight performances of *Henry Five*. And I have now officially run the entire circumference of Manhattan."

Ooohs and aaahs.

"Of course I did it in bites. And that leads into tonight's discussion. We've talked about meaning being the end result of accumulation, yes? And I have now accumulated, through multiple runs, the singular achievement of running this island's perimeter. Tonight I want to challenge all of you to think deeply about *character*."

Gideon pulled a chair to center, sat.

"It's a beautiful quirk of the English language that a 'character' is a single mark or letter. And only by combining nine individual letters—nine *characters*—do you get the word 'character.'"

Raised eyebrows. Scribbling pens. Tilted heads. Typing thumbs.

Gideon happened to glance at Rheia. Electric. And suddenly this mini-lecture he'd given a hundred times sparkled with new clarity.

"You observe someone. Real life, the stage, same thing. Each individual action. Each singular choice. They add up. Trends emerge, coalesce into traits. You begin to anticipate and even predict their behavior, what they are most likely to do when confronted with a challenge. And ultimately you assign a moral or ethical quality to this person. You have determined—through accumulation—their character."

He rose. He stalked. He felt tiny beads of sweat on his temples.

"This means character is descriptive, not prescriptive. Not a fixed state of being, but ever-evolving. So as actors, we must interrogate the character of our characters. Because character does not exist outside the human vessel. Characters don't exist on the page. They frankly don't even exist during rehearsal. They require witness. A character exists only when a flesh and blood actor is observed by an audience."

Kaida raised her hand. He gestured her to speak. "My dad always says that character is what you do when no one is watching. But you're saying character *requires* someone watching...?"

"Both. Your dad was talking about integrity there. But awful people can play saints on stage. Co-stars can loathe each other and still portray sizzling chemistry."

Rheia spoke with a pointed smile. "So acting is lying."

Gideon replied in kind. "It's storytelling. Take Hamlet. I'm not a Danish prince with a murdered father but once I step on stage we all agree to play along with the story—the lie—so we can collectively seek out the truth."

"But what if I play him wrong?" asked Rasheed. "Do I break the truth?"

"No, Rasheed. There's not some perfect, singular Hamlet floating out in the ether for you to capture or channel. Hamlet is just words on a page. He only comes to life when a live, breathing actor speaks him into existence. Every one of you could play Hamlet, and if you played that role with integrity, you would be right."

A collective scoff from Tosha, Kaida, and Emma. Tosha spoke for all three. "Every one of us?"

"Absolutely. Why not? Women played Hamlet as early as the 18th century. Sarah Bernhardt played Hamlet in Paris and London in 1899 and then on film in 1900. The truth belongs to everyone."

Kaida flipped open her tablet. "I am googling the heck outta that!"

Eager Evan: "Have you ever played Hamlet?"

"Yes, I had the great luck to play Hamlet a couple years ago."

"Cool, man!"

"Actually? It was terrifying. You feel this... pressure. To 'get it right.' The audience has expectations. Everyone knows the 'Greatest Hits,' y'know? So they basically sing along as if you're a cover band. *To be or not to be. Alas, poor Yorick. Get thee to a nunnery. O that this too too solid flesh would melt—*"

Marcel cleared his throat. "Actually, the early quartos say 'sullied.'"

"Ooooh, Marcel, you and I are gonna fight! I'm First Folio and 'solid' all the way."

"What the heck are they talking about?" Imani whispered loud enough for everyone to hear.

Joan said, "Shakespeare nerdgasm."

Dan thrust his fist into the air. "Demand satisfaction! Bard battle! Duel to the death with sticks!"

"Thanks a lot, Marcel," Gideon said. Marcel chuckled and held up his hands in comic apology. Gideon forged on. "Anyhow, *Hamlet* has been called Seven Soliloquies and a bunch of filler."

Evan was aghast. "Really??"

"It's like everyone is waiting to see if you mess up those speeches. The stuff in between is go-to-the-bathroom, refill-your-drink time. That pressure can be debilitating."

Alfonso said, "So how did you deal with that?"

"Well..." Gideon reflected. "Every night, after stretching out and warming up and fight call, I would sit at my station in the dressing room, look into the mirror, and line bash the entire show."

Imani again. "Line bash? The hell?"

Rasheed said, "Say all your lines as fast as you can."

Imani thumbs-upped. "Thanks." Rasheed thumbs-upped back.

Gideon continued. "At first it was out of fear of forgetting something. But as I repeated this practice, I realized I had turned the entirety of Hamlet's text into a mantra. I'm sitting half-dressed, half-Hamleted as it were, and saying these words that so many others have said before me. It became meditative. I used to be religious, but I never understood the idea of the 'communion of saints' until I chanted *Hamlet* into the mirror eight times a week for two months. My voice was being added to the mist, the cloud, the... the..."

Rheia. "The snowflakes?"

He looked directly at her.

"Yes. I became a part of something so much larger than myself." Rheia gave him a tiny, knowing nod.

He stood, grabbed the chair, cleared the space. "But none of those Hamlets—not mine, not Branaugh's, not Olivier's, not Sarah Bernhardt's—are PERFECT. The one and only. Anything you ever need to feel you have to copy. Since it's *your* voice and *your* body up there, Hamlet is *you*. When you act you do not become someone else, you become a clarified version of yourself."

Dan spoke, his tone surprisingly serious. "The mask does not conceal. It reveals." Everyone looked. Dan shrugged. "Hey. I can be deep."

The class chuckled but Gideon felt it too. One of those moments when a light bulb collectively switches on. He groped for the words.

"So. If character is an observable accumulation, what happens if you turn your observation upon yourself? Are you able, with humility and openness, to accept what you see?"

He paused. Looked down at his own hands. "Am I?"

Silence.

"What if you don't like what you see?"

He looked up. Everyone was reflecting. Some were holding back tears.

Imani. "If you don't like it then friggin' change it."

Evan. "How?"

Imani. "Actions accumulate into character, right?"

Gideon nodded.

"So take action."

Rheia waited outside The Hatchery's stage door as Gideon tidied up inside. Kaida and Tosha waved to her as they headed off together. She waved back. Apparently karaoke was on the docket. Any other night watching Tosha sing her heart out on "I Write the Songs" would have been an easy invite to accept.

Other students variously dispersed. But Dan and Joan lingered. "Soooo what are you up to tonight?" Joan asked.

Dan was less elegant. "You and Gideon… grabbing a drink?" He contorted his face into a cartoonish wink.

Rheia chuckled. "Not what you think." *Not even close.*

"If you say so."

Joan grabbed Dan and dragged him away. "Well have a good time, whatever you do. See Dan, I *told* you." Arm in arm they merged into the bustling city.

Rheia slipped on her shades.

"Adler?"

The sound of someone sucking up every last drop of milkshake slurped into her ear.

"Hey Rheia." *Sluuuurp.*

"Geez, Adler, seriously, the sound quality on these things is exquisite."

"Of course. I engineered 'em."

"So maybe take it easy with the straw?"

"Hey you want me on call all night, I gotta fill the tank."

Rheia snorted.

Adler hiccuped. "You on your way? Bringing along boy wonder?"

"Yep. Everything set? Stan there?"

"Rehearsal room ready to go. Stan the Man's in the wing. He wants to make a dramatic entrance." Adler slurped. "You nervous?"

Way more than I expected.

Outwardly: "Oh, you know, normal jitters. I mean no one's expecting a whole lot anyway, right?"

The stage door opened. Gideon stepped through, flashed "just a minute" at her with an upraised finger, set about locking up.

"He's here, Adler. Gotta go. See you in a few."

"Standing by."

She started to take off her shades but Adler cleared his throat. "Hey Rheia?"

"Yeah?"

"Just... well. Break a leg."

"Not my leg I'm worried about tonight. But thanks. Anything else?"

"Just one thing."

"What?"

Adler let loose a skull-rattling, lactose-dripping belch. Rheia yanked the glasses off but even held at arm's length she could hear the tectonic resonance of Adler's insides. Even Gideon, turning the deadbolt, perked up and looked around for the source of the strange rumble.

She muttered something murderous, ignored Adler's foamy chuckle, and stuffed the sunglasses into her bag as Gideon walked over.

"Was that Adler?"

"Yeah. His skill set is... eclectic. All locked up?"

Gideon nodded.

"Then off we go."

"Where?"

"To your audition."

"My...?"

"That's what you wanted, right?"

She took a step.

"Rheia."

She turned back. Saw his nerves swarming him. He took a shuddering breath. "Thank you."

"For what?"

"For..." He rubbed his face. Crossed his arms. Stuffed his hands in his pockets. "For listening last week. For showing up tonight."

She saw how desperately he needed encouragement.

Make him fight.

She said in her coldest voice, "Last chance. I'm gonna walk away. If you follow, it's on you."

She walked away.

A few steps later, she felt him follow.

46

GIDEON FOLLOWED Rheia off the 6 Train. They exited the Cypress Avenue Station. She broke the silence that had enveloped them the entire ride.

"I take it you haven't run the Bronx yet?"

Gideon shook his head.

"Welcome to Port Morris."

They walked east on 138th.

"Morris? As in Gouverneur Morris?" Gideon asked.

Rheia shrugged. "How should I know?"

Gideon craned his neck, looking up and down the side streets. "I think he's got his own Square around here."

"Why? What'd he do?"

"He's the Penman of the Constitution. Wrote the Preamble."

She shook her head. "Is your running playlist just the Jeopardy theme on repeat?"

"I like to know where things come from, why things and places are named the way they are. Says a lot about us. Our history. Our values. Our myths."

Rheia hung a right on Walnut Avenue. Gideon followed. He sniffed. "Is there an ironworks nearby?"

Rheia nodded. He sniffed again.

"And a brewery?"

"If gentrification had a cologne. Smelting and hops."

"East River's over there?" Gideon asked, pointing off to their left. "Making sure I've got my bearings."

"Yep."

"You know it's not actually a river?"

"Oh god."

"It's a saltwater estuary. Flow changes direction. Strong currents. Lots of barge traffic."

"Are you for real?"

"You didn't read the kayaking brochure in the theatre lobby?"

"We're here. Thank god."

Rheia led Gideon toward a warehouse. A large "For Lease" sign shouted from above the door.

"The Troupe owns this?"

Rheia flipped open a panel. Shiny keypad. She punched in a lengthy code.

"For now. The Director knows how to invest. We move our bases of operation around a lot, stay under the radar. Couple years? This'll be condos, coffee shops, and curry joints, just like Oak Point over there… " A thumb jabbed over her shoulder. "And the old Clock Tower over there." An extended finger pointed the opposite way. "But for now…" A beep from the pad. A series of muted metal thunks. She pushed the door open. "It's home sweet home."

She gestured Gideon in. He squinted, trying to make out anything in the dark. Moonlight bounced around a cavernous space. She closed the door and the echo chased the moonlight up into the rafters. Shadowy shapes loomed. A walled-off windowed office crouched in the corner, blue computer glow leaking through closed blinds.

Rheia called out, "Adler? A little light?"

The moonlight froze, then scurried away as rows of industrial lights buzzed and flickered. Gideon's jaw dropped as he took in the Rehearsal Room.

47

SOME OF WHAT Gideon was looking at made sense. Some of it looked wildly out of place. Some of it he had no context for.

A huge wrestling mat to practice hand-to-hand combat.

A pyramid stack of variously shaped actor blocks: wooden cubes, rectangles, even a couple L's that could form a couch when shoved together. Next to the pyramid, a collection of IKEA-flavored furniture. Tables, chairs, a kitchen island.

A collection of typical gym equipment. Dumbbells. A couple TRX straps hanging from suspended beams. Heavy bag. Sparring pads.

A haphazard collection of hand props. Could have been a booth at a community yard sale. Books and magazines, mugs, salt and pepper shakers, sports equipment, clothing accessories. The stuff that populates the average daily life.

He approached a table loaded with blocks and cylinders of what looked like sulfury jello. He poked one particularly long rectangular block. Smooth, gelatinous, incredibly dense. He could barely make an impression, even as his nailbed turned white from pressing.

He sniffed. Leaned in, sniffed again. The aroma was intensely off- putting, but also...

"Cinnamon?"

Rheia was watching Gideon explore, her eyes—as always—assessing.

"Stan's secret recipe."

"Stan?"

"Our Choreographer."

"Choreogra... oh c'mon, Rheia!"

"Or think of him as the Fight Captain. Either way, he's gonna put you through your paces."

Gideon leaned in closer. The block was translucent but not transparent. He could make out a shape inside. For all the world it looked like...

"Is that a *bone*?"

"Yes and no. Sized and shaped to the average male femur. Plaster encased in ballistic gel."

"Say what??"

"He cooks it up over there."

Gideon looked past the table, caught sight of a high-end, industrial, five-foot wide gas stovetop. Huge pots, funnels, a cordless drill with stirring extension, a pallet of AP flour, buckets of salt, and Willy Wonka-esque candy thermometers precisely organized on and around the stainless steel beast.

Chains clanked as Rheia yanked. A pulley system engaged and a pile of ballistic gel forms rose from the floor. They hung in the air, linked together, eye level. Gideon blinked and they snapped into focus. A segmented human body. Hanging there like a side of beef.

"Introducing him to Carlos?"

Gideon turned. The chewy voice belonged to a wiry, wild-haired, young white man emerging from the office. Buddy Holly glasses balanced precariously on his nose, and thankfully he was wearing chili pepper boxers and a Pac-Man t-shirt because the fuzzy bathrobe encasing his whip-thin form flapped open with every step.

Rheia tied off the chain. "How many times does Stan have to tell you not to name the target dummy?"

"But Rheeeeiaaaa, I love watching you break Carlos over and over. It's therapeutic. Stan the Man just frankensteins him back together anyway. Isn't that right, Carlos?" He patted the dummy between its gelatinous thighs.

"There is something seriously wrong with you, dude." Rheia moved to a locker and pulled out workout clothes.

The dude turned to Gideon. Crunched a Cheeto. Wiped the orange dust on his robe. "You must be Rheia's pet." Stuck out his hand.

Gideon shook the offered hand and glanced at Rheia. She rolled her eyes in apology. "Yeah I shoulda warned you. That's Adler."

Adler dipped a curtsy. "Ta-da!" Crunched another Cheeto.

Gideon noted some rogue orange powder on his own palm, snatched a nearby rag. "Who's Carlos?"

Adler heaved a sigh. "My asshole ex. Ripped out my heart. Stomped on it. Pissed on it. Ran it over with his Harley." *Crunch.*

"Stay off those online dating apps, Adler," Rheia said as she brought a bundle of gear over to Gideon. "You know how many names that dummy has had?"

Gideon accepted the athletic shorts, tank top, and wrist-bands. "You actually asking me?"

"Wild guess."

Gideon looked Adler up and down.

"Carlos is numberrrr... six."

Adler gasped. "I am offended, sir!" He swirled away and

pulled one of the IKEA chairs to the side of the wrestling mat. Sat with dramatic aplomb.

"Close guess," Rheia said. "Carlos was seven."

"Carlos was *special*. He was the one." *Crunch.* "Can't wait to watch you pummel him."

Gideon quietly asked Rheia, "This guy is the Stage Manager? He designed your sunglasses?"

"I know, I know. But in the lab? Genius isn't a big enough word."

Adler threw a Cheeto at the dummy.

An unseen door banged in the shadowed recesses of the warehouse.

Rheia nudged Gideon toward a bathroom.

"Better get changed. Stan doesn't like to be kept waiting."

GIDEON STOOD on the wrestling mat, dressed to move, facing Stan. Rheia watched warily.

Adler squirmed impatiently on his actor block. The Cheetos were gone, magically replaced by a Chinese take-out box.

The only sound was Adler's chopsticks clicking. Stan had yet to speak. At six-foot-one, Gideon rarely had to look up to meet someone's eye. But in the case of Stan... the 40-something, Black, former Green Beret gazed down from Olympus, easily six-four, hair short, beard tight, faded "Army" t-shirt stretched to seam-popping extreme by a chiseled physique that could have been modeled on one of the Greek statues at the Met Museum.

And like those sculptures, his stillness exuded a massive amount of potential energy.

Click clickety clack click. The chopsticks seemed incredibly loud to Gideon as the silence stretched. He felt Stan's eyes poking, prodding, prying for all potential weaknesses.

Stan abruptly stepped to the props table and picked up a

baseball bat. He marched back to the mat and tossed it. Gideon snagged it out of the air.

"Attack me," Stan said, his voice the rumble of distant thunder. Gideon looked to Rheia. She flicked her head toward Stan. Adler'swet chuckle bubbled up—*"hehehehe"*—but at least the chopsticks had paused.

Gideon took a deep breath, dropped into a classic broadsword stance, and slickly double-stepped forward as he swooped the bat around-his-head-behind-his-back and slashed it at Stan's face. His fully extended arms zipped the barrel to perfect rest six inches from Stan's sculpted jaw.

Stan hadn't flinched. "What the hell was that?"

"Um." Gideon pulled back, awkwardly demonstrated with the bat. "It's called 'casting,' like a fishing pole? You send the energy past your target, no actual follow-through. That way even if your fight partner misses his parry you don't cleave his head in two. Like, well, Stan, you didn't move to defend yourself, so... so I stopped."

"Geez, Gid, don't worry about him," Rheia said. "It was obvious you had no intention of striking so why waste energy defending?"

Adler slurped a noodle.

"What's with the wind-up?" Stan said.

"Oh." Gideon fidgeted. "Well, it tells the story to the audience. And it telegraphs to your partner that the choreographed strike is coming. So they can parry accurately. Keep everyone safe. Eight shows a week, y'know?"

Adler cackled. "Plus it looks badass cool."

"I could have incapacitated you five times just during your windup." Stan looked Gideon up and down. "You say he can wrestle?"

Rheia nodded. "So he says. I saw him sink in a textbook rear-naked choke on the train."

"I'm right here," Gideon muttered.

Stan flickered his fingers in a *c'mon* motion. "Let's go, grappler."

The gaslight deep in the core of Gideon's rage made a soft *whoomp* as it lit. He tossed the bat aside and sprang at Stan. The makeup of his college team had been such that he almost always got paired with the one guy bigger than him—good ol' Leon, all smiles off the mat, all business on—so Gideon understood leverage against a larger opponent. He feinted, let Stan swat his first grasp away, creating an opening to drop down and capture a leg—

But suddenly Gideon's wrist was locked. His shoulder torqued, his feet left the ground, and his breath wooshed out as his back hit the mat.

"Bravo!" Adler hollered around a mouthful of gray-tinged sesame broccoli.

Gideon wheezed. "Those moves... against the rules..."

"Rules??" Stan said. "You're kidding, right? This is a joke? Rheia is this guy for real?"

Rheia grumbled to herself, ran a hand back and forth over her scalp.

"It's crap. He's gonna have to relearn everything. You sure about this?"

Gideon struggled up to a knee. "Stop talking about me like I'm not here!"

"Then BE here!" Stan spat before cold-shouldering away to examine his gel blocks.

"What does he mean, Rheia?" Gideon stood, put his hands on his hips, kept breathing deep.

"Think of your stick exercise, Gid. That level of focus. You're not in the moment right now. You're thinking. About safety and rules and impressing us and a million other things that don't matter. Because in the Troupe it's not illusion. The fighting is for real. And yeah it's still 'eight shows a week' for us, we don't want to get injured, but those guys I tumbled at the Bear and Fawn? And the ones on the train? Adler, you were poking around in the hospital system, what happened to all those guys?"

Adler opened his mouth. Rheia held up a hand. "Swallow first."

Adler swallowed. "Stitches and casts and splints. T will probably never play Xbox again after what you did to his hand. One or two may have permanent limps. The Tooth Fairy is out a few quarters. I know at least one had to get his nose rebuilt."

Rheia shrugged. "See? The safety of your scene partner is no longer your concern. So can you strike without a windup? Commit to the follow-through? Inflict actual injury?"

Gideon looked over at Stan's expansive back.

"I don't know."

"That's what we're here to find out. C'mon." She picked up the bat and led him toward the dummy.

Stan pretended surprise. "Oh. You're still here, grappler?"

Gideon felt the gaslight leap. His furnace caught. He grabbed the offered bat from Rheia, took a couple quick steps toward the dummy, lined up.

Adler put down his food and clapped his hands. "Oh goodie goodie good..."

Gideon swung for the fences. The bat hit the dummy right in the ribs. The fleshy *thwack* vibrated up his arms. The dummy wobbled on the chain but was otherwise intact.

"YES! Take that, Carlos!"

Stan was less enthused.

"Rheia, this guy is way too polite. He'll never stop anyone handing out those love taps."

"Talk to ME, man!"

"OK, grappler, lemme guess. You lost more matches than

you won because you were reckless. You favored blunt force over strategy because the mat wasn't competition for you, it was therapy. You may know how to be exquisite in your theatre world but you haven't realized you can bring that same precision to *my* world. Don't just club the target, STRIKE it. Break the bone inside the meat. Rheia?"

Gideon flinched as Rheia slashed forward. The steel baton had snicked into existence in her hand. Her arm blurred twice. Gideon heard two gel-muted *cracks*. The dummy's left wrist and knee jutted at unholy angles.

"Oh yes yes YES! You like how that feels, Carlos??!" Adler stood on the actor block, gyrated his hips.

Gideon peered into the gel. Splintered plaster. At the knee a shard protruded.

Stan whistled. "See that? Joints. Weak points. Precision. That opponent is toast. And she didn't even break a sweat."

Gideon glared.

"Don't be mad at *me*, grappler. Put that fire to use."

"Gid." He turned. Rheia was there. Close. The baton had disappeared.

She grasped the bat and pulled it up between them. She shook it, forcing him to grip hard.

"You've gotta let it out."

Gideon's insides cooked at temperatures he hadn't felt since...

"Imagine the dummy is Coach Carl."

His vision narrowed to a pinprick.

"Just as an exercise. I've got your back."

He saw in vivid detail a spot on his thumb where he had chewed a cuticle.

"Think about how you cast a broadsword. The power is in there."

He saw a vein pulsing on the back of Rheia's hand.

"Put the target point six inches inside the skin instead of six inches outside the skin."

He heard as though broadcast from outer space Stan telling Adler to sit down and shut up.

"Look at the dummy." Rheia floated away. Gideon's vision had gone red. The bat gasped in his grasp.

"There he is. Don't let him get away. Don't lose to yourself."

All Gideon heard was his own heartbeat. All he felt was the rage coursing through his veins. But instead of being dragged by it, he mounted it.

"*Release.*"

The bat was the stick. It moved of its own accord. Gideon simply followed. He stepped back, trembling. Adler shrieked with delight. Rheia's hands were back on the bat, helping him to lower it.

"Gid. Look."

The dummy's right wrist was obliterated. The right knee matched the left, stabbing shard and all.

"OK then," Stan said. "He's not hopeless. Bring him back tomorrow."

Stan walked away.

Gideon was perplexed. "Wait. That's it?"

Rheia popped him on the arm. "Yep. Chin up. You got a callback. Go home, get some sleep. You're gonna need it."

SUBJECT: Rehearsal Report Day 1

BODY: Rheia's pet got his ass kicked by Stan, no big surprise there, but then he totally massacred Carlos. So Rheia might be on to something, too soon to tell.

I've unpacked all the intel from Rheia's performance a few weeks back. That cell was part of a larger group, "One White Nation." Call themselves the Owners. Yeesh. Tracked down as many members as I could and left the dossier in the PO Box. *Dossier.* Isn't that a cool word?? We could say "file" but "dossier" just sounds so much more superspy. I printed out a second copy and gave it to Rheia. I'm guessing she'll want to put together a show soon. These Owner whackos need a talkin' to.

Still think it's a pain in the butt to stay analog and kill trees. I could email or file share this stuff so easy. My encryption is sweeeeeet. And going to the post office is such a drag cuz I have to put on pants.

Also the coffeemaker is totally on the fritz. I need caffeine!!

SUBJECT: Fix the Coffeemaker Yourself

BODY: Dossier received.

Yes. It's a cool word.

Yes. The Owners are dangerous. Keep digging. Track their chatter. Yes. Rheia has started writing a script. Be ready to design.

Please wear pants to the post office.

Gideon had never gone through a conditioning program like the hell Stan unleashed on him. High school cross-country? Collegiate wrestling? Grad school tumbling and fight choreography?

Tiddlywinks.

Day after day. Running. Crawling. Climbing. Jumping. Push-ups. Pull-ups. Sit-ups. Everything-ups.

Pre-sun runs. Late mornings and afternoons in a perpetual state of breathless agony as Stan concocted athletic tests and cross-training circuits and obstacle courses.

Tires.

Rope ladders.

"Monkey bars??"

"Get moving, grappler."

Late afternoon ice bath, its own special agony that by day three became an addiction. Dinner at home. Get to the show. Hold on for dear life through the fight scenes, every muscle shrieking. No post-show bourbons, just bruised blackouts in bed.

He came to know every nook and cranny of Port Morris as Stan made him ruck with a fifty-pound kit.

Burpees.

Jump rope.

Kettlebells.

Adler constantly jitterbugging around, eating and chortling and smacking Carlos.

"Doesn't he work?" Gideon managed to ask Rheia during a five-minute break that Stan timed to the precious second on his massive G-Shock watch.

"He works overnight. Like a vampire. Don't disturb him when he's plugged in."

Bench press.

Vertical jump.

Shuttle run.

"Think I'll get drafted in the first round, Coach?"

Stan stared at him.

"Y'know, cuz this feels like a combine."

Stan stared at him.

"Cool. Good talk. What's next?"

Row machine.

Wind sprints.

Medicine ball.

"Lunch. Thirty minutes." Stan disappeared.

Gideon collapsed into a chair. "He's not especially social, is he?"

"Drink your smoothie, Gid."

He gulped it down. Tore open an energy bar.

"You do realize this is the longest callback ever?"

"You can leave anytime."

He chewed. Rheia scanned a sheaf of pages, made notes with a purple pen.

"Whatcha readin'?"

She glanced up. Assessed. "Script for my next show." Went back to reading.

He chased the bar with a thermos of water.

"So, Rheia..."

She huffed and looked up again. "What."

He held up a conciliatory hand. "Serious question."

She put down her pen. "OK."

"Did you really want me to lead a workshop?"

"Yep."

"For other Troupe members?"

"Yep."

"To teach them to be better actors?"

"To help them more effectively impact the audience, yes."

"And by audience you mean spectators to their street fights?"

Rheia sighed. "Sure."

"But we're past that now?"

"Way past."

"Because I saw you go all Batman with my belt?"

"Yes. And because I showed you my baller sunglasses."

"PLEASE CALL THEM SHADES!" Adler yelled from the office.

"So I'm no longer just a side gig?"

Rheia sat back. "Oh you're still a side gig, Gid. Maybe now more an experiment."

"That's a step up I guess."

"Hey. You said you wanted 'in.' We're open to new ideas. You're the first actor we've auditioned."

Gideon cocked his head. "I'm confused."

"The current cast of the Troupe is all ex-military, former athletes, a couple martial artists. The Director built upon a foundation of combat experience. Thought it would be easier to train up the acting side. Results have been... mixed."

Gideon leaned forward. "Whoa. How big is the cast?"

"Can't tell you."

"C'mon, I'm trustworthy."

"No, I mean I literally can't tell you. Only the Director knows. Siloed smaller companies. Use entertainment industry as cover, plant ourselves as consultants or crew in different locations."

"Like, undercover?"

Rheia nodded. "But soldiers stick out in the regular world. They can't help it."

Gideon barked a laugh. "Yeah. Stan is memorable, that's for sure."

"Memorable is detrimental to the mission. So the experiment is, in addition to training fighters to act, can we train actors to fight."

"You are blowing my mind right now."

"You asked."

Chewing. Drinking. Pen scratching.

Stan appeared. "Wrap it up, grappler. Five minutes." Gideon groaned.

"But it's only been ten!"

"Time is relative." Stan disappeared.

Gideon wolfed down the last of his pathetic lunch. Rheia shuffled her papers.

"Gid."

"Yeah?"

"You should know, the Director is ok with us breaking you."

"Um. What?"

"Your callback? Stan's just getting started."

51

SUBJECT: Rehearsal Report Day 3

BODY: Stan is putting the pet through his paces this week. You know how it goes. All the baseline tests for speed, strength, reflexes. Boot camp Stan-the-Man-style. He hasn't dropped the Bruce Lee quote yet, but it's comin'. The pet is keeping up for the most part.

I'll wear pants to the post office, but ONLY if you send a new coffeemaker.

SUBJECT: Coffeemaker for Pants

BODY: No deal.

SUBJECT: Rehearsal Report Day 6

BODY: Rheia's pet finally snapped today. My money was on Day 4, she had Day 5, so neither of us bulls-eyed it but she still won. So I'm down ten bucks and that sucks. But this Gideon fella... I assume you're checking out the footage? He's raw but the dude has guts.

Also have you seen Rheia's script? I've got some sweeeeet designideas!

Also do sweat pants count?

SUBJECT: Submit Designs

BODY: Rheia's script approved for performance. Submit designs asap.

Owners moving fast. Time of the essence.

The footage is intriguing, yes. Put together a safe room. I'd like a sit-down with him.

And sure, sweat pants count.

52

Plank.

And plank.

And plank and plank and plank and—

Gideon collapsed. Stan clicked his G-Shock.

"Added five seconds. At least you're headed in the right direction, grappler. One minute breather. Then meet me at the heavy bag."

Gideon rolled onto his back, saw Rheia looking down at him. "How much more?" he croaked.

"We all went through it, Gid. Don't be late to the heavy bag or he'll make you do penalty burpees."

Gideon shuddered. She offered a hand, hoisted him up. He greedily accepted a water bottle and chugged.

"Small sips, Gid."

He sipped small. Shuffled to the heavy bag. Stan handed him gloves.

"Put 'em on and let it rip. Ninety second rounds."

"Any particular combo? Jab-hook-uppercut?"

"Negative. Just wanna see what you've got. What your instincts are."

"More observation."

"Affirmative."

"But come ON." He slammed the gloves to the floor. "What are we doing here? Why aren't you teaching me to fight? I thought that was the whole damn point!"

Adler grumbled and passed Rheia a ten-dollar bill.

Stan was granite. "Here's the deal, grappler. You've gotta teach me how to teach you."

Gideon's entire body shook. From frustration, from lactic acid, from being pushed to its absolute limit. "Cut it with the Yoda crap, man!"

Adler called over, "I think Stan the Man is way more Mr. Miyagi than Yoda, dude."

"Mr. who?" Rheia asked.

Adler gasped. "Wax on wax off? Paint the fence? Sand the floor?" Rheia shook her head.

"*Crane technique??*"

Rheia shook her head again. "Nope. No idea."

"My god. I feel sorry for you."

Gideon grudgingly pulled on the gloves. "*Karate Kid.*" Punched the bag. "Pat Morita." Punch. "1985 Academy Award Nom." Punch. "Best Supporting Actor." Punch.

Stan whistled. Gideon looked up, pitiful hope on his face.

"Your form is pathetic."

"So TEACH me! Show me correct form or a fight move or something!"

"You think you're ready for a 'move'? Rheia, c'mere."

Rheia glided over. Stan slapped a wooden prop handgun into her hand.

"First move. Disarming a scene partner."

Gideon pulled off the boxing gloves. "You come up against a lot of guns?"

Rheia rolled her shoulders, shook out her legs. "Hope for the best, plan for the worst."

"And the point of a 'move,' grappler, is that principles work across varied circumstances. Doesn't matter what the weapon is. Gun, knife, bottle, stick—"

"Nunchucks!" They all looked at Adler. He blew them a kiss.

Rheia and Stan faced each other. Rheia pointed the gun. Stan narrated as he demonstrated in slo-mo.

"Mirror the weapon hand. Rheia's got the drop on me, a weapon in her *right* hand, so I start the move with my *left*. Push it offline, out and away from center body mass. Opposite arm comes under, pushes up, then you twist back hard, maintaining your grip on the weapon. Final torque and their wrist should be so stressed the weapon ends up in your hand."

Gideon watched closely. Stan and Rheia demoed twice more, a bit faster. Smooth and easy.

"Your turn, grappler."

Gideon and Rheia faced each other. Again she took a threatening stance.

"First time slow," Stan said. "Just like you theatre people do in fight call."

"Got it." Gideon flowed through the move. Push offline, under and up, twist and torque and *pop* the gun was in his hand. "Sweet!"

"Again. Up to speed."

"Yessir!"

"Don't *sir* me. Again."

Gideon handed the prop back to Rheia, gave her a lopsided grin, took his position. He missed the look that passed between Stan and Rheia.

"OK. She's got the drop on you. Disarm."

Gideon bounced on the balls of his feet, stared at Rheia's hand, and lunged.

He grasped air. Blinked. Looked around for a witness to the unfairness of it all. "She... she dodged!"

Adler cackled. "You expect your scene partner to make it easy?"

Stan. "Again."

This time Gideon kept his eyes on Rheia's, tried not to tele-graph the moment he would execute.

He reached fast. So he thought. Nothing but air. Gun in his face.

"You gave it away, grappler. Fake. I thought you were an actor. Again."

Rheia's expression granted no quarter. Gideon feinted, Rheia bit, he lunged, his fingers brushed the gun but Rheia twitched away and even flicked a sharp shove into his sternum. He woofed and backed up.

He rubbed his chest. "So that's how it is?"

She shrugged. "Reflex."

"We aren't here to play pattycake, grappler. You asked for this. Again."

Adler dipped Fritos in a chocolate milkshake. "Better'n Netflix!"

Lunge. Miss. But he slapped away her shove.

"Ooooh it can learn!" Adler exclaimed around the choco-latey-corn mush in his mouth.

Lunge. Miss. "Again."

Lunge. Miss. "Again."

Lunge. Grasped! But Rheia stepped forward and shoved down. Gideon lost his balance. She nudged him with a shoulder and he tumbled.

"Get up, grappler. Go again."

Sweat dripped from Gideon's every pore. They had to move to different parts of the mat to avoid slipping. Stan was implacable. Rheia relentless. Adler insatiable.

Gideon bore down. But Rheia's hand and the wooden gun danced and bobbed, elusive and mocking. Welts from blocked counterstrikes blotted his forearms. He panted. He lunged. Missed. Slipped. Fell to the mat.

"Get up. Again."

"Dude, he's toast," Adler said. "Cut him a break already."

"No," Stan said. "Bruce Lee. 'I fear not the man who has practiced ten thousand kicks once, but I fear the man who has practiced one kick ten thousand times.'"

Adler hooted. "*There* it is!"

As Gideon stood, a couple synapses deep in his lizard brain observed Rheia also sweating and breathing hard. Gideon rope-a-doped the next few grab-misses, trying to lull Rheia into fuzzier response times.

He launched an intentionally slow lunge, the weakest yet. Rheia barely had to move to avoid.

Stan inhaled but before he could say "Again" again Gideon sprang, catching Rheia completely unaware. His hand clamped on the gun. His other arm slammed under and up, he twisted back, textbook, and now Rheia's instincts kicked in but too late. Gideon torqued the gun out of her hand and stepped back triumphant.

He bellowed. A wordless, raw *yawp* that echoed through the rafters.

Adler leaped up, spilling milkshake all over his bathrobe. "Yeah Gideon! Woop woop!"

Rheia toweled off her face. "Gid." He looked over. "Nice."

"Nice? More like about time, grappler." Stan extended his hand. "Weapon."

Gideon handed it over, raised his hand for a high five. Stan left him hanging. Stepped back two paces. "Now me." He pointed the prop. "Again."

Gideon deflated. "C'mon, Stan. I got it."

"You got nothing. One more time. Prove it."

Adler raised an inquiring finger. "Um, couldn't he at least take a moment to celebrate? Or, y'know, get hooked up to an IV?"

Stan, void of mercy. "One more time."

Gideon looked to Rheia. She didn't speak but he saw the challenge in her eyes. *You gonna break?*

"Listen closely now, grappler. An amateur practices till they get it right. A professional practices till they can't get it wrong. No scene partner you ever encounter will stop to acknowledge your slick-ass moves. The audience won't understand that you're tired, that you need a break. Once you're on, you're on. So congratulations. You got it right. You are now officially an amateur. You want to be a pro?"

Gideon breathed. Stripped off his t-shirt, wiped his face, threw the shirt to the side. Exhaled hard.

Stepped forward.

Adler went "whoooooa."

"Good then." Stan twitched the gun. "One more—"

Gideon exploded. Left hand on the gun, pushing offline. But he added a surprise, just for Stan. A tight right elbow *thud* on Stan's solar plexus. Then under and up and twist—

But good god *damn* Stan was strong. Gideon felt Stan's hands clamp onto his and sensed the forward drive that Rheia had used earlier. He sidestepped and avoided getting shove-tumbled.

But he sidestepped the wrong way.

Stan aborted the shove, pivoted his hip so it snaked under Gideon's, and yanked. Gideon barely had time to think *shit-*

judo-throw-shit before his feet were off the ground and above his head.

Stan made no effort to cushion Gideon's fall.

"Nice elbow, grappler. That's instructive. I'm going to build you a personalized combat system. This week of observation? Only way I could get what I needed to make you your most dangerous you. Hit the ice bath. I'll see you next week for final callback."

He walked away but paused to grab a towel.

"Yo. Price."

Gideon sat up in shock at hearing Stan use his actual name.

"Heads up."

The towel flapped through the air and landed in Gideon's lap. Stan vanished.

Rheia brought over some water. "Need anything else, Gid?"

Gideon took three huge swallows. "Adler?"

"What's up, dude?"

"Got any more milkshakes?"

53

Spearhead barely ate. He drank only when parched. He left his double screens only when his bladder screamed.

The software spun and spun.

He compared faces. So many faces. Hopscotched from link to link, tracking through social media pages and testimonials of "victims" and "first responders."

He fell asleep in his chair more than once. Woke up imagining the hand of AlphaSupreme squeezing his shoulder.

I have been chosen. I must not fail.

He stumbled across a blog. Meta-data revealed it had gone public only recently but its online presence had grown exponentially. Stories of victims were always more popular when children were involved. Transparent manipulation.

He read: "I will not try to make sense of the senseless, but oh how I will testify."

Think mighty high of yourself, don't you? Spearhead clicked through the pics. *Fake.* Click. *Fake.* Click. *Fake.* Click.

The mother's face... something jumped out.

His breath caught. He flicked the mouse, stabbed the cursor

into folders. PDFs erupted. Click. *There!* Click. *And there!* Click. *And THERE!*

Spearhead sat back. His heart jackhammered joyously. He had found one! Here he had actual visual evidence that a *single* so-called victim had been present at *multiple* so-called shootings.

Fucking crisis actors. And now she's profiting off a blog filled with lies.

"We did it, Grandad. We did it!"

In seconds he had set up a fake account and opened a private message box. He typed: "You are a liar."

54

Aniyah—her seal broken—flooded her blog with memories and stories and pictures. The digital monument to Jazzie grew and grew.

She discovered that people outside her inner circle responded, too. Within days Jazzie had circled the globe. Friends of friends of friends clicked through Jazzie's life, clicked "like," clicked heart and smile and prayer-hand emojis. Left comments:

"What a heartbreaking story."

"Your courage is inspiring."

"Thank you for sharing."

"My little boy died of cancer, I feel your pain."

At first the comments from those she had never met made her feel *too* vulnerable. Like she had ceded control of the narrative. But then she came to crave the validation, the sense of being seen and understood.

Some people even left pictures of their own children who had died far too young for reasons just as incomprehensible.

Several private messaged her. Some looking for a connection; she responded based on her gut. Others looking to interview her for follow- up news stories; these she ignored.

Mostly she rediscovered purpose. In sharing her joy and her pain she discovered the strength to wrestle the demons into submission. They would never be eliminated but they could be subdued.

She heard Imani coming up the stairs, bringing her a nighttime tea, regular as clockwork. She smiled and dragged another photo into the blog. *What would I have done without her...*

Another private message pinged. She opened the inbox.

You are a liar.

She gasped. She rubbed her eyes. The words sizzled on the screen.

"Hey Ani, you ok?"

Aniyah jumped and double-clicked, opening a photo to hide the inbox. "Oh, hey, yeah, all good. Don't you knock?"

Imani brought over a steaming cup. "Hrrmph. Don't deflect. What's up?"

"I'm not deflecting." And then Aniyah, knowing Imani's weak spot, totally deflected. "You finish your journal assignment for acting class?"

"Oh god yes I can't wait for next Monday, I hope Gideon goes off on one of those tangents again, I loooove when he gets worked up, the way he MOVES, all that Shakespeare supergeek fan stuff I had no idea but he can sully *my* flesh ANY day!"

Aniyah blew on her tea as Imani monologued. A couple minutes later Imani had kissed her on the head, exchanged "good nights," and headed back downstairs.

Aniyah closed her bedroom door. Faced her laptop across the room. Stand-off.

She approached the desk. Set down her tea. Took a breath. Closed the cloaking picture.

You are a liar.

She sat down. Sipped the tea. Clicked the name of the accuser: SH11. Nothing else. No real name. No identity. Anonymous troll.

She blocked the ID. Sipped again. Went to the bathroom and washed her face. Over the gush of the faucet she heard the computer ping. She came back, patting her cheeks with a towel. New private message. From SH22.

You are a liar.

Her guts twisted. Beads of perspiration sprang up on her freshly washed forehead. She blocked the ID. Stepped back from the computer like it was a coiled snake.

Steam lazily rose from the tea mug. The computer pinged.

Private message from SH33.

You are a liar.

She reached out, extending her arm long to keep her body as far away from the glowing screen as possible. Block. Almost immediately—

Ping. SH44. *You are a liar.*

Aniyah realized she was moaning softly. She snapped her mouth shut. Back to the bathroom. Hung up the towel. Looked at herself in the mirror.

"Screw this troll."

Back to the laptop. Sit. Scalding swallow of sleepy time. Reply, typing with deliberate strokes: "And you are a coward." Send.

Three throbbing dots signified the troll composing his response. His? Yes. His. Only a man would have the gall—

Ping. *How am I a coward, liar?*

Aniyah wiped her brow. Typed. "You hide behind a code name. Anonymous coward." Send.

Throbbing dots.

Ping. *And you hide behind a fake name, a fake story, a fake daughter. I'm calling you out. That makes me the opposite of a coward. And you're still the liar.*

"Don't you dare talk about my daughter." Send.

Dots. Ping. *Why not? It's not like she existed.*

"What is WRONG with you??" Send.

Ping. *You are what's wrong.*

And then SH44 unleashed a torrent. Cruel waters raged. Her screen filled like a levee overwhelmed.

False Flag Operation...

"Jazzie" is a completely made-up character...

Never existed...

Lying to the world...

No "gunman" no tragedy no dead kids...

Conspiracy. Fake news. Media and pedophile elites manufacturing pretend

families they can pretend murder on the pretend news...

Strip our liberties our guns our rights our freedoms...

You're paid to act like you're in pain...

You're a blight you're a plague you're a fake...

Aniyah strained to get her head above the surface and spluttered, "Who *are* you?" Send.

Throbbing dots. She imagined him panting on the other side of the chatbox, spittle dangling from his lips.

I'm Spearhead. Spearhead14fucking88. And I'm going to expose you for what you are.

She clicked BLOCK and slammed the laptop shut. She knew blocking wouldn't work, this troll had already proven that, but it still felt like having a sliver of the last word.

She trembled. She went into the closet and grabbed the large ziploc bag stored safely on the shelf. Opened it. Pulled out what had been Jazzie's favorite stuffed animal. Held it oh so gently against her heart.

She looked out the window through her reflection into the night. He was out there. Somewhere.

The tea steam swirled in the disturbed air as she yanked the curtains closed.

55

Spearhead cackled to himself as the notification popped up: "You have been blocked by this user."

So easy to build fake IDs. He had a pack of them ready to go, straining against the leash.

He glanced at his other screen. It was filled with images that proved this "Aniyah" (*stupid name, how 'black' do you need to sound?*) was somehow miraculously present at a dozen "mass shootings."

There she was as the friend of a victim, cradling a head with slick-ass blood and gore sculpted by a Hollywood special effects make-up artist.

There she was as a reporter, ambulances and EMT extras perfectly choreographed in the background.

There she was as a teacher shepherding huddled child actors into the playground as an alleged SWAT team stormed an elementary school armed with prop guns filled with blanks.

And here she was as a mom weeping on the shoulder of her hired husband.

Spearhead had to admit... she was *good*. She sold it. If he didn't know how to look for the tells he would believe her in every circumstance.

He also had to admit... this was terrifying. The budgets involved, the amount of dark money necessary, the size of the conspiracy...

He sent up another prayer of thanks that AlphaSupreme had foundhim, chosen him, given him clarity of purpose.

Spearhead turned back to his primary screen, refreshed "Aniyah's" blog. No new reply. He had driven her off-line. For now. She would be back to push more lies. And he would be ready.

He would torment her until she confessed.

56

"How is our prophet?"

The man known as AlphaSupreme stood behind his children, facing the bank of screens, idly twirling their hair.

Agnes and Jude saw all. Having hacked Spearhead's system they could see the righteous young man through his own webcam, even when he thought it was turned off. They noted how he sat, how he fidgeted in his chair, how often he went to the bathroom, the frequency of his prayers, the violent swings in his emotions.

They could also see everything on his two screens, both of which were mirrored on dedicated monitors in their workstation. They clocked every search, every site visited, every ID and password.

Agnes shivered as Father's finger curled a lock of hair around her ear. "He has engaged with the whore, Father."

"But she disconnected before I could fully invade her system." Jude felt Father's hand pause on his head. He stiffened. Punishment or reward?

"But you planted the seed?"

"Yes, Father. Next time she logs on I'll get a notification and I can have control in under a minute."

Father caressed. Jude relaxed.

"Good. Her confession must appear to come from her own hand. I am proud of you, my children."

A screen to their right blurred with a series of scrolling messages. AlphaSupreme leaned in to read.

"I see our Owners are hard at work. Is their plan coming together?"

"Yes Father," Agnes said. "Since they reached critical mass Jude and I haven't had to do much. Just the occasional nudge."

"But we keep our eye on them, just in case."

AlphaSupreme stepped away to another pair of screens where Agnes and Jude had built the series of deep fakes of the whore.

"You are certain our prophet does not suspect your work?"

Jude and Agnes glanced at each other.

"No, Father," Jude began.

Agnes continued. "I was able to pull everything from her social media accounts—"

"—and we spliced her image into the various news reports—"

"—if the video qualities were too far apart we just focused on the stills—"

"—but we were able to find believable bodies to superimpose her face on—"

"—and the stills especially I photoshopped out any inconsistencies."

They looked at their Father as he studied their work.

"Then we tracked his searches in real-time, and Jude was able—"

"—I could anticipate where he would navigate next—"

"—so he planted the pictures and videos where our prophet was most likely to stumble over them—"

"—Agnes reminded me to make him work for it. If it was too easy he would get suspicious—"

"—I also tweaked the code in his facial recognition software—"

Jude impulsively clapped his hands. "Oh Father, Agnes was amazing!"

She blushed. "Simply doing the Lord's work."

"But based on everything we've seen him do and heard him say—"

"—he definitely believes the whore is a crisis actor—"

"—and part of a false flag operation."

They looked to their Father for approval.

He frowned. "Pride is a sin."

They deflated. Their eyes flicked to the whip on the wall. Agnes reached underneath the console and clutched Jude's hand. Their breathing synced.

"But I forgive you." They exhaled quietly as their Father returned and laid his hands on their shoulders. "It is almost time for the next step. You will be able to lead our prophet to his purpose?"

Jude and Agnes nodded vigorously.

"Good. The Day of Judgment approaches. Inform me once you have control of the whore." AlphaSupreme squeezed their shoulders, headed for the stairs.

Agnes blurted, "Father. Spearhead believes as we do. Is it wrong to lie to him?"

Jude closed his eyes. Father did not like being questioned.

"Agnes. Look at me." Jude sensed his sister turning in her chair. He squeezed his eyes tighter. "You are old enough now to understand something I have not explained to you before. We are not lying to him. Does the shepherd lie to the sheep? We are telling him what he needs to hear. In pursuit of holy work, the truth bends to the Lord's will."

They listened to their Father's steps ascending. The heavy door opened. Closed. The locks clanged.

Jude opened his eyes. His sister was already looking at him. She shivered. They leaned in and touched foreheads.

A notification sounded. Jude clicked open a press statement. Stacy Mallory, yet another whore of Babylon, would be holding a press conference later in the week to announce the introduction of her bills. They would watch, analyze, report to Father.

They turned back to their keyboards. The Lord's work was never done.

Jude monitored the activity of Spearhead and the whore. Agnes pulled up schematics for homemade IEDs.

57

THE LIGHT on the keypad blinked red to green. The muted metal thunks played their familiar bass line. Gideon opened the Rehearsal Room door. No one trusted him yet with the code but Adler could buzz him in from anywhere.

No one around. Gideon dumped his backpack on the table. A chain creaked. "Hey Carlos."

Adler burst out of the office. Robe. *"Han Shot First!"* T-shirt. Boxers covered in red puckered lips.

"Giddy Gid! You are in a for a treat!"

"Oh yeah?"

Adler reached into a robe pocket and yanked out a pair of his shades.

"Behold!"

"Seriously??"

Adler cackled, ceremoniously extended his arm.

Gideon received the shades reverently. "Does this mean...?"

"No it doesn't," Rheia said, appearing from somewhere.

"Those are loaners. You need them for your meeting with the Director."

"My meeting…?"

Rheia ignored him. "Adler. Safe room ready?"

"Almost. Final render is spinning, security protocols running one last diagnostic. Call it five minutes."

"What's all that?" Gideon asked.

Adler put a finger to his lips. "Shhhhhh. Privacy."

"Oh yeah? Just how big is Big Brother these days?"

Rheia snorted. "You ever talked to someone about, say, wanting to buy a new pair of running shoes and then ads for shoes show up in your email? Social media? Newsfeed?"

Gideon thought for a moment. "Actually… yes."

"Tip of the iceberg. Siri and Alexa don't just google shit for you and play music, guide you through your scone recipe. They listen. If something is free that means you're the product."

Adler pulled a bear claw from his other robe pocket, went to town. "You know the only two pieces of software on this planet that have yet to be hacked, Giddy? The algorithms for Google and Facebook. Those'r buried so deep no one's even sniffed 'em. That's not just proprietary, that's paranoia. Makes you wonder what they're hiding." He hacked up some fried dough that had gone down the wrong pipe.

Rheia said, "But we the Consumer, as long as it's fast, we don't care. Sacrifice liberty for safety—"

"You get neither," Gideon said.

Rheia nodded. "So we keep Troupe stuff off the grid. Analog is always first choice—"

"Analog?"

"In person. Handing things off. Chain of evidence. Dead drops. Everything digital leaves breadcrumbs."

"Facebook is forever."

"Absolutely. Employers google search all interviewees. Why wouldn't they?"

Gideon snapped his fingers. "So you use burner phones?"

Adler groaned. "You even know what those are?"

Gideon gave a face-saving shrug. "Sorta."

"Uh-huh sure, Mr. Hollywood. We have no need for burners. For I am the Lord of Workarounds."

Rheia shoved Adler toward the office. "Get a move on, Lord."

"Alright, alright." Over his shoulder as he disappeared he said, "We use email for non-time-sensitive stuff."

Gideon held up an accusing finger. "E-mail?? What about digital breadcrumbs?"

Rheia pulled a notebook out of her bag, paged through it. "Relax. You set up a browser-based account. Like Hotmail."

"Or Juno?"

Adler's head popped out. "Yer shittin' me you still have a Juno account."

"It was the first email I ever set up. I keep it now just for spam."

"Huh. OK, Hollywood." Adler's head popped back in.

Gideon pressed. "But Rheia, you send an email even on Juno or Hotmail, can't someone, whatever, *ping* it? Capture and crack it?"

"Sure. Once it's *sent*. So we compose a message and leave it in the draft box. Never send it. We all have designated accounts with each other. Both know the password. Log in. Check draft folder. Read. Delete. Compose. Never send."

"No breadcrumb."

"If something's time-sensitive but we can't get face to face we use the chat function inside an MMORPG."

"A what?"

"A massively multiplayer online role-playing game. Open

worlds with quests and complex economic systems. You can even transfer real money into goblin gold and back again."

"Damn."

"Hundreds of thousands of people around the world with avatars. Chatting through the game is basically untraceable. Especially because the one we use Adler programmed from the ground up."

"What's it called?"

Adler hollered from the office. "*Hinterlands!!*"

"That's where you're gonna meet the Director."

Gideon held up the shades. "You said I'd need these?"

Rheia smirked. "Yeah. Those are optimized. Be careful."

"Careful?"

Stan appeared, carrying a duffle. "Rheia, you ready?"

"Almost. Just gotta get Gideon into the safe room, then we can go."

"Big plans tonight?" Gideon said.

"Call it a dress rehearsal," Rheia said.

"Cool. Break a leg. Before you go, I've got one more Hinter-lands question."

"What is it, Gid?"

"And this is important."

"*What?*"

"Can I be a night elf?"

They stared at him.

Stan said, "I'm going to assume you're being serious because if not I might have to break your face."

"I'm absolutely serious. Night elves are awesome. Plus they are fleet of foot and that's sorta my thing, right?"

Rheia shook her head, slid her notebook into her bag. "Sorry, Gid. Adler built it so he's the only night elf. Wait till you see the size of his codpiece."

Gideon tilted his head.

Rheia shrugged. "Don't say I didn't warn you."

"So what else can I be?"

"You don't get to pick. Adler assigns. Keeps your ego out of it."

Gideon sighed. "Fine. So what am I?"

"I think he made you a Paladin. Like a Ranger. Think Aragorn."

Gideon nodded. "Works for me. How will I recognize the Director?"

"Highest-ranking mage in the Hinterlands."

Gideon was getting into it. "What're you?"

"Thief slash bounty hunter."

Gideon hooted. "Oh yeah, that's perfect! And Stan what are you? A giant? A centaur? A titan??"

"I'm a gnome."

Gideon blinked. "You're a...?"

"A gnome." Stan grinned. "No one *ever* suspects the gnome."

"You're six foot four."

"It's fucking *virtual*, Price."

A beat. They could hear Adler humming to himself in the office. Gideon cleared his throat.

"What, Price?"

"What's your gnome name?"

Stan spoke with exquisite elocution.

"Dipple Togglesprocket."

Gideon bit down hard on the inside of his cheek.

Stan spoke with exquisite elocution.

"You laugh, Price, I *will* break your face."

Thankfully just then Adler bopped out of the office.

"We are good to gooooo!"

58

Stan and Rheia left. Adler fiddled with the sunglasses.

"OK put 'em on. You're logged in to the waiting room. I'll join you from the office. Just follow the path to the village. Oh you'll need these, too." He handed Gideon a pair of wristbands. "Can't play a video game without a controller, Hollywood. See you in a minute!" Adler scampered to the office.

Gideon grabbed his thermos of water, sat, slipped on the wristbands. Then he put on the shades and the Rehearsal Room disappeared. Stirring fantasy music played as he plunged into the virtual waiting room.

His avatar looked *good*, oozed new car smell. Rheia had been right: a Paladin in kick-ass knee-high boots and a flowing hooded cloak stared back at him.

A voice proclaimed, "Welcome to the Hinterlands, Bard the Stick-bearer of Thespis!"

"Subtle, Adler," Gideon thought.

He waited. Bard waited. Bard started to tap his foot. Gideon looked around, saw a floating, blinking button that read "Enter!"

He lifted his arm. Bard's arm followed.

"Whoa. Slick."

Gideon experimented, moving his arms, turning his head. Bard followed but maintained his impatient expression.

Gideon/Bard reached for the floating button. Touched it. The game launched.

Gideon's jaw dropped.

The graphics were unbelievable. Not so realistic as to cause the queasiness of uncanny valley, but *hyper*-real. A dream state.

Bard walked along a path on the outskirts of a countryside village. Smoke curled from chimneys. Breezes and birds. Bleating of sheep and goats. A traveler passed, the creak of her wagon and snicker of her horse pristine in the bone conduction speakers. It wasn't hard to imagine the weight of Bard's leather purse bouncing against his hip. Or the smooth grain of the well-polished quarterstaff in his hand.

No wonder people spent thousands of dollars and countless hours plugged in. A world like this?

He entered the village. Walked in wonder through the collection of thatch-roofed shops and inns. Came upon a tavern that looked strangely familiar. He couldn't quite put his finger on why the architecture spoke to him, but then he caught sight of the carved wooden sign hanging above the door.

A small deer prancing on the back of a ferocious grizzly.

A horse cantered up behind him. He turned and saw a tall, slender elf leap lithely from the saddle. Rich blue skin, pointed ears, silver armor, hair dancing not so much *in* the wind as *with* the wind. And a bulging metal codpiece inscribed with magical runes.

That on closer examination were actually exquisitely detailed depictions of elf porn.

"Welcome, Bard, to the village of Lemuria!"

"Thanks Adler."

The elf shook his head. His hair made achingly beautiful shapes in the air.

"Please, here in the Hinterlands, I am known as Peregrin the Endowed."

"So I see."

Peregrin née Adler rapped his knuckles on the codpiece. It rang like a church bell calling parishioners to prayers. "It's good to be the programmer. And hey!" Adler pointed at the sign. "You like what I've done with the place?"

"Oh I got it, Adler."

"Ahem."

"*Peregrin*. The Bear and Fawn."

Adler pushed open the door. Gideon followed him in. And his jaw dropped again.

The dimensions were identical to the real watering hole downtown. Tables in same places. Bar running along same wall. Somehow Gideon felt the sensation of the same beer stickiness on the floor. Could practically smell the bowls of stew and fresh-baked bread being served. Even live music in the same corner. A leprechaun combo—fife, drum, and harp—tooted out a pastoral version of *Love Machine*.

"Barkeep! Two meads!"

"Right *hic* away, Peregrin, sir!" replied a hiccuping, glittering ball of light that hovered behind the bar, lurching this way and that, carrying mugs five times its size.

Gideon squinted through the sparkle. "A fairy bartender?"

"A sprite, my good Bard. Narissa the Inebriated. Best mixologist in the Hinterlands."

Peregrin led Bard to a booth. On the way they passed a quartet of dwarfs engaged in a belching contest.

They sat. Narissa zipped over with two froth-sloshing mugs. "So this *hic* is he?"

"This is he, my darling sprite."

"May the *hic* ghosts of your ancestors smile upon you, Bard."

"Um. Thanks, Narissa. You too?"

A giggle like tiny wind chimes. Interrupted by a ruckus stemming from intense disagreement over which tectonic burp had achieved the most resonant undertones.

"Pardon me, boys." Narissa weeble-wobbled away to play peacemaker with the dwarves.

"Bottoms up, Bard!" Peregrin said, lifting his mug.

Wondering what the point was to drinking virtual mead, Bard cheers'd back.

And Gideon realized that simultaneous with Bard gulping animated mead, he was taking a huge swallow of real water from his thermos back in the Rehearsal Room. He spluttered and coughed.

Adler howled with glee. "He has been baptized!"

The dwarves, leprechauns, and Narissa bellowed back, "All must be baptized!"

Gideon caught his breath. "What's all that?"

"You took a real drink, didn't ya?"

"Yeah! So weird."

Peregrin chuckled. "Happens to all the noobs."

The door banged open. All heads turned. *Love Machine* petered out.

The dwarves started starstruck whispering. "It's the Mage!"

"The Mage!"

"The Mage is here!"

And for the third time, Gideon's real jaw dropped.

59

THE MAGE STOOD seven feet tall in a floor-length cape that shifted continuously through the color spectrum. Like Peregrin's hair it had a life of its own, floating in the air as though underwater. The Mage itself didn't step so much as float across the floor, and its face was... *blurry*. Only that wasn't quite right, it wasn't a glitch in Adler's programming. It was more like the Mage had dozens of faces, all overlapping, looking in various directions, expressing various emotions, all at once.

The dwarves' whispered conference came to a quick consensus. They stood as the Mage glided past.

"Oh mighty Mage," the spokesdwarf proclaimed. "Might we, your humble servants, request a boon of blessing upon our battle axes!"

The Mage stopped. A wand appeared in its hand, traced an intricate pattern.

Gideon belatedly noticed Narissa hiding inside an empty mug and Peregrin averting his gaze.

The spell erupted with a deep *thump*, felt more than heard, a mountain's heartbeat. The light, however, was cosmic. Bard was blinded. Gideon too, the lenses of his shades going entirely white for several seconds.

The tavern re-emerged, like fog lifting. Gideon saw Peregrin's elf- grin.

"Pretty cool, huh?"

Gideon looked around. The dwarves were gone. The band was gone. Narissa still buzzed behind the bar but otherwise the joint was empty.

Except for the Mage, studying Bard, faces upon faces.

"Did the Mage just kill them??" Gideon whispered.

"No no no, that was a Spell of Apparition. All those users will find themselves in some far corner of the Hinterlands. Will mean a couple hours of traveling back to civilization but oh what a story they will have! Hehehehe. And now for introductions!"

Peregrin stood. Yanked on Bard's sleeve. Bard stood, awkward and unsure.

The Mage slid forward.

Peregrin lifted an arm, orator-style. "Oh Mighty Mage, I present to you Bard the Stickbearer of Thespis!" He swept into a bow.

Bard gave a small wave.

The Mage gave the merest inclination of its head. "Sit, Bard of Thespis."

The Mage's voice was an auditory twin of the Mage's face. Multiple voices overlaid each other. Not one voice echoing but several voices in concert, weaving through shifting harmonics.

"Peregrin the Endowed," the Mage continued. "My gracious thanks for arranging this meeting. I bestow upon you a blessing."

The wand crackled with lightning.

This time Gideon-Bard averted his eyes.

Thump.

Peregrin's codpiece glowed, the "runes" wriggled, and the metal bulge expanded a half-inch or so.

"I thank you, Mighty Mage!" Another sweeping bow and Peregrin was out the door, surely to share the blessing of his blessing with some lucky centaur.

The Mage gestured at the door. "Narissa?"

"On it." The sprite flashed directly to the door—no wobble—set the locks. "We're clear."

"Thank you."

The suddenly sober barkeeper got to work cleaning up spills.

The Mage sat, gestured for Bard to sit across, folded its hands on the table. "Now then. Hello, Gideon. I'm the Director."

It was as equally strange to hear multiple voices use the first-person singular as to hear his real name uttered.

"Oh. Hi. So no more role-playing?"

"Oh we keep up appearances when Adler is around. But when 'Peregrin' is otherwise engaged, we just talk normally."

"Great."

"How's your body?"

"What?"

"Stan's hell week."

"Oh. Brutal. But I'm still in one piece."

"So I see. Narissa?"

The ball of light zipped over. "Yes?"

"What do you think?"

Gideon could feel both the Director and the sprite analyzing him. His hackles rose. "You said to talk normally. Who is 'Narissa' for real?"

"Not your concern, Gideon," the Mage-Director said.

"Seems like it is."

"Less you know the better."

"Who'd believe me anyway, though, right?"

"True."

"I'm having my ass kicked by a Green Beret in a secret warehouse and drinking with elves in a video game and being told by someone I thought was an acting student that we can change the world one bully smackdown at a time."

"Clear summary."

Narissa clucked her tiny tongue. "I think he could go either way."

The Director "hmmmmm'd."

"You ok with all his doubt?"

The Director waved a hand in dismissal of that particular anxiety, inadvertently swatting Narissa out of the air. "Hey!"

"Oh geez, sorry. But no, his doubt does not disturb me. Doubt is the ants in the pants of faith, as they say. I don't want unthinking zealots. And I don't want Troupe members devoid of empathy."

"But if his doubt paralyzes him?"

The Director shrugged. "We cut him loose. Hopefully still in one piece."

Gideon broke in. "I'm right here! Now I see where Stan gets it. Hey! Is that you in there, *Narissa?*"

The ball of light snickered. "Not even close."

"Why are you angry?" the Director asked. "You've made it to the final callback."

"Though you're sorta blowing it," Narissa said.

Gideon bit back a sharp retort. Spoke deliberately. "Look. We wouldn't be talking now if I hadn't shown potential, right?"

The Director nodded.

"I understand there are risks. I understand you don't want to be on the hook for my safety. That's fine. I'm a big boy."

"Why do you want this?" the Director asked.

"So this is the interview portion?"

"There's no room for vengeance in the Troupe, Gideon."

"Rheia told me the same thing."

"You won't make up for your sister here."

Gideon again bit back a retort.

"And you're a marvelous teacher, I'm told. You've got a solid career going, which is nothing to sneeze at in the theatre biz. You're a tremendous actor. I thoroughly enjoyed *Henry Five*."

"You saw my show? You're in New York?"

"Of course I did. Had to see you for myself. Stan saw it too, though he's less enthused about this whole experiment. But even he was impressed with how you didn't crumble. I believe his exact assessment was 'not entirely hopeless.'"

Gideon snorted. "Ringing endorsement."

Narissa jangled. "You always such a jackass?"

Gideon wished for a flyswatter.

The Director said, "So I come back to why would you want this. The shall we say *clandestine* lifestyle will cost you far more than it pays."

Gideon clenched his real hands. Bard's virtual hands mirrored. "It is about my sister. But it's not revenge."

Narissa jingled.

"OK it's partially about revenge, but it's more about..." Gideon turned his head so that Bard could look out the tavern window. A fantastical world rendered and re-rendered on the other side of the digital glass.

"I expect I could go out there on a quest and slay the dragon. And it would feel grand. But there would be no tangible consequence beyond my own endorphin rush. That world out there, the one Adler built? It doesn't actually exist."

"Doesn't it?" the Mage asked. "Don't the worlds you build on stage actually exist?"

"I used to think so." Gideon ran Bard's hands across the

smooth wooden table. "I got into theatre because I thought the catharsis of storytelling could change people. But if I'm making even the tiniest dent, I can't see it. What I've seen Rheia do... She's slaying dragons in the real world."

Gideon tried to catch a pair of the Mage's many eyes.

"The true tragedy of what happened to my sister? To my family?" He tasted bile. "It's *common*. Happens somewhere every day. *That's* why I want in."

The distant clock bonged again. Narissa buzzed for a moment in the Mage's ear. The Mage nodded. Narissa zipped away through the keyhole.

"Where'd she go?" Gideon asked.

"Troupe business. If you've got questions, ask now."

Gideon gathered his thoughts. "You've clearly got significant resources at your disposal. Why the bottom-up approach? Why not top-down? Take on the *big* bullies? I'm not saying this well, but you could be a Goliath. A Goliath for good."

"Tried it. Doesn't work." The Mage pulled out a long pipe, puffed smoke. "You're correct, Gideon. I've got wealth. Worked hard, got lucky at the right times, retired early. Like you, I wanted to change the world. And that means changing the system. So I went after city commissioners, state representatives, didn't care about party or creed, if I saw someone I thought could pull a lever, I went after 'em, checkbook open. I even nabbed a sit-down with a US Senator. Change the system from within the system, right?"

"Right."

"Bull puckey. Can't change the system because it doesn't want to change because it's not broken. It's rigged. Works exactly as designed. It incentivizes being an asshole, and the higher up you go the bigger the incentive. The playing fields aren't level, Gideon. Be the change? No no no. Be the *karma*."

The Director blew a smoke ring.

Gideon asked, "Anything happen with the Senator?"

"I terrified him, truth be told. He made a couple empty promises, I watched my money get siphoned off into pet projects and shell games. So I shifted gears. Orphanages. Community and after-school programs. Tutoring. Scholarships. Spent *time* with people instead of just spending money. Know what I learned?"

Gideon shook his head.

The Director leaned forward. "A thousand bucks effectively targeted outweighs half a mil in the mail. I should've realized that from the get-go. I received an anonymous scholarship when it looked like I wouldn't be able to afford college. Made all the difference in my life. Change the life of one person and you have changed the world. Viewed from the outside that change is incremental, hardly noticeable. Viewed from the inside, though, for that individual? The world has changed."

"Your present is your past for your future," Gideon muttered.

"Hmm?"

"Something one of my students said. Snowflakes. Ripples. Small things now causing big things later."

"Exactly. I use money, you use teaching and storytelling. We scatter seed, water it, move on. No idea what may bloom but you do it anyway." The Director coughed. "Damn. I'm not even smoking offline but Adler's graphics play with my mind."

"So how does the Troupe fit into this?"

"Like you said, Gideon. So much of the evil in this world is common. Banal weeds. And my money isn't infinite. Nor is my time. Once again I got lucky. I met Stan."

"When? Where?"

The Director waved the pipe. "Another time. Stan taught me about 'rooftop leadership.' Green Berets insert themselves behind enemy lines. Live with the locals. *Spend time* with them. Village under attack? Green Berets are the first up the ladder to the rooftop to defend the village. Demonstrate tactics. Ask for nothing in return. Earn trust. Eventually? Teach the locals to fight for themselves. So. The Troupe emerges in bars. In trains. Demonstrates. Hopefully inspires."

"Catharsis."

"So that's why we're talking, Gideon. I can see that you get it. But I'm still concerned for your safety and, frankly, your soul, whether you believe in that or not. The Troupe has no expectation of you. And you are under no obligation to us, beyond secrecy."

Narissa popped back in through the keyhole. "Director. Time."

"OK, we're done for now. Show me something. Maybe we'll talk again."

The wand waved.

Gideon reached out. "Wait wait wait what about—"

Thump. The lenses went white. Re-pixelated. Bard found himself on the summit of a mountain. He looked out over the vast Hinterlands. Through perfect cirrus clouds he made out a sinuous reptilian shadow gliding above a distant valley.

He took off the shades.

Rehearsal Room.

He took a swallow of water, peeled off his shirt, and went to the pull-up bar.

60

WASHINGTON D.C.

"There's a difference between 'American History' and the history of America." Stacy Mallory paused. "Do I start with that? It's a bit mental. Maybe start with the Ellison?"

Amelia made some quick adjustments on her tablet, flicked the updated speech to the teleprompter set up in their hotel suite.

"Try this, Stacy."

Stacy reset herself. "Ralph Ellison, the towering intellect who wrote *Invisible Man*, had it right. America has two histories. The first is stylized myth, and it's the one we all know, the one that's written down, taught in our schools, portrayed in our movies, called upon in our aspirational speeches. 'American History.' America as a shining light on a hill."

Stacy shifted. The merest adjustment in her center of gravity. Her voice slid down two notes. The effect never ceased to amaze Amelia.

"The second is messy. It's real life. It's the blood and guts, and it's full of contradictions. The *history* of America. And that's scary because so much of what we do as Americans contradicts who we say we want to be. As Ellison put it, there are disheartening discrepancies between our social reality and our democratic ideals."

She paused and looked again to Amelia.

"Well?"

Amelia chewed her lip.

"Well??"

"Something's off, Stacy."

Stacy muttered one of her mother's favorite curses. "*Sea*biscuit."

"Too many big words. Sounds like an essay. You gotta get back to journalism and—"

"I know I know. Hemingway. Seventh-grade vocabulary. Straight- forward sentences."

"You roll your eyes but look back at the campaign. The speeches that worked were the ones with sound bites built in."

Stacy growled. "The curse of the modern attention span."

"We can have our cake and eat it, too, Stacy, we just gotta find the hook for this one."

A shy throat cleared. Stacy and Amelia looked at the door.

"Come on in, Samar," Stacy said.

Samar tip-toed forward. He still hadn't worked through his awe of the rockstar Congresswoman.

"How long were you standing there, Samar?" Amelia asked.

"Um..."

"Never mind. What do you need?"

"Well," another throat clear, "two things. First. There's no story."

Amelia squinted. "What?"

"The Congresswoman is best—I mean, she's ELECTRIC— when she tells a story. Like at the monument."

Stacy and Amelia waited. They both knew to accept feedback from as many sources as possible. Samar also waited. He didn't yet comprehend that a rockstar could care what he thought.

The waiting got awkward.

"Go ahead, Samar." Stacy waved her hand. "Say what you mean."

"Well... it's just..." He took a calming breath. "I applied for this internship because of your story. And what I've noticed is that whenever you tell stories, it doesn't matter what thesis or hook or sound bite you've planned. It *rocks*. What do we keep learning from polls and social media? Humans don't respond to data or evidence. Like, at all. They respond to narrative. Spoonful of sugar, right? Hide the data and evidence in a story."

This was the most Samar had ever spoken around the Congresswoman. He suddenly seemed to realize it. He snort-giggled and froze.

Amelia glanced over at Stacy. They shared a rueful grin.

"Thank you for the reminder, Samar," Stacy said. She walked to him and extended her hand. He looked at it, uncomprehending. She reached down and took his, shook it in both of hers.

"My momma used to tell me there is no path without the jungle. It's easy to get lost if you don't have trustworthy guides. You keep on keeping me honest, ok?"

Samar nodded like a kid on Santa's lap.

Amelia interrupted. "Sorry, Samar, you said you had two things? What's the second?"

"Oh! Right. Yes. Representative Wilder is here."

Amelia reeled. "Bury the lead much, Samar?? Go go go get him up here!"

Samar saluted, realized he was saluting, bowed, realized he was bowing, made a choking sound and scampered from the room.

Stacy smoothed her jacket and moved to the sitting area. Amelia followed, muttering something vicious about interns.

They tidied, arranged the drinks, fluffed the pillows. All the tiny, innocuous things one does before portentous moments. Stacy placed a red velvet box in the shadow of a Scotch bottle.

Amelia said, "You sure about this?"

Stacy blew air out her lips and massaged her jaw. "Oh my brilliant Amelia. Have we been sure about anything the last two years?"

"I've always been sure of you."

"Well. Times like these? That's enough."

A knock at the door.

"Sky's the limit, Stacy."

"Damn straight. Let him in."

61

Spearhead opened the brand new soldering kit.

THE SCOURGE railed in the background. The guest was a higher-up in a growing resistance group, the Owners. Spearhead double-checked his recording software was capturing the details of upcoming protests and underground communication, since social media companies were starting to bow to the will of the New World Order and censor pages dedicated to racial purity.

It sounded like something big was brewing. But up north. If only he could be there!

But no. He had his own purpose.

AlphaSupreme hadn't spoken to him since that glorious night. At least not directly. But his browser kept leaping to pages of its own accord, guiding him in a crash course on bomb-making.

He studied the schematics that flickered to life on his screen. Meticu- lously constructed his workspace. Plugged in the iron. Moistened the sponge. Pulled out a practice circuit board. Tested the temperature of the tip... a satisfying *hiss* as he wiped the heated iron on the sponge. Slipped on safety glasses. Targeted a lead. Placed the tip on the connection. Applied the solder. A couple seconds. The metal flowed, shiny lava.

Fumes rose to the ceiling like a prayer.

62

Congressman Francis Wilder, fit, full head of dashing gray hair, dressed casually—because he could—in jeans, comfy walking shoes, and a lightweight pullover, swirled his glass. Inhaled deeply.

"Highland Park 15." His iconic gravelly voice effortlessly commanded the room.

Stacy wondered... *How many speeches has that voice made on the House floor over the past forty years?*

Out loud she said, "I used to sell the heck out of this stuff at my momma's restaurant. Whenever someone wanted Scotch but wasn't sure what they were in the mood for, this was my recommendation."

Wilder nodded. "Perfect balance of peat, spice, and floral."

"Fun fact: northernmost distillery in Scotland."

"True. Located on the Orkney Islands. Rocky crags surrounded by whirlpools. The winds are so constant and fierce that trees can't grow."

"Sounds intense," Stacy said.

"No more so than D.C., surely."

Polite laughter all around.

They sipped, seated across from each other in plush chairs. Amelia stood behind Stacy, puttering with papers and her tablet. An athletic, mid-30s white man in a runway-ready three-piece suit stood behind Wilder, his severe jaw impeccably shaved even at this later hour. Stacy gestured at the open bottle.

"Tyler, would you care for some?"

The athletic man shook his head once. "No thank you, ma'am. And you can call me 'Ty.'"

"OK, Ty."

Wilder sipped again. "Ty does not indulge in spirits. I admire his self-control."

No one really had anything to say to that. Only Wilder seemed at ease.

"I also admire *you*, Congresswoman Mallory."

"Stacy is fine, Congressman."

He inclined his head. "Whoever did your background work hit the bullseye. Highland Park 1 5 has long been my favorite."

"I'm sure I rely on Amelia as implicitly as you do on Ty, sir."

"Well done," Wilder said, lifting his glass in Amelia's direction. "Know thy enemy, yes?"

"Are we enemies?" Stacy said.

"Aren't we?"

"Do we have to be?"

"Ah." He rested his glass on the top knee of his crossed legs. "The reason you've asked me to an under-the-radar, off-the-books, late-night drink. Ty strongly discouraged this chat but I was curious. You want me to co-sponsor your bills, yes?"

Stacy set her glass down on the table between them, leaned forward. "Yes. I'm trying to get some bi-partisan energy going. Reach across the aisle."

"Admirable. Just be careful. You may have to reach so far you lose your balance. Fall into the lava."

"That's why I'm reaching to *you*, sir. You're right. We did our homework. Your track record is that of an honest conservative. Your party has skewed away from you."

Ty's eyes flashed. "I guess that depends on where you're standing."

Amelia snapped back. "On any objective spectrum Congresswoman Mallory lands barely left of center. If she seems extreme to you then that says everything about the state of our education, media, and your party's scorched earth tactics."

Ty smiled. His teeth were perfect. "Takes two to tango."

Amelia smiled. Her dimples were disarming. "Please continue mansplaining, it's irresistibly charming."

Ty's smile widened. Wilder twitched a finger. Ty came to heel.

"You'll have to forgive him," Wilder said. "He is programmed to protect me. Gets his hands dirty so I can keep mine clean. May I?" He gestured his empty glass at the bottle.

"Of course." Stacy shot Amelia a *stand down* glance. The two Chiefs of Staff simmered.

Wilder leaned back, his glass filled. Stacy sallied forth.

"Historically, Congressman, you've been moderately right of center. Left wing, right wing, a plane needs both to fly, yes? The extremists clinging to the wingtips scream loudest but most of our passengers sit in the fuselage."

Stacy felt Wilder x-raying her.

"You studied journalism, yes?" Wilder said.

"Yes, Congressman."

"Another bare-knuckle business."

"I actually kept working at my momma's restaurant all through school—"

"And during your first staff writer gig. You didn't stop pouring Scotch till you started freelancing."

"You know a lot about a freshman Congresswoman from a state half the country away from yours," Stacy said.

"In journalism school you studied Hearst? Pulitzer?"

"Of course."

"You remember what Hearst said to Pulitzer in the build-up to the Spanish-American War?"

"I know they both published whatever they wanted, fact-checking be damned."

Wilder chuckled. "Sounds like social media today, no? Anyhow, Hearst sent Pulitzer a challenge. A head-on contest to —and I believe I am quoting here—'attract the largest number of *undiscerning readers.*' Isn't that something?"

Stacy tried to read Wilder's blandly bemused face. "Are you saying we should have contempt for the voters?"

"Not at all. There is wisdom in the audience, as it were, but they are also easily manipulated. Repeat a lie enough and it becomes true. This is simply a fact of the human condition. As a first-year Representative you may not have learned it yet but surely in your campaign you started to sense it."

"In my first year I've seen nothing but politics prized over mission and it's driving me nuts. I want us to *govern*, not play a zero-sum game." Stacy held up her hands to pause whatever packaged bon mot Wilder had at the ready. "But yes I also understand optics. My bills have many co-sponsors but they're all from my party."

Stacy pointed at the red velvet box waiting on the table between them. Wilder nodded.

"Ah. I was wondering when you were going to get to that."

"That box is why I asked you here."

Wilder's eyebrows raised. "For me?"

Stacy nodded. Ty shifted into curiosity, Amelia into antici-pation. Wilder set down his glass. Picked up the box.

"Too large for a ring. I thought for a moment perhaps you were going to propose."

"In a way I am."

Wilder stroked the velvet. "Marriage of convenience?"

"Of necessity."

He opened it.

He gasped.

63

Stacy, Amelia, and Ty all held their breath.

Wilder finally said, "Leave us."

Ty was perplexed. "Sir?"

"Out."

"Should I sweep for recording devices?"

Wilder didn't look up from the box. "Should he?"

"No need, Congressman," Stacy said.

"Sir, I really think—"

"Ty, I'm old enough to be your grandfather. I can have an off-the-record chat with my colleague without you hovering."

"Amelia, will you show the Congressman's Chief of Staff out and wait in the other room, please."

"Absolutely."

Ty and Amelia exited. The door closed Stacy and Wilder in together. Time curled up in the corner like a cozy cat.

Wilder said, "I haven't seen one of these..." His fingers oh so gently plucked an aged campaign button from the box, its edges scored with flakes of rust. "My basement flooded years ago, I lost many treasures."

He turned the oversized button around so it faced Stacy. She already knew what it said but looked again anyway. In bold red font, with blue stars lining the circumference: *I'll always be FRANK!*

Wilder turned the button back to himself. "This is from my first ever campaign."

"For county commission."

He nodded. "Looking back, it all seems inevitable. But in the moment nothing ever feels certain."

"You rocketed to the state legislature and barely caught your breath before launching national."

"And here I've stayed, all these years."

They sat. The time cat in the corner arched its back, settled back down.

"You know my wife designed this?" Wilder said.

"No I didn't, Congressman."

"Please, it's just you and me now."

"OK. Wilder. You went by 'Frank' for years, didn't you?"

"Oh yes. I could never abide 'Francis.'"

"*I'll always be Frank.* It's catchy for sure."

"A bit naive. At least it would be today. Certainly nothing as aspirational as *Sky's the Limit*."

Stacy topped off both their glasses. The time cat purred.

"You know, Stacy," Wilder began, his gravelly voice weaving a spell, "nothing costs anything anymore. I remember my aunt got me my first camera when I was, oh, maybe nine years old. It was one of those old rectangle Kodaks, a pocket Instamatic or some such. You have any idea what I'm talking about?"

Stacy smiled, shook her head. "Afraid not, Wilder."

"Yes, well, we had to use actual *film*. And a roll for my treasured Instamatic was only twelve or twenty-four shots each.

Then you had to put it in an envelope, mail it off, and wait. There were stakes. A cost of time and money. Suspense. What did you actually capture? You didn't know until that package of pictures came back to you in the mail. It felt like a birthday when they arrived. And every image had… weight. Today?" He snorted. "Immediate gratification. Filters. Digital, retake, trash it, retake till you get the lie right. There's no suspense. No cost. No surprise. No weight." He rubbed his thumb across the button. "Albums now are just gigabytes in a cloud."

Wilder stared at the button in his hand. Stacy sipped. Then she asked, "When did you stop being 'Frank' and start being 'Wilder'?"

Stacy was surprised at how quickly he answered. "After Marilyn died."

"Oh. I'm so sorry, I didn't mean…"

He waved away her apology. "Some things you can't find even in the most invasive background check. Politics forces you to have two marriages. One private. One performative."

Wilder reverently placed the button back in the velvet box. "Thank you for this. I can't imagine how you dug it up."

"Samar."

"Hmm?"

"That terrified intern you met outside?"

"Mmmhmm?"

"He's an eBay warlock."

Wilder laughed his first sincere laugh of the evening. Slipped the box into his pocket, took a healthy swallow of Highland Park, sat back and slapped his thigh.

"OK. Take your best shot. You earned it."

Stacy opened her mouth but then paused. Wilder and the time cat both looked at her expectantly.

"You had a slick pitch ready to go, didn't you?" Wilder said.

"Yes."
"Rehearsed it in the mirror?"
"Oh yes."
"Trash it. Just talk to me, Stacy."
So she did.

64

Wilder had asked for it. Stacy shot from the hip. Amelia would have been mortified.

"Something you just said, Wilder, about inevitability? Look. I'm a rookie Rep who happened to surf the right wave at the right time. My first year is almost done, next year most of my time will be spent fundraising and campaigning. Who knows how many seats flip, the House is nothing if not volatile. There's no guarantee I'm still here after next year."

"I remember that feeling. I miss it."

Stacy guffawed. Wilder shrugged. Stacy continued. "So I'm gonna go big or go home. I'm not gonna accept that some wall has been built between parties. I'm gonna trust that my constituents see progress on the issues they care about matters more than some cockadoo ideological purity."

"So what happens if you lose re-election?"

"I go back to work in momma's restaurant and kickstart the freelance muckraking."

"Solid plan. Thank you for being so forthright."

"Then you'll love this. You must have a war chest stuffed

full of favors and political capital. I want you to spend some of it on my bills. On me."

Wilder chuckled. "Brazen."

"Well I've had a couple Scotches."

"No no. Don't apologize. But—and I mean no disrespect—you're not the first bright-eyed first-termer to talk this way. I've heard this eager pitch many times. And for issues far less volatile than voting rights and scrubbing the Confederacy from statues and bases."

"Those shouldn't be volatile issues," Stacy muttered.

Wilder snapped, "You want to join me in the real world here, Stacy? D.C. eats good intentions for breakfast. Why should I stick my neck out for you?"

"It's actually not about me, Wilder. I know what I am in the grand scheme here."

"And what's that?"

"A mollifier. I create the illusion of diversity. The establishment can point to me as an example of the ol' American b.s. of pulling yourself up by your bootstraps, hard work and grit. Bunch of lies. It's math. White kids as a whole get better education. Have better nutrition. Lead safer and more privileged lives."

"Typical. Blame the players for the game being rigged."

Stacy gritted her teeth. "I'm not blaming those white kids, Wilder. Not their fault they were born wherever. Like I said, even me, I happened to catch the right wave, but I'm the exception that proves the rule. I grew up with a lot of kids that in a true meritocracy would be pulling the strings by now instead of being danced on 'em. But the system is smart enough to drop scraps, keep full-fledged revolution at bay."

Wilder said, "You're quite cynical for an idealist."

"I'm neither. Racism is baked in. Do eggs look like a cake? No, but it sure doesn't look or taste right without 'em. When you get that hint of vanilla, can you SEE it? No, but it's mixed right in."

"Vanilla beans are black."

"Nature has a sense of irony," Stacy said. "If the flour isn't gluten-free, can you tell that by looking? No, but if a celiac takes a bite you better believe they're gonna have a bad reaction. And just because you may not have that reaction doesn't mean the racism isn't there."

"Homey metaphor."

"My momma knows how to spin 'em."

Wilder regarded her, his face unreadable. She waited him out.

"You know, Stacy, my party's National Committee came calling a couple times many moons ago, asking me to give the Senate a whirl."

"But you chose to stay in the House."

"I did. Even though it means being on the bottom rung of the federal ladder."

"How's that?"

"We're taught in school that our government has three equal branches, yes? But that isn't true, practically speaking. There are four distinct bodies. And it's not a mistake that only one of those four was originally designed to be elected directly by the people. Only Congress. The Presidency? Insulated by the Electoral College. The Supreme Court? Appointed. And the Senate? Chosen by state legislatures all the way up to 1913."

Stacy nodded. "Seventeenth Amendment."

"The Founding Fathers, for all their courage and brilliance, didn't have much faith in the common citizen's judgment. Term lengths? Supreme Court for life. Senate six years. President four. The House, as you've pointed out, a volatile two. Those numbers aren't accidental. They keep the only directly

representative portion of government in the chaos of accountability."

"Wow." Stacy's surprise was genuine. "Now who's the
cynic?"

Wilder wasn't done. "Also note the inverse math. The
House may have the most members but that just means a
Senator from the least populous state is far more powerful than
a Representative from the most populous. Only two Senators
per. One President. Nine justices."

"Started at five."

"True."

"Been as high as ten. Been set at nine since 1869 except in
cases when it was eight while a replacement was rustled up."

"Trying to impress me?"

"Better believe it. Is it working? I can juggle, too."

Wilder chuckled.

"So what you're saying, Wilder, is that the House, by
design, is the *least* powerful component of the system, precisely
because it's the one *most* guided by the people."

He nodded. "All the other players are protected. To keep
power in the hands of—"

"Rich white men."

Wilder sighed. "Of the privileged few. Yes."

"So why didn't you jump to the Senate?"

"Accountability. You scoffed earlier, but I mean it. You
aren't the only one who sees problems with the system. If the
Senate is meant to be deliberative and the House to be
raucous... well. Raucous sounds like a hell of a lot more fun."

Stacy started to smile but Wilder fired a fastball.

"Speaking of the Supreme Court, how many women
should be on it?"

"Assuming they're qualified?"

"Of course."

"You testing me?"

"Of course."

"Nine."

"Why?"

"Why not? It was all white guys till Thurgood in 1967. That's almost two hundred years of uninterrupted testosteronic whiteness."

"*Testosteronic?*"

"First woman wasn't till O'Connor in '81. So why not all nine women? As you pointed out, they aren't elected so they don't have to be representative. So why not even all nine people of color? We had an all-white, all-male Supreme Court for over a hundred and seventy- five years. Just because."

Wilder fired another. "Electoral College. Go."

"Gotta rethink it if not outright kill it. Think it was random that four of the first five presidents came from Virginia, the slaviest slave state?"

"Goddamned three-fifths compromise."

"Baked into the cake, Wilder. American commerce and industry hadn't been built yet so where was the wealth? With landowners and slave owners. What do wealthy people do? Protect that wealth. Build systems whereby their wealth can grow and be safe from the grubby paws of the hoi polloi."

"I'm wealthy, young lady, careful how you're painting with that brush."

"I'm making observations on the aggregate of human behavior across time, not trying to throw the baby out with the bathwater." Stacy risked fastballing back. "Bill of Rights, I assume you're familiar?"

"Now you're being persnickety."

"Want me to put my gloves back on?"

Wilder shook his head. "My skin's plenty thick."

"Our glorious Bill of Rights originally had twelve amendments, not just ten. The first two smartly didn't get voted in. Know what they were about?"

"I do but tell me anyway."

"Salaries for senators and representatives," Stacy said. "Makes you wonder about their priorities."

"And yet the Bill of Rights is a quantum leap forward, Stacy. First time in history a federal government recognized human rights in its founding documents. Credit where credit is due."

"Sure, Wilder, on the one hand that's true. But on the other, it originally got voted down. Twice. Twelve states to one. It took a bunch of 'room-where-it-happened' horse-trading—"

"Saw that musical three times on Broadway. So good."

"How much were your tickets?"

Wilder blanched. "Point taken." He gestured for her to continue.

"So the Bill of Rights didn't even pass on its own merits, it was used by a couple states to hold the Constitution hostage. Ratification was dependent on a Bill of Rights being taken up in the first congress. It took months of bickering—we forget how much our Founding Fathers despised each other—but the big ten got thrashed out. But then—and you're gonna love this, Wilder..."

"Can't wait."

"The Senate voted that the Bill of Rights *should not be binding on the states*."

"They've always been assholes over there. And my beloved House voted opposite."

Stacy nodded. "Oh yeah. The House endorsed the Bill of Rights big-time. But—"

"The Senate won. I know. Bill of Rights didn't become binding on the states until after the Civil War. Ridiculous."

Wilder stood up, ambled to the window, looked out at the lit-up Capitol. He pulled the red box back out of his pocket.

"How'd I do, Wilder? Pass-fail or you grade on the curve?"

"Stand down, Stacy. Keep that powder dry."

The time cat padded over, rubbed against Stacy's leg. She scratched it behind the ears as Wilder gazed out the window, idly caressing the velvet.

"Stacy. Do you know how many times I've run unopposed?"

"No, Wilder."

"A depressing number. And did you know that last year my stiffest competition was from my own party? Those extremists your Chief of Staff is so worked up about? They're coming for me as well."

He turned around. Something about his posture caused her to stand.

"You know what else didn't exist when our founding documents were written, Stacy? *Political parties.*"

He tapped the box against his other palm.

"I haven't been entirely forthright, Congresswoman. This meeting was actually my idea."

"What?"

"I wanted to see if you actually knew your stuff. But more importantly I had to know if 'Stacy' and 'Congresswoman Mallory' were cut from the same cloth. I'm glad to report you are."

"But we badgered your staff for months!"

Wilder shrugged. "Power 101. If someone wants something don't just give it to them. Make 'em work for it. Welcome to D.C."

Stacy plopped down into the chair, her mind whirling.

"And if you thought that was something, Stacy, you've gonna love this."

She smiled ruefully. "Can't wait."

"No one knows. I'll deny it if you leak it. But I'm retiring after this term."

Stacy shot back to her feet.

"Yes, it'll be a shock to many. But I'm done. I have to get out while I still have time to just be. See my grandkids, check some items off the bucket list. And I'm just so tired of breathing swamp air." He took a couple steps toward her. "So once again you got lucky with your timing. I do have a brimming war chest. And I have a year to put the final stamp on my legacy. No reason not to spend it all. So what the hell. Odd couple. Let's get *raucous*."

Stacy stammered, "I... You..."

"But understand something. Getting what you think you want can be a curse. This'll put a huge target on our backs. You sure?"

She fetched their glasses, handed him his, lifted hers.

"Yes, Wilder. Absolutely."

He lifted his Scotch.

"You know what? Behind closed doors, you call me *Frank*."

65

THUNK. *Thunk. Thunk thunk.*

Gideon entered the Rehearsal Room, groaned as he dumped the weighted rucksack. Sucked on his thermos. Toweled his face.

Rheia gave him a quick nod, went back to thwacking Carlos with baton combos.

Stan scribbled in a pocket-sized notebook. Didn't bother looking up. "That where the ruck goes, Price?"

Gideon groaned again. "No sir."

"Don't *sir* me."

Gideon re-shouldered the pack, took it the last twenty feet, dumped it again.

Stan paused his scribbling, clicked his G-shock. "Acceptable time today, Price. Would've been better if you hadn't dicked around with the ruck. Lack of discipline." Unpaused his scribbling.

"Permission to puke, sir."

"Don't *sir* me. Take a seat." Stan put a finishing touch on the notebook. "Here."

Gideon took it, flipped it open. Diagrams. Rules of engage-ment. Impressively detailed sketches of combat strikes. The primary combatant even sorta looked like him.

"Geez. You freehand these drawings?"

Stan nodded. "Every Green Beret learns anatomy in detail. We're all top-shelf medics. Have to be. Train on goats."

"Goats?"

"Not the goat story!!" Adler shouted from the office. "C'mon man, I'm eating!"

Thwack! "Adler's eating," Rheia grunted. *Thwack thwack!* "I'm shocked."

Stan said, "A goat's anatomy is incredibly similar to that of a human. Instructors inflict a variety of battle wounds on your goat. You fix it up. It dies? You get cut. It lives? Congrats. You do it again. Those goats save soldiers."

"My god."

"It's intimate. Easy to get emotionally attached. Can mess you up." Stan's voice shook the office windows. "That's why I tell Adler to STOP NAMING THE MOTHERFUCKING DUMMY."

Gideon paged through. Noted a particular attack.

"This an elbow strike?"

Stan nodded. "You surprised me with that. It'll serve you well. One of Rheia's favorites, too. Study that manual. I built it specifically for you."

"So." Gideon bounced to his feet, grinned large, shadow-boxed. "The day is finally here! You're gonna teach me to fight."

"Rule one, Price. Fighting is our last resort. First aim always is deescalation."

Thwack thwack! "Remember the bar, Gid?" *Thwack!* "The train?" *Thwack!*

"Yeah?"

"How many times you hear me give all those jerks second and third chances?" *Thwack thwackity thwack!*

Stan stood. "Hope for the best, Price. Plan for the worst."

"Yessir!"

"Don't *sir* me." Stan cracked his knuckles. "Let's get to work."

66

Imani was worried. Aniyah's energy the past couple weeks was more and more *off*. Quiet at meals. Preoccupied. Every day when Imani came home from work Aniyah was closed off up in her room.

Maybe Reggie had called, divorce stuff? But if that was the case Aniyah definitely would have said something. She had never hidden from Imani before.

On the train to work Imani always checked Aniyah's blog so she knew Aniyah was still active there. Pictures and stories and reflections. The number of readers and commenters just kept growing.

Oh that beautiful girl. Jazzie. How I miss you.

Imani settled into her train seat after another bizarrely silent breakfast with her dearest friend. Pulled out her tablet and opened the blog. Scrolled. Smiled at the newest picture, one that actually included Imani herself laughing with Jazzie at some ridiculous dance move Reggie had just busted out. Her eyes fluttered down through the comments filled with laughing emoji faces and *ROTFL* text speak.

"Fake cunt liar bitch."

Imani startled, shook her head, blinked repeatedly as though her eyes were playing tricks. The three *I'm typing* dots appeared. Another comment flashed.

"You are evil. Jazzie is fake. You poison the world with your lies."

Imani's hand covered her mouth to stifle the cry in her throat. She hit refresh. The first comment was gone. Blocked? Deleted? The second still throbbed.

A third appeared, even uglier.

A fourth, viler yet.

Refresh.

The second and third were gone. A fifth had reared its head.

Imani realized she was watching a pitched battle in real-time. Aniyah and this commenter—*Spearhead1488*—typing and clicking in furious tandem, one posting, one scrubbing. Aniyah trying to protect Jazzie from the profane, defending her monument from an onslaught of unfathomable hatred. An onslaught that Aniyah could not keep up with.

The comments rained acid.

Refresh.

The blog was gone.

Refresh. Refresh. Refresh.

404. Error. Page not Found.

Jazzie had disappeared. Imani's rational mind understood that Aniyah must have simply switched the blog to private but her guts felt like Jazzie had died all over again. She rocked in her train seat, keened quietly, the passengers nearest her shooting wary glances.

She wiped her eyes and fumbled out her phone, speed-dialed Aniyah.

Aniyah's voice was fake-cheery. "Hey you! Commute ok?" Muffled sniffles. Imani cut to the chase.

"What's going on with the blog, hon?"

"What do you mean?"

"Who's 'Spearhead'?"

The name shattered Aniyah's facade. "I don't know! Imani he's violated everything, this morning he even sent emails to my personal address, I don't know what to do—"

"OK OK shush now." Imani's guts rallied, cold rage dousing her initial shock. She repacked her tablet, stood, tensed herself at a door like a sprinter in the starting blocks. "I'm gonna call into work and get off at the next stop. I'm coming right back."

Aniyah's weeping was terrifying but also good. Imani could hear the relief. Nothing poisons like secrets.

"You stay put. Leave the blog private. We'll figure this out."

67

GIDEON SUBMERGES.

When he does come up for air it's only to make sure he's still swimming in the right direction.

The Rehearsal Room, his bed, the train, the Hatchery, performance, training, class, on a run.

Alarms shove him toward doors. Apartment door. Stage door. Warehouse door.

The Green Beret pushes him to a point past resistance or thought. Gideon demolishes Carlos over and over. Stan rebuilds Carlos over and over.

"When de-escalation is impossible—don't look at me, look at your target, elbow then parry—the fighting principle of the Troupe is simple. Deliver maximum harm in minimal time while taking no damage. Pain is not enough. Hell, doctors cause pain. Pain enrages. You don't want your scene partner angry or even merely subdued. You want them *incapacitated*."

"Yessir."

"You *sir* me again and I swear to mother-loving…"

Stan tumbles Gideon to the ground. Again.

"Get up. You're outnumbered. Take out the dummy but know where I am, too."

Gideon takes out the dummy, pivots to parry but Stan takes his back. Hisses in his ear, "You're toast." Throws him to the ground.

Slam cut. Hot shower. Ice packs. Smoothie. Adler and Rheia in the office arguing about something lighting up a computer screen.

Or lighting up the stage?

———

The audience quiets.

"O for a Muse of fire!"

Tennis balls.

Invading France.

"We happy few!"

Sweaty from swinging broadswords. *Or was he sweaty on the mat?*

———

A break. Gulping air, gulping water.

Adler chatters. "You know bone is freakishly strong? Ounce for ounce bone is stronger than steel." His teeth decimate an apple fritter. "A cubic inch of bone can bear a load of nineteen thousand pounds. That's like five pickup trucks. Four times tougher'n concrete. Evolution is amazeballs."

Stan stomps by lugging fresh dummy parts. "Bones break. All about how you deliver the force. Knock out your opponent and they can't fight back."

Frosting glistens on Adler's lips. "Yeah like CPR. Quick,

targeted compression? Ribs crack, sure. But slow pressure? Pile on the trucks!"

Gideon manages to ask, "And knockouts?"

Adler: "Not about raw force. You've gotta cause enough rotation—"

Stan: "Hit 'em on the button."

Adler: "—get that head going zero to forty-three thousand rpm in under a second—"

Stan: "Hit 'em on the button."

Adler: "—and the brain stem shuts down. That's why you see boxers build up such big neck muscles—"

Stan: "Just hit 'em on the goddam button. Hinge of the jaw."

Rheia passes through: "But not with your fist."

But where is Rheia?

Because two seats over from her there's Tosha raising her hand. "Gideon, please, why is it called 'rehearsal' and not 'practice'? What is difference?"

Rasheed seconds. "Yeah, it's always play *rehearsal* but basketball or soccer *practice*."

Gideon answers. "Practice is focusing on a single element. Rehearsal is putting those various elements together in different shapes till you find the most effective version."

Rasheed processes. "Like, I'm going to practice my free throws, or practice a footwork drill or something, but a scrimmage is more a rehearsal?"

"Exactly. Athletes don't glom on to the term 'rehearsal' but it's the same idea. A quarterback and wide receiver will *practice* a particular passing route over and over. But once you add a defender or do a walk-through it's basically rehearsal. I practice my lines at home. I rehearse with my cast in the studio."

Hands in the air.

A hand shoves him forward.

"Take out the dummy, know where I am. GO."

Gideon whirls. Elbow to dummy jaw. Lights out Carlos, Adler *woo- hoo's*! He ducks, avoids Stan's first grab, pivots. But Stan is always two steps ahead. Gideon's arm captured in Stan's implacable grip. Torqued. Pain. Not harm. But definitely pain.

Hello there, mat. Clambering back to feet. Pissed.

Adler cackling. Rheia's face in draft three of a script. Stan not even sweating.

"Go again, Price."

Mat.

"Go again, Price."

Mat.

Gideon stands...

...and finds himself facing the class. "In French the word for *rehearsal* actually means 'repetition.' Because repetition is the key to learning. Repetition is the key to learning. Repetition is...?"

The class in chorus: "The key to learning!" "You got it. There's no shortcut to expertise."

"Go again, Price...

...Keep it tight. Maximum harm, minimal time."

The mat licks Gideon all over. Stan calls a break, stalks away to the prop table. Rheia helps Gideon up, sits him down, drapes a towel over his head, offers a water.

"Rheia." *Gulp.* "What the hell is going on? I get it, I get it. Maximum, yes, but why the minimalist strategy?"

"Eight shows a week, Gid. Those long, flashy fight scenes in movies? Bullshit. The amount of energy expended, damage taken? False. Impossible. Why do you think boxing rounds are three minutes? MMA five minutes. Wrestling?"

"Seven."

"Yep. And what if you have multiple scene partners? What if you have to give chase? If you're outta breath you can't perform. Think mechanically. Cold. Precise. Take your ego out of it. The longer a fight goes the less control you have over the outcome. You make a mistake. Your scene partner gets lucky. Someone calls the police. The longer it goes the less likely you exit clean."

"You ain't fighting for points, dude!" Adler cracks open a neon-green energy drink. "No bells, no rounds, no judges, no refs!"

Gideon sips water. His breathing and heart-rate stop sniping at each other.

Stan barks. "Price. Break over. Again."

Break over. Marcel with his usual insightful observations. "Gideon, that word 'rehearsal.' Etymologically speaking—"

"Ety-what's-it-who-now?" Evan says.

"The origin of a word and how its meaning evolved," Marcel says. "Cool."

"Thanks for asking," Alfonso whispers to Evan.

"Etymologically speaking," Marcel continues, "that word 'rehearsal' contains 're-hear,' yes?"

Gideon taps his index finger on the tip of his nose. "Yep. Rehearsal is re-hearing. A form of repetition."

Little light bulbs pop on above student heads. Student heads tilt down to scribble and type.

"And note that it's to re-HEAR. Not re-do or re-see. Not even re-act. The Elizabethans talked about going to *hear* a play, not to *see* a play. It's not just words that evolve. Human behaviors evolve, too."

───────

Gideon's body learns first. His mind plays catch up.

Whirl. Elbow to dummy's jaw. Duck. Pivot. Parry. Immediate counter. Stan so incredibly fast and strong.

But suddenly—is Gideon imagining it?—his fingers find purchase. His muscles fire of their own accord. Time slows. Movement flows. It's like he and Stan are dancing but now, finally, Gideon is leading.

His center of gravity is lower than Stan's—

The leverage tilts in his favor—

Stan's feet leave the ground—

Stan's back hits the mat—

And Gideon is the one standing.

"Holy hip toss, Batman!!" Adler cries, spraying half-chewed fruit roll-up. "You figured it out, dude!"

Rheia is silent. But she raises an eyebrow to the ever-watching camera mounted high in the corner.

───────

And she shows up to class. Every Monday.

Gideon continues. "And then in German 'rehearsal' translates as 'investigation.' Actors have to interrogate the script, interrogate each other. Investigate. Play Sherlock Holmes, seek out clues left by the playwright, bring behavioral analysis to bear on the characters."

Emma: "Like *Criminal Minds!*"

Dan: "Or *Silence of the Lambs!*"

<hr>

Gideon makes a mistake. He takes the merest moment to bask in his success. He eases the pressure. And Stan?

Well. Stan *erupts.*

Gideon's body flails through contortions. Reversal. Two points. The mat. Home away from home. Gideon facedown. His moment of victory mangled.

"Uncool, dude! Personal foul! Yellow card!" Adler's bathrobe flaps in indignation.

"Cool it, Adler," Rheia says.

"That was totally unfair."

"No such thing as unfair," Stan says. "Bullies fight fair? I didn't tap. He didn't incapacitate me. The world isn't fair. The systems aren't fair. You spend all that time digging in the dark web, Adler, you see those degenerates acting fair? You see any honor?"

Gideon growls. "Honor is a mere scutcheon." He presses his palms into the mat. They look at him.

"Can honor set to a leg? No. Or an arm? No."

He gets to his hands and knees.

"Can honor take away the grief of a wound? No."

He sits up. Stares the three of them down.

"What is honor? A word. What is in that word 'honor'? Air." Gideon stands.

"C'mon Rheia. You brushed up on your Shakespeare?"

She faces him. "Falstaff. *Henry Four.*"

Gideon challenges. "Honor."

Rheia accepts. "Who hath it?"

"He that died o' Wednesday."

"Doth he feel it?"

"No."

"Doth he hear it?"

"No."

"'Tis insensible, then?"

"Yea, to the dead." Gideon resets. Turns his darkened gaze on Stan. "But honor will not live with the living, because retraction will not suffer it. Therefore, I'll none of it. Honor is a mere scutcheon."

Stan smiles his dangerous smile.

Gideon smiles back. "I won't make that mistake again. *Sir.*"

Stan's smile vanishes.

Gideon's doesn't. "Let's go. Again." The two men move forward.

"And Kaida, if I can pick on you for a second, how does 'rehearsal' translate in Japanese?"

Kaida's face screws up in thought. "Huh. Well, the best translation is 'practice.' But it has a different flavor."

"How so?"

Kaida's face unscrews like a lid popping open. "Oh! Like, think about martial arts. Or yoga. Physical practice connected to spiritual practice."

Tosha says, "Oh! Is like your phrase, 'practice makes practice,' yes?"

Gideon nods. "Full transparency, I stole that phrase from

my yoga teacher in college. And I struggled with it for a long time. It clicked for me on a run one day when I had set out to break my 10K personal record but just didn't have it, not a speed day, so I downshifted and did a nice easy twelve miles instead."

Imani rolls her eyes. "Nice easy twelve miles? Good lord."

Gideon smiles. "Today, my body is what it is. My mental and emotional states are what they are. I will never be precisely the same as I am at this very moment. Which means my humble warrior or my upward dog or my crow—or my run—does not have some perfectly prescribed version that I have to aspire for."

Emma nods vigorously. "Yes! My yoga teacher says there's no such thing as a perfect pose, only your fullest expression of a pose!"

"And that's just like the performance of a play. It happens, it's moonlight in your hands, and it's gone. You can't hold on to it. No pose can be perfected. Poses are guides. Manifestations of principles, proven over time, that can ground you. Practice makes practice. You are never finished. You can only ever be ready."

The mat.

"You weren't ready, Price. Up. Again."

But at least Stan is sweating now, too.

Rheia's hand raises. "If I could riff on this idea of readiness."

"Sure, go ahead."

The class focuses. Rheia rarely shares. But when she does it's well worth listening.

"Readiness is a mental and emotional state more than even a physical state. In Aikido, there's this idea: *irimi*. It means 'to enter.'"

Evan: "Like entering the stage?"

Rasheed: "Or entering the scene?"

"Both. Either. But the idea is grounded in violence, like Gideon has talked about. There's stillness... and then you shatter the stillness by moving. By entering. But *irimi* also translates as—"

Kaida blurts, "Choose death."

Rheia nods.

Alfonso: "Holy crap."

Dan: "Well that's intense."

Rheia continues. "In a fight, at any moment, there are only ever two options. *Irimi*, entering, or *ura*, going around. Choosing death means you have accepted that the only way to win is to enter fully, to leave yourself exposed and hope your strike lands first."

"Hope??" Gideon is pissed. Sore. He eases a shoulder and shoots a sweaty glance at Stan and Adler who are in the office comparing notes on draft five. "Hope is not a strategy, Rheia, especially if we are talking about maximum harm in minimal time while taking no damage so I can do a freakin' eight-show week!"

Rheia captivates the class.

"Which is exactly why rehearsal, repetition, practicing your practice are so vital. Like you said, Gideon. There are no short-cuts."

Gideon knows her words are for him. But as she finishes she seems to be talking to herself.

"Not when the stakes are so high."

68

IMANI'S FIST pounded Aniyah's desk.

"But why can't you trace him? He is harassing and threatening my friend! Every time we block him he just comes back as a new user."

The bland voice on the other end of the line droned.

Aniyah paced behind her, chewing a thumb. "More customer service apologia?"

Imani nodded, rubbing her temples. Hollered, "No no NO do not transfer me AGAIN, please just—"

An insipid instrumental version of *Sir Duke* started playing.

"Oh they did NOT turn Stevie Wonder into elevator music!" Imani disconnected and slammed things. "Clearly they can't help. Here. You keep compiling screenshots. I'm calling the damn FBI."

But the FBI was also no help. Not a judgment, just a fact. Aniyah had nothing really to give them. An agent visited, looked over her laptop, poked around her blog, backdoored the code.

Spearhead hadn't left a trail.

Aniyah thanked the agent while calming an increasingly irate Imani. Imani called in some favors, got in touch with an ex of a friend of a colleague who once ran in gaming circles and had dabbled in some light hacking.

This ex spent an hour or so in Aniyah's room, hacking away at her computer. His head bobbed to the K-pop tunes blasting in his headphones. He brought in a distinct aroma of body odor and patchouli but left behind only the conclusion that "whoever this 'Spearhead' jerk is, he's got mad skills."

Aniyah talked Imani off the ledge. Made Imani promise to stop losing sleep over this. Imani cursed and went to bed.

Aniyah stayed up. She roiled inside. The desecration of her little girl was part of it, but also...

Becoming a mother had opened up parts of herself she didn't even know existed. Everything in her intuition told her Spearhead was a man, but just barely. He was a boy. He was someone's son. Something must have happened to him to make him this way.

She opened up her blog. Settings. She had watched the agent and the ex like a hawk. Learned a few tricks.

Launched her blog back out into the world but kept the privacy on lock. Couldn't let Imani know what she was up to. She wouldn't approve. And Imani's disapproval was a force unto itself.

She opened a chatbox. Took a deep breath. Started typing.

"Hello, Spearhead. You are wrong about me. You are wrong about Jazzie. She existed. And I will prove it to you if you're strong enough to give me the chance."

Send.

69

Adler and Rheia poured over draft eight. Stan held kick pads, circled the mat, barked commands, caught Gideon's knees and shins. Gideon misplaced a kick, winced.

Stan's G-shock buzzed. "Time! Two minute rest."

Gideon limped a couple steps, shook out his foot.

"Careful with those kicks, Price," Stan said. "Impact with lowest part of your shin, not your ankle or foot."

"I know, I know."

"Eight-show weeks, Price."

"I *know*."

"Same reason we avoid punching, dude!" Adler said.

Gideon snorted. "*We?* You throwing some fists of fury in your downtime, Adler?"

Adler sparkled his fingers into jazz hands. "Must protect my precious phalanges. Keyboards to caress!"

"By the way, Rheia," Gideon said.

She didn't look up from the script. "Yeah?"

"Remember my belt?"

"What about it?"

"Bloodstains won't come out of the leather."

"I'll buy you a new one for your birthday." She looked up. "So *Henry Five* closes this weekend."

"It does."

"Got anything lined up?"

Gideon met Rheia's gaze. Felt Adler and Stan watching.

"Not yet. But I thought I'd extend my sublet. Y'know. Finish off acting class and then... see what happens."

Silent assessment. Rheia, Stan, and Adler communicating telepathically. Gideon waited them out. Sipped from his thermos.

Rheia went back to her script. Adler popped a pork rind. Stan smacked the kick pads together.

"Ten seconds, Price."

Gideon rolled out his neck. "Quick question. I totally get protecting our hands and ankles—"

"Tiny bones, dude!"

"So why not use real weapons?"

"Look around you, Price," Stan said. "Anything can be a *real* weapon." Stan's finger jabbed. "That prop table? Everything on it is a *real* weapon." His finger jabbed again. "Book. Broom. Beer stein." And jabbed. "The floor." And jabbed. "The wall."

"The wall is a weapon??"

Stan snarled. "Walls, floors, furniture. All of them are harder than your fists and feet. Why do you think we practice on a damn mat? Walls, floors, furniture. All of them are also larger than your fists and feet. They can do a lot more damage across a lot more area of your scene partner's body. One throw, shove, or trip can cause multiple impacts. And unlike your fists or feet, it doesn't matter if they break."

"Walls, floors, furniture. Got it."

Stan raised the kick pads. "So let's go."

But then Gideon said, "But I meant knives. Guns. You keep saying incapacitate, but when are you gonna show me how to, I guess, field strip or fill a clip?"

Stan turned to stone. Rheia and Adler froze.

Gideon sensed the shift. "What? What did I say?"

Stan's whisper was death on the breeze. "You child. Bullets and blades don't just kill today. They kill tomorrow." He walked away. "Without tomorrow, nothing changes."

The door to the locker room suffered Stan's wrath.

Adler and Rheia glared at Gideon.

"I'm guessing he saw some shit on his tours," Gideon said.

Adler and Rheia nodded.

"And for what it's worth, dude, stabbings and shootings bring down major heat. The Troupe doesn't want attention. We wanna disappear. Like the Von Trapps into the Alps, y'know?"

"And Stan isn't wrong, Gid. Someone bleeding out overshadows your message. Also, you bring a *real* weapon? You escalate, put your scene partner on high alert, lose any sense of surprise. Maybe they pull theirs, maybe YOUR tomorrow is threatened. So. Just break their kneecap. You make your point today, they still get a tomorrow. They can heal. Learn. Change. Grow."

"Limp."

Rheia shrugged. "Everything costs something. Time for bullies to pay up. Just giving 'em what they deserve. It's called justice."

"What about mercy?"

"Oh god, you gonna go all *Merchant of Venice* on me? Enough with 'the quality of mercy is not strained' crap."

Adler cackled, tossed his head in a *Brady Bunch*-y singsong: "Portia Portia PORtia!"

Gideon held up his hands. "Just sayin'. Mercy and forgiveness can—"

Rheia slammed the table. "Mercy is simply *not* getting what you deserve, and bullies already live in a world where *not* getting what they deserve is a daily occurrence. Entitlement. Privilege. Society shows them mercy at every turn. The Troupe shows the audience something novel. David and Goliath, right?"

"And David's slingshot is part of his novelty."

"Knives and guns suck up all the oxygen. But you transform an everyday item into an object of power? It becomes more than a weapon. It becomes a totem."

Gideon went to the prop table, ran his hands over the various items. Rheia and Adler went back to editing the script.

Gideon said, "Has the Troupe ever…"

They looked up at him. Gideon chewed his lip.

"Ever what, Giddy Gid?"

"Ever… taken someone's life?"

Adler shook his head but Rheia said, "Not yet."

Gideon and Adler both blinked in surprise.

"What do you mean *yet*??" Gideon said.

"Yeah, whoa, *what*?!" Adler took a step back from her.

Rheia slammed the table again. "Protect tomorrow. Fine. But if a bully threatens the life of an innocent then they've set that rule of engagement. Will I do everything to avoid killing them? Of course, but it's not the morality of it. It's the logistics. Murder is messy, even when justified."

"Justified??" Gideon said.

Adler rubbed his eyes, ruffled his hair, stomped a foot. "OK, hold on, you talking from experience here or…?"

Rheia's jaw clenched. Adler spun around.

"Holy hell, Rheia! I never saw this in your background check!"

"Not as a Troupe member, Adler. This was—"

An alarm wailed from the office. Rheia and Adler stiffened.

"What's that about?" Gideon asked.

They ignored him. The wailing echoed. Adler slipped on his shades.

Rheia gathered the script.

"Oh shit," Adler said. "Get Stan. You gotta boogie."

"I thought we had another couple days, Adler!"

Adler moved faster than Gideon had ever seen. "Well they moved it up, Rheia! GO NOW." He slammed the office door behind him.

"Looks like you get the afternoon off, Gid." She shoved the script in her bag. "Break a leg at your show tonight."

"What's going on? Can I help?"

Rheia answered by sprinting for the locker room.

70

NEAR PLEASANTVILLE, NEW JERSEY

Rheia crouched in the alley. Put on her costume. Wig. Jacket. Wristbands. Shades.

"Adler. Check check."

A potato chip crunching answered her. "Places please."

"All set. Stan make it too?"

"Oh yeah. You two made crazy good time."

Rheia ran over the script in her mind one more time. The Owners had planned simultaneous mob-style attacks of several minority-owned businesses in the area. The goal, according to the thread on the deeply buried One White Nation online message board, was simple. Intimidation and destruction. Drive non-white people out of the neighborhoods that used to enjoy the protection of "racial covenants" between developers and private owners.

Adler had worked his magic and ID'd the locations of the attacks as well as which Owners would be executing each.

Loaded maps into the newly installed GPS in the tactical sunglasses. Script was airtight.

But for some reason the Owners had launched their operation early. Meant a level of improvisation had been added but them's the breaks.

Hope for the best. Plan for the worst.

According to the script, Rheia was about to confront the third highest- ranking "Centurion" and two of his "Legionaries" who were tasked with vandalizing a halal grocery store. Stan was a few blocks away taking on Centurions four and five and their gang, who were targeting a Black Baptist Church.

"The church," Stan had queried at first read-through. "What's their plan?"

"Ummmm..." Adler scrolled. Whistled through his teeth. "Firebombs."

The temperature around Stan plummeted.

"Mine."

"I hear ya, Stan the Man, but there's gonna be like nine guys there. They're planning a media blitz and will have a security perimeter—"

"*Mine.*"

"OK, OK, chill, all good, just sent the map and message thread to your tablet."

Stan had disappeared in a swirl of ice and Rheia had subtitled Act Two: "Stan." Left the page blank. She had personally witnessed the ex-Green Beret take out seven scene partners in under a minute. She felt far more fear for the Owners' skeletal integrity than for Stan's safety.

The other three attacks outlined on the message board Adler had packaged into various anonymous tips that even now were landing in key inboxes and hotlines. Though the accelerated timeline wouldn't allow for all-out ambushes, authorities should have the drop.

But these two attacks they kept for themselves. Nabbing some alone time with three of the top five Centurions? Well now. Some *gentle coaxing*—Stan's term—could lead the Troupe straight to the top of the food chain. Called himself "Primus Pilus," the highest-ranking Centurion in the Owners.

Rheia shook her head in disgust as she tucked her bag behind a garbage can. *God, such morons, don't realize the Roman Army was an ethnic free-for-all.*

She made a final adjustment to her wig. Double-checked her steel baton was cozy in its thigh sheath.

Good to go.

"Adler. Lights up."

"Break a leg."

Rheia stepped not so much quickly as deliberately. Rushing would draw unwanted eyes. Better to be precise. She'd arrive faster anyway.

Dress me slowly, I am in a hurry.

She wove through the parking lot, using the cars for cover.

"You got eyes on the stage?"

Chips crunching. "Store's security cam is inside. Your scene partners have just rounded up the family." Crunch crunch. "Once they're outside I've got a good field of vision from the traffic cam across the street. Can't see you yet."

"How's Stan?"

Crunchy chuckles.

"Reminding me of this video game I used to play, *Splinter Cell.* You know it?"

"Not my jam."

"All stealth. Sneaking through shadows and silent take-downs. I know where Stan is and I still don't see him. Nine guys down to six. None of them yet the wiser."

Wow, Rheia thought as Adler reloaded his mouth with whatever chip brand he was victimizing tonight.

"OK, warning, stand by, they should be coming out the front dooooor... now."

Sure enough the front door of the family-owned halal grocery store slammed open. Two men in old-school hockey goalie masks—garishly painted red, white, and blue—dragged a struggling 30-something Muslim man. They were followed by a woman who had to be the grocer's wife. She was crying and clinging to her two young children. Bringing up the rear was a third masked man, who laughed and idly prodded the mother and kids with a metal baseball bat. His mask had been painted to look like a shrieking bald eagle.

Hello, Centurion.

The first two men threw the grocer to the pavement. He tried to get up but they kicked the ever-loving crap out of him. He turtled on the ground. The family pleaded.

To no avail. The eagle-masked Centurion whirled his bat and smashed out a store window. He turned back to the cringing family.

"Fucking Muslim FILTH! I bet you celebrated when the Towers fell, didn't you??"

The pleading continued. The grocer in his panic switched from accented English to fluent Arabic.

"SPEAK FUCKING ENGLISH!" Eaglemask smashed another window. The two foot soldiers resumed kicking. The mother and children redoubled their wailing.

"So much for subtlety," Rheia muttered.

"That's their plan. They want to send a message. You ready to rock'n'roll?"

The disturbance indeed had the desired effect. An audience was gathering, built from foot traffic and a few cars that had stopped to rubberneck. But they all stayed at a distance, just outside some instinctive, invisible boundary.

Rheia saw a few phones coming out. Most would selfie and

post a self-serving social media update later. Some would film and hope to go viral on YouTube. Maybe a few would livestream. One or two might call 911. Those concerned her. She needed time to interrogate.

"Scramble the cells. Keep an eye out."

"I'm all yours. This just in: Stan has incapacitated all nine, secured the church, and taken the two Centurions to the woodshed."

"Already??"

"Yep. Your turn."

She moved.

71

EAGLEMASK SCREECHED A COMMAND. The two kickers spat on the grocer and cleared.

Now five parking spots away. Rheia angled for a gap between two SUVs.

The bat lofted high. Eaglemask spewed a vile speech. One of his henchmen had his phone out, capturing the glory. The wife scrambled on hands and knees, threw herself across her husband, protecting his battered body with her own.

The audience grew. But not one by-stander dared intervene. No shouts. No stepping forward. No calls for help or threats to summon the authorities.

Rheia allowed herself a burst of speed and the SUVs spit her out behind Eaglemask as the henchmen pulled the wife off her husband.

"We are One White Nation!" Eaglemask proclaimed.

"One White Nation!" the red, white, and blue masks echoed. Eaglemask took aim, a bird of prey about to dive. The grocer cowered. The audience sucked on their horror like straws in a supersize soda.

"Yo! Centurion!" Rheia said.

Eaglemask turned. The bat lowered. Rheia felt the eyes and phones shifting her way. Good. Time to jujitsu these assholes' media blitz against them.

"Don't you think whatever your point is you've made it?"

"Get lost, mongrel bitch," Eaglemask said. He also sensed the phones. He inflated and preened. He was gonna trend all night, spread the Owner gospel far and wide. He turned back toward the diseased Muslim.

"Blindsiding a family with a bat, scaring kids, what kind of coward are you?"

The crowd could've come from central casting. They "ooooh'd" and "aaaaah'd" and nudged each other. Rheia shoved back her judgment. You have to meet the audience where they are.

Eaglemask spun. Tale as old as time. "You want a piece of this, too? HUH??" He shook the bat, took some sort of Jedi-lightsabery fighting stance.

Time to leverage the SUVs.

"You're ridiculous. Your patriotism is pathetic. And that mask? Seriously? Your mommy regurgitate into your mouth when you were a little chickadee?" Rheia puckered her lips and smacked an air kiss across the pavement.

If that hadn't been enough, the tittering reaction of the audience sent Eaglemask over the edge. Abandoning his two henchmen—mistake—he charged at Rheia, clearly intending to decapitate her. Rheia pretended to be intimidated and reversed two steps, putting herself between the SUVs. Eaglemask instinctively adjusted his swing out of the horizontal plane. Now the bat attack was coming vertically, his arms extended high.

This of course left his midsection entirely exposed.

Just before Eaglemask began his downward strike, Rheia

launched forward and snapped a front kick into his belt buckle. Newtonian physics and mathematical calculations conspired to focus almost a ton of force into the few square inches momentarily connecting Rheia's heel with Eaglemask's belly.

He may as well have driven his car thirty miles per hour into a tree.

His diaphragm contracted, blowing out his breath like a bellows. He staggered back, gasping and retching. Rheia followed tight, surprised he had managed to hold on to the bat.

The audience rumbled with bloodlust.

Eaglemask mustered another swing but Rheia was inside the arc. She caught the bat down near the grip with one hand and snapped her other elbow into Eaglemask's jaw.

More Newtonian number-crunching. Mass. Vectors. Acceleration. The mask cracked. Human blood leaked from fractured feathers.

"Right on the button!" some wannabe ringside commentator howled from the crowd.

Rheia again suppressed her impatience with the average citizen while noting that the commentator had accurately assessed her strike. Eaglemask was out cold on his feet. She pulled the bat from his numb fingers, caught him by a jacket sleeve, and lowered him to the pavement.

The two henchmen hustled her way. They fanned out, trying to surround her. Rheia saw one of them digging into a pocket.

Knife. So be it.

Rheia feinted at the other to freeze him, felt Pocket-Digger get excited and start to rush. Typical. She pivoted and chest-passed the bat at Pocket-Digger, not trying to harm with the improvised projectile, just distract.

Pocket-Digger skittered to a stop and raised both hands to deflect. The bat caromed harmlessly off his forearms. He reached again for his knife—*oh he was gonna cut this mystery bitch UP*—but then he felt something... odd.

Rheia had stomped her heel to the outside of his knee.

The *crack* of dislocated kneecap was a sound containing no Hollywood glamour. The cheers building up around the commentator choked and left a vacuum of wincing silence that Pocket-Digger obligingly filled with primal howls.

He slashed at her with the knife that finally had found its way out of his pocket. She sharply parried with the baton that had leaped from thigh to fist. The knife hopscotched away. He stood there empty-handed, hobbled, humiliated.

So be it.

Rheia loaded up a Wimbledon-worthy backhand, heavy on the topspin.

Newton tapped out. No math necessary here.

The sound of carbonized steel on painted plastic was sunlight glaring off chrome, forcing your gaze away. Pocket-Digger timbered. His mask lay in shattered pieces next to his unconscious body.

The grocer and his family stared at her. The second henchman stared at her. The audience stared at her. Phones reflected at her. This would be the time for the speech.

"How'm I looking, Adler?" she sub-vocalized, moving her lips as little as possible.

Crunch crunch.

"Sorry, Rheia, someone in the hookah bar across the street landlined 911. I missed it."

"But Stan corralled two Centurions?"

"Oh yeah. You can totally exit stage right. We got what we came for."

Rheia head-faked at the second henchman. He flinched away so hard he tripped over his own feet and parked his ass perfectly in the "Expecting Mothers Only" spot. As the phones all followed the henchman's descent, Rheia pulled out her own, held it high, and panned across the audience as though taking her own video.

She once again heard the commentator: "Hey, the ninja lady is filming us." Fingers pointed, phones refocused, Rheia waited a few tense seconds—straining to hear any approaching sirens—willed the audience into a quivering quiet.

Rheia lowered her phone and looked at it as though reviewing her footage. She shook her head with deliberate slowness, the iconic image of parental disappointment. She looked up at the audience, her reflective shades making it seem she was picking each of them out individually. Some glared back. Some avoided her gaze. Some actually looked down. She carved a disgusted snort out of the air.

The audience shifted, shamed by her silence. Commentator spoke up. "What are you gonna do with that video?"

Rheia pocketed her phone. "What are you gonna do with yours?"

Eaglemask stirred and sat up. Rheia picked up the bat and popped a jab to his beak with the knob. He re-sprawled. She reached down, yanked his mask off, pointed it at the second henchman still on his butt.

"Take it off."

He did.

"Turn around. Go on, now. Let 'em all see you."

He did. They did. If the sudden gasps were any indication at least a few of them knew him. Delicious.

"See? White supremacists hide behind our flag. It's up to all of us to call bullshit. Make sure you film their real faces. I'd love to see them all on the news losing their jobs."

She walked away toward the alley. Now the first siren was audible. The audience shifted again, some deciding to get while the gettin' was good, some congregating to compare notes, others adjusting to better vantage points to watch the next act.

Rheia ignored them all and kept walking.

"Adler, anyone following me?"

"Stage door clear, no autograph seekers. But Starsky and Hutch are close, don't dally. Also can you pick up some salt and vinegar Pringles on your way back? I've OD'd on cool ranch, need something tangy."

"Only if you kill that traffic cam for me."

"Deal!" Crunch crunch. "Done! Parking lot is flying blind. Enjoy your public!"

She cleared the corner of the grocery store and shifted into a higher gear. Retrieved her bag. Kept moving. Sunglasses, wristbands, and wig all in. Nondescript ball cap out and on. Microfiber cloth—not just for cleaning reading glasses—wiped carefully but quickly up and down the bat and mask. Both tossed into a stack of empty produce crates.

Rheia reached the end of the alley and turned left, sticking tight to the building. Peeled off her jacket, pulled the sleeves through, reversing it from solid black to shamrock green. The sirens had multiplied. The first sounded a couple blocks away.

She curled around the corner and came up behind the crowd. Mingled with the audience to wait it out.

Commentator got his moment of glory, recounting every detail for an officer taking statements.

Phone recordings were uploaded and downloaded.

Eaglemask and Pocket-Digger groped back into conscious-ness and joined Henchman in vigorous protests, but eyewitness testimony cuffed them all into cruiser back seats.

The grocer and his family, after a quick interview, zoomed away in an ambulance. Looked like he'd be OK, if sore for several days. Coulda been a lot worse.

Most importantly Rheia saw multiple fingers pointing cops

across the parking lot toward the far corner of the store and alley entrance. The bat and mask were quickly dug up and two squad cars zipped away, tracking the pony-tailed woman in the black jacket and reflective sunglasses.

According to Commentator the woman was apparently "some kind of badass."

72

"God bless you, my sister."

Pastor Steve embraced the sobbing woman. Recently widowed. House in foreclosure. Children hungry. Targeted when she came to the weekly food bank. Ushered into his office. A few kind words. An offering of shelter. Water in the desert.

She would make a fine addition to his collection.

"Brother Timothy, show our newest sister to her quarters. Get her children enrolled in our school just as quick as you can."

"Right away, Pastor Steve! Sister, right this way."

The door closed. Pastor Steve slipped through a hidden hatch in the back corner of his office. Emerged into his private sanctum as AlphaSupreme.

Security feeds blanketed the compound. News scrolled. Multiple stations carried the same press conference. He unmuted one screen. Congressman Wilder's unmistakable voice.

...proud to co-sponsor these bills with my colleague,

Congresswoman Mallory, and walk beside her at the upcoming Unity March...

AlphaSupreme scowled. How many more would be contaminated by this non-White welp? She was proving troublesome.

...We must stop thinking of politics as a zero-sum game. Because here's the truth—we all want the same things. Neither party is trying to destroy America...

But AlphaSupreme absolutely wanted to destroy America. Because America was no longer pure. No longer belonged to those who had fought for and founded and built it. No. America was beyond saving. It needed to be razed to the ground so that AlphaSupreme and those others God had chosen could rebuild it.

...I'll be FRANK (the heathen reporters obligingly chuckled), *that's just silly. We all want more and better jobs. We all want good health care and strong education for our children. We may disagree on the precise policies that will achieve those goals but as long as we focus on the commonality of the goals themselves we can surely find ways to work together...*

Ah yes. The children. AlphaSupreme gazed with wonder upon the images of his children working all across the compound.

Jude and Agnes... by far the most special. Though Agnes would need to be brought to heel sooner than later. The Enemy could so easily warp those brilliant minds. So he protected them. Kept them hidden and focused on the work. They knew they had siblings but not the true extent of the Flock. Their dozens of half-brothers and sisters. Each measured and tested and set to the tasks best suiting them.

Some cooked, cleaned, laundered. Others maintained the various buildings: nursery, classrooms, living quarters, sanctuary, dining commons, gymnasium, factory. Nurses, teachers, gardeners, mechanics. Some hired hands. Some volunteers from the congregation. Some refugees, like the sobbing woman and her children who would soon find their places.

But most tied together by AlphaSupreme's blood. His eyes flicked from screen to screen picking out his paternal features in the faces and figures of the various Flock buzzing with daily activity.

...If there's one thing the lockdown taught us it's that we all have much more in common than we realized...

The lockdown! Such a blessing. Supplies. Infrastructure. Preparations. So much further along now and with far less fear of being discovered. While the weak cowered in quarantine, AlphaSupreme and his Flock had put nose to grindstone and achieved years of progress in mere months.

...and being a one-issue voter isn't enough. No one wants more abortions but I'll own up to the facts on this one. Abortions go down during Democratic administrations and either hold or go up during Republican administrations. So we need to ask the real question—what policies are more effective at achieving our shared goals? And then get our damn agendas out of the way and get to work...

"Oh Wilder," AlphaSupreme thought. "I shall pray for your soul. But if you are not for me, you are against me."

Although AlphaSupreme had also learned the inverse is just as true. If you aren't against me, you are FOR me.

AlphaSupreme saw one of his younger sons leaning against the barn, enjoying a break from toil in a patch of sunlight.

Except break wasn't for another seven minutes.

He made a note to cleanse the pre-teen that evening at vespers. Public example.

He sighed. Humans were lazy. In constant need of a shepherd even as they resisted being told what to do. Most of them wanted nothing more than to stay home and have their affairs and self-medicate and bathe in the glow of their screens, consuming and ever consuming.

AlphaSupreme often wondered if inertia was the true nature of the Holy Ghost. *The majority of your followers don't possess the constitution to be Apostles, to live on the mountaintop. But as long as they sit in their La-Z-Boys and express "concern," their cumulative inaction gathers into a force. And that force... might that be the Holy Ghost? The smoke that gets into your clothes and refuses to wash out?*

Because inertia has a vector. Even the laziest face a direction. So get them pointed in the direction you want, then even standing still they serve your work. Like a *chevalier de frise*, glistening spikes and spears repelling the Enemy's charge.

...My colleague Stacy talks a lot about the underbelly of our history. Those events we'd rather forget because they show our country in an unflattering light. But here's the thing. She is at heart an optimist. She is not denigrating our nation by bringing up the less savory details of our past. She believes we can do better, can BE better. But only if we understand where we come from. As my high school history teacher loved to say: history doesn't repeat itself, but it sure likes to rhyme...

AlphaSupreme nodded. He recognized principles. Principles don't pick sides, thus it is a mistake to underestimate the intelligence of the Enemy. The Enemy knew as well as he that history is built of *tiny* moments, not large ones.

Consider the metropolis of Kyoto, spared the fate of Nagasaki simply because Secretary of War Henry Stimson crossed it off the shortlist. Reason? He had honeymooned there before the war. And thus did Nagasaki burn under a mushroom cloud while Kyoto survived. Tens of thousands of lives on a knife's edge. No foreknowledge, no control, no agency.

History is forged with nudges.

As is human behavior. When they think they are deciding

for themselves yet do what you want, that is when you truly have them. Imperceptible yet constant pressure.

...We must find the humility to see the bad in ourselves as well as the good in those who disagree with us. No human or country is all one or the other. George Washington heroically stepped down, first as Commander of the Continental Army, then as President, when no law or precedent required him to do so. He could have been a king but put the nation first. This is true. Yet it also is true that George Washington enslaved other humans, who were only released upon his death. Paradox is the only basket large enough to hold truth...

But Wilder. Don't you understand that God created certain humans to serve others? Women to serve men. The White Race to rule, others in their appropriate places.

AlphaSupreme opened a journal, drafted notes.

"Even Paul, the greatest apostle, did not fundamentally change. God understands this about us. God appeared to Saul on the road to Tarsus. Blinded him. Three days later Ananias visited. The scales fell from Saul's eyes. He became Paul. But had he changed? NO. His personality was the same. His zealotry was the same. His ego. His charisma. The same. God just nudged him in a different direction. You already believe. You are already washed in His blood. He is not asking you to turn one hundred and eighty degrees. He is asking only for two or three. What direction might God nudge you in, what might you accomplish for His glory, if only you would let Him?"

Basic idea, rough. He would craft it to be homey and comforting for his Flock, violent and convicting for THE SCOURGE. When you realize the spectrum of human nature is a circle as opposed to a straight line, you see that recruits can come from either direction.

...Stacy and I disagree plenty. But we are willing to have the necessary conversations. We are willing—and I know this is a

dirty word—to compromise a little to gain a lot. Because we overlap on far more than we don't. Common ground. Frankly (titter titter), *it does exist.*

Reporters softballed questions. AlphaSupreme switched a screen to Jude's brilliant social media aggregate tracker. Average, uninformed citizens who considered themselves expert commentators, right and left, started ranting and raving about what Wilder had just said. Where most would hear a cacophony of self-righteousness, AlphaSupreme heard a symphony of opportunity.

Again he thanked God for the lockdown. Being forced online had been a boon. Jude and Agnes, at first tasked simply with ensuring that the wider Flock could still partake of Sunday sermons from their living rooms, discovered that virtual worship could explode their real numbers.

Inertia. Convenience.

Parishioners seized onto the ease of clicking "like" or "share." Why bother getting dressed, driving, sitting next to each other, feeling trapped through the entirety of a service? Why not sit in comfort, in your underwear, eating snacks, avoiding traffic, avoiding the boring parts by dragging a slider through a time-stamped video?

And another manifestation of the Holy Ghost: why waste time and effort evangelizing real people when you could marshal fake people to do it for you?

Jude found you can buy twenty-five thousand fake Twitter followers for $225.

Nudges. Smoke creeping into woven fibers.

Agnes deep-dived on troll farms and bots. Inundated the social media of the Flock with alleged friends and enemies and commentators and "likers."

Fabrications. Ghosts.

The Flock swelled. Inertia multiplied at exponential rates.

Extremism rooted in potential Apostles. All because of some 1's and o's.

AlphaSupreme idly wondered if a prayer offered by a virtual person found its way to the real God.

He had been skeptical at first. Jude and Agnes devised an experiment to convince him. They created two online groups of opposing views out of thin air. Paid a measly couple hundred bucks to post a handful of ads.

They scheduled real protests for both fake groups on the same day, in the same location. One protesting guns, the other gun control. They left the specifics vague. Humans are genius at enraging themselves.

Nudge. Nudge. Nudge.

Agnes and Jude took their hands off the keyboards. Told their Father to sit back. Watch. Nothing up our sleeves.

The two protests went viral.

Two batches of protestors gathered. They saw each other. They clashed. Many protestors bled. Several spent the night in jail. Membership in both fake groups skyrocketed.

The scales fell from AlphaSupreme's eyes.

He had Agnes and Jude set up scores of fake pages, most religious or patriotic, tapping into the already simmering militia groups. Some of them, though, he skewed toward the social justice and cancel culture crowd. Know thy enemy.

The most active group had been One White Nation. Agnes had the idea to create a mythical figure to lead the group, "Primus Pilus." And Jude played the role perfectly, dropping cryptic hints, making hazy promises, nudging the Owners to overt action.

In fact, in just a couple days, the Centurions and their Legionaries were scheduled to launch the first of what Alpha-Supreme hoped would be an ongoing series of grassroots attacks that would—

A message from the basement pinged on his central screen and a couple of the news channels blared with breaking news.

"...Authorities report that multiple white supremacist plots were foiled near Atlantic City..."

Father. The Owners have been thwarted tonight. We are investigating.

AlphaSupreme's journal flew across the room. The story of Saul-Paul splattered against the door. Brother Timothy, on the other side and about to knock, backed away.

He knew better than to interrupt Pastor Steve's prayers.

73

It didn't matter what Aniyah sent, what she scanned or pho- tographed. Spearhead rejected all evidence.

Obviously fake.

Jazzie's birth certificate.

Nice forgery.

Baby pictures. Report cards. Crayon-art that had hung on the refrigerator like a Monet in a museum.

Photoshopped. Edited. Any kid could have drawn that.

Aniyah blazed. Pounded brutal keystrokes.

"FINE. But even if Jazzie didn't exist—WHICH SHE DID!—that doesn't prove I'm a 'crisis actor.' What proof do YOU have of THAT?"

Her inbox vomited attachments. Pictures upon pictures. She gasped. If she hadn't known for a fact that she hadn't been present at these horrific scenes, she herself would have believed it.

"That's not me."

Lie.

"I wasn't there, I wasn't at any of these—"

A jpeg. Jazzie's school. Lines of confused, crying children. Shell-shocked teachers. Hollow-eyed parents cordoned by cops. Weary ambulances. Top left corner. Her husband. His face photographically frozen in a rictus of pain. His arms holding up a woman who forever shrieks into his chest. Her profile just visible through disheveled hair.

That *was* her.

"This one." She sent it back. "This one IS me. That's Jazzie's school. Third ambulance from the right. Jazzie is inside."

So you admit it??!

"That's the only one that's real!"

Suuuuure.

"The others aren't me!"

Sure do look like you.

Aniyah saw an opening. "Then they must be fake! If you can believe that all the pictures and evidence I send you are faked, why don't you have any doubt about these??"

There was no way Aniyah could know it, but that thought had never occurred to Spearhead. His fingers froze over the keyboard.

But the human creature is designed to crush cognitive dissonance. Just as quickly his fingers thawed.

Typical libtard doublethink.

Aniyah stifled a scream, not wanting to bring Imani running. The crushing internal pressure turned the rough coal of an impulse into the bright diamond of an idea. An idea she immediately knew was foolhardy and dangerous. But necessary.

She typed before she could talk herself out of it.

"MEET ME."

74

Spearhead pressed deep into Florida's interior. The belly of the beast. You can feel it in Florida… humans aren't meant to live here. At best humankind exists in an uneasy truce with the massive, hungry peninsula. But turn your back? You can feel nature creeping up to reclaim whatever "civilization" you've had the gall to erect.

But Spearhead knew how to navigate. Granddad had raised him to recognize the grunting bellow of the gator, to read currents of inlets and bays and swamps. To find his way in, and more importantly to find his way back out.

As he maneuvered the skiff Spearhead told himself that he'd left the lying bitch hanging. He could never admit that her challenge—"MEET ME"—had twisted red hot in his gut.

What could she want? Was it a setup? Had she been playing him this whole time? If he showed up would he find himself swarmed by cops and disappeared into an interrogation center??

Admitting to him that one of the pictures *was* her? He had to admire the audacity. Sly sly sly.

He breathed deep. Salt air and isolation. He was the only human for miles, floating on the little skiff under a moonless night. The engine puttered.

Florida watched him. Tensed to pounce.

Spearhead should have expected such a move from a professional liar. Was he already too overexposed? He should have—

A jaguar roared close by, an unmistakable sound, like a saw chewing through wood. Spearhead hunched down, searched the overhanging canopy. The sawing faded but Spearhead knew the large, invisible cat was watching.

And it clicked.

What if HE set the trap for HER? After all, a face-to-face with a flesh and blood crisis actor? Just think what he could learn! Think of the opportunity not only to unmask the Deep State but to lift himself in the esteem of his White Brothers, and even in the eyes of AlphaSupreme!

The skiff caromed off a half-submerged fallen tree. Water and branches grasped at him. Florida's maw opened. Spearhead scrambled to balance and pushed back into the relative safety of open water. He cursed himself for his lack of vigilance. Refocused. Test first. Tomorrow he could start setting his ambush for the liar.

He wiped his brow, licked his lips, tasted brine. Felt his heart accelerating with anticipation.

The hand of AlphaSupreme had guided him here.

The soldering had come easy. The electronics even easier. The chemistry was trickiest. Gathering all the necessary materials had taken some fancy footwork, covering tracks and bouncing transactions through multiple accounts.

Never leave a trail. He had learned that from Florida.

The engine puttered.

He settled upon a particular stretch of mangroves. Set

several devices. Checked wires. Acquired signals. Ignored the hordes of tree crabs scuttling over the bark. They didn't have long for this world anyway.

Puttered away. Thought about it. Puttered further. Better safe than sorry.

Spearhead opened his phone, swiped to the appropriate screen, offered a prayer, pressed a button.

Crocodiles, panthers, red tail hawks, all manner of life fled from the fireball.

The heat reached for him, fell just short. A fine mist of water returning to earth, however, *did* reach him.

Spearhead waited as long as he could, his eardrums ringing and his blood pounding, then puttered back to the mangrove.

It was obliterated. Dead fish floated everywhere. Birds unlucky enough to have been nesting in the blast radius hung like tattered flags in mangled branches. Hell, he'd even gotten a fucking manatee.

He puttered away, test passed, ready to act as Alpha-Supreme's strong right hand. And eager to lure the liar.

Florida licked its wounds and let him go.

This time.

75

Four tumblers of Highland Park 15 and one tumbler of sparkling water clinked together.

"Terrific speech, sir," Ty said, sipping his Perrier.

"Thank you, Ty," Wilder said. "Though I must give credit where credit is due. Thank-you, Stacy, for the loan of your intern. He's quite the editor."

Samar, already choking on Scotch fumes, choked again.

"We're quite fond of him," Stacy said, giving Samar a wink. He smiled weakly, tried to speak, coughed again, gave a wobbly thumbs-up.

Wilder said, "That 'history likes to rhyme' bit, where did he come up with that? So good."

Amelia chuckled. "That's actually one of my stories, Congressman. My history teacher blew my mind open. Inspired me toward a career in politics."

Ty toasted her. "Don't let the facts get in the way of a good story."

She toasted back. "The lie that tells the truth."

"Picasso," Ty said.

"That's right," Amelia said.

"I know."

Amelia's dimples and Ty's smile exchanged phone numbers.

Samar had finally stopped coughing. "It's just stand-up."

They all looked at him. He squeaked.

"What do you mean, Samar?" Stacy asked.

He took a huge breath. "When I was a kid I wanted so bad to be a comedian. For my birthday one year my parents got me a week at a stand-up boot camp. The lead instructor ran her own comedy club. She told us that the best comics connect with the audience by being vulnerable. And that vulnerability comes from poking fun at yourself instead of punching down on others. So a first-person story is way funnier than telling a story about someone else."

He took a big swallow, forgetting it was Scotch. He spluttered. "Mmmm. This is... this is really good." Everyone hid their grins.

"Go on, young man," Wilder said. "I think I see where you're going, but finish your thought."

"So if you hear a funny story, in stand-up your best move is to—"

"Steal it," Ty said.

Samar wiped his brow. "Well, yeah, or, y'know, just *claim* the bit as your own. Make yourself the central character. Have that odd thing happen to *you* as you work it into your set. It's still the truth, just funnier."

"Well I'll drink to that," Stacy said, and the five tumblers clinked again.

"So. Stacy."

"Yes, Frank?"

"This Unity March."

"Amelia's brainchild. Multiple cities, same day. And within each city... Amelia, you explain."

"Within each city, rather than a singular route, we've identified a central destination. We're organizing local leaders to lead smaller marches from their own neighborhoods to that destination, so the several small marches meld into one large gathering. Truly come together and unify. A stage. Music. A speech or two. Food trucks."

Wilder refilled his glass. "Yes, all that I understand. I think it's terrific. I wanted to suggest that you and I, though, Stacy, change where we make our appearance."

"Oh? You don't want to do Richmond? Former capital of the Confederacy, we can push hard against all the Robert E. Lee and Jefferson Davis monuments."

Samar was Scotch-loosened. "You know Lee him*self* was against Confederate monuments?" He hiccuped. "Yeah, he didn't want any statues and streets and busts and stuff, he wanted the country to moooove ooooon. None of that 'Lost Cause' poppycock." He took another slug. "WOW this is good!"

Amelia traded Samar's tumbler for a bottled water. "Here ya go, kid."

"You have another place in mind, Frank?"

"I do. Ty came across something. Ty?"

Ty put down his water, picked up his tablet, flicked open a saved browser tab, handed it to Stacy. Amelia read over Stacy's shoulder.

"Last election," Ty said, "Florida voters overwhelmingly supported an amendment to their state constitution that restored voting rights to over a million people."

"Ex-cons," Amelia said. "I read about that. People who served out their time on felony convictions but weren't having their right to vote restored."

"Exactly," Ty said. "Now, I'm a huge champion for election integrity—"

"Nice euphemism," Amelia said.

"But when my side wins—"

"IF."

"—I want it to be on the up and up. Gerrymandering. 'Stop the Steal.' Crock of crap. No honor in cheating your way to victory."

"I agree."

"I know."

Even Samar noted the heat between dimples and smile.

Wilder cleared his throat. "But now Florida's state legislature is pulling every string to undo the will of the voters."

Stacy's knuckles turned white on the tablet. "They're instituting a poll tax??"

Ty nodded. "Even when someone serves out their time, they aren't allowed to vote until they've paid off their LFO's."

"Flying saucers??" Samar gasped.

Amelia patted him on the arm. "Drink your water."

"Legal financial obligations," Stacy muttered. "Outstanding court fees, fines, restitutions, whatever."

Ty said, "Not only that, Congresswoman, but the state has no central database for returning citizens to even figure out their LFO amount. The records are scattered. Piecemeal. Inaccurate."

"And the cherry on top," Wilder said, "is that Florida also requires returning citizens to swear under penalty of perjury they are eligible to vote."

"And how are they supposed to know if they're eligible when Florida can't even tell them if or what they owe," Stacy said.

"Classic FUBAR catch-22," Ty said.

"*Sea*biscuit!"

The room seethed. Samar guzzled water.

"So. Frank."

"Yes, Stacy?"

"This Unity March."

"Mmmhmmm."

"Let's you and me go to Florida."

76

THE NEXT COUPLE DAYS, Gideon kept showing up to the Rehearsal Room. Adler buzzed him in but never came out of the office. Not a peep from Rheia or Stan. Gideon had Carlos and the props all to himself.

He worked. He practiced. He mulled.

He knocked on the office door.

"Adler? Seriously man, what's going on? Is there something I could be doing?"

No response, even though he could hear Adler inside muttering and flapping.

Back to breaking Carlos' bones.

The weekend arrived. Final five shows in fifty hours. Closing night party. Bittersweet.

Monday morning. Run. Rehearsal Room. Buzzed in. Empty. Not even Adler in the office.

Sweaty afternoon experimenting with props. *How do you strike with a book?* Extra-long shower. Headed to class.

No Rheia.

Imani rushing in just before warm-ups, solo.

"You ok?" Gideon asked.

"I'm good, just got held up at work. By the way, you're looking good." She blushed. "I mean, like, ripped."

"I'm... what?"

"You been working out or something? I mean your jaw, your shoulders—"

"Oh, yeah, thanks." Couldn't very well explain Stan. "Some extra push-ups with my runs."

"Well whatever your secret is, it's working. Do share." She waggled her eyebrows.

He laughed but felt her eyes probing. "No Aniyah tonight?"

"Yeah, no, she woke up with a migraine, so she stayed in all day."

"Ugh. Brutal."

"Yeah, I gotta let Alfonso know."

Gideon had forgotten. Tonight after class was Alfonso's show. Dan and Joan presented flowers and apologies. Grandkids. Surprise visit.

"We'll catch you next time! Promise!" Dan said.

Joan gave Alfonso a big big hug. "Break all the legs, sweetie." Everyone else shared cabs from the Hatchery to Brooklyn. Opening acts. Appetizers upon appetizers. Rounds and rounds of drinks. Gideon allowed himself one. It was good. *Too* good. Switched to soda with bitters and lime.

Then Alfonso appeared. And Salsa Verde owned the stage.

The students hooted and hollered. The little cabaret theatre stretched at its seams to contain the exuberant performer and delighted audience. Gideon noted Alfonso applying lessons from class. Salsa Verde shimmered and glowed. The performance rollicked through a pristine set of lip-synced songs, from Rosemary Clooney to Lady Gaga to yes indeed Barry Manilow.

They congregated outside on the sidewalk post-show, waiting for Alfonso to change. Emma entertained with an on-point imitation of Salsa Verde's take on "Come On-A My House." Rasheed sang a surprisingly harmonic back-up. Marcel answered rapid-fire questions from Tosha and Kaida, who weeks ago had claimed him as their adoptive grandfather. Evan and Imani clapped along.

Alfonso emerged. Adulations burst forth. Selfies and hugs galore.

Gideon found himself wrapped in Alfonso's arms. Glitter that had evaded the hurried backstage wipe-down pollinated his clothing. Salsa Verde's voice murmured in his ear, "Thank you thank you thank you."

Gideon grinned big and patted his overjoyed student on the cheek. He was about to offer his own congratulatory words...

But a harsh sonic squelch pierced the night.

And here came a roiling group of chanters waving flags and home-made placards painted with calls to repent and pray. A braying bull- horn amplified the terrified hatred spewing from the mouth of their shaggy-haired leader.

"ADAM AND EVE, NOT ADAM AND STEVE! THIS IS NOT ENTERTAINMENT! THIS IS DEPRAVITY AND ABOMINATION! REPENT OR FACE GOD'S WRATH IN THIS WORLD AND THE NEXT!"

"Well shit," Alfonso said. "The cabaret manager told me this might happen. This homophobic gang keeps showing up to harass the performers and patrons."

Gideon glanced at the front door. Sure enough, the manager was already on the phone outlining the nature of his emergency.

A righteous finger pointed. "There's one, right there!" The bullhorn zeroed in on Alfonso, who still sported green eye make-up and carried a menagerie of feathered accessories under one arm.

"YOU! ABOMINATION! FILTH! REPENT NOW! YOU HAVE BEEN LED ASTRAY!"

"I go to mass every week!" Alfonso yelled back. He noted Gideon's raised eyebrows. "Seriously, every week. Love me some saints."

The bullhorn squealed.

The cabaret manager stomped out, bellowing that he had "had enough goddammit!"

The bullhorn brayed.

Rasheed and Evan stepped forward shoulder to shoulder, trying to intimidate the increasingly frothy-mouthed leader.

The bullhorn squelched.

Tosha tried to keep Imani from sticking her finger into faces as Kaida and Emma pleaded with everyone to *calm down calm down please calm down!*

The bullhorn called to arms. The chanting mutated into shouting.

Marcel, trying to keep his new granddaughters out of harm's way, squeezed into the simmering scrum. And someone, whether inadvertently or with intent, shoved him. Marcel tumbled into the street.

Sudden quiet as everyone looked.

The calm...

Marcel's temple was striped with blood. His glasses were shattered.

...the storm.

Screams. Accusations. Counter-accusations.

Tosha and Kaida helped Marcel stand and shepherded him to the side as shoving erupted in earnest. The bullhorn was ripped from the leader's hand and smashed to the pavement. Indignation tipped into fury. Battle lines drew up. A no man's land emerged, all parties instinctively forming a cage of bodies inside of which those willing to trade blows could once again test the theory of might making right.

Gideon shielded Alfonso at the fringe. He saw Rasheed, Evan, and Imani squaring up against the leader and a few of the more menacing protestors. He desperately wished for Rheia.

Instead he got Stan's voice in his head.

Hope for the best, plan for the worst. Try to deescalate. But if that proves impossible...

"Alfonso, stay here."

...then strike not to cause pain, but to inflict a wound.

Alfonso's protests bounced off his back as Gideon stepped forward.

Incapacitate.

77

Stan's voice continued.

Always move forward. Most scene partners wilt under pressure. They're not accustomed to aggression. Get your counter in first. Use a parry to advance.

Gideon willed the cacophony to fade. He imagined entering a stage, lights rising, house full. His every nerve tuned in, reached out.

Gideon saw his students shifting into athletic stances. Saw the leader and his gaggle of protestors likewise dropping their centers of gravity. He could read the future like choreography. Angles of bodies. Positions of feet. Vectors of fists.

Hands and feet are weapons. How are weapons propelled? Via joints. Take out joints. Weapons become dead weight.

The characters snapped into focus.

Rasheed had every intention of striking first. He had been under pressure his whole life. A dam always about to burst.

The thick-necked protestor to the leader's left would hold back, look to get in close and squeeze, while the whippet-thin protestor to the leader's right gave off the vibe of a frenzied puncher.

The leader himself, buzzing like a possessed prophet? Would he actually fight, or just let his lackeys do it for him?

Unclear. Martyrs are the most dangerous.

Or disrupt mobility. Break a hand, it can't grab you. Break a foot, it can't draw power from the earth.

Gideon hesitated on the edge of no man's land. How best to leverage all the data pouring in? Stan's voice like an operating system spinning in the background.

Or disrupt the senses. Four of the five are located in the face and head. Especially target vision. Theatricality. Misdirection. Surprise.

Gideon took a breath.

And always move forward.

Gideon invaded no man's land, striding between Rasheed and the whippet. The volume dipped. Gideon pulled on all his diaphragmic training.

"This is everyone's chance to walk away."

He spoke loud enough to be heard but didn't strain or try to shout over. Those in charge don't need to yell. Everyone listens when the boss whispers.

For a moment the tide receded. Gideon hoped the calm surface didn't mask churning depths. He knew he could strike in defense. But incapacitating? Carlos was an unfeeling dummy. These protestors, for all their bile and hate, were already hurting.

It had been an illusion. The tide had pulled out only to gather into a wave. Gideon saw the whitecaps forming and initiated his counter a beat before the whippet sprang at him.

Yep. Frenzied puncher.

Gideon flowed through a variation of the disarm move Stan

and Rheia had browbeaten into him. The whippet's fist darted at him. *Deflect outward. Underneath, up and over.*

But instead of the final twist popping loose a firearm, it popped the whippet's wrist into a wince-inducing angle. The whippet instinctively turned his back to ease the pressure on his joint, so Gideon planted a firm shove into his shoulder. The one-and-a-half-second flurry of movement ended with the whippet right back where he had started, massaging his wrist and looking lost.

The crowd murmured.

"Walk away," Gideon said. "Go home."

The leader, the thick-neck, and the whippet looked at each other.

The tide pulled. And this time the thick-neck rode the wave forward. Reached out with beefy hands.

Gideon held his ground. Slapsticked his own hands onto the thick-neck's wrists, gave a tiny tug as though intending to pull and throw. A bluff. The thick-neck instinctively resisted and pulled back hard. Gideon simultaneously pushed, adding all his strength to the thick-neck's chosen vector.

The thick-neck staggered backward. His arms flailed like an old-timey cartoon character. Down he went on his backside.

Laughter from the spectators.

Shit, Gideon thought. Wounded pride would not lead to de-escalation. Nor would emboldened others jumping in to rumble. He had to end this.

As the leader helped the thick-neck up, Adler pushed past Stan and cackled in Gideon's brain.

You ever watch America's Funniest Home Videos? Or those 'fail' videos on YouTube? Pain is funny, dude. Kid whacks daddy in the balls. Backyard stunt goes bad. Hilaaaarious. But the video always cuts away before you see bone sticking through skin, y'know? You want the audience to laugh? Cause pain. You wanna shut 'em up? Cause injury.

Rheia joined Stan behind Adler, watching in Gideon's mind, waiting to see if Gideon had it in him.

The tide pulled. The thick-neck and the whippet surfed together.

The audience leaned in.

Gideon moved forward. Which absolutely no one had expected, outnumbered as he was two to one.

He went straight at the whippet, who froze in indecision at Gideon's decisiveness. He unfroze when Gideon landed a perfect kick—lowest part of shin to outside of knee— bending over with a howl. His face became low-hanging fruit. Gideon's knee plucked it.

The whippet crumpled. Gideon waited an interminable half-second for the thick-neck to arrive and wrap him in a bear hug from behind.

Exactly as Gideon expected.

Gideon flicked his head backward, the back of his skull love-tapping the thick-neck's nose. He intended only to stun but his adrenaline was surging. Based on the response of the audience, he'd drawn blood.

Gideon latched his hands onto a thick-neck forearm, pirouetted, and torqued the trapped arm high between the thick-neck's shoulder blades. He tangled his foot into the thick-neck's legs, shoved hard, and the thick-neck for the second time tripped and plummeted. The pavement delivered a series of blows to face, chest, shoulder, palm, and knee.

The floor is a weapon.

"Gideon!"

Alfonso's voice reached Gideon three steps ahead of the leader, who had been biding his time, looking to land a cheap shot. But Gideon, while thankful for Alfonso's warning, was already turning. Time had slowed. Edges were crystal clear. He assessed the leader, still two steps away. *Overcommitted haymaker.*

Gideon realized this is how he must have looked to Stan when he first "cast" the bat. All for show.

Again Gideon advanced. Slow and smooth, easy two-step. The leader couldn't pull his punch. It missed by a mile. Gideon used the leader's momentum to slam their rib cages together. Gideon expected it, his breath was fine. But the leader's breath was knocked clean out.

Close quarters, heart to heart like this, Gideon could fight blindfolded. Wrestling is all about feel.

He found handfuls of the leader's jacket. Easy.

He lowered his center of gravity. Yawn.

He turned and tossed the leader over his shoulder like a sack of laundry. Whee!

The whippet was groggy on the ground. The thick-neck rolled around mewling. The leader lay on his back, gasping for breath. His hand and wrist were knotted in the jacket sleeve clenched in Gideon's implacable grip.

Gideon didn't have to raise his voice. "I say again. All of you. Walk away. Go home."

The protestors shuffled in place. But the leader was having none of it. He screamed, pointing at Alfonso and Gideon from his back.

"DO NOT YIELD! ERADICATE THIS FILTH! SAVE ME AND—"

Rheia snapped her fingers. The leader's voice faded and Gideon felt time slow almost to stopping. The Troupe stepped out of his mind's shadows.

Adler clucked his tongue. "You're holding back, dude."

"And you've given them every chance," Stan said.

"Them?" Gideon asked.

"Incapacitation isn't really about your scene partner, Price. It's for the audience."

"This moment won't stay frozen for long, Gid," Rheia said. "I told you. This would be your rubicon. Look at them."

Gideon did. So many dilated pupils. All focused on him.

"The audience needs the climax, Gid. The release. On stage, they expect it. Out here, they don't. But without it, the situation will only get worse."

Rheia was right. Gideon sensed the protestors building themselves up into a tidal wave.

Stan said, "Do it or don't."

Adler said, "There's a cost either way, dude."

Rheia said, "So own your choice."

He chose.

Rheia nodded. "See you on the other side, Gid." She snapped her fingers. The Troupe disappeared.

Time restarted.

Gideon flexed.

The leader's wrist snapped.

And it snapped so *easy*. Way easier than he expected. Like a twig. Like bubble wrap.

Gideon released it. It hung oddly.

The crowd went... not just quiet... but still.

The tidal wave evaporated.

And Gideon was suffused. His nerves sang. His heart pounded. His blood pumped with an elixir of opening night and runner's high and orgasm.

Silence shrouded no man's land. Even the leader was quiet, staring at his strangely angled wrist.

"Take your friends to the hospital," Gideon said. "Everyone else go home."

He walked away. He heard the leader sniffling, sucking air, working his way up to shrieking. He heard calls being made, cabs being hailed. He heard his students confused. He had transformed in front of them. He didn't know what they thought but he knew he couldn't face them. Not yet. Maybe not ever. Alfonso called out, "Gideon! Mr. Price!! Wait! WAIT!!"

But he didn't wait. He turned a corner and broke into a sprint. Turned more corners. Kept sprinting. One more corner.

He slowed to a shaky walk. Sweat coated his skin. If anyone was following, he had lost them.

Had he lost himself?

Or found himself?

He didn't know. And this *feeling*... wouldn't tell him. Couldn't tell him. The feeling simply WAS. It was electric. It was holy.

It was terrifying.

He may have willed everyone else to go home. But he could not.

He trembled on the train all the way to Port Morris.

78

Agnes and Jude hadn't slept for days. And they hadn't been able to give Father anything but bad news.

Their backs and shoulders sizzled with fresh wounds. A pool of their congealed blood stained the floor beneath the exhausted whip hanging on the wall.

"Jude, are you not Primus Pilus?"

"Yes, Father."

"So who commanded the Owners to move up their attack?"

"It was the idea of the Third Centurion. The one who wears the eagle mask."

"And you did not dissuade him?"

"Father I tried—"

sizzle

"Agnes, where are the Fourth and Fifth Centurions?"

"Father, we've not been able to locate them. Everyone else is accounted for in arrest reports and hospital records."

"So they are still missing?"

"Yes, Father."

"Did they run? Were they taken?"

"We haven't been able to—"

sizzle

"What about our Prophet?"

"His test was a success," Agnes said.

Jude played the footage from Spearhead's GoPro. The mangrove fireball.

"Finally. Get me in touch with him. It is time he heard the voice of AlphaSupreme again. The Owners' failures have shown us that a firmer hand is necessary. What is the Prophet doing now?"

Jude pulled up the transcript of Spearhead's messages. AlphaSupreme leaned toward the screen. His breathing quickened.

"He has set a meeting with the whore?"

"Yes, Father."

"Who told him to do that??"

"No one, Father."

Jude *sizzled.*

"He risks everything!!"

Agnes *sizzled.*

"I must pray on this. Find those Centurions. Be ready to connect me with the Prophet."

The metal door at the top of the stairs clanged closed.

Agnes and Jude moved to a corner. Crouched on straw-filled mats. Took turns applying salve to each other's backs. Pressed their foreheads together and prayed.

A news alert pinged.

The half-siblings could have wept with relief. At last. A piece of good news.

They forwarded the link to Father. Headline: *Representatives Mallory and Wilder will be leading the Unity March in Sarasota, Florida.*

The metal door at the top of the stairs clanged open.

Father's footsteps descended. They sat at their stations with their raw backs to him. Felt him approach.

"God smiles upon us." His hands gentle on their heads. "You were already prepping groups to attack this march, yes?"

"Yes, Father. We have disciples marshaling in all of the cities."

"Very good. And now God sends two perfect targets into the arms of our Prophet. Show me what he sees."

The half-siblings worked their magic. A monitor burst with green grass and blue sky.

Jude slumped, relieved his feed had connected. "Captured from the Prophet's GoPro, Father."

"This is real-time, Jude?"

"Yes, Father. Right now."

A scene was playing out in a sunny field. "Agnes, what am I looking at?"

"Father, that is Payne Park. In Sarasota."

"Shall I break in on the Prophet's cell phone, Father?" Jude asked.

AlphaSupreme monitored the monitor. "Not yet, my son. Let this play out. Call him on my command."

"Yes, Father."

They watched.

79

THE TAVERN DOOR OPENED. Peregrin trooped in, followed by a curly-bearded gnome with a tall pointy hat and a green-skinned woman in a long gray cloak.

Narissa twinkled in welcome but no one spoke. Real-world tension thickened fantasy-world air.

More creatures entered. A phoenix on the wing. A gorgon in whispered conference with a minotaur. A faun. A cyclops. A couple wood elves. A trio of goblins.

Everyone sat. No one spoke.

The Mage entered. No niceties. "Postmort. Adler."

"Ahem."

"Oh for god's... *Peregrin*."

"Yes, oh Mighty Mage?"

"The Owners."

"Yes!" Peregrin stood, his protruding codpiece bonging against the edge of the table. "Fellow heroes of myth—"

"Nutshell."

Peregrin huffed. "Fine. Basically, those five coordinated attacks last week?"

Nods all around.

"Tip of the iceberg."

Peregrin sat.

"Stan," the Mage said.

"Yes, Director," the gnome replied.

"Are you still entertaining our two guests?"

"Wrung 'em dry."

"Location still secure?"

The gnome snorted. "C'mon."

The Mage shrugged. "Had to ask. You can let them go once we finish here."

The gnome nodded.

"Anything actionable?"

"Affirmative. I've already forwarded all the intel to Adler and Channing."

"It's *Peregrin* and *Havok*," the night elf grumbled.

"Channing, what've you got?" the Mage asked.

The cyclops stood. His bristled head brushed the ceiling. "Here's the skinny, everyone. Peregrin is correct."

"*Thank*-you, Havok."

"Last week was like a test drive."

"Who's driving?" the green-skinned woman asked.

"That's the million-dollar question, Rheia. The Centurions are puppets, only they don't know it. Primus Pilus is a ghost, pulling the strings not just on the Owners but on multiple militias and white nationalist groups. Even that cell you took out a couple months ago in New York? Same network, but none of them know they're connected. It's all smoke."

"That's a big fire," Rheia said.

"With one hell of a sophisticated arsonist."

"Thank you, Channing," the Mage said. The cyclops sat.

"You left out one thing, Havok," Peregrin said.

"No I didn't, Peregrin."

"Ummm, yeah. Ya did."

"Because we haven't CONFIRMED it yet, *Adler*."

"I'll have confirmation any minute, dude!"

"*Dude*? Since when do night elves say 'dude'?"

"Suck it, one eye! I'll get you a monocle, maybe you can see what's in front of you."

The Mage waved its wand. *Thump*. Peregrin and Havok both stiffened and their mouths vanished.

"Boys, boys," Rheia said. "Bet you wish you hadn't programmed that spell, Adler."

"We don't have time for you two to have one of your spats," the Mage said. "This another of your hunches, Adler?"

Unable to speak or move from the shoulders down, Peregrin nodded yes.

"Impending large-scale attack?"

Peregrin nodded yes.

"Bigger than last week?"

Yes and yes and yes.

"But you don't have hard confirmation yet, Channing?"

The cyclops shook his head no.

"Stan. You've been with our guests. What's your take?"

The gnome pulled at his beard. "You know Adler drives me nuts. But my gut is with him on this one. Those two Centurions were clueless. But they were ready to be martyrs."

"OK. Chase down the hunch but get the details rock solid. I need you two working together on this. Can you please do that?"

Three eyes glared at each other. But two nods yes.

"Thank you. Go."

The wand waved. *Thump*. Peregrin and Havok disappeared, ejected from the game.

"Anything from anyone else?"

"Yes, Director," Rheia said. "We may have to do something about Gideon."

Goblins grumbled. The gorgon and minotaur snorted. The faun muttered, "Oh geez come on."

Stan said, "Now what?"

"I got a bunch of texts from the acting students just before this meeting," Rheia said. "Apparently Gideon..."

"Gideon what?" the Mage said.

"Well, he performed. Stepped into a messy situation, tried to defuse it. But ended up sending three people to the emergency room."

"Three??" Stan said. Rheia nodded. Stan whistled.

Others not so impressed. A wood elf asked, "Who told him he could perform? Was he at least in costume?"

Rheia shook her head. "No one told him, he just reacted to the situation. But no. Not in costume. All the students saw it."

The room got hot.

The phoenix said, "Director, why are we risking ourselves for this guy??" Others echoed.

The Mage held up its hands. "Rheia, what are the details here?"

Before she could respond, an alarm sounded. Narissa flittered behind the bar, slid open a wooden panel. A completely out-of-place touchscreen blinked with warning lights.

"Which Rehearsal Room?" the Mage asked.

"Port Morris. It's Gideon. He's at the door."

All eyes swung to Rheia.

"You there, Rheia?" the Mage asked.

"Yeah. I'm here."

"Deal with him. Everyone else, we're waiting on Adler and Channing. Go-bags ready."

80

RED LIGHT GREENED. Locks thunked. Gideon pushed through the Rehearsal Room door. Saw Rheia removing her shades and standing up from the table.

"Where have you been, Rheia??"

"I hear you had a busy night."

Gideon marched to the fridge, yanked it open. "Not a word, no instruction, nothing."

"Nothing personal, Gid. Bigger fish."

"Yeah yeah yeah I'm a *side gig*, I get it." He chugged a sports drink. Rheia leaned on the edge of the table, arms folded. "You know most of the Troupe thinks we're wasting our time on you. And after tonight they think you actually put us at risk."

"What was I supposed to do, Rheia??"

She held up her phone. "Alfonso. Imani. Rasheed. Emma. Blowing up my cell. All of them *saw* you, Gid."

"You let me see you. On the train?"

"And I caught hell for it. And was already thinking about bringing you in to consult. Situational awareness."

Gideon stalked around, shaking his head. "You didn't see these people, Rheia, these *bullies*, as you call them. And I did it just like you and Stan told me. Tried to deescalate. Maximum harm in minimum time. Took no damage. I was there, I made them pay—"

"Did it feel good?"

Gideon froze.

"It did, didn't it? Crossing that line. You felt powerful. Still do, don't you?"

Oh my god he did. Did he ever. He wanted to shout it, to yawp, to kick in more teeth. But all he said was "Yes."

Rheia stepped in close. Whispered, "You can't give in to that feeling. You've gotta stay cold."

He whispered back, "I don't want to. The world... it finally makes sense, Rheia. Right and wrong. Good and evil. And I'm good. WE are GOOD."

"No, Gid." She pressed a fist against his chest. "We are justice. Not vengeance. You start chasing this feeling? You'll lose yourself."

"Sounds like you know what you're talking about."

Rheia tapped him with her fist.

"This is the cost, Gid. This wasn't how I meant for you to learn it. But now that you know, you know. Still think you want in?"

The locks on the door thunked.

"Expecting someone else?" Gideon said.

"No..."

Adler burst out of the office. "I didn't buzz them in!"

"Kill the lights." Rheia was already moving.

"Don't know how but they overrode—!"

"Adler! Lights!"

Rheia snatched the bat off the prop table, slipped on her shades, and the room plummeted into darkness.

Gideon heard but couldn't see the Rehearsal Room door opening. Couldn't hear or see Rheia but sensed her taking up a flanking position. He backed up until he felt the prop table against his legs, worked his way around behind it, groped blindly for a weapon, latched on to a candlestick—it would have to do—and crouched.

He heard footsteps shuffling forward. He tightened his grip on the candlestick, wished he had his own pair of shades so he could see through the thick darkness.

Then he heard Rheia gasp.

"Adler! Lights."

"You sure?"

"She's sure, Peregrin," said a familiar voice.

The lights snapped on. Gideon blinked twice. First for his eyes to adjust. Second in shock.

Joan and Dan Forth stood squinting in the sudden light.

Rheia was behind them, lowering the bat and slipping off her shades. She glared at Gideon. "What are *they* doing here?"

"How the hell should I know??"

Adler again burst out of the office. Came up short. "WHOA. Aren't they...?"

"Yeah, they're in Gid's acting class with me."

"DUDE. You let them follow you here??"

The familiar voice had been Dan's. "You can talk to us, y'know. Maybe put down the bat and candlestick? Unless we're playing a hopped-up version of Clue?"

"We did catch them a bit by surprise now, didn't we, dear," Joan said, patting Dan's arm.

"*What is going on here??*" Rheia said.

Dan grinned. "Isn't it *hic* obvious?"

"Holy crapola," Adler said. "*Narissa?*"

"**hic**"

Adler pointed at Joan. "Does that mean...?"

"Yes, dear, I'm the Mage."

The Forths looked at each other. Looked back at the stunned trio. Spoke together.

"We're the Director."

81

THE NEXT FIFTEEN minutes were a blurred cross-examination.

Adler: "Weren't you just in the Hinterlands?"

"Yes, dear, but we keep a condo nearby."

Gideon: "So your grandkids aren't visiting?"

Dan chuckled. "Grandkids are the perfect excuse for anything."

Rheia silent.

Adler: "Does anyone know?"

The Forths conferred with a glance.

"Only Stan," Joan said.

"I met him by chance, many moons ago," Dan said. "He inspired us to start the Troupe."

Gideon: "How much of what you told me as the Mage is true? The money? The Senator? Orphanages?"

"All of it, dear."

Rheia silent.

Adler: "You two seriously need to do something about the coffeemaker. You can afford R&D on my shades, this warehouse, a condo in Port Morris, but not a new Breville?"

"Adler you're a world-class hacker and engineer," Dan said. "You can't fix a coffeemaker?"

"Just use the French press, dear, those don't have any wires or buttons."

Adler gagged.

Gideon: "Why did you take my class?"

Rheia finally spoke. "Good question." She turned a stony gaze on the Forths. "Why *did* you take Gideon's class? You spying on me?"

"What a silly question, dear. Of course we are."

Rheia spluttered.

Dan said, "When we saw Gideon in *Henry Five*—and again, Gideon, it was so good! You were great."

Gideon beamed in spite of himself. "Thank you."

Dan turned back to Rheia. "We saw what you saw, Rheia. So we thought we'd make two sundaes with one scooper, as they say."

Adler squinted. "Nobody says that."

Joan took Rheia's hand. "By being in class with you, dear, we could take stock of Gideon, yes, but also observe how you handled recruitment. Plus it was something fun for us to do together."

"Date night!" Dan said.

Rheia returned to silence.

Gideon cleared his throat. "So, why reveal yourselves now?"

Joan suddenly got weepy. She pulled out a tissue and dabbed at her eyes as Dan rubbed her shoulder.

"Joan and I can't lead the Troupe forever," Dan said. "And we may have to transition leadership sooner than later."

"Why's that?" Gideon asked.

Dan smiled. "The big C. I watched my dad go through chemo. None for me, thanks."

"I'm so sorry," Gideon said.

Dan shrugged. "Hey hey, ho ho, everybody's got to go. Not next week or anything, but you better believe I'm gonna blow the everlovin' heck outta my next birthday."

Joan took a shuddering breath. "So you see, Rheia dear, we weren't spying on you because we don't trust you. We actually have the highest hopes for you."

Rheia spluttered again.

"And you, Mr. Price," Joan said, "you had to go and make a spectacle tonight. Forced our hand a bit, didn't you?"

"Joan... Mrs. Forth... I didn't... I mean—"

"No no, we can handle everything but the students. You'll have to address them at some point to keep them from over-sharing. But what are we going to do with you?"

Everyone looked at each other. Silence stretched. Gideon's phone rang. He checked. "It's Imani."

"What are you going to say?" Dan asked.

"I have no idea." He let it go to voicemail.

More silence.

"Well this is awkward," Adler said. He pulled a ziplock baggie of mixed nuts from somewhere out of his bathrobe. He munched.

A series of pings sounded from the office. Adler jumped and coughed on a cashew. "Gotta check that!" He flapped away.

Gideon's phone rang.

"Imani again?" Rheia asked.

He nodded. Voicemail.

Adler hollered from the office. "Channing confirmed my hunch!"

Dan hollered back, "Then let's get to work!"

Gideon's phone erupted with texts. "Imani again."

"She must really want to talk to you," Joan said.

"She's saying it's an emergency, something about Aniyah. I'm gonna…"

Gideon stepped away, called Imani.

Adler flapped back. "Mr. and Mrs. Forth, Mage Director sir ma'am—"

"First names are fine now, dear."

"What's up, Adler?" Rheia snapped.

"The timeline on this is tight. Like two days. We've got multiple attacks in multiple cities—"

"The Unity March," Dan said.

"Bingo."

"Imani hold on hold on hold on." The urgency in Gideon's voice pulled everyone's attention his way. "Aniyah didn't have a migraine? She wasn't there when you got home? What? What's a 'Spearhead'?"

Adler practically backflipped and ran to the office. Rheia gestured Gideon back, put a finger to her lips, took his phone, put it on speaker. Imani's voice tumbled. "I broke into her blog, Gideon, I totally violated her privacy, her password of course is Jazzie's birthday, she *told* me she wasn't messaging with this Spearhead asshole anymore but I just knew she was hiding something, why wouldn't she come to me??"

"Wait wait, slow down, go back to the beginning."

Imani blew her nose and went back to the beginning. Brought Gideon and the eavesdroppers up to speed. Told him about the most recent exchange between Aniyah and Spearhead.

"You think she's on her way to Florida to meet this troll?"

"I *know* she is. Some of her clothes are missing. My car's here, though. She must've called a cab to get to the airport—oh my god, Gideon, what is he going to do to her??"

The next fifteen minutes were a blurred script-drafting. Gideon promised Imani he'd call her back asap with a plan.

Dan pulled up Unity March schedules on a tablet and checked airline options with his phone. Rheia and Joan talked strategy over maps of Unity March cities. Adler connected dots until the shape of Spearhead emerged.

"Knew I'd heard that name, he's popped up here and there in connection some look-at-me vandalism."

"What's his connection with Aniyah?" Gideon asked.

"He's been carpet-bombing her blog. He's a true believer. False flags and conspiracies. Platinum-level, storm-the-Capitol kook. And there's some overlap with the Owners, I'm gonna confab with Channing, he's tracking that chatter." He put on shades and scurried to the office. "Havok, you one-eyed jerkwad, whatcha got?"

The rough draft came together. Sprawling epic. Scripts were sent. Every Troupe member cast in a speaking role. Rheia disappeared into the locker room, reappeared with loaded backpacks.

The printer whirred. Dan handed Gideon two boarding passes. "Tell Imani to meet you at LaGuardia, you've got a 6am to Tampa."

Gideon checked his watch. "That's in four hours."

"Better hop to."

Joan handed Gideon a tablet. "Here's everything Adler dug up on Spearhead, his messages with Aniyah, where they're meeting, maps of Sarasota."

Dan handed Gideon another paper. "Rental car. Three-hour flight. Tampa to Sarasota about an hour drive."

Rheia handed Gideon a backpack. "Go-bag." She held one for herself. Dan handed her a boarding pass.

"You coming too?" Gideon asked.

"I'll be on the flight right after," Rheia said. "Imani shouldn't see me involved. You go with her, keep Aniyah away from this psycho. I'll be scoping out the march route."

"Then what?"

"Then nothing, dear," Joan said.

Gideon realized the size of his role. Supernumerary. Non-speaking. Barely a cameo.

"But what if I can get my hands on Spearhead? Or I can help with the march?"

Joan shook her head. "This is for real, Gideon. Stay in your lane. Let the Troupe do our thing."

"Speaking of which," Dan said, "I'm gonna get started looping in law enforcement. Time to flood the tip lines!" He cracked his knuckles and headed for the office.

Joan handed Gideon a pair of shades. "No small roles, dear."

"Only small actors," Gideon muttered. He regarded the shades. "So these are mine?"

"Think of them as loaners for your final callback. Get Imani and Aniyah home safely. That's more than enough."

Joan patted him on the cheek. Gideon slipped the shades into his pocket and the go-bag over his shoulder.

"Gid," Rheia said.

"Yeah?"

"Break a leg."

"You too."

He thumbed his phone and headed for the door. "Imani? It's me. Pack a bag quick."

The locks thunked behind him.

"Rheia."

"Yeah, Joan?"

"Think he'll stay in his lane?"

Rheia hefted her backpack.

"Not a chance."

82

He sat on a bench in Payne Park. The Sarasota sun stabbed through tree canopy gaps.

He wore sunglasses and big headphones. Bopped his head in time to music that wasn't playing. Flipped pages of a guns-and-ammo magazine he wasn't reading. Took bites and sips from a meal deal he wasn't tasting.

Just a young fella idling away a beautiful lunch break. Birdsong. Whoops and hollers echoing from the skate park. Squeak of swings. Explosive exhales of disc golf players teeing off a few yards away.

He had arrived a good forty-five minutes early. Drove around the perimeter. Walked the red-gravel loop. Scoped out every corner of the playground, cafe, and parking lot. Stayed on alert for anyone or anything out of place. All clear. So he picked a bench near the top of one of the gentle rises—great sightlines—and watched for Aniyah.

A car door thudded shut. He looked that way.

Speak of the devil.

He kept bopping as Aniyah emerged from a shiny rental

sedan. He pulled out his phone. She looked precisely like the pictures. He pressed "call," watched it connect, and placed the phone in his shirt pocket.

Aniyah entered the park. She looked around, getting her bearings. She ambled away from him. He lost sight of her behind the playground, a mini-metropolis of primary-colored climbing walls, slides, and rope bridges.

He bopped and waited.

A minute or so later she appeared on his other side, coming around. He hadn't seen anyone shadowing her and everything about her body language seemed legit.

She might really be alone.

She carried a purse and a large, loaded bag. One of those reusable grocery bags made from recycled two-liter bottles or whatever.

He flinched. Her eyes had locked on him with almost physical force. He realized he had been studying her so intently that he had stopped bopping.

Don't approach till I take off the headphones.

He deliberately removed the headphones.

Aniyah walked straight toward him, up the mild grade of the path. He could hear the red gravel grinding beneath her feet.

He stood. Stuffed the magazine and headphones into his pack.

She stopped several yards away. They eyed each other suspiciously, then curiously. Both were surprised to see the other had actually showed.

He fidgeted.

"Oh my god," Aniyah sighed. "You're so young."

He opened his mouth to speak the scripted line...

...but the hairs on the back of his neck leaped upright.

A split second later another car door thudded shut. No.

Two car doors in quick succession.

He and Aniyah both looked that way.

Another shiny rental. Another black woman. But also a white man who moved like a predator tracking.

Every evolutionary alarm system in his brain stem shrieked its warning.

The newly arrived duo hurried into the park. He watched them split up. The black woman followed Aniyah's path, disappeared behind the playground. The white man canvassed two disc golf players, showed them a photo. The golfers looked, shook their heads.

He snapped back to Aniyah. She clearly recognized them but didn't seem happy. She looked shocked and embarrassed and angry.

Adrenaline overload. This wasn't part of the plan. He fumbled out his phone and raised it to his ear.

"What do I do??!"

A voice hissed, "Run, asshole."

83

Spearhead's binoculars tracked the kid scramming off the red gravel, through the grass, toward the duck-filled pond.

The partially finished apartment complex across the street from Payne Park—"*Live Where You Play!*" screamed a flapping banner—had plenty of empty balconies facing the playground and disc golf course.

Breaking in to one? Easy. Setting up a blind? Also easy. Beach chair. Binoculars. Earbud. Convincing a cash-strapped college kid to sit in a park, wear headphones, and meet some lady with his phone on?

Craigslist. Fifty bucks. Super easy.

Spearhead chuckled to himself as he watched the college kid scrambling. The call was still connected. He could hear the kid gulping breath as clearly as he had heard Aniyah's voice for the first time... *You're so young.*

But his chuckle withered as this who-the-hell stranger rocketed into the binocular's field of vision and closed distance with an effortless stride. Amateur gazelle, meet professional lion.

The stranger's hand grabbed the college kid's backpack and

yanked him to a shuddering stop. Then the stranger straight-up lifted the kid into the air, twisted, and slammed the kid into the dirt.

Holy shit, who was this guy?

The kid's terrified whimpering dribbled through the earbud. Spearhead sweated cold. Setting up the blind and sending a proxy had proven his paranoia correct.

Except this guy didn't seem like a cop or FBI. There was no sense of a sting operation or trap. Spearhead swept his binoculars all over. No sirens. No other agents closing in. And Aniyah and the other black woman were embracing and crying.

What the hell??

The kid blubbered. "Please man please man please I didn't do anything!"

Spearhead zoomed in. The stranger had cranked the kid's arm almost to tendon-popping.

"I don't believe you, *Spearhead,*" the stranger said.

"I don't know what you're talking about, man!!" Rivulets of snot cut through the torrent of tears on the kid's face. "I answered a Craigslist ad, just meet some lady and tell her where to go next, like a scavenger hunt or something! I'm telling the truth!"

Spearhead saw the stranger's energy shift. Watched the stranger's head radar the park. His fight-flight instinct red alerted. He was seated in shadow. He had yesterday scoped the park and looked up at the apartments to make sure of his blind. He knew he was invisible.

But still he went utterly still.

The stranger's sunglassed eyes swept over his blind. They felt like spotlights.

"What else?" The stranger's voice so intimate in his ear.

"Nothing else, man, I'm serious, please, my arm NO

WAIT! I called him! I was supposed to call him and leave it on so he could listen in! My phone! Here! Take it!!"

The stranger lifted the kid's phone. Words converted to signals and bounced off towers and one-and-zeroed in and converted back into words that burrowed into Spearhead's ear.

"I know you're watching. Don't ever contact Aniyah again. Or next time, I'll be the one watching you."

84

Down in the basement, AlphaSupreme, Agnes, and Jude watched the whore and her friend get into the first rental sedan and drive away. They watched the stranger help the college kid up, dust him off, send him on his way.

But the stranger kept the phone that connected to Spearhead.

"Father?"

"Not yet, Jude."

They watched the stranger get into the second rental.

They watched the stranger sit there.

They watched the stranger watch the park.

The Sarasota sun oozed into the afternoon. The disc golf players finished their round. Babysitters and young parents chased children through the playground.

In the balcony blind, Spearhead's body cramped. His bladder shrieked. His throat was parched. But he dared not move. Not even to take a sip from his canteen. He kept the binoculars glued to his face, watching the stranger watch the park.

In the rental, Gideon caught his breath. That powerful feeling flowed through him again. His every instinct insisted Spearhead was still nearby.

Stay cold. Think clearly.

Rheia should be landed and driving to Sarasota by now. The shades. Conference call.

Adler chuckled. "No way dude! You body-slammed a body double??"

But Rheia was implacable. "Good work. You're done."

Gideon pleaded his case. "Aniyah and Imani are safe. I can help, dammit!"

"Your part is played, Gid."

"But I've got Spearhead's phone!"

"Hold up there," Adler said. "Not exactly Spearhead's, it's more like—"

"A burner?"

"Sure, Hollywood. Now get that dongle out of the front pocket of your go-bag. Connect the phone to your shades, I can maybe pull something useful."

Back in the basement, Jude and Agnes squirmed. But AlphaSupreme was patience carved.

"Father, do you want to speak to our Prophet?"

"Not yet, Agnes. God will give us a sign."

They watched.

In the blind, Spearhead wet himself. But still he did not move. The sun oozed further. Its light angled into the rental's windshield, reflected, blinded the binoculars. Spearhead lowered them—ever so slowly—into his lap.

He watched.

In the rental, the dongle connected. Conference call on hold as Adler pillaged the burner.

Gideon studied the maps on the tablet. The Unity March would end at Five Points Park in downtown Sarasota. That would provide the largest, densest target for any sort of attack.

But something nagged at him.

This Spearhead... sending a double... he was paranoid but smart. Dangerous combo. And he wouldn't see himself as a conspiracy crackpot or terrorist. He would see himself as the HERO.

Think of him as a character in a play. Analyze. Super-objective. Get in his head.

He would want his attack to be symbolic. Iconic. Specific targets rather than general mass casualties.

Gideon scrolled through the Unity March's start points. Five neighborhoods: Rosemary District, Gillespie Park, Alta Vista, Burns Square, Newtown.

Yes. More likely Spearhead would target a start point. Closer to homes. Make it personal. Make it hurt more. But which?

Gideon decided to drive around the neighborhoods. Scope out the routes. Get a feel. Alta Vista was just a few blocks away. He'd start there.

In the basement, AlphaSupreme watched the rental sedan pull out of the parking lot and turn south. Directly toward the Prophet's blind. Agnes and Jude held their breath.

The stranger drove past. Disappeared into side streets.

Agnes and Jude started to exhale but a notification pinged on Jude's monitor.

"Father! Someone is trying to break in on the Prophet's GoPro feed."

"This is the sign. Connect me."

In the blind, Spearhead shuddered. Eased himself out of the beach chair. His foot was asleep. His body ached. His pants stank of ammonia. His phone pinged. A text. "Answer when I call." No number. His phone rang. No number. His stomach turned over. He answered.

"Yes?"

I did not tell you to engage with the whore.

Spearhead's knees gave out. He collapsed back into the beach chair.

"AlphaSupreme?"

Yes. Turn off your GoPro.

"What? How do you—?"

NOW, Dustin. The enemy is trying to track you.

Spearhead turned it off. Yanked out the battery for good measure.

In his bathrobe, Adler grinned around the slim jim jutting from his teeth. "Too little too late, asshat. Livestream again, I double-dog dare you."

In the basement, Jude confirmed the feed was dead. Nodded to his Father.

In the blind, Spearhead awaited judgment.

Who was that man?

"I don't know, AlphaSupreme."

Who was that lamb you sent in your place?

"Some college guy, no one."

Did you meet? Did he see your face?

Spearhead was silent.

I see. You are a fool.

Spearhead wept.

But I am forgiving. I offer you a chance for redemption. You have failed here but succeeded elsewhere. Your bombs are ready for tomorrow's sacrifice, yes?

"Yes, AlphaSupreme!"

And you have the strength, the faith, the will to use them on our enemies?

"YES. I will blow Mallory to hell."

Go home. Pray. Prepare. Tomorrow you will strike such a blow.

"What should I do about the crisis actor, AlphaSupreme?"

In the basement, Agnes and Jude cringed as Father covered his mic and screamed in righteous fury. "Fucking CHILD!"

AlphaSupreme took a breath. Offered a contrite prayer. Spoke into the mic.

Leave the whore to God.

85

Driving the neighborhoods, the hint of an idea started to form in Gideon's mind. He left it alone. If he chased it, he'd lose it.

He checked on Imani and Aniyah. They were safe in a vacation condo near the Gulf that Imani had scored with a last-minute online deal. They had decided to stay overnight, maybe even check out the Unity March the next day. They invited him over.

He declined. Manufactured his first cover story. His guts clenched at how much a little but necessary lie actually cost. *Thank-you, no problem, enjoy the beach, travel safe, see you for final class next week.*

He got a room in a motel on the Tamiami Trail near the airport. He grabbed a sub. Loaded it up. He was Adler-ravenous.

He sat on the hotel bed. Wolfed his sub. Surfed websites detailing the histories of the various communities he had driven throughout the afternoon. Let the idea play hopscotch on the edges of his consciousness.

Late edition of the local news on the motel TV. Unity March of course the lead story. Something the lady anchor said caused Gideon and his idea both to look over.

"Representatives Mallory and Wilder will be the featured speakers in Five Points Park. They will be marching with the group starting in Newtown."

The idea sprang into existence fully-formed. *Like Athena from the skull of Zeus,* Gideon liked to say when students made intuitive leaps like this in class.

Shades. Conference call.

"You shouldn't still be in Sarasota, Gideon," Dan said. Joan and Rheia grumbled in agreement.

Gideon realized they truly were concerned for his safety. "My choice. Even if you don't end up casting me in the Troupe, right now I can help. I can do something."

"Oh come ooooon, hear him out, what can it hurt?" Adler said. "Y'all took a chance on me, remember? And that's worked out beauuuuutifully."

A beat. Adler munched something crunchy. Joan sighed.

"Go ahead, dear."

Gideon outlined his thinking. Spearhead psychology. Paranoid and smart. March start point easier to target. Fewer authorities. Cleaner escape routes. But more importantly, the need for glory. Personalized victims. Make it about himself.

"So which neighborhood?" Rheia said.

"He'll zero in on the intersection where the Newtown march joins with the Gillespie Park march."

"Why?"

"Newton is Sarasota's historically Black neighborhood. Gillespie Park is mostly Hispanic. And Newtown is also—"

"Where those two tear-down-the-Confederate-statue Reps are starting!" Adler finished.

Gideon heard their collective minds whirring through

calculations. "Holds water," Dan said. Joan and Rheia again grumbled in agreement.

"See? Giddy Gid ain't just a pretty face," Adler said. He cackled and munched.

Gideon's guts flipped at how much their approval meant. "So now we know where to focus, right?"

Joan had already moved on. "Adler, any idea yet what form Spearhead's attack will take? Guns? Bombs? Suicide vest?"

"Bombs," Gideon blurted.

"Why?" Rheia said.

"Because he is fundamentally a coward." Gideon dug deep. *Empathize. You're him. What drives you?* "He'll need to watch. He'll want to bask in it after, not go down in a blaze. He won't *try* to get caught, but if he does get caught he won't mind. Because he'll become a celebrity."

"So we're looking for IEDs," Rheia said. "Hidden along the march route."

Adler said, "As soon as he starts live-streaming—"

"Oh yeah, he'll totally broadcast this," Gideon said.

"—I'll have him on lock. We just gotta be ready to pounce. Means you'll have to get your hands on one fast, show it to me so I can figure out how to defuse and track the rest."

"Five," Gideon said. *Athena.* "There'll be five."

"You need more bodies," Dan said. "Countering groups is cake, but this lone wolf solo terrorist bullshit—"

Something pinged in Adler's office. "Well well well, ask and ye shall receive. Just heard from Stan. He's already neutralized the Owner gang that was gonna attack the march in Savannah."

Gideon whistled. "That guy is unbelievable."

"You don't know the half," Dan said. "He hits the road now, he could be there in six hours."

"Looping him in," Adler said.

Seconds later, Stan's voice. "You really take out three, Price?"

"Sir, yes sir."

"Bite me, grappler."

"You're both very pretty," Rheia said.

Joan laid it out. "Dan and I will be quarterbacking marches in other cities. So Sarasota is on you. Stan takes the intersection point between neighborhoods. Gideon, you start at Gillespie. Rheia, Newtown."

Adler cackled. "Three Musketeers ain't got nuthin' on you!"

86

"Jude, are you asleep?"

Her half-brother's snoring hitched then fell back into its soothing rhythm.

Agnes shifted on her mat, struggling to sleep. Father would need her sharp during the Unity March. Monitoring the attacks in the various cities. Protecting their digital flanks. Tracking their Prophet.

And watching for the stranger.

She shifted again, one side to the other. She preferred to sleep on her back but the freshest stripes were still too raw.

She sat up. Prayed. Usually she could feel her words ascending through the metal door and into the sky. But tonight they gathered at the top of the stairs, unable to find passage. They fell back unheard to the concrete floor.

"Jude?"

Again his snoring hitched.

"How many people are going to die today because of us?"

Jude didn't snore the rest of the night.

Gideon tossed. Turned. Tossed.

Threw the blanket off. Stuck one foot out of the sweated-through sheets.

Flipped the pillow. Fluffed it.

Tossed. Turned.

He got up. Washed his face. Drank some water cold from the mini-fridge.

Waiting. Nothing was more exhausting than waiting. Yet sleep would not come.

The timeless, salty air of Florida clung to him.

He cranked the rickety a/c unit. It wheezed. He flicked the ceiling fan to high. It gasped.

He stripped down. Got in the shower. Cold water shrieked from the heat in his skin.

He toweled off. Pulled on shorts. Tried to study the maps. The march routes.

But other images arose unbidden.

Was it just last night he had been inside the cabaret watching Alfonso then outside the cabaret snapping a wrist in his hands?

Was it just a couple months ago he had been in the Bear and Fawn and seen Rheia face down three bullies with a pool triangle?

Was it just a dozen years ago Finley had hugged him on opening night and told him how proud she was before disappearing from his life?

Ghosts are memories trapped in timelessness. That's what makes a ghost a ghost: no sense of the passage of time. Without time, there is no context. Without context, there is no consequence. And without consequence, there is no meaning.

He laid on the damp bed spread-eagled. Stared up at the

ceiling fan fighting its losing battle against the thick air. And he wondered... *How many people are going to die today?*

The moon crept over the Gulf.

Spearhead kayaked to the moon-bathed dolphin statue. Turned and disappeared into the mangroves. Beached. Sat on the stone. Tried to commune with Granddad.

"This might be the last time I can come out here for a while," he whispered. "So I wanted you to know. You were right. And tomorrow I will make you proud."

But Granddad wasn't there.

Spearhead counted the number of strokes it took to paddle back to the shack. Packed his backpack ever so carefully. Double-checked. Triple-checked. Traveled in his mind the routes between the five targeted trash cans. Imagined the glorious carnage, especially at the intersection where Stacy Mallory would meet her fiery end.

A breeze off Palma Sola Bay found its way through a shack window. It caressed the nape of Spearhead's neck and whispered Granddad's voice into his ear. A final gift. An inspiration. A way to work back fully into AlphaSupreme's good graces.

Ask forgiveness, not permission.

As Spearhead worked into the early hours, he tried to calculate the number of people who would die today. More than the number of paddle strokes from secret stone to sacred shack?

Spearhead finished. Then quadruple-checked everything. Then slept like a baby.

The sun climbed out of the Atlantic.

87

Thousands of feet thunderstormed into the pavement. Homemade signs stabbed at the overcast sky.

A bullhorn called. *"No Justice...!!"*

The throng responded one-throated. "NO PEACE!!"

"No Justice...!!"

"NO PEACE!!"

Gideon pressed through the crowd. Kept his head on a swivel. Gaps in the Unity March opened and closed. He slipped through a sudden eddy and stepped onto a bus stop bench.

The protestors stretched blocks in both directions, packing the street and spilling onto the sidewalks. Rows of businesses, mostly mom'n'pops, to the north. Historic church and cemetery to the south.

Cars idled at green lights as the host marched past, most honking in support, a few in protest of the protest.

Then Rheia's voice in his shades. "Mallory and Wilder have started to march." Gideon pictured her over in Newtown a few blocks away.

"Adler we need intel now."

"Almost almost, Spearhead's live but he's scrambling and bouncing, one sec..."

"If we don't defuse all five before they make the inter-section—"

"I know I know I KNOW."

A marcher and her young son stomped past Gideon. The boy grinned up and pumped his fist. Gideon looked down and flashed a peace sign in return. The boy fist-pumped past.

"Got him! Heads up, Giddy, he's tracking toward Gillespie. Rheia, Stan, I'm backtracking now, looking for points where he paused, those'll be where he hid the—"

"Located one," Stan said. "Public trash receptacle."

Gideon's vision went double as the inside of his lenses ghosted with the image of Stan's hands holding a Spearhead-built IED.

"Those look straight-forward enough," Adler said.

"Amateur," Stan said. His fingers poked and pried. Gideon held his breath. "Internet bomb-making one-oh-one." Stan's fingers yanked a wire. "Defused. Everyone see that?"

Gideon almost fainted, caught himself before tumbling off the bench.

"Stan the MAN!!" Adler hooted. "I screenshotted all that, kids, so now when you find yourself a boom-boom you've got a how-to-defuse flipbook."

"That won't mean jack if we don't—"

"Oh Rheia, you must have faith in me. If y'all would kindly turn your attention to your heads-up displays you'll see I've marked the next three Spearhead farts with blue dots. Stan there's another just south of you. Rheia, two in your domain. Giddy I'm guessing he's bringing number five right to ya."

"Headed to my first target," Rheia said.

"Headed to my second," Stan said. "Find him, Price. We need all five."

"On it," Gideon said. He fiddled with his shades. The double vision was impeding his view of the crowd. He got the HUD to flicker off. The women and men and teens and children, all heights and colors and backgrounds, swept past. White bodies ringed the edges, an intentional wall, privilege transformed into protection. Gideon felt every footfall. His heartbeat red-lined. Where was Spearhead??

Remember, he's the hero of this story. He's already set four bombs. He's feeling invincible. He'll be strutting, he won't be able to help it...

Adler grunted.

"What is it?" Stan said.

"There's a gap."

"What do you mean, a gap?"

"I mean Spearhead must've turned off his GoPro for a hot sec, Stan, there's a gap. Like he disappeared and reappeared."

"How long was he off the grid?"

"Timestamps show about three minutes."

"Did he travel?"

"No, but I can't speak for the three minutes he was offline."

"After I defuse my second, I'll investigate."

"Just marked that location in green for ya, Stan."

"Target procured," Rheia said. "Gid you got anything?"

"Not yet."

"Dude, look for backpacks," Adler said. "Best way for him to carry his toys while blending in."

But scanning for backpacks didn't help, they were everywhere. Cold dread crept up Gideon's sweaty back. Time was an imp, dancing and cackling just beyond his reach.

"Defused," Rheia said.

"And then there were three," Adler said.

Gideon looked toward the head of the Gillespie march. The leaders stepped in unison, arms linked. The bullhorn brayed. The crowd roared back.

The shades vibrated against his temples. Stan's voice. "Price? Anything?"

"Nothing."

Adler's voice. "His signal's practically on top of you, dude!"

"Dammit, I've got nothing!" His adrenaline spiked. Sweat dripped into his eyes.

"Gid." Rheia's voice. "It's you and the stick. Stop looking and start seeing."

Gideon focused on a telephone pole across the street. A mammoth version of his two-dollar dowels. He slowed his breathing. Let his peripheral vision go soft.

Gideon sensed the leaders halting and raising their arms into crossed Xs above their heads. Felt the vibration in the pavement as the march braked. Heard the rustle of sleeves and skin as raised crossed arms swept toward him like a late-inning wave at a baseball game.

The bullhorn squelched a plea. White people flowed forward, the protective wall adjusting amoeba-like to defend the march leaders from whatever threat or obstacle had emerged ahead. Whether it was a police blockade or a counter-march Gideon never knew...

...because in the fuzzy edges of his vision a shape moved against the tide. He flicked his eyes away from the pole. The shape snapped into a focus.

A young man. A kid, really. Also white, backpacked, ball-capped, chin high, *strutting* along the opposite side of the street.

"I've got him."

The kid stopped at the corner trash can. Tactical pants. Work boots. Lightweight jacket over a white T-shirt. Gideon watched the kid pretend to tie his shoe as he cased the corner. The kid swigged from a water bottle, swung his backpack around, unzipped a pocket. As the water bottle went into the bag, another package came out. It disappeared into the trash and the kid reslung his bag.

"He just placed the fifth bomb."

"Location marked," Adler said.

The kid gazed around the crowd, a smirk smearing his face. His eyes passed over Gideon. Stopped. Rewound.

"I'll get that one while Stan checks out the gap," Rheia said.

Gideon saw the kid recognize him.

Hello there, Spearhead.

"Gid."

"Yeah?"

The kid turned and ran.

"Go get him."

88

Gideon sprang off the bench. Landed awkwardly. One of his ankles barked. He ignored it and pursued. He stutter-stepped as he passed the trash can.

"Sure you don't want me to defuse? I'm right here."

All three voices: "NO!"

"Stan makes it look easy but bombs are persnickety," Adler said. Gideon gritted his teeth and broke into a sprint. He pinpointed Spearhead, locked on like a heat-seeking missile, did his best not to knock anyone over.

The kid didn't give as much thought to avoiding the marchers. His zigs and zags turned into shoves. Shouts and curses were flung at the kid's back, auditory breadcrumbs for Gideon to follow through the chaos. He closed distance.

"Bomb three defused," Stan said. "Headed for the gap."

The kid looked back over his shoulder. His eyes widened at seeing Gideon so close so fast.

"Bomb four located," Rheia said. "Will neutralize and head for the fifth."

Gideon's ankle growled. He bore down.

"Get his phone!" Adler said. "Two to one that's the detonator. Get that, we're in the clear no matter what."

Ten more steps, he'd be able to reach out and—

A middle-aged couple stepped in his path. He cut hard. Too hard. His ankle snarled. He stumbled and collided with them. Tried to cushion his fall but the pavement was unforgiving. He tumbled and rolled. Pants ripped at the knee. Elbows scraped to bleeding. Palms sanded with grit. *The floor is a weapon.* He scrambled to his feet and watched the kid slash left around a corner.

Realized he was watching without shades.

They were bent and broken on the ground. He snatched them up and tried to fit them to his face.

Blank cracked lenses. Radio silence.

Gideon leaned over, hands on knees. He gulped air and ignored the buzzing around him. Some offered assistance, some cursed him for not watching where he was going. His subconscious deciphered that the middle-aged couple was pissed but uninjured, while his conscious mind focused to a pinprick.

You're on your own but not alone, Gideon thought. *Just get his phone.* His ankle howled. His blood spotted the pavement by his shoes. *You can't catch him, you've gotta get in front of him. Analyze the script. Get in his head. Where do you go next?*

Gideon glanced at the corner where the kid had disappeared.

I'm a prophet. I'm a soldier. I laugh and weave this narrow escape into my heroic narrative.

Gideon straightened up. The corner where the kid had turned was preceded by a series of business. Hairstylist. Coffee shop. Phone repair.

I can circle back and witness my triumph. I want to see Mallory's face as she realizes she's dying. I NEED TO WATCH.

Gideon dashed to his left, straight at the entrance to a diner. The little bell rang brightly as he burst through the door. The line cook and waitress barely had time to register his presence before he was past the counter. Through a door. Deliveries stacked along the wall. Hard right. Immediate left. Blew past the bathrooms.

Bathrooms that served *two* businesses.

The back of the diner connected with the back of a yoga studio that faced the street one block over from the grumbling couple Gideon had just tumbled. He sprinted past three rows of downward dogs and came to a panting stop by the front window.

"Can I help you?"

Gideon looked back. Faces gaped at him from under armpits. The instructor approached, her mouth set.

"Sorry to disturb your practice, I'll be out in a sec." He eased back the bamboo shade and peeked up the street.

Spearhead was there, four doors up, coming Gideon's way. Circling back to watch. Gideon ripped off his ballcap, just enough of a transformation to buy him a couple precious seconds.

"Sir, you really need—"

"The light in me honors the light in you," Gideon said as he handed her his cap and slipped out the door.

The kid had his GoPro held up on a selfie stick, live-streaming his legacy. And in his other hand... a phone.

Gideon turned his back, grabbed a protest sign that couldn't have been more conveniently discarded on the sidewalk, and jabbed it upward.

Finally... time slowed. Gideon pictured the kid's every step. He exhaled. Inhaled. Held. The readiness is all.

The kid's voice reached Gideon a few steps in advance. "What I do, I do for the survival of the White Race. This day will always be remembered, as will my name. My *true* name. Spear—"

Gideon whirled and clotheslined the kid with the sign. Corrugated cardboard on a stick wouldn't do much damage but the shock dropped the kid to the ground. He started to scurry away on all-fours. Gideon step-ball-changed forward and kicked the kid's backside, sending him sprawling.

The phone clattered onto the sidewalk.

89

"I've lost Gideon!"

Rheia and Stan kept weaving through their crowds. "What do you mean lost, Adler?" Rheia said.

"His shades, his signal, he's gone!"

"Technical malfunction?" Stan asked.

Adler huffed. "No way, man. Something's happened to him."

Rheia accelerated. "Everyone stay on target. Stan, figure out that gap."

"Affirmative."

"Adler, try traffic and security cams, pick up social media, someone around here has eyes on Gid whether they know it or not."

"Yeah yeah yeah, good good."

"I'm closing in on five. Gid'll have to take care of himself."

She arced around a family. At least three generations' worth.

Stan reached the green dot marked on his HUD. Realized

he wasn't even twenty yards from where he had defused the first bomb, just off the intersection where the two marches were going to merge. He looked north over the hundreds of bobbing heads, saw the phalanx surrounding the two Representatives headed his way.

What did you do for three minutes, you little racist fuck?

"Hup hup!" Adler yelped.

"What is it?" Rheia and Stan asked together.

"I've got Giddy running through a diner. Security cam. OK I've got a traffic cam on the backside, yep, he just stepped out of a yoga joint and grabbed a sign..."

Rheia made a hard right. "I'm three blocks out."

"Holy shitballs! Look at this!"

A GoPro feed popped up on the inside of Rheia and Stan's shades. "My *true* name. Spear—"

The image spiraled through sky and sidewalk and crowd. Jolted to a stop. Feet marched up the side.

"What the hell are we seeing?" Stan asked.

"I'm trying to piece it all together! But I think he got to Spearhead!"

Gideon's voice cut through on the GoPro. "Adler! Adler! I've got his phone!"

"Oh you smart smart lad, you know I'm watching."

"No suicide vest, his backpack is empty!"

Rheia kept cruising. "Two blocks. Stan what's up with the gap?"

"Defuse that bomb then get to Price and interrogate the kid. Too large an area here."

"Oh no," Adler said.

Gideon's voice again, urgent and loud. "No! You don't understand! Let go! LET GO!"

"Some Good Samaritans have pinned Giddy down!" Adler

said. "The kid is screaming like he dropped his ice cream. They think Gideon attacked him. Oh no oh no oh no."

Rheia shifted into overdrive.

"They gave Spearhead his phone back."

$$90$$

Rheia ignored Adler shrieking in her ear. Ignored Stan repeating "abort, abort, abort!"

Choose death.

Final block breathless sprint. Arrived at the trash can. Looked down. Number five. She reached in and grabbed it. Slid her fingers in to defuse. But something different. She stopped.

"Stan do the wire colors matter??"

"Adler goddammit patch me into her visuals!"

"Here here there you go!"

But Rheia had looked up.

Stan cursed. "Eyes on the package, Rheia!"

"Sorry Stan, got a couple curious cops closing in. Plan B."

"So go already!"

"Plan B??" Adler said. "What the hell is Plan B??"

Rheia ran right at the cops, the bomb football-tucked in her elbow. They startled. She juked an ankle-breaking head-fake. One cop bit hard and fell. The other pivoted away like a bull-fighter avoiding the horns.

"Adler help her out already!!"

"Oh Plan BEEEE. Got it! Rheia. Cemetery ahead to your left. Reflecting pond in the middle."

She angled that way, hurdled a headstone, heard the cops chasing. Also heard a voice ranting on the GoPro still beaming into her shades.

The devil is at our door! I will show you the truth!

Spearhead.

He stood on the hood of a car, phone lifted like Excalibur.

Today I fulfill the Fourteen Words!

He built toward his climax. She cut a straight line across the meandering cemetery path, racing through grass and flowers and freshly dug dirt.

We must secure the existence of our people and a future for white children!

The reflecting pond mirrored the overcast sky.

All of you, hear me and know my name.

She broke stride and heaved. Turned and sprinted. Screamed a warning at the cops.

I am SPEARHEAD!

She dove behind a century-old oak as the bomb splashed into the pond.

91

As the words of Spearhead's poisonous tirade began to sink in, the hands holding Gideon eased their grips. He broke loose and lunged.

Too late. Spearhead pressed a vicious finger to his phone.

Tremors in the ground caused everyone to look down. Then a towering spume of water made everyone look up.

Roiled heat and boiled pond and shredded branches and sharded marble rained down.

People ducked. Covered their heads. Screamed and ran and huddled. But injuries were minor.

Until Spearhead, still standing on the car hood, realized his triumph had been undone.

"There should have been more!" He stabbed at his phone, again and again. "There should have been five!" His furious gaze turned on Gideon. "What have you done??"

The people who had rescued Spearhead realized the error of their ways. Alchemy 101. Fear into rage. Gideon stepped aside. They were too many. They would not be denied.

Spearhead too late understood the shift. He clambered off the hood but was immediately engulfed by the mob. He disappeared from Gideon's view like a stone into the sea.

His injuries were going to be severe.

92

*T*HERE SHOULD HAVE BEEN FIVE.

Fists and feet pummeled. Spearhead turtled on the ground. Dustin, though, detached and floated above the fray. While he noted every kick, punch, and stomp, he didn't feel them. He felt only one thing.

Confusion.

There should have been five.

At some point, the beating stopped. And then the pain came, along with police and EMTs. The pain was everywhere. Healing hands scurried over his body. Harsh voices battered with relentless questions. But he couldn't answer through puffy, bleeding lips. His tongue probed gaps where teeth had previously rooted.

He couldn't focus. Seeing double. He concentrated. An image swam out of the haze. The man from the park. Looking at him from behind yellow police tape. The man who had somehow tracked him down and ruined his plans.

There should have been five. Why weren't there five?

A woman joined the man. She was limping. Blood and dirt

streaked her disgusting brown skin. They put their heads together, talking, staring at him. He could tell they wanted something from him. But the yellow tape held them back.

The woman checked her watch.

And he remembered.

There weren't five.

Spearhead checked his own watch. It hurt like hell to tuck his chin the necessary couple inches to see. But it was worth it.

AlphaSupreme, I am sorry for deceiving you. I knew you would be watching. Please accept my offering. Any second now...

He had researched local response time for first responders. Adjusted his calculations to account both for the heavy foot traffic and for the fact that many police, medics, and reporters would already be nearby, lining the march routes.

It was a strategy he had read about in the darker corners of the web.

He smiled at the man and the woman. He saw them see him smile. Their heads tilted like a couple of stupid dogs. He grunted through the pain, lifted his arms, pointed to his watch, and stuck his fingers in his ears.

The man from the park and the mongrel woman shuddered with understanding.

Even above the sirens and radio chatter and stampeding news crews he heard the woman yelling, "STAN! STAN! GET OUT OF THERE!"

The last thing he saw before his eyes swelled shut was the man from the park terrified and helpless.

Spearhead sighed and passed out content.

A moment later his final bomb—the one he had put on a simple egg timer—dinged zero.

In the faraway basement, a fireball flickered across many monitors.

Father, was that part of the plan?

No, my children. But all things work together for the good. Let us pray and give thanks for our Prophet.

93

Almost a week later, Stacy Mallory swung her legs off the hospital bed. No one was going to stop her. No nurse, no doctor, no orderly, no staff.

She dressed. It took a while. Her body was still stiff. Aches within aches.

She gave orders. Her PR and media teams hopped to. Cars were summoned.

She accepted a supporting arm from the most no-nonsense nurse on the floor. Made her slow way through the halls. Stopped at an intersection. Down the corridor to her right she could see federal agents stationed outside a door.

His door.

Her insides turmoiled.

The no-nonsense nurse shepherded her left. To the ICU. Stacy placed her palm on Amelia's forehead. *You come back, you hear me?*

They reached the elevator. Rode it down. Exited.

She thanked the nurse and claimed a car for herself alone.

The driver remained quiet as she wept in the back seat. He parked. Waited as she composed herself.

Ty appeared at her window. He had been in the follow car. She lowered the window halfway.

"How you holding up?" she asked him.

He unconsciously smoothed the bandages on his temple.

"Pain is mandatory." He forced a grin. "Suffering is optional."

Her voice was so soft. "Ty, please know—"

He shook his head. "Later, Congresswoman. Right now..." He glanced over his shoulder, saw the reporters converging, turned back. "I've got you."

"Let's go then."

The driver appeared at her door, opened it, ran interference with Ty through the reporters. Other staff spilled from other cars, orbited the quickly growing group.

They moved toward the memorial. An antique, wrought iron streetlamp, gifted by the nearby salvage store, held vigil at the cemetery entrance. At its base spilled a pile of flowers, stuffed animals, hand-made cards and posters, candles, even a couple *I'll Always Be FRANK* buttons. A small portable generator hummed, lighting the lamp dusk to dawn and back again.

The flickering light illuminated not only the memorial but also the scoured sidewalk pavement, the shattered store windows band-aided with plywood, the sooty streaks on the street.

As the sun set, the cemetery's ghosts peaked out into the lamplight, adding their breathless voices to the community's keening.

Stacy shuffled through the overflowing mementos. Arrived at the lamp. Leaned against it with one hand. Listened. And waited.

The cameras and noise attracted attention. Neighbors and

families with haunted eyes rubbed shoulders with on-air personalities with meticulous coifs.

The driver stood a few feet to the side, his crossed arms and paternal glare maintaining a moat around Stacy.

Ty conferred with the staff scurrying from outlet to outlet. When he was sure they had a critical mass ready to go, he shot Stacy a thumbs up.

She was about to break in on every channel.

                                94

There was no television in the tiny sublet. Gideon hadn't cared to scrounge one up during his stay. But he and Rheia listened to the Congresswoman live on social media as they packed up his few belongings.

...Like this light, we hold back the encroaching darkness...

Gideon's palms, knees, and elbows sported new scars. He had gone through three tubes of ointment.

...Like this light, we know the night will pass and the day will come...

Rheia's limp was fading but she still kept her ankle wrapped. Thankfully the ringing in her ears had stopped after only a couple days.

...This past week, you have been my light. Your outpouring of support and concern, the cards and calls and emails, just... thank-you. Physically I am healing well. But my heart... well, like you, my heart weeps...

Gideon's jaw clenched and unclenched. His stuffing of socks into backpack took on a violent edge.

...Amelia, my peerless Chief of Staff, is stable but still in the ICU and has yet to awake. Our intern Samar, who daily inspired us, succumbed to his multiple injuries late last night. His family was with him. A scholarship has been set up in his honor...

Gideon slammed down the backpack. Stalked to the window. Looked out at the world. Rheia let him be, continued packing.

...And as you all know, Frank—

Her voice hitched. Gideon and Rheia looked over at the tablet. A voice flung itself from the crowd: "We love you, Stacy!!" The owner of the voice started to clap. The clapping multiplied. Grew into a storm. It wasn't applause. It was defiance.

...Thank-you. I love you too. And I don't understand why I'm standing here with you and Congressman Francis Wilder isn't. Why I survived that horrific explosion while he died instantly. I myself am unsure what awaits us on the other side. That's one of the reasons I work so hard today, in THIS life. But wherever Frank is now, I hope he is with his beloved wife, I hope he is content, I hope he knows that we acknowledge and honor his life's work on behalf of our nation—

Gideon stabbed the tablet off. Went back to the window.

"Hey."

He didn't look, but Rheia knew he was listening.

"We did good. YOU did good. A win."

"A *win*??" He spun to face her. "Fifteen dead! Including a *Congressman*. Dozens injured. And that neighborhood? That sort of trauma??"

Rheia held up her hands. "Think how much worse it could've been. And not just there but all the other marches. No other casualties."

He twisted away. Stared through the window.

"Wins and losses are rarely cut and dried, Gid. That world out there? Hope and sadness walk hand in hand."

They stayed that way for a bit.

Rheia held up the pressure cooker. "Staying or going?"

Gideon glanced. "Comes with."

He rubbed his eyes as she packed it into a box.

"How's Adler?" Gideon asked.

"He's terrible," Rheia said as she taped the box shut. "I've never seen him like this. He blames himself."

"A lot of that going around."

"But he's also digging into everything that kid has ever touched. There's someone behind him, behind the Owners."

"Primus Pilus."

"Adler's on the hunt." She hoisted the box. "So you gonna help me out with all this or what? It's not even my stuff."

He approached. Reached out for the box. Stopped. "Rheia?"

"Yeah?"

He chewed his lip. "How are you so ok?"

"Playing the long game, Gid. Doesn't mean I'm ok. It'll sound ridiculous but think of it as closing night. Curtain falls and you've gotta let go, yeah? Move on to the next."

"You're right. It does sound ridiculous." He tried to smile bravely. He failed.

She set the box down. "You're not in class. You're not on stage. You don't have to wear a mask with me."

He tried to turn away but she wrapped her arms around his neck. His face collapsed into her shoulder. His breathing heaved. She squeezed him tight. He sobbed, his body racked. He clung to her. She kept him from drowning. Stan had done the same for her, not so long ago.

It took some time. It always does. But his sobs subsided.

He pulled back. She held him. Forced him to look her in the eye. "No shame, Gideon Price."

It took a moment. It always does. But he nodded.

"Thank you, Rheia."

They released. She picked the box back up. Offered it to him. He accepted. Hefted it under one arm, shouldered his backpack, looked around the tiny apartment for any left-behinds. "So what comes next?"

"So glad you asked." Rheia slung a duffel, grabbed the handle of a rolling suitcase. "Stan is striking the Rehearsal Room."

"With one arm?"

"Sling comes off in a couple days. And he can do more one-armed than you and I put together."

Gideon shook his head. "Lucky."

"Not his first rodeo."

"What about you and me?"

"The Director thinks the Troupe may have gotten over-exposed."

"Dan and Joan."

"Yeah."

"What the hell."

Rheia snorted. "*Yeah.* Being in class with them earlier tonight? Geez. So weird."

"They might be the best actors I've ever seen, no joke."

"You handled it well, by the way. *Stickman.*"

Gideon chuckled. "Wasn't sure how Alfonso and everyone were gonna be. But they just seemed... grateful."

"Yep."

"I thought... when I broke that guy's wrist... they were seeing right through me."

"Hide in plain sight, Gid. And hey, why weren't Aniyah

and Imani in class? Especially Imani, can't believe she'd miss her last chance to do tongue-twisters with you."

Gideon smiled. "She texted. Still in Sarasota. They marched from Burns Square, made Five Points before the explosions. Got a bit jostled in the panic but they're ok. Not sure why they stuck around down there all week."

"You should check on them."

Gideon composed a quick text while Rheia did one more scan. She spotted the tablet, nabbed it, stuffed it in his backpack as he pressed send.

Rheia said, "Anyhow, the Director thinks it's time to go to ground, regroup, reassess. So you and me, we're gonna set up the new HQ."

"Where?"

She winked. He rolled his eyes. "I'll know when we get there?"

"Exactly."

Rheia opened the door. Gideon stepped forward.

95

In the basement, the face of the blood-tainted Congress-woman defiled one of the monitors.

...Something else this light shows us? White supremacy is the greatest threat to our safety and democracy today. I'm not so sure anymore that the arc of the moral universe does indeed bend toward justice. It needs us to push. And many will push back...

Agnes and Jude cowered. They had never seen their Father so *calm*. It was terrifying.

It didn't help that the three ArchAngels also were present.

Mike was zooming in. His bland, corporate face filled another screen. You would glance right past him. But his eyes... if you spent an extra second looking into his eyes you'd see the insatiable fire of the zealot blazing hot.

Gabby had shown up in person. Everything about her screamed "suburban white-flight soccer mom." But the half-siblings knew she had sacrificed at least eight of Father's enemies.

Raph never showed himself. Never. They had no idea what he looked like, how tall he was, how old he was. He was nothing but a voice, processed and auto-tuned into a digitized monotone.

AlphaSupreme muted the harlot.

"Jude."

Jude obeyed. His fingers trembled so badly it took him three tries to press play.

The shaky GoPro footage. The boy who called himself SPEARHEAD1488. The Unity March in Sarasota. The chase. The escape. The boy crowing.

—*This day will always be remembered, as will my name. My true name. Spear—*

The attack. The GoPro clattering to the ground. Sideways feet. Hands scrabbling. The struggle. A frantic collage of bodies, faces, sky, ground. The boy on the hood of a car. The single distant explosion. The boy's disbelief. The boy swallowed by vengeful marchers. The GoPro stomped in the scrum. The screen black.

"Jude. Again. The moment of sky."

Jude willed his fingers to move steadily. Cursor. Timestamp. Play.

AlphaSupreme commanded all. "Listen."

A voice. Calling again and again amidst the chaos. Calling *Adler! Adler!*

"Freeze it."

Jude froze it.

The face of the man in the sunglasses. The man who had somehow disrupted the boy's plans. AlphaSupreme's plans.

"Agnes. The other."

Agnes clicked. A recorded voice hissed.

I know you're watching. Don't ever contact Aniyah again. Or next time, I'll be the one watching you.

"The same man," Gabby muttered.

"Who is he?" Mike demanded.

AlphaSupreme ignored his ArchAngels for a moment. He caressed Jude's cheek, twisted a finger through Agnes' hair. "Well done, my children."

"Who *is* he??" Mike asked again, his pasty face mottling red.

"We don't know. That's why I've gathered you. Find him. Vengeance is a virtue."

Gabby moved to the screen showing the man's face. She studied. Jude thought she looked hungry. "We find him through this 'Adler' he was speaking to."

"Or *Aniyah*." Mike sneered the name like it tasted disgusting.

"My children are already tracking them. As soon as we have their locations, you'll know."

Raph's void of a voice slithered from a speaker.

"*What about the boy?*"

Jude and Agnes shivered, but AlphaSupreme was a burning bush.

"Martyr him."

96

In the hospital's waiting room, Aniyah and Imani sat side by side. All three televisions, though tuned to different channels, carried Representative Stacy Mallory.

...The young man who caused all this destruction and pain? He was not born a racist. People, truly, are not racist...

"Don't know that I agree with you there, sister," Imani said.

...Choices can be racist. Beliefs and habits can be racist. But those are learned behaviors, and so I have to believe they can be UNlearned...

"Wish I shared her optimism," Imani said. Aniyah remained silent. "Hey. You don't have to do this."

"I do though."

"You want me in there with you?"

Aniyah shook her head no. "Not part of the deal. He'll only see me."

"Such crap."

Imani fumed. Aniyah adjusted the recycled grocery bag on her lap.

Imani's phone chirped. She pulled it out. A tiny grin peeked through her scowl.

"Must be Gideon," Aniyah said, nudging with a playful elbow.

"You hush now," Imani said, elbowing right back. "Says everyone missed us in class, telling us to get home safe."

"That's nice."

"Mm-hmm." Imani's thumbs blurred.

Aniyah was about to tease but the federal agent and the lawyer approached.

"It's time," the agent said.

Aniyah and Imani stood.

"Whoa, no, uh-uh. What's in the bag?" the lawyer said.

Aniyah handed the bag to the agent. The agent looked in. She looked up and raised an eyebrow. Aniyah's return gaze revealed nothing.

The agent handed the bag to the lawyer. The lawyer looked in. He also looked up at Aniyah puzzled.

Imani snorted. "Seriously?"

The lawyer blew some air through his lips. "OK."

He handed the bag back to the agent, who passed it back to Aniyah, who clutched it to her heart.

"The second he says he's done you're out of there," the lawyer said. Aniyah nodded.

Imani squeezed Aniyah's shoulders. "I'll be right here."

Aniyah nodded again.

Imani stuck a finger in the lawyer's face. "Your *client* even breathes on her wrong, I will end you."

Aniyah followed the agent and the lawyer to the elevator. They got in. The agent pressed a button. It lit up. A ding sounded. The doors started to close.

Aniyah felt time thickening. In the seconds it took to ride

up four floors she could have run a marathon. Written a symphony. Relived her entire relationship with Reggie.

She had felt this way only once before. Outside the school, screaming into Reggie's chest, Jazzie's body under a blood-spotted sheet. Each heartbeat a century. Each breath a millennium. Trapped in the never-ending present.

She squeezed her eyes shut. Bit down on the inside of her cheeks. Willed time to thin out. If it got too thick, she'd be suspended in amber.

Her resistance was for naught.

Time...

...shifts.

An age passes.

They arrive at room 507.

The agent opens the door.

Aniyah walks through.

Spearhead—*Dustin, Dustin, his name is Dustin*—lies in a bed. His right hand cuffed to the rail. One leg elevated in a cast. Eyes bandaged over. His discolored, splotchy skin a detailed report of every blow the terrified and furious crowd had rained down upon him. His head turns at the sound of the door opening.

The agent says something. The lawyer says something.

The door closes behind her.

She feels rage because he is unable to see her. She feels gladness because his injuries are deserved. She feels disgust because humans can hurt each other so. She feels eagerness to make him confess. She feels pity because he's so young and how the hell did he get this way?

She feels fresh rage because she feels pity.

He says, "Why did you ask to see me?" Split lips mush his words.

She says, "Why did you say yes?"

Neither has a reasonable answer.

A TV is mounted high on the wall. The Congresswoman wraps her speech at the streetlamp by asking for a moment of silence.

Spearhead says, "Take your silence and shove it, bitch."

Aniyah says, "Child, you will shut your goddamn mouth."

He huffs. But he quiets.

The silence stretches. And stretches. The heart monitor beats steadily in the background, measuring out life in little dollops. Then the Congresswoman says, "When my momma is tired, or angry, or hurt, this is what she does." She starts to sing.

...I sing... because... I'm happy...

The crowd joins her, transforms into a harmonized congregation.

...I sing... because... I'm free...

Aniyah hums along.

...His eye... is on... the sparrow... and I know—

Some producer in some control booth somewhere jumps the gun. The TV cuts to a panel of talking heads. They start hot-airing and checking all the preordained infotainment boxes.

Spearhead says, "So what do you want?"

Aniyah says, "I have something to show you."

She places the bag on the bed beside him.

He says, "I can't see."

She says, "Maybe now you will."

He reaches blindly. He finds the bag. He reaches inside. He asks, "What the hell is this?"

She answers, "A stuffed animal, genius."

He pulls it out. He can't see the raucous colors of the fuzz but he can tell by feel that it's lumpy and misshapen from years of being squeezed. "Dinosaur?" he asks.

"T-Rex."

"Dinosaurs are the shit."

"Jazzie thought so too."

He drops the dinosaur like it bit him. It roars on his lap.

She says, "I was going to show it to you in the park but you chickened out, so..."

He chooses to snort. "You could have bought this at any store on the way here."

She sighs. "OK. Sure. You're right. I could have."

The TV blathers.

"But I didn't."

She watches his hands. Those hands had built bombs. Those same hands pick the dinosaur back up. Explore the thick tail, the ferocious felt teeth, the humongous legs, the absurdly small forearms.

He asks, "What's his name?"

She answers, "*Her* name is Rosa. Rosa Rex, Queen of the Dinosaurs."

The TV blathers.

Aniyah says, "Jazzie couldn't fall asleep without it. After she was killed, I slept with it. Because it smelled like her. Then I realized my smell was wiping out hers. So I keep it bagged in the closet. I only bring Rosa out... when it hurts too much."

He says nothing.

She says, "Go ahead. Smell her."

"Smell...?"

"Smell Rosa. Smell Jazzie."

He's taken aback. But then his lip curls. He smooshes his nose into the dinosaur and takes a huge, dramatic sniff. He shrugs and says, "I don't smell shit."

She says, "If you did, would you have the balls to admit it?"

He's about to snarl a curse when, for once, all the TV talking heads agree.

"*Monster.*"

"*Psychopath.*"

"*Makes me reconsider my stance, maybe the death penalty is appropriate here.*"

Spearhead pulls the remote out from under his blanket and changes the channel. It's righteous outrage everywhere. Click.

"*...racist...*" Click.

"*...murderer...*" Click.

"*...terrorist...*" Click.

"*...monster...*"

"Morons," he says. "No one understands."

"What don't we understand?" she says.

"I'm a fuckin' *patriot.*"

"You're a...?" She laughs out loud. "Setting a secondary bomb to target firefighters and ambulance drivers isn't patriotic, Dustin. Terrorists do that."

"They're the terrorists! And my name is *Spearhead!*"

"You know what? *Dustin?* I don't even care about your bombs. I know I should but all I want right now is for you to admit Jazzie lived, and if that makes me a horrible person then fine. But my daughter was real. And someone like you murdered her. Why? *Why?* Because you're angry? Because your precious little feelings got hurt? What is wrong with you??"

"Nothing!" he yells. "I see the TRUTH!"

He throws the dinosaur. It bounces off her shoulder.

She is aware of the door opening behind her. Of the agent asking if everything is alright, the lawyer blustering that she's agitating his client. She is aware of the TV looping for the bazillionth time its curated cuts of aftermath footage. It's so familiar.

She is aware of the sightless young man calling her every foul name he can muster.

She is aware of bile in her mouth and hatred coursing through her. Aniyah picks Rosa up, brushes her off.

And she prays. Hard. Through gritted teeth. To God and gods and goddesses. To the Universe. Anyone. Anything.

If you're out there... please... grant me grace. Grant me grace. Oh god, I beg you, please oh please oh please, grant me grace.

Only Jazzie answers.

I'll do that. Thank you, baby.

Time...

...shifted.

She left. Didn't look back. Rode down. Embraced Imani.

"You forgot your bag," Imani said.

"No I didn't. Let's go."

Back in the hospital room, Rosa Rex, Queen of the Dinosaurs, sat on Spearhead's bedside table, waiting for Dustin to see.

97

Leaves changing color, crisp air perfect for sweatshirts with shorts, spiced apple cider, and playoff baseball all conspire to make October easily the best month in the Midwest.

Any who say otherwise are Commie bastards.

Another October tradition, though one no longer glowing with autumnal sheen for Gideon, was Homecoming.

He pushed through the gymnasium's double doors. The pep rally was in full swing. *Born to Run* blasted from the speakers. Coach Carl stood on stage leading the clapping. Principal Simmons danced to the side, chronically off half a beat.

Everyone on their feet. Students, parents, teachers, the whole town crammed into the gym. Visiting extended family members squished in with last year's reunited graduates swapping stories of college dorm life and other momentous freshman year discoveries.

Gideon scanned the press of bodies. He knew every in and out of this gym. He'd been a star-struck middle-schooler at the ribbon cutting for this shining monument to Coach Carl's success.

There. The gap between the bleachers leading to the exit closest to the parking lot. If and when Coach Carl ran, that was the exit he would rabbit toward.

Gideon rode the crowd like a cork on a tossed sea. He sensed the double doors opening again a few moments before the final wave landed him gently by the gap.

Gideon watched Rheia mount the stage like she belonged there. Adler's shades reflected the crowd back to itself. School-colored cap tight on her favorite wig. Varsity jacket—like the cap—snatched from the onsite swag shop.

She waved off a couple questioning assistant coaches, claimed the microphone, pumped a fist in time with the Boss's final refrain. The assembly roared.

"Today is a special day! We're gonna bring new meaning to the word *Homecoming*!!"

Cheers.

"But I'm just here to introduce the real heroine. Alison, get on up here!"

A savvy sound board op, reacting to this unrehearsed interruption, had the wherewithal to tag in some Bryan Adams. *Run to You* shook the gym as a stoic, 30-something white woman climbed the steps and marched past Coach Carl to the podium.

Gideon marveled. How Rheia had tracked down Alison all these years later—Adler surely played a part—and then convinced her to participate in such dramatic fashion...

Gideon also seethed. He wanted to be up on that stage, close enough to wrap his hands around Coach Carl's throat. But Rheia had reminded him: "Stay cold. This is gonna go viral. We don't wanna blow your cover on your first scripted performance, now do we?"

So he swallowed his bile and conceded to rear-guarding.

Rheia took Alison's hands and gave them an encouraging

squeeze. Alison gripped the podium. Bryan Adams faded away beneath the curious murmurs of the crowd.

Everyone sensed the temperature shifting. Only Gideon, Rheia, and Alison knew why.

"My name..." Alison gritted her teeth. Had a quick conversation with herself. Re-launched.

"My name is Alison. If you look up, you'll see it stitched on a couple of those cross country championship banners."

Whoops and *"We're number one's!"* echoed off the ceiling as faces up-turned and scouted the fabric testaments.

"But you know what name you won't see up there? Even though it should be right next to mine?"

Gideon braced himself.

"Finley Price."

Mute button.

Everyone knew. Even those who had only been kids those many moons ago. Even those who had moved to the small town after the Prices had left. Everyone knew.

"I'm not surprised those banners still hang, even though her name has been unstitched."

Principal Simmons scurried toward Alison. Rheia intercepted, spoke a curt few words. Principal Simmons deflated. The room coughed and shuffled and muttered. Principal Simmons sat. It looked to Gideon like he was mentally composing his resignation letter and taking stock of every lawyer he knew.

Alison for the first time looked at Coach Carl. He looked back, oblivious.

"Everyone. Look at this pathetic man." Alison had found her voice. Gideon again gave Rheia credit. She had been adamant that Alison would deliver the best killing stroke.

Alison pointed. "Even now he is too narcissistic to see that his end has begun. Coach Carl is like those Covid patients who with their dying breaths still insisted the virus was a hoax. Cognitive dissonance is a son-of-a-bitch."

Coach Carl understood Alison's tone even if her words were nonsensical. He puffed up and strutted toward the mic.

This time Alison didn't need Rheia's intervention. "You don't recognize me, do you?"

Coach Carl stopped dead in his tracks. Gideon noted phones coming out of pockets. Livestreams flowing. Rheia had called it. This was going viral. The town would be left a smoldering ruin.

Alison hissed at Coach Carl. "My name is Alison Talbot."

Coach Carl's eyes bugged out.

She proclaimed to the packed room, "Coach Carl raped me. My friend Finley Price confronted him. Because he had raped her too. He put her in the hospital. Then paid for my abortion."

Coach Carl's panic heated to a simmer. Gideon licked his chops. Made sure his own shades were secure, his own school cap and jacket on tight.

"Finley Price wasn't the first. And I wasn't the last." And Alison listed off the names of all those that she and Rheia had been able to talk to, those who had agreed to the inevitable publicity. She listed off just the dates of those who confirmed Coach Carl's actions but who wanted to stay anonymous. She listed off every rape and molestation and—

"Fall 1997. Beth Simmons. Yes, Principal, your own niece. And you knew. And you did nothing."

Blood lust oozed from the bleachers. But Alison cold-showered it. "ALL of you already knew. And all of you did exactly nothing."

Then something unexpected happened. A current student, her face garishly painted for maximum rally pep, stepped out and walked to the front of the stage. She reached up. Alison crouched and reached down. They clasped hands.

David and Goliath, Gideon thought.

She took a shuddering breath. And even without the microphone—

"Last year..."

—even speaking up into Alison's eyes—

"...after Regionals..."

—she made sure everyone heard.

"...Coach Carl raped me."

The dam burst. Half a dozen other current and former students streamed forward. Each of them bullseyed Coach Carl. Alison clambered down and tried to wrap her arms around them all. Cleansing tears washed the paints from their faces.

Shock. The attention swung to Coach Carl. His panic had reached a roiling boil.

Gideon tensed. *C'mon you asshole, make a run for it...*

And run for it he did. Away from Rheia, of course, down the stage steps, skirting wide around Alison and the seven young women...

...directly toward Gideon.

Carl bulldozed through the gobsmacked Homecomers. Saw a man standing in his path. Reached out to shove him aside.

Gideon trapped Carl's outstretched arms, pivoted, and flipped Carl Stan-style with his hip. Carl's feet flew through the air. He landed hard on his back. Gideon was instantly down on one knee, spitting in Carl's ear, "You can't outrun this. *Coach.*"

Gideon reared back and missile-launched his fist.

In the ensuing chaos, Gideon and Rheia vanished. School caps and jackets discarded in the dumpster. Shades and wig tucked away into pockets. Rendezvous at the car. Gideon slid into the passenger seat. Rheia eased them out of the parking lot, meandered toward the highway.

A couple cop cars screamed past them and raced toward the school.

Gideon watched the trees flashing by. Fiery orange and yellow leaves leaped from branches, danced in the wind, proclaimed that yet again to everything there is a season.

"Thank you," he said.

Rheia nodded. Drummed her thumbs on the steering wheel.

"You punched him," she said.

"Yes I did."

"With your fist."

"Uh-huh."

"Stan'll be pissed."

"Oh I know."

Rheia decelerated, turned onto the entry ramp, reaccelerated.

Gideon wriggled his fingers, winced. Flexed them, winced again.

"How's your hand?" Rheia asked.

He held it up. Red swollen knuckles. Couple spots of split skin. He grinned.

"Hurts like hell."

She grinned back.

"Good."

The car hit the highway at speed. The small town and its ghosts were left behind.

ACKNOWLEDGMENTS

No one in this world accomplishes anything truly worthwhile all by their lonesome.

Big picture I must first thank all my previous publishers. My mom MaryLu and her two sisters Melli and Von, who published my "book" about a mother chicken when I was about three feet tall.

And Mr. Torrence, quite possibly the best fourth-grade teacher ever to grace the public school system, who constructed in his classroom a climbable and sittable "book nook" from leftover lumber and poached carpet remnants. This homemade library he populated entirely with books written by his students that he selflessly published, taking home our scribbled notebook paper and pounding out clean copies on his typewriter, then binding them in colorful cardboard covers. I still have my two first editions, almost forty years later, including THE BIG FIVE HORSE RACE, my shamelessly plagiaristic homage to Walter Farley and his series of Black Stallion stories.

And then Mrs. Seybold, who kept a straight face when I pitched the idea of writing a novel for my 12th grade English project, and cheered me on all the way to its, um, sure, let's say completion.

Looking back, my god, how lucky I've been. Mr. Rooker (from whom I learned adjectives, adverbs, helping verbs, and sentence diagramming... and I mean down to the cellular level). Dr. Hart. Dr. Shaw. And I haven't even touched on my theatre mentors. Yikes. It's like I'm giving an acceptance speech and forgot to put my cheat sheet of names in my tux pocket.

I sincerely hope this effort does you all proud.

Coming back to present day, all my deepest thanks to Kathy and Joe Rinaldi for the initial advice and encouragement. And the members of the Rabbit Room (Alex, Amanda, Doug, Sam, Sylvia) for all their incalculable real-time feedback.

Thank-you as well to Thomas Gibbons, a tremendous playwright whose work I have been honored to act in and direct, who turned me on to the very real and troubling belief out there in crisis actors.

Dad. For never letting me off the hook.

And all my love and gratitude to my Hyde Park Pack—Rebecca, Gaia, and Odin—for supporting and encouraging me all the way. Looking at you all sleeping and snuggled together every morning at 5am, before making my way to the coffee and the Troupe, is the most heart-filling inspiration I could ask for.

ABOUT THE AUTHOR

Jason Cannon is an award-winning theatre artist and teacher. He has an MFA in Directing, a Masters in Drama, and a quarter-century in professional theatre.

When not on stage or in rehearsal Jason devours every Lee Child, James Rollins, Mark Dawson, Vince Flynn, Brad Thor, and Randy Wayne White book in the cosmos.

As an actor Jason has portrayed everything from a rapping dinosaur to a robot and from a hitman to Hamlet. He has written plays about J.R.R. Tolkien and Aesop, directed plays about hiccuping dragons and foul-mouthed puppets, and once while improvising he was attacked by a stage light.

He lives in Florida just a holler from the Gulf with his partner Rebecca and their two silly pups, Gaia and Odin. He makes a killer key lime pie and runs lots of 10Ks and half-marathons.

Jason believes storytelling in all its forms—whether seen on the stage or read on a page—has the power not only to entertain but also to comfort, provoke, and inspire us to be better humans.

GHOST LIGHT is his first novel.

If you enjoyed *GHOST LIGHT*, please consider leaving a review. They are super helpful!

Jason is also available as a teacher, speaker, and emcee.

Learn more about Jason at jason-cannon.com and watch for the next three stories in the TROUPE series—*THE UNDER-STUDY, BLACKOUT,* and *RULE OF THREE*—at ibis-books.com.

THE TROUPE SERIES

The Understudy

Ghost Light

PLAYS

Wheelchair Chicken

Last Rights

Old Enough to Know Better

The Eagle and Child: J.R.R. Tolkien and C.S. Lewis

Windsor Live!

Aesop's Greatest Hits